THE DARK

by Bob Hodgman

Cover designed by Bob Hodgman

Bob Hodgman
Visit my website at www.BobHodgman.com

Printed in the United States of America

First Printing: April 2019
Independently published

ISBN-9781728926605

To my wife, my most-sweet Jan, who does not like this sort of story but who read it, nonetheless.

PART I

CHAPTER 1

The first shot hardly registered, just a door slammed somewhere out in the night. A dog barked, furious. The door slammed again and the dog stopped barking. Jamie looked up from his biology text and rubbed his eyes.

Out his window, a full moon sailed through broken clouds and the street below was moonlit and then dark and then moonlit again. Bare tree branches cast shifting shadows in the early spring breeze, and his block, familiar since grade school, seemed transformed by the night into something restless, foreign, and menacing.

The door slammed yet again, closer this time. A car alarm shrieked. Jamie looked down the hill, but the street below was empty.

"Turn off your light," said Nate Bonney from the hall outside Jamie's bedroom. Jamie turned and looked at his step-dad. "Quick," said Bonney.

Jamie hit the switch on the desk lamp and his bedroom went dark. Bonney came and stood next to him. He bent down to look out the window, craning his neck to see.

"What is it?" asked Jamie.

Bonney put his hand on Jamie's shoulder. "Look," he said. Jamie looked down the street, down the hill toward town. A lone figure walked up the hill in the middle of the street. Something in his hand glinted from the streetlight as the man crossed into Jamie's block. He lifted his hand – a casual gesture – another bang and a flash.

Jamie jumped up and knocked over his chair. "Holy shit! He's shooting!" They both backed away from the window.

"Call the police," said Bonney. "I'm going to lock up downstairs. Stay away from the window." He rushed out the door.

Jamie looked at his phone, lying on the desk near the window. He licked his lips and then stepped forward, picked up the phone and retreated to the doorway. 9-1-1... "What is your emergency?" a woman's voice with a country twang.

"Someone is shooting," Jamie whispered.

"Yes, sir," said the dispatcher. "Your name, please."

"Jamie Montane."

"Your location?"

"3707 Oak Street."

"We have multiple reports of active shooters downtown. Can you hear the shots? Do they sound close or far away?"

"They're close," said Jamie. "He's right here, on our street. I saw him!"

"He's up on Oak Street? And you're at 3707?"

"Yes!"

The dispatcher said something muffled and another voice responded in the background, then she came back on the line. "All right, sir. Are you safe?"

"I don't know. What am I supposed to do, go out and ask him?"

"Please stay calm, sir. We recommend that you lock your doors and shelter in place. Turn off lights so you don't attract attention. Is there only one shooter?"

"I only saw one guy."

"OK. Can you tell us where he is now?"

"Hang on..." Jamie crouched low and approached the window. The dispatcher's voice was saying something quick and emphatic, something about staying away from windows. Jamie lifted his head slowly until he could see the street below. The man was in front of his house, walking. Without breaking his stride, he raised the gun again and fired at the house across the street. Jamie ducked down and sat on the floor. "He's right there, right outside my house." He whispered. "He just shot Mr. Schultz's house."

Now Jamie could hear the sirens. They came closer, screaming up the hill. Jamie couldn't help himself. He looked.

The police cars blasted through the four-way stop at the end of the block and the man with the gun in the middle of the street turned to face them. He raised his gun and fired rapidly at the approaching cars. The windshield of the lead car shattered and the car swerved, bumping up over the curb. It smashed into a big maple in someone's front yard.

The cop in the second car floored it and came straight on. He rammed the shooter without slowing. The shooter's body rolled over the hood and windshield, flew off the roof and smacked down on the pavement behind the car. Tires squealed as the squad car came to a stop.

Jamie turned and slid down the wall to sit on the floor. Red and blue emergency lights flashed across his bedroom, transforming the sturdy walls of childhood into a tumbling, chaotic space. He covered his eyes.

* * *

It was sunny. Morning light streamed through the window and for a few seconds Jamie drifted in the warmth and comfort of the heavy blankets. Then he remembered. He stumbled out of bed and went to the window to look out. Traffic cones closed off one side of the street out in front of the house. Short poles poked out of some of the cones supporting a cordon of yellow police tape. He craned his neck. The grass was chewed up where the police car had plowed into the tree, but the car itself was gone.

Jamie pulled on jeans and t-shirt and went into the bathroom. He dragged a comb through his hair and considered shaving but gave it a pass: his blond stubble was still downy and nearly invisible. He splashed water on his face, toweled off and went downstairs.

Bonney was sitting at the kitchen table, watching a newscast on his laptop: explosions and running people. A woman covered in dust rocked the still form of a child. The scenes were of a distant place and Jamie hardly glanced at them on his way to the refrigerator.

"Any news of last night?" he asked.

Bonney looked up. His longish hair, gray at the temples, had not been brushed yet and there were shadows under his eyes. He rubbed his face and the week's growth of salt and pepper beard. "Yeah. It was some local guy. He lived just a couple blocks down the hill."

Jamie sat down and poured milk on his cereal. "Wow. What happened? What set him off?" he asked.

Bonney shook his head. "They don't know yet. Looks like he shot his wife first and then he just walked down the street shooting randomly."

Jamie made a face. "What an asshole," he said, but as soon as he said it, he regretted it. It was so inadequate. He glanced at Bonney.

Jamie's mother, Ellen, came in and headed for the coffee pot. "Language," she admonished.

"Sorry," he said.

Ellen put her coffee mug down on the table and kissed Jamie on the cheek. "How you doing, sweetie? Get any sleep at all last night?" she asked.

"Some... Dreams kept waking me up."

"Apparently there were more shootings last night downtown," said Bonney.

"Must have been a busy night at the emergency room," said Ellen. "Glad it wasn't on my shift."

Jamie put his spoon down and looked at his mother and then at Bonney. Bonney glanced up at Jamie from the laptop and the news, a stream of disaster and war. "Sorry," he said, and snapped the lid of the laptop closed. "You OK?"

Jamie blinked. "Yeah, yeah, I'm OK. Just tired."

Bonney watched Jamie for a few seconds. "Maybe you'd rather stay home from school today?"

And it struck Jamie that more than anything, he wanted to go to school today, to get away from the yellow police tape fluttering in the early spring morning breeze outside his house. He longed for the flood of young faces in the halls far away from the death and destruction of the outside world.

He shrugged. "Biology quiz," he said. "I gotta be there." He pushed back from the table and started up the stairs.

"I need to talk with you when you get back from work," said Bonney to Ellen. Jamie stopped half way upstairs, out of sight, and listened.

"What's up?" asked his mother.

"This project I'm working on for the CDC... It looks like they're studying violence like a disease, like you can catch it and spread it."

"So?" prompted Ellen.

"It's a rush job," said Bonney. "They're acting like it's an emergency, like the epidemic has already broken out and they don't know how to stop it."

"It sure feels like it," said his mother's voice.

"What do you mean?" asked Bonney.

"Well, last night. And work... The way it's been at the emergency room. Darnell is just a small town, but it doesn't feel that way anymore."

"We need to think about this," said Bonney. "We need to be ready."

A chair scraped across the kitchen floor. Someone was getting up from the table. Dishes clinked. Jamie went on up, taking the stairs two at a time.

He brushed his teeth and pulled on a hoodie and a faded jean jacket. He loaded his books into his backpack and paused at his desk. Outside in the street below his bedroom window, the police tape fluttered yellow around the blood-stained spot in the pavement. And although Jamie knew it couldn't be, the stain appeared larger than before, like it was spreading. He turned and went down the stairs. "Bye," he called and escaped out the door and down the hill to school.

* * *

Ebola was hot. Lassa, Marburg, all the hemorrhagic fevers. Eleven thousand dead tended to concentrate the mind. And open the wallet. Rose could feel it as she walked the crowded hallway at the CDC conference. The excitement, the laughter, the testosterone. They were all getting funded. Enjoy it while it lasts, she thought.

She walked up to one cluster of bearded, tweedy attendees. "Hey, Rashid."

"Hey, Rose." Rashid turned to her. "How's it going?" Rashid was visiting from Al-Jazeera University in Syria. They had been friends since grad school.

"Not bad. Pressure's off now that my presentation is cancelled."

"Oh, yeah. I was sorry to hear that. I was going to go. I thought you might be interested in some field testing we did."

"Oh, yeah?"

"Yeah. You heading for lunch? Can I join you?"

"Sure." They turned and followed the flow toward the cafeteria.

"We went in to Dura after the riots and tested for Insanus Lyssavirus," said Rashid. "All the tests were positive. Everyone had it. No surprise to you, I suppose."

Rose shrugged. "How did you test?"

"We used bDNA," said Rashid.

Rose stood for a moment, looking at Rashid. "Everyone tested positive? And you used bDNA?"

"Well, we tested 523 bodies. Or body parts, actually. But we're pretty sure we tested 523 individuals. All the samples were positive."

"Isn't Dura that village where everybody was massacred?"

"Yeah, that's the one. But now they think it was some sort of blood feud or food riot or something. There's no evidence of an outside attack."

Rose walked over to a bench against the wall and sat down. Rashid followed and sat next to her. "You OK, Rose?" he asked.

"Were they stressed, the people in Dura?" She ignored his question.

Rashid nodded. "They were hungry. Babies were dying."

Rose licked her lips. "That much virus and that much stress... That would trigger the violence." She looked up at him. "It's starting, Rashid."

"Ah, Rose. Don't go there." He shook his head. "They will fire you for sure if you start on this again."

"I can prove it. I've got a guy building a database."

"They don't care, Rose. They'll just refuse to believe it. And that'll be it for your career."

"They won't be able to ignore it, Rashid. We're talking Dura times a million, all over the world."

Rose stared straight ahead as if stunned by her own words. Then she spoke, so softly that Rashid leaned in to hear. "Don't go home, Rashid. It's already started.

You don't want to be there." But she didn't say what came to her next: was anywhere safe? Would anyone escape?

* * *

Jamie made his way to class and sat down at his desk. Mrs. Johnson was setting up a slide show so he pulled the shades, and someone hit the lights. The classroom was dark. Jamie dropped back into his seat and pretended not to notice Adele, who was sitting across the aisle. Mrs. Johnson showed her first slide, and the image of a bullet-like Rabies virus lit up the screen.

"All right, everyone," she said. "Stay awake. The midterm will definitely have a question on epidemics." Some clown at the back of the room made snoring sounds, which Mrs. Johnson ignored.

Everyone was wide awake by the end of the lecture. The last slide was a picture of a crowd of people with a big question mark over it. Mrs. Johnson's comments suggested she thought the question had been answered, and that it was just a matter of time. There were too many people, too tightly packed, and something – Ebola, Swine Flu, Rabies, or something we hadn't spotted yet – was going to lay waste to humanity and put an end to it, possibly in the lifetimes of some of the young people sitting here now in her class. "It might have already begun," she said.

Jamie got the impression that Mrs. Johnson was somewhat tired of the human race and felt that its end would not necessarily be a bad thing. He thought of the shootings in town and the news clips on Bonney's laptop and wondered for just a second, sitting there in the dark, if in fact she might be right.

The lights came up and someone raised the blinds. Adele glanced at Jamie and caught him looking at her. He turned to the front of the room and studied the now blank screen, as if its empty expanse held an important message. Adele shifted, sat back in her chair and folded her hands in her lap. She had long, slender fingers that seemed forever stained with paints and charcoal from her art classes. She looked down at her hands, frowned and rubbed at a charcoal smudge. Today she wasn't wearing army boots and she wasn't all in black. Today was not a goth day, he thought. He glanced out the window. A line of dark clouds was pushing up the valley from the coast and the town was taken by deep shadow.

* * *

Fifth period, and Jamie rushed to Physics. The halls were jammed. Locker doors slammed and groups of kids pushed past each other to get to class before the bell.

Jamie sensed a change in the flow up ahead and craned his neck to see. Three guys who were on the football team were coming down the hall, like a wedge, one in front, two behind. They made no effort to pass smoothly through the crowd but marched straight ahead. Kids stepped aside or flattened against the lockers to make room, and the three moved in a bubble of silence.

Jamie recognized them. Caleb, the point man, had been sort of a bully since grade school. Jamie had faced him down once on the playground during recess, but that was before Caleb got big. Jamie was as tall as Caleb, but very lean, skinny really. Caleb had bulked up like a super hero. Or maybe like a super villain, because he had a mean streak. Maybe it was the steroids, Jamie thought.

Caleb had always been that way, but somehow this semester the whole school felt different. The hallways were harsher, riskier. Some boys had been suspended for fighting, and just last week a substitute teacher had been hauled off in handcuffs when he lost it and beat a smart-ass kid senseless. And it wasn't just school, was it? It felt like something dark and vicious had gotten loose in the world. Or had it always been this way, and I'm just seeing it for the first time, he thought. Maybe I'm the one who's changing.

Jamie caught Caleb's eye, a stupid mistake. Caleb smiled, and Jamie felt uneasy. Caleb turned his head and said something to the footballer on his left, another big kid named Dwight. Now both Caleb and Dwight were looking at Jamie, and Jamie felt a stab of alarm. They were almost on him, and Jamie looked around for a doorway or someplace he could escape. He moved as far to the right as he could, out of the way, but the kids standing at their lockers left only a narrow passage. Caleb, Dwight and the third guy had moved out into the center of the flow and as they passed Jamie, Caleb leaned over and shouldered Jamie into the wall, hard. Jamie went down, books flying, taking several innocent 10th graders down with him.

"Whoa! Sorry, dude!" said Caleb, and the three laughed as they made their way on down the hall.

Jamie picked himself up and started helping the others he had knocked down. "Sorry," he said, but the other kids pulled away from him. Jamie was a target now and being friendly with him could invite the same.

He started to gather up his physics notebooks and someone handed him his textbook. Jamie looked at the paint-stained hand that held it out to him and then up into Adele's gray eyes. There were flecks of amber in the gray.

"What a bunch of assholes," she said. "Are you OK?"

How much had she seen, he wondered? Had she watched his attempt to escape? Had she seen his fear? His face was hot with the shame of it.

"Yeah, yeah. I'm fine." They both stood up and Jamie took the book from Adele's hand. "Thanks," he said, looking down at the book. There was an awkward pause. Jamie wanted to say something witty and brave, but his mind was a complete blank. "Well, ah, thanks," he repeated.

"No problem." Adele smiled. She waited a beat too long and her smile faded in the silence. Then she smiled once more, a big smile. "See ya," she said and stepped around him and walked on down the hall. Jamie turned to watch her walk away. He cursed the footballers. He cursed himself.

CHAPTER 2

It wasn't dark, yet, but the heavy cloud cover of the early spring afternoon cast a pall over the streets of downtown Darnell. Jamie leaned into a raw wind, hunched against the cold, as he walked home from school.

He slowed as he passed one small house. Angry voices from inside reached him out on the sidewalk. A little girl sat alone on the front step, coatless in the chill afternoon, and watched him as he walked by. Something in the scene felt wrong, and Jamie wondered if he should call someone, but couldn't think of who. His mother was an ER nurse. She would know, or maybe Bonney, he thought. He hurried on.

Jamie crossed the street to his block. The yellow police tape was gone but the dark spot on the pavement was still there. A door opened, and Mr. Schultz emerged with his golden retriever, Spot. Spot had no spots and Mr. Schultz, an old, retired guy with thinning gray hair that stuck up all over, had explained once to Jamie that the name was a joke. Spot bolted out the door as if pursued by the walking dead and was brought up short, hard, by the leash. Mr. Schultz stumbled and grabbed the storm door.

"God damn it," he yelled at the dog, who hunkered down as far from his owner as the leash would allow. Mr. Schultz rushed out and kicked at him. Spot yelped and dodged, jerking the leash out of the old man's hand. Now free, Spot turned and sprinted past Jamie across the street. Mr. Schultz took several steps after him but stopped in the middle of his front yard. "Goddamn dog," he yelled, again, as Spot disappeared between two houses making for the woods, the leash trailing behind him.

Jamie stood on the sidewalk, gaping at Mr. Schultz who glared back.

"What the fuck are you looking at?" the man demanded, and Jamie turned away and walked quickly across the street to his house. He took the steps to the front porch two at a time. The light in the window of Bonney's home office was on, and Jamie threw down his coat and backpack in the entry way before he went up the stairs to the upper floor. He knocked on Bonney's door.

"Come in," said Bonney. Jamie opened the door and stepped into a book-lined room with a small, twin bed and a huge, messy desk. Bonney sat at a cleared spot, working on a laptop computer. He twisted his lean body in his chair so he faced back toward the door and Jamie. He was in classic work-from-home form. It looked like he had not combed his hair yet today and beneath dark eyes and a beak-like nose the growth of salt-and-pepper beard looked almost intentional. He wore a ratty flannel shirt unbuttoned over his favorite "Being Peace" t-shirt. He had on a pair of dad-jeans, way faded with a hole in one knee. Jamie flopped down on the bed and stared up at the ceiling.

"Hey," said Bonney. "How was school?"

"Great," said Jamie.

Bonney waited.

"What's with Mr. Schultz?"

"Why?" asked Bonney. "What happened?"

"Couldn't you hear him? He was screaming at Spot."

Bonney frowned and studied the design of a small, oriental rug on the floor. He nodded and looked back up at Jamie. "I heard something. A minute ago."

"He loves that dog," said Jamie. "Why would he kick him?"

Bonney looked surprised. "Yeah, that doesn't sound like Mr. Schultz," he said.

"So, Spot ran away. He's somewhere in the woods."

"Hmm," said Bonney and nodded again.

"I feel like we should do something," said Jamie. "Like maybe call the police?"

"I don't know... What can they do? It's not like they're going to launch a search party for a dog." Bonney shook his head. "Spot's big. He can take care of himself. He'll come back in a bit. Mr. Schultz isn't normally like that. It'll be OK."

Jamie was silent for a few seconds. "It doesn't seem right. Things just don't feel right," he said.

"How so?" asked Bonney.

Jamie sat up and stared at the bookcase on the wall in front of him. He threw up his hands. "Everything seems more...violent, more out of control, you know?"

Bonney studied Jamie. "Did something happen at school?"

Jamie grimaced and shook his head. "Oh, I got knocked down in the hall today."

Bonney sat up. "That's not good. Was it on purpose? Were you hurt?"

"Nah. I'm not hurt." Jamie rubbed his elbow. "But it was totally on purpose."

"Who did it?"

"Some football players. Caleb, Dwight, and some other guy. Caleb shoved me against the lockers and I fell down. It was totally unprovoked."

"I'll call the school." Bonney picked up his phone.

"Don't do that, Bonney," said Jamie. "You'll just make things worse. It's no big deal, really. I'll work it out."

Bonney hesitated.

"Don't worry, Bonney. It's just been a funny day, you know?" said Jamie. "The stuff last night, school. And I saw a little kid sitting outside a house down the hill with her parents screaming at each other inside, and Mr. Schultz screaming at Spot. And the news, and all. Sometimes it feels like we're all just tearing ourselves apart." He stood up. "It's OK. I'm OK." He looked at Bonney's computer screen. "What are you working on?" he asked. If you got him going, Bonney could talk about his work all day.

"Super rush, top-secret thing for the CDC." He turned back to his keyboard. "They won't tell me what it's for, but it looks like they're analyzing the spread of violence like an epidemic, like a virus."

"Cool. Why the rush?"

Bonney was silent for a few seconds, then he laughed. "Every project's a rush job. That's why they call in consultants, so they can blame someone else for missing deadlines."

"Ah," said Jamie. He shrugged and started for the door but paused and looked back. "Did mom buy more mint chocolate chip?"

"Yeah," said Bonney. "I left you some."

"Awesome," said Jamie and went downstairs to the kitchen.

* * *

Bonney sat staring at his office door where Jamie had just stood. Jamie had left the door open, as usual, but this is not what was on Bonney's mind now. His conversation with Jamie had left him with a sense of unease, a sense that he had not responded well, that he had failed to get it, to really hear what Jamie was saying. Sometimes Bonney himself felt that the world was spinning out of control, descending into a new dark age of tribal violence and vendetta. Just think of the news coming out of the Middle East and dead people in the street in their nice, middle class neighborhood. But bad news is what grabs your attention, isn't it? And the media was all about selling eyeballs, right?

He glanced at his laptop screen and then over to the white board on the far wall, filled with notes, shapes and lines that defined the software he had to deliver by tomorrow noon. High school can seem like the whole world to a seventeen-year old boy, he thought. A bad day, and it's the end of humanity. A good day, and it's spring-time forever. I'll see how he's feeling at dinner. He turned back to the keyboard and started typing.

He heard a whistle outside on the street and leaned forward to look out the window. Mr. Schultz was walking down the sidewalk on this side of the street. He called to Spot in a voice that was pure sweetness and love. In his hand, he carried a baseball bat.

CHAPTER 3

Adele sat at her kitchen table. She held a slice of sourdough bread slathered with crunchy peanut butter. She spread a thick layer of raspberry jam over it and took a bite. The garage door opened and closed, and a car door slammed. Her mother bustled in, juggling purse, briefcase, coat and a small bag of groceries.

"Ah. I see you've found something for dinner," she said. "Sorry I'm late, Sweetie."

"No problem," said Adele through a mouthful of PB and J.

Her mother was in her early forties and was looking a bit thin and worn, hints of silver showing in her thick dark hair. Her eyes were gray like Adele's and had a way of looking at you as if she could see everything there was to you, right into your very soul. This evening, her mother's gaze contained a touch of doubt that Adele had seen before, but only tonight did it really register. The weeks since Adele's father, Mike, had moved out had not been easy weeks.

Her mother put the grocery bag down on the table and considered her daughter. She touched the corner of her own mouth and Adele scrubbed a little smear of jam from her cheek, taking the hint.

"How was work?" Adele asked. She positioned another spoonful of jam on the bread.

"Work was good, sort of. My presentation was cancelled, but the conference was good. Busy. Lots of meetings. Bunch of people here from the other CDC labs. Some virologists in from Europe and the Middle East. How was school?"

A look of distaste flitted across Adele's face. "School was school," she said.

"How's the kinetic sculpture coming?"

"Yeah, it's good," said Adele. "I solved the problem with the articulated arm."

"What problem was that?"

"Where it ripped the pantyhose and then froze." Adele's artwork was going through a complex, 3-D, mixed media, mechanical, conceptual phase. Her work moved, transformed and even interacted with the viewer. No more passive viewers, declared Adele in her artist's statement, to the delight of her art teacher and the consternation of the school risk management committee.

"So, it'll be ready for the art and science fair?"

"Could be."

"That's really great, Deli," said her mother. She gave Adele a quick hug and started putting away the groceries.

"Do you think you'll be able to make it? To the fair?" asked Adele, careful to keep her tone casual.

"Sure," said her mother over her shoulder as she put some cans of soup up in the cupboard. "If things don't get too crazy..."

"Dad said he'll be there."

Her mother turned around to face Adele. "Yeah. Good," she said. "What's your dad got to say?"

"He says he's OK. He still doesn't have any furniture. Says the futon isn't as comfortable as it was twenty years ago."

"Not much is," said her mother, staring out the kitchen window at the dark woods in back.

Adele followed her mother's gaze. The evening breeze pushed and pulled at the bare trees. Something down low to the ground moved through the brush, a glint. Or perhaps it was just the wind in the early spring foliage.

"He says Power City is way too small. Everyone knows your business."

"Sounds like a lot of fun," said her mother. Power City was a company town, and everyone there worked with Adele's dad at the power plant or the hydroelectric dam.

"Dad's going to let me drive the Jeep when I have after school activities." Adele smiled at that.

"What's he going to do when you have the car?" objected her mother. Adele looked up at her, then, because the answer was obvious. Power City wasn't just a small town, it was a tiny town. Everything was within walking distance of everything else.

"You know Power City, mom. He can walk it, easy."

"Oh. Duh," said Rose. "Is your room all set up, then?"

"He said the bed would be delivered tomorrow."

Her mother looked vaguely unsettled by this exchange, as if her husband was finding it way too easy to assemble a functional life without her. Was she having second thoughts about the separation, wondered Adele. Her eyes were stinging for some reason, and she brushed her fingertips over them.

"I know, honey," said her mother. She stepped over to Adele and put her arms around her. "Don't worry," she said. "Everything will work out." But her mother's voice lacked conviction.

"Well whadda we got to eat, here?" said her mother. She stepped over to the fridge and opened both doors like a hostess greeting guests. She scanned the shelves and pulled out a Tupperware container. "Mmmm, pot roast."

Adele put the peanut butter and jam back in the fridge and her dish and tableware by the sink. She started for her room. "Excuse me," said her mother, pointing to the dirty dishes.

"What?" Adele gave her a wide-eyed innocent look.

"What am I? Your maid?" demanded her mother. "In the dishwasher, please. And don't forget to wipe up the table."

Adele considered several sharp replies, most suggesting her life would be easier during the weeks with her dad, but held back. She sighed, straightened up her dishes, and then made her escape to her room and homework.

* * *

"OMG", typed Adele, and pressed Send. This was, of course, meant ironically. She despised the goggle-eyed, airheaded bimbos who dropped this line at school. For a brief second, she considered the possibility that Rachel would not get the irony and think that Adele had texted "OMG" for real. She heaved a sigh of relief when Rachel's "No shit" came back, and Adele could hear her friend's utterly bored voice and see the tired, dismissive flip of her hand. All was well.

"Snack time," Adele punched in and pushed back from her desk without waiting for a reply. She went out the door and headed for the kitchen, scuffling along the hall runner in her pink bunny slippers. These were the height of irony too, of course, but in the occasional unguarded moment, she could feel a certain fuzzy comfort from them, all irony aside.

Adele stepped out of the hall into the great room. Her mother was sitting on the couch in front of the TV, a plate of warmed-up pot roast in front of her on the coffee table, half eaten. She was leaning forward, her eyes on the TV where a perfectly groomed news anchor spoke urgently to the camera. Adele walked in and leaned against the back of the couch behind her mother.

"What's the news?" asked Adele.

"The Middle East," said her mother.

Adele felt the pull of the strawberry yogurt in the fridge, but her mother's locked-on gaze kept her attention on the news report.

"Drone footage suggests that the battle for the city is over," said the TV news anchor, "but it is unclear who won. Both the rebels and the government are claiming victory. Our drone cameras have not been able to locate any significant military operations this morning, although it appears that small groups of irregular troops or perhaps just armed civilians are moving through the city and the drone microphones are still picking up what sounds like sporadic gunfire. Our foreign correspondent Mickey Delaney is on the outskirts of the city."

The anchor turned to a screen in the news studio and addressed a tired and somewhat smudged woman who was holding a microphone. Her hand was shaking. "Mickey, what's the situation there?"

"Well, Ralph," said Mickey. "This final battle for the city was the fiercest I've ever witnessed. We were lucky to escape with our lives. The fighting was incredibly bitter. We saw uniformed, regular army troops open fire on unarmed civilians and civilian men and women attacking soldiers with their bare hands. Children were not spared." Mickey paused and blinked. She looked off-camera and then back. "The fighting looked less like a battle and more like some sort of riot, all against all. Government soldiers were shooting at each other and... It was just all against all. We lost Mahmoud, our sound guy. It just felt like the end of the world, Ralph." Mickey started to cry and dropped the microphone. The TV switched back to the studio and the news anchor.

"Thank you, Mickey, for that report on a society tearing itself apart. Stay safe out there," he intoned. "We'll be right back after these messages."

"Wow," said Adele. "The Middle East... What's the matter with those people?"

"Actually, the CDC is trying to find out," said her mother. "It isn't just your basic dysfunctional society, Deli. There's something really wrong over there. And it's spreading."

"What? Like a disease? Spreading where?"

"Yeah, just like a disease. And it seems to be spreading outward from a couple of trouble spots in the Middle East." Adele's mother looked up at her from the couch. "The news media hasn't caught on yet, you know. It's been so gradual. We're all just used to the violence, right? Just another terrorist attack or whatever. But there's something different, now. That all-against-all thing. That's completely different. There have been some outbreaks in Syria, Yemen, Somalia."

"Thank god we live in Darnell," said Adele.

Her mother turned back to the TV. Off in the woods, a pack of coyotes yipped, and a cat screamed.

* * *

Adele came striding down the sunlit hall, arms swinging and boots making a satisfying clomp, clomp, clomp. The whole house was morning bright, and Adele smiled at the new, spring day. The school art and science fair was this afternoon, and she had decided to actually invite Jamie to come see her piece, not just mention it in his presence. To hell with being coy. She had dressed in artist's black - sophisticated, not goth - and her dark hair was held back in a French braid showing off her long, slim neck, her skin shocking white after the long, sunless, northwest winter. Her mother was leaning against the counter in the kitchen, her phone pressed to her ear.

"Uh-huh. Uh-huh," she said. "Istanbul?" Pause. "OK. Up a thousand percent?" Her mother listened. "Yeah, it's what I would expect." The voice on the other end asked a question. "Don't know," said her mother. "This is the first time we've had good numbers on violent crime, you know, so we can't compare it to the other places. What's the latest from Somalia?" Pause. "What do you mean, it's all gone? Where did it go?" Pause. "Sweet Jesus," her mom's Southern accent was coming back, always a bad sign. "OK, look. I'm on my way in. I've gotta drop Deli off at school, but I'm leaving now. Yeah, yeah. I'll be there."

She ended the call and turned to Adele, standing still in the doorway. "Hey, Deli. Are you ready? We have to leave right now."

"Like now, now? What about breakfast?"

Her mom frowned. "Sorry, sweetie. I've gotta get to work, ASAP." She opened the fridge and scanned the shelves. "Here," she said, and handed Deli the remains of a six-pack of snack-sized yogurt containers. She opened a drawer and pushed a spoon into her hands. "You can eat in the car."

They hustled out the side door, grabbing coats as they passed through the mudroom, and got into the car. Her mom backed out the steep drive and accelerated down the hill toward town.

"What's going on, mom? You're being totally scary," said Deli around a mouthful of blueberry yogurt.

"Sorry, honey. There's nothing to worry about here, but things aren't looking so good in the Middle East." She slowed for a stop sign at the bottom of the hill. "Things have really blown up. Just in the last twelve hours." She pulled to a stop exactly on the line. "That all-against-all violence is popping up in new places. And the old places - like that city on the news last night - are silent."

"What do you mean, silent?" asked Adele. She scooped a spot of yogurt off the corner of her mouth with the spoon.

"We've lost contact with our people in Somalia. And it's not just us. No one is answering their phones. Our consulate is offline. Satellite photos show smoke pouring from the building."

She started into the intersection but another car from the right - an old beater - pulled out at the same time. Adele's mom stopped and waved the man on and he stomped on the gas, mouthing cuss words and giving them the finger as he went by.

"Geez, what an asshole," said Adele.

"Hey," her mother said. "Don't be like that."

"What? Even when some random asshole gives you the finger?"

"Absolutely." Her mother glanced over at her. "Hear me, Deli," she said. "Anger isn't just something that comes and goes, anymore. Something is different, now. It's like every flash of anger leaves a residue, and it gets worse and worse. People give in to it, and they go down some dark hole somewhere and they don't come back."

"Come on, mom. Darnell's not exactly the Middle East."

"That guy who gave us the finger? That was the Middle East, Deli. That was exactly the Middle East."

"Huh," said Adele, and licked her spoon clean. "So, what's this got to do with you? Why's the CDC all excited?"

"Violence is like a public health issue. You can study its spread like a contagion."

"Yeah, but why you? You're just a virologist, right?"

Adele's mother gave her a quick look, eyebrows raised. "I know something about the spread of disease, so I'm on the team." Adele knew understatement when she heard it. Her mother was an internationally recognized expert. "I think they're barking up the wrong tree on this one, though," her mother went on. "I've got some ideas of my own."

"Like what?" asked Adele.

Her mother frowned. "If you look at what's happening and you try to define a set of symptoms," she put air quotes around symptoms, "you come up with a symptomatology that reminds me of a virus I studied."

"OK," said Adele. She did not blink at the word symptomatology. Dinner table conversation in her house ranged from the Seattle Mariners to the importance of the standing wave ratio in radio transmissions to viral symptomatology, a chancy topic when eating mashed potatoes and gravy although the performance of the Mariners could depress your appetite significantly, too.

"There was a virus that they thought caused Alzheimer's, but they messed up on two points: the symptomatology and the statistics."

This was a story Adele had heard before, but only from her father. Some major drug company had touted a big study that showed Alzheimer's was caused by a rabies virus variant. This was not a cure but identifying the cause would have been a great first step on the way to a cure. But Adele's mom was the rabies expert at the

CDC, and something about the study did not smell right. She looked at the original data, ran some new statistical tests and published a series of papers and studies that contradicted the drug company's findings. Adele's dad said that after that, her mom got re-assigned to this west coast lab, the boonies as far as a career with the CDC was concerned. And then the head of her department back at the CDC home office - the guy who had reassigned her - retired and took a cushy job at the drug company.

"How so?" asked Adele.

"Alzheimer's patients experience progressive confusion and loss of cognitive function." Adele steeled herself: her mother was in lecture mode. "They might go through an angry stage or a depressed stage, but the main thing is the cognitive loss."

"And?" Adele prompted.

"A subset of the subjects in the study didn't progress through the angry or depressed stage. They just descended into fury or despair and stayed there." Adele's mom slowed for a corner. "They were so sunk in it, that they stopped eating. There didn't seem to be any loss of cognitive function, but they lost all interest in daily activities. They would have starved to death without a feeding tube. That is totally not typical of Alzheimer's."

"So, what's the connection with the Middle East?"

"It's the fury. That all-against-all behavior."

"What about the despair? No one's reporting a huge number of cases of terminal depression, are they?"

"No, but we probably wouldn't see them unless we did some sort of systematic survey. They would be invisible, inside, wasting away in a chair staring at the wall or curled up in bed." She paused, and then went on as if speaking to herself, "Assuming the violent ones hadn't already torn them to pieces."

They approached some little kids at a crosswalk on the left, and Adele's mom took her foot off the gas, watching them carefully. Sure enough, the kids misjudged and bolted across the street in front of the car. Adele's mom slammed on the brakes and the kids made it to the sidewalk, safe.

Adele rolled down her window. "Hey, Stevie," she yelled. "I'm telling your sister you're playing chicken with cars."

Stevie grinned and waved. "Hi, Deli!" he shouted as the car pulled away.

"Who was that?" asked her mother.

"That's Rachel's little brother. He'll be lucky to make it to fifth grade."

"What about the statistical mistake they made?" asked Adele, glad to leave the symptomatology discussion behind.

"That one was a classic," said her mother. "The researchers confirmed that everyone showing Alzheimer symptoms tested positive for the virus."

"What's the matter with that?"

"Well, a few years ago I was at a conference. And one of the researchers on the study was there. A really sweet guy I knew in grad school."

Adele glanced at her mother.

"One night, we were reminiscing, and he was knocking back the drinks. And we got on the study, and he admitted that my critique was exactly right. He said they had confirmed that everyone with symptoms had tested positive for the virus. But they missed the strongest correlation which was between high viral load and the violent behavior. And they never checked to confirm that people with no symptoms tested negative for the virus."

"Ah," said Adele. She started opening another yogurt.

"So, just for kicks, Rick tested himself." Adele's mother looked over at her. "He tested positive. He started testing everyone he could. Everyone tested positive."

Adele looked down at her yogurt.

"When I got back from the conference, I tested myself. Positive. I tested your dad. Positive. Everyone I've tested, tests positive."

"Did you test me?" asked Adele.

"Yeah. I tested you, too. Positive."

"How did I get it? From you?"

Her mother was silent for a few seconds. "I think it's everywhere, Deli. Everyone we've ever tested has it, without exception. I think everyone in the world has the virus."

"That doesn't sound good."

"It gets worse," said her mother.

"Oh, joy," said Adele.

"I retested a couple of people. The later tests showed an increase in the viral load. It's growing, and there's a point where it's like it reaches critical mass. People go off like a bomb."

They rode the rest of the way in silence.

CHAPTER 4

The bell rang, and Jamie made for the door with the other kids. He was acutely aware of Adele who was just ahead of him, and he pushed forward a bit, not really with any plan in mind but just to be there. Stepping into the hall was like stepping into whitewater rapids, all rush, push and noise.

Adele turned to him and the crush of the hallway bumped them together for a second, a soft impact on his arm.

"Oops. Sorry," said Jamie, and smiled. Adele smiled back, but a seriousness was in her eyes that the smile did not chase away.

"Hey, are you showing anything at the fair today?" she asked.

"Yeah. I'm doing an exhibit on the transition from the Upper Paleolithic to the Neolithic in Europe." He pushed on. Experience taught him that he had about five seconds to say something interesting before the glazed look would come into the eyes of his listener. "That's when we fell from grace, you know, when we went from hunter-gatherers to farmers."

"Cool," said Adele. "I'll come by and see it."

"Great," said Jamie. "Are you doing another moving piece?"

"Yeah. It's called Torn Down Under. It's about how modern life does violence to women. I'll run it for about an hour, or until the pantyhose give out. Come by and see it. They wouldn't let me show the porn clips or do the propane torch thing but it's still pretty cool." She stopped abruptly, as if afraid of talking too much. They were at an intersection of halls and she turned to face Jamie.

Jamie remembered when they were kids on the playground, how during games he would chase her but she was too fast and he could never catch her. Now as he looked at her, she seemed to change before his eyes, woman, girl, woman, girl. And like a light-sensitive mechanism, he felt his blood rise, fall, rise, fall.

She was looking at him. He knew he was supposed to do something.

"OK?" she asked?

"Yeah. Yeah, sure," he managed.

It was the right thing. She smiled, high wattage, all shadows gone now, and he smiled back, it seemed to him, with his whole body. And she turned and walked away. And he stood there without moving as she disappeared into the crowd.

"Hey, man. Beep, beep!" someone said.

"Sorry," he mumbled, and turned and hurried on to class.

* * *

Bonney pulled his old pickup into the circular drive and peered through the sliding glass doors into the emergency room. Medical staff were rushing back and forth, but there was no sign of Ellen. He put the truck into neutral and pulled on the emergency brake, but left the engine running so he could get out of the way quickly if an ambulance pulled in. He waited.

The glass doors slid open and Ellen stepped through. She had changed out of her uniform and into something suitable for the student fair at the high school. She crossed in front of the pickup and jumped up into the front seat. She scooted across until she could reach Bonney and gave him a kiss on the lips.

"Get me out of here," she said.

"Hmmmm," he said, and looked her up and down. She settled back onto her side of the bench seat and fastened the belt.

"Sorry I'm late."

Bonney put the truck in gear. "Looks busy in there."

"Yeah, it's just been crazy today. It's like a Saturday night. We had a car accident – some guy tried to blow through the stop sign down at the highway and hit a pickup truck broadside. Some people injured in a fight at the tavern. A woman brought in a little girl with a sprained wrist – says she fell off her tricycle." She rolled her eyes and blew out a big breath. "I thought I recognized her so I checked the paper work and she's the little girl who lives in the next block, you know, just down the hill."

"Oh, yeah," said Bonney. He shifted into second as they passed the sporting goods store. "That's too bad. She seems like a real sweetie."

"She was brave, really brave, like stoic. Like almost too stoic, like she's been punished if she cries."

"Ah. Do you suspect abuse?"

Ellen stared through the windshield at something far away. They pulled up to a stop sign. "I called Child Protective Services," she said.

"What did they say?"

"They said leave a message at the tone."

Bonney frowned. "Don't you have some sort of unpublished number for medical professionals? Like, they're always supposed to answer?"

"That was the number I was calling. They must be flooded with calls."

"Is this because of the budget cuts?"

"I don't think so. I got through just fine a couple of weeks ago, and they got right on it."

They rode in silence for a couple of blocks.

"I'm so lucky to be on day shift. I mean, it's getting worse and worse. Day shift is starting to feel like the three to eleven shift used to be. But I hear that the night shift is getting really crazy. Did I tell you Miriam quit?"

Bonney shook his head.

"Amy in HR says it's going to be hard to hire a new night shift nurse to replace her. She says she read a study that says the number of unfilled positions for nurses in the United States grew last year but the number of nurses actually shrank. They're all burned out."

Bonney glanced over at his wife. "I guess that makes you even more valuable."

"Yeah, as long as I'm willing to do the work. But I don't know, Bonney." She looked at him and then went on. "It used to be that we'd get a kid with a high fever or an old guy with flu. Occasionally we'd get the broken arm when a kid fell off the swing set or maybe a logging accident or a car crash. But now we're flooded, even on the day shift. And there's so much violence. Domestic arguments that become fist fights, and fist fights at the bar that become shoot outs." She shook her head. "Sorry. I just had to vent."

"No problem, babe."

Ellen seemed to pull herself together. "So, how was your day? Project done? What time did you come to bed last night?"

"I got to bed around 3:30. Did I wake you?"

"You're a little old to be pulling all-nighters, aren't you?" Ellen ducked the question.

"Amen to that. But the local CDC office would be a great client."

"Success, then?"

"Yeah." Bonney grinned. "But they didn't get me the test data until like 8:00 last night. Huge file, tons of data. Took me a couple of hours to build the database and run the statistical routines. Ran it through the reporting modules and about had a heart attack."

"How come?"

"The projections on the report were way out of whack. I texted Rose Prada at the CDC and she called right back. At first she seemed upset, like the test results were all wrong. But then she calmed down and said not to worry, that the trends in the test data probably would show everyone in the world exhibiting symptoms in a matter of weeks. I said ha-ha, this is just made up test data, right? And she said of course, that it was against CDC policy to distribute real data to contractors. And she sort of laughed. Which sort of worried me. I'm not real sure what she's up to with this project."

"What do you mean?"

"Oh, like I wonder how official this project is. You know, does her boss know what she's doing or is she just out on her own with this work?"

Bonney turned into the school parking lot and started the search for a parking place. "You want me to drop you?" he asked.

"Nah, I'm good," said Ellen.

Bonney squeezed the truck into a spot between a battered Jeep Cherokee and an ancient Subaru station wagon.

"Do all the kids have cars these days?"

"Of course," said Ellen. "Where have you been?"

They entered through the main doors on the west side of the building and checked in at a table where a policeman sat. "Hey, Ellen, Bonney," he greeted them both.

"Hi, Peter," said Ellen.

"Hey, Pete," said Bonney.

Ellen knew all the city police from her work in the emergency room. Bonney knew most of them from a bowling league he and Ellen had joined when they first moved to Darnell and were just exploring small town life.

"How's it look, tonight?" asked Ellen.

"Looks good. Big crowd for the exhibition. Probably even bigger for the game. Lots of people in from Arlington. Jamie's got a nice exhibit. Little off on the dates, though." Pete was a fundamentalist Christian and Jamie's timeline for the transition from Upper Paleolithic to Neolithic was, of course, the work of the devil.

"He's using the standard scientific dates," said Ellen. She gave the policeman an extra big smile with wide, innocent eyes. The policeman frowned and started to say something, but Bonney grabbed Ellen's arm and pulled her away.

"Catch ya later, Pete," he called over his shoulder. Ellen pulled her arm free.

"You don't need to protect me from Peter," she said.

"I was protecting Pete from you," replied Bonney. Ellen snorted.

The signs for the fair directed them to the gym, and the halls became busy as they approached. When they stepped through the big, double doors, the noise and commotion stopped them in their tracks. They blinked and surveyed the room, looking for Jamie's table.

"There he is," said Bonney. Ellen followed his gaze to a table on her right. Jamie stood in front of several large screens and moved his hands around, swiping, pointing, touching the air, like an orchestra conductor. The displays on the screens blinked and panned, switching rapidly in response to his motions. A small crowd had gathered around the table and Jamie stood aside when a man reached out and tentatively waved his hand. The screens flickered in response. Jamie stepped forward, demonstrated a set of motions, and a pair of skeletons appeared, the one on the left screen labeled Upper Paleolithic and a smaller one on the right labeled Neolithic.

"Wow," said Bonney. "He got the gestural interface working. That's pretty amazing."

Bonney and Ellen started across the room toward Jamie's exhibit. Bonney rested a hand on Ellen's back, as if to stay close in case they lost visual contact in the press of the crowd. They skirted a particularly large group around an exhibit that was all mechanical arms in motion, pulling and tearing at some filmy fabric to a heavy rap beat. A beautiful, dark haired young woman dressed all in black with high boots and very skinny jeans stood in front of the installation. She threw her head back and laughed at something someone in the crowd said and then replied with a smile.

"Yeesh," said Ellen as they made their way past. "Amazing how skinny jeans can attract a crowd."

"Looks like a very creative installation," said Bonney. "We should check it out before we leave."

"You mean check her out," said Ellen.

Bonney laughed.

* * *

"This is really awesome, Jamie." Bonney was standing in front of Jamie's exhibit, waving his hands and watching the screens change. With each sweep of his hands, the image of a clearing in a forest changed, layers of dirt peeling off to reveal an arrangement of large stones in a straight line, the remains of a wall of some ancient structure, then beneath that smaller stones in circles, and beneath that discolored spots in the dirt, all that remained of the wooden post framework of wattle and daub shelters from when people initially settled down at the beginning of the Neolithic.

"Look at this, Bonney," said Jamie. He stepped up and lifted his hands like a preacher telling the congregation to rise, and the framework of the huts rose from the spots in the dirt, sticks were woven through the uprights and then a mixture of mud and grass covered that, showing finally a reconstructed Neolithic dwelling.

"Computer, tell me about it!" Jamie spoke in a commanding tone, and a Siri-like voice gave a short lecture about the construction technique they had just watched.

"Just think what you could do with this and virtual reality," said Jamie.

Bonney blew out his breath appreciatively. Ellen stood with her mouth open.

"I am so impressed with this, Jamie," she said. "Did you do this all on your own?"

Jamie glanced at Bonney. "Bonney helped with some of the programming logic, but I created most of the content."

"I think I put in about fifteen minutes total on one programming problem," said Bonney. "This is really all Jamie's."

"That is so cool, Jamie," said a young woman's voice.

Bonney and Ellen turned and Adele gave them a big smile.

"Hi, Deli," said Jamie. "Take a look at this."

Adele squeezed past Bonney and Ellen and stood next to Jamie, who proceeded to demonstrate with decisive gestures and firm voice commands, his back now to his parents.

Bonney and Ellen looked at each other. "Excuse me," said Bonney. "Weren't we just in the room with your son?"

"Skinny jeans rule, I guess," said Ellen. "And don't forget, you adopted him."

Bonney turned back to Jamie and Adele and smiled. Jamie was standing close to Adele, touching first her hands and then her arms, moving them in a series of gestures. He put his hand on her back, low down, as if to steady her.

"Modern technology really opens up some possibilities, doesn't it," said Bonney. Ellen jabbed her elbow in his ribs. "Oof," he said.

Jamie and Adele looked back, and Adele stepped away from Jamie.

"Aren't you going to introduce us?" asked Ellen.

"Oh, yeah... Mom, this is Deli, Adele Prada. Adele, this is my mom and my dad, Nate Bonney."

"Pleased to meet you Mrs. Montane, Mr. Bonney," said Adele. She held out her hand to each and shook.

"Just Bonney is fine," said Bonney. "Everyone just calls me Bonney."

"Then Bonney it is," said Adele, smiling.

"Any relation to Rose Prada? She works at the CDC?" asked Bonney.

"Yeah. She's my mother. Do you know her?"

"Bonney is working with your mom on some CDC project. He's a computer programmer," said Jamie.

"You're working on her secret project? The violent behavior thing?"

"Yeah, that sounds like it," said Bonney.

"She just got you the data late last night, right?" said Adele. "She was so embarrassed. She said she finally had to give you a copy of the real data because she couldn't generate a good test dataset."

"The data she gave me last night was real data?" asked Bonney. The smile was gone from his face.

"What's secret about it?" said Jamie before Adele could reply.

Adele looked at Jamie and then back to Bonney. She seemed unsure of herself and clasped her hands together. "Oh, it's not a big secret. She's just not sure she'll find anything. Would you like to see my sculpture?" she offered.

"Sure," said Jamie, before Bonney could press his questions, and they followed Adele through the crowd to her exhibit. The sculpture was motionless when they got there, an odd thing of shapes draped in the sheer fabric of dark panty hose, now shredded and torn.

"Normally it moves," said Adele, "but once the fabric tears, it's basically done." She looked at Bonney and Ellen, who appeared puzzled. "So, I turn it off then," she explained.

"Ah," said Bonney with an expression of comprehension, more polite than convincing. Ellen cocked her head and frowned.

"I saw it when it was moving," said Jamie. "It was really cool."

Adele beamed, and Jamie's face lit up in response. Bonney couldn't help but smile back, as well. Ellen took in the reactions of her men to the young woman and gave a tight smile.

"Well, we need to get going," said Ellen. She turned to Jamie. "Dinner's at 5:30."

Adele turned to Jamie. "Hey," she said. "Rachel and I are going out for pizza after the fair. Want to come? You can tell me about how you did the gesture detection thing. I could really use that for my next piece. Maybe we could do a collaborative piece."

"That sounds like a great idea," said Bonney. He turned to Jamie. "You'd be glad to help, wouldn't you?"

"Yeah, sure," said Jamie.

"Let us know if you need a ride," said Bonney. "Where are you getting pizza?" he asked Adele.

"We'll be at Guido's Place."

"I know where that is," said Bonney, as if any place in Darnell might be unknown to anyone.

"Well, I guess I'm cooking for two, tonight," said Ellen. She took Bonney's arm and pulled him toward the gym doors. "Don't be late," she called over her shoulder.

"I won't," said Jamie.

"We could pick up some pizza. Crack open a bottle of chianti. Kick back," Bonney suggested when they emerged from the gym and started down the school hallway. "Might be just the thing after a tough day at work."

"Oh, maybe another night," said Ellen. "Why were you so quick to tell Jamie OK? Do we know anything about Adele and her friends? That silly sculpture!" Bonney lengthened his stride to keep up with her.

"OK, I admit that I kind of get it," she went on. "Everyone hates pantyhose. But the titillation of the piece – the younger women think they can play with being a sex object, you know? Exploring the power of it without realizing the trap? They don't know the struggle my generation of women went through, they don't appreciate our sacrifice."

Bonney looked at Ellen. Her face was tight and her hands were clenched on her purse.

"And we don't know anything about her family, really. You notice neither her mother nor her father came to the fair?" Ellen glanced up at Bonney. "I just don't like the look of her. She's so obvious, with those skinny jeans and her bellybutton exposed. She appeals to the worst in him. He's too young, doesn't know what he's dealing with. The slut." And then she stopped in her tracks, looking straight ahead as if peering down some dark tunnel with no light at the end. She turned to him, a troubled expression on her face. "Listen to me. What am I saying?" she demanded. Then she laughed. "Two bottles," she said, holding up two fingers. "Offer me pizza and two bottles of chianti, and you've got a date." She grinned up at him.

Bonney looked into her eyes and then grinned also, but they drove back to the house through dark streets without speaking, and Bonney wondered about data and violence and the next few weeks. A sense of helplessness came over him, a sense that even two bottles failed to ease.

* * *

Guido's Pizza Joint was a weird combination of old and new. On the one hand, it had a dim interior, where the diners sat in scarred, dark wood booths with narrow bench seats and high backs left over from when the place was a rough and tumble logger bar. On the other hand, the food was the latest pizza fare: wood fired, any crust you'd want, and all the goat's cheese, salmon, and pesto you could wish for. Sun-dried this, artisan-that, and all locally sourced. Gluten-free options for everything, of course. The old Darnell families wouldn't be caught dead there. It was a favorite among the newcomers, though, professionals and techies who worked in the city down on the coast but couldn't afford to live there.

The line to get in stretched out the door. Rachel waved to someone and Jamie turned to see. Caleb and Dwight were ahead of them with a rowdy group that seemed to take up a lot of room in the waiting area. Caleb smiled and waved back.

"Don't wave to him. He's a creep," said Adele. Rachel just shrugged and tossed her head. Adele turned to Jamie. "She's hopeless," she said. "Likes the bad-boys." Jamie pushed his fists into his pockets and shrugged.

When the hostess finally led them to their booth, Adele hung back until Jamie sat down and then sat next to him. Rachel sat opposite. She fiddled with her phone for a second and a text popped up on Adele's phone. "Smooth move," it read. Adele didn't deign to reply.

They ordered and ate and now the table was littered with the remains of their pizza and grease-stained, crumpled up napkins.

A young man with dark hair and complexion approached their booth. "Is that it for tonight?" he asked.

"That's it for me, Juan," said Adele. She looked at the others.

"I'm done," said Jamie.

"Yep," said Rachel.

Juan put down a ticket. "I'll be right back for that," he said and turned to the booth where Caleb and his crew were sitting.

"Hey, Juan," said Caleb. He smiled up at the waiter.

"Hey, Caleb," replied Juan.

"I see you finally found a job. Helps that your dad owns the place, huh? I didn't know your family was Italian. I thought you were Mexicans."

"We're American, Caleb. Guido's is just the name of the restaurant."

"Oh, sorry, man. My mistake," said Caleb.

Juan tore off a ticket and held it out. "Who gets it?" he asked.

"Ah, shit," said Dwight. "Can you divide it up?"

Caleb slid out of his booth and came over. He leaned on the high back and turned to Adele. "Dwight and I are going to the game tonight. You girls wanna come along?"

Jamie's face reddened. He had no interest in sports and the last thing he wanted to do that night was go to the baseball season opener, but the snub remained an intentional insult. Adele hesitated, seemed slightly taken aback.

"Oh, sure," said Rachel.

"Sorry, Caleb," said Adele, "Jamie's already invited me. Maybe we'll see you there." She smiled and hooked an arm through Jamie's.

Jamie and Rachel looked at Adele. "Right, Jamie?" she prompted. She turned to Jamie and looked him directly in the eye. Her face was calm, with a slight smile. She waited.

Jamie met her gaze. He smiled. "Yeah," he said. "We're really excited about the game. Kill those Badgers."

Caleb straightened up and looked from Adele to Jamie, the displeasure plain on his face.

"Beavers," he said. "We're playing the Arlington Beavers tonight," but Jamie and Adele didn't seem to hear.

CHAPTER 5

It was cold as they walked back to the ball field at the high school. Rachel was a few steps ahead with Caleb and Dwight, one on each arm, doing a great job of making sure Adele and Jamie had some space. She appeared to enjoy the task.

They got through the gate and stepped out of the flow of the crowd to look around. It was the first game of the regular season for Darnell, and there were high hopes for the team this year as younger players matured.

"Jesus! Looks like the whole town turned out," said Jamie.

"Who are these people?" asked Rachel. She looked at the press of fans. Some were students from Darnell, but there were also family groups, moms and dads with little kids in tow, blankets and sleeping bags under their arms. Mixed in were groups of young men, boisterous, carrying coolers filled with soft drinks and bags of chips. Security at the gate opened the coolers and checked the bags but seemed unaware of the many bottles of liquor and cans of beer tucked in pockets or hidden under coats that made it into the stands.

"Big game," said Dwight. "Lots of fans in from Arlington tonight."

"Let's grab our seats," said Caleb. He looked anxiously toward the tiny bleachers behind the backstop. "Some guys are holding four seats for us. Wow, Jamie, I don't think there's room for you." Caleb looked regretful. Dwight grinned.

"You guys go on," said Adele. "Jamie and I are sitting up there." She motioned to the only other seating around the diamond, a modest set of bleachers along the first base line. Baseball was definitely second-string when it came to sports at Darnell High. Tradition and a well-connected coach ensured that the football team got most of the institutional support, despite a mediocre record.

"Come along, boys," said Rachel. She hooked arms with Dwight and Caleb and swept them along before they could protest.

Jamie and Adele made their way up the stands, stepping carefully on the aluminum stairs. A group ahead of them paused repeatedly, pointing to open spaces and debating vigorously. There seemed to be strong opinions on the matter and when the dilemma was finally resolved, the group — mostly young men with faces painted Arlington gold and green — shuffled awkwardly by the feet and legs of earlier arrivals and settled down with their coolers. Jamie and Adele continued on up to an area that was mostly still open, instinctively putting several rows of seats between them and the painted men.

"Whew," said Adele. She scooched closer to Jamie across the cold, metal bench. "Kind of breezy up here."

"Do you want to move?" offered Jamie.

"No, no. This is good." Adele leaned in and smiled up at him. Jamie smiled back.

They sat for a minute without speaking, taking in the scene. The stands below them were packed and the seats around them filled quickly. Everything was illuminated by the glare of the lights. It was harsh and unkind where it touched the faces of the fans and left deep shadows where it could not reach.

"Are these games always this noisy?" asked Adele. She put her mouth close to Jamie's ear to be heard, perhaps closer than necessary.

"I guess it's a big game," said Jamie. He wondered why Adele was yelling into his ear. He looked around and frowned. Not that he knew anything about it, but it seemed awfully loud. And there was a tone to the noise, an edge that was out of place. Perhaps the Darnell ball field had this effect, forcing fans of both teams to sit side-by-side in the single set of bleachers.

Everyone stood for the Star-Spangled Banner, Darnell and the other up-river communities being fairly traditional in many ways. A sophomore girl sang, and the bleachers were stilled for a moment as her young voice sailed through the cold, clear air, carrying the highest notes with power and ease. For a few seconds, all were silent, and then the crowd exploded, cheering and stamping, shaking the stands beneath them, united briefly by the heroic vision of the nation's past. Then the Darnell team took the field, and the game was on.

The score stayed close for five innings. First Darnell and then Arlington took a one run lead. Calls were hotly contested by the coaches until an Arlington coach was ejected when he pushed the first-base ump. The crowd howled.

Jamie and Adele had given up trying to carry on a conversation. They stood when the crowd around them stood and clapped when Darnell made a play or a run. In all the commotion, it was easy to hook arms without really noticing what they were doing as the fans around them jumped to their feet and sat back down.

Below them, the young men with the green and gold painted faces were obviously enjoying themselves, drinking, hooting and yelling. They were the quickest to jump up and the last to sit back down, filling the space around them with their noise and motion and irritating the hell out of any Darnell fans sitting near them. Words were exchanged and finally, in the top of the sixth, an old guy in an ancient Darnell letter jacket shoved one of the young men from behind. Cold beer spilled across an older woman sitting in front of the young man, and she turned and slapped him hard across the face. The young man actually apologized to the woman and then turned around to deal with the old Darnell fan behind him. But before he could do anything, the older man hauled off and punched him in the jaw. The young man sprawled backward across the benches below him, and the older man launched himself onto him, screaming obscenities.

Chaos ensued as fans pushed and shoved to get away from the fight, and the painted faces jumped in. It was unclear, at first, what exactly the young men were doing in the melee, but then they pulled the combatants apart and broke up the fight, although the older man appeared to have gotten banged up a bit in the process. He did not calm down, and it took four guys to restrain him.

Several beefy security men rushed up the stairs and took control of the older man who continued to struggle and curse. Once, he almost broke free and it was only because one of the security men was the high school wrestling coach that he did not succeed. They dragged him down to the foot of the stands and held him on the ground until Pete, the policeman, arrived and cuffed him.

Even then the man fought on, a vicious kick connecting with the knee of the wrestling coach who fell heavily. "Jesus, Hugh!" he yelled, calling the struggling man by name. "What the hell are you doing?"

One of the other security men started hitting the cuffed man in the face and only stopped when Pete put his body between the two. It took all four to finally restrain Hugh with a pull-tie like thing around his ankles, and Pete put a knee on the man's back and gripped the cuffs in one hand while he called for backup. The game was paused, and everyone in the bleachers was on their feet watching the spectacle.

Adele turned to Jamie. "You know, I think I'm done with the game."

"Yeah, let's go," he said, and turned to the stairs.

"Excuse me... Excuse me," said Jamie as they shuffled past the stunned fans on their row. They could still hear Hugh raging, and now there were murmurs of disapproval from the crowd as the security guards became more forceful in their attempt to subdue Hugh who appeared to be trying to bite them. Jamie and Adele descended the stairs, squeezing to the left as they approached the grunting and thrashing men on the ground ahead of them.

A can of beer spun through the air, the harsh lights glinting in the spray of liquid that spattered the crowd below. The can struck Pete full in the face. "Fucking enough, already!" yelled a voice from the stands. The crowd booed and jeered. A jumbo drink followed and then Pete, the security men, and Hugh as well, were all pelted with things thrown from the stands. Jamie and Adele ducked as they pushed past the scrum at the foot of the stairs but were splashed by the cups and cans that rained down around them.

A few more steps and they were safely away from the mess, but a new sound above them in the stands made Jamie look back. Multiple fights had erupted in the bleachers as those splattered with the thrown drinks turned on those who had thrown them, and the Darnell fans turned on the Arlington fans. Families with young children abandoned their blankets and sleeping bags, trying to escape flailing tangles of men, and the whole scene descended into a screaming, shouting chaos while Jamie watched, his mouth hanging open.

"Holy shit," said Jamie. "What is this?"

"It's a riot!" said Adele. She gripped Jamie's arm with both hands. They were buffeted by a rush of people going every which way. Some were running away from the violence but many were rushing to join the brawl. Sirens pierced the din and several police cars screamed up, bumping over the curb and rolling across the grass to get close to the stands. The policemen jumped out, formed a wedge and attempted to push through the maelstrom toward Pete and the security men who were now somewhere beneath a vicious pile of angry fans.

"Let's go!" shouted Adele. She pulled at Jamie's arm. He turned, gripped her hand, and started toward the street. Two young men with military haircuts were just ahead of them, making their way through the mob. One led the way, running interference, while the other stayed close behind and carried a little girl who wrapped her arms around his neck and buried her face under his chin. A young woman stumbled after him, clinging to his belt with both hands. Jamie and Adele stepped into their wake and stayed as close as they could as they made for the gate.

The riot engulfed them now, like a wildfire in the woods. Furious knots of men and occasionally a woman or two flailed away at each other all around them. Once Jamie was almost taken down by a man who staggered up and grabbed him, but Adele sank her teeth into his arm until the man cried out and let go. Finally, they all emerged through the gate in the chain link fence. Jamie and Adele sprinted to the street and slowed to a fast walk when they reached it. Jamie turned and walked backwards for several steps and then stopped. Adele stopped too, and they both looked back at the field.

People poured out through the gates in the fence around the field, running, stumbling, back-lit and dark against the glaring arc-lights. The flashing lightbars of the police cars were a red and blue strobe on those closest to them, freezing the fleeing figures repeatedly in a nightmarish tableau of desperation and fear as they rushed to escape the eruption of violence. Silent, they streamed by Jamie and Adele, hurrying on to the safety of car and home.

The scene inside the fence was mostly obscured by the escaping crowd, but above the heads of these, in a pool of light, was an area of violent agitation where a raised fist flashed and an aluminum bat glinted briefly in a vicious arc. The fight extended up the bleachers in isolated knots of tangled bodies that tumbled from bench to bench.

"Oh, god," breathed Adele.

Dwight, Caleb and Rachel emerged from the crowd. Dwight looked grim and pressed a wadded-up scarf to the side of his face. Rachel ran up to Adele and threw her arms around her.

"Deli! Are you OK? Oh, Jesus, we almost didn't make it. Some old creeps grabbed me, and Dwight saved me." Her voice was shaky.

"Yeah, Dwight really nailed those fuckers," crowed Caleb. He kept scanning the crowd around them, a fierce grin on his face.

"What happened to your face?" asked Adele.

"It was bleeding. I think it's stopped," said Dwight. "I'll be OK."

"You should go to the Emergency Room," said Jamie. "Does anyone have a car?"

"I've got one," said Caleb. "I'm over here." He motioned down the street which was lined with cars parked on either side.

"I'll ride with you guys," said Rachel. She turned to Dwight. "You can sit in the back with me."

Caleb pulled out his keys. "Let's roll." He turned to Jamie and Adele. "You guys need a ride?"

"No. You go straight to the hospital," said Adele. "We can walk, no problem."

"Let's move it," said Dwight. He put a hand on Caleb's arm and then Caleb, Dwight and Rachel started down the street. There was something slightly off about how Dwight was walking, and Rachel gripped his jacket, steadying them both as they went.

"Text me, Rache," called Adele. Rachel brandished her cell phone with her free hand in response.

Cars were coming by now, inching through the walkers. One driver was honking his horn and flashing his brights. People gave way slowly and someone banged on the trunk of the car as it pushed through. The driver rolled down the window and made a rude gesture.

"Let's get out of here," said Jamie. They linked arms and walked down to the corner where they turned right and then left onto a quiet street that ran parallel to the one jammed with cars and pedestrians. Behind them, more sirens cut through the low rumble from the ball field, and an ambulance — lights flashing — zoomed by them on its way from the school to the hospital. The lights flickered. All the lights, streetlights, porch lights, the windows of all the houses, all went dark, and for a split second, the world was utterly black. Then they all came back on again.

"I should call my parents," said Adele. She pulled out her cell and speed-dialed her mother. She took another couple of steps, holding the phone to her ear and then stopped. She looked at the phone and frowned. "No bars," she said. "Do you have bars?"

Jamie dug his phone out and pressed the power button. The screen stayed dark. "Shit. I think the battery's dead," he said. He pressed and held the power button but there was no response. They looked at each other and then Jamie looked up and down the street. "I guess we're hoofing it," he said. He held out his arm, and Adele took it. They walked without speaking. The sounds from the baseball field faded as they got farther away, and finally, their silence was broken only by the sound of their own footsteps and the wind in the trees.

* * *

Jamie was working his way home, up the hill, his long legs moving quickly. He had a sense that things were utterly different, somehow, that he had been asleep but now was awake, that he had been a child, living a charmed, small town life of school clubs, forts in the woods, and family camping trips, but no longer. The cold wind of that spring night seemed to blow in from a distant and very big world and his sheltered life in Darnell with his mother and Bonney appeared fundamentally altered. Did he belong here anymore? Had he ever belonged here? Had this place ever really existed, or was it just a comforting facade on an uncomfortable world created by the care of his mom and Bonney? They had seemed so powerful, once, but now his parents seemed vulnerable, smaller, less.

Standing on the corner of Main Street, they had said goodnight. The street lamp cast a harsh light over them, giving Adele's skin a yellowed cast and making a gaunt mask of her face. Somewhere along the way, she had acquired a black smudge on her right cheekbone, and her tidy French braid was barely a memory in the tangle of her dark hair. A gust of wind blew a strand across her face. It brushed her lips and she reached up and captured it and tucked it behind her ear, but another gust immediately blew it free again.

They stood for a moment, not speaking, and Jamie looked down into Adele's face. It came to him that she was the form of that night, that the night stood in front of him in all its wild power and disarray, and he felt that the world had expanded, become vast and alien. And then Adele kissed him, on the lips. A quick light touch, and then she was gone, crossing the street and the railroad tracks beyond. And that cold breeze from far away had found that touch of wet on his lips, a second, chill kiss.

He frowned and pulled the collar of his jacket up around his neck. It was not what he had expected. The entire night was unexpected. The world was unexpected. She was unexpected.

And how could it be that Adele was unexpected? He had been aware of her for months, since the start of the semester when she was assigned the seat next to him in English Lit. And, of course, he had known her for years, like everyone knows everyone in Darnell. So how could she keep surprising him?

He took the front steps two at a time and the door unlocked with a click at his approach. He pushed through and tossed his backpack onto the floor of the entryway. The warmth and light of the house enveloped him and he sighed in relief. The dark thoughts that had visited him on his lonely walk up the hill retreated to a far corner of his mind. The front door, with its smart lock that Bonney had installed, the light and warmth of home, seemed to reestablish the charmed circle.

"I'm home," he announced. He walked to the hall closet and hung up his jacket. "Hello?" he called.

CHAPTER 6

Jamie took a quick tour of the first floor of the house. No one was in the living room. The TV room was dark and silent. The only sign of life was an open bottle of micro-brew beer on the kitchen counter. He picked it up and held it up to the light. The bottle was almost full, but only cool, not cold to the touch. He considered tasting it but put it down and resumed his search.

"Hello?" he called again and ran up the stairs to the second floor. The hall was dark except where light spilled out of Bonney's office, illuminating one spot of the well-worn hall runner. Jamie walked down to the door and looked in. The usual piles were in the usual places and the laptop was sitting on the desk. The screens were dark. He went back out into the hall and checked each of the bedrooms which were also dark and empty.

He came down the stairs, fast as usual, and retraced his steps through each of the first-floor rooms, looking for a note. He checked the answering machine on the landline to see if there were any messages or memos. None.

Somewhere in the house, there was a scratching noise, and a low moan or whine. Jamie inclined his head slightly and held his breath, waiting to hear the sound a second time. There it was, coming from the back of the house. Jamie moved in that direction, stepping into the kitchen and looking around for anything out of the ordinary. All seemed in order. He stopped again and waited, and again the sound came, a gentle scratching at the back door and a definite, low whine. Jamie walked to the sink and leaned forward to look out the window, craning his neck so he could see what was on the back porch, but he couldn't see anything.

He went to the door, flicking on the back-porch light on his way, and put his hand on the knob. He paused, and then placed his foot on the floor a few inches back from the door, put his weight on it and slowly turned the knob. The latch clicked and the door swung open as far as his foot. Jamie leaned to the left and looked around the door through the crack out to the back porch. A low whine drew his eyes downward, and there was Mr. Schultz' dog, Spot, muddy, trembling, his leash still trailing from his collar, dirty and tangled in a clump of branches. The dog sat, looking up at him.

Jamie opened the door all the way and knelt down on one knee. He held his hands out to the dog. "There we go. Good dog," he said gently. "Come on in."

Spot got up and walked forward, pushing his head into Jamie's hands. Something was off in how the dog walked. He appeared to favor a hind leg, but his tail wagged as Jamie stroked his head and made clucking sounds. The dog's head left a grimy smear on Jamie's t-shirt, and his hands came away dirty and wet.

Jamie unhooked the leash and threw the tangled mess back out onto the porch. He guided the dog into the house and closed the door, turned on a light and led the dog down the half flight of stairs into the walkout basement. Once Jamie's playroom, the lower level was now storage. The cement floor and tattered rugs would not suffer from the dog's muddy paw prints.

Each step on the stairs brought a short whine from Spot, and it took a while to reach the floor. There, Jamie checked him over quickly. A gash, recent by the look of it, cut across his left rear flank. The coat was matted down with clotted blood. Jamie touched it as gently as he could, but the dog yelped and turned back toward his hand, teeth showing for a second but then hidden. The dog licked Jamie's hand, pushing it away from the wound.

Jamie sat back and wiped his hands on his jeans. "OK," he said. "You stay here. I'll get you some water and something to eat."

The dog watched him as he got to his feet slowly, making no sudden moves. He put out both his hands, palms out. "Stay," he directed. Spot looked at him and then laid down. Jamie went to the stairs, looking back to make sure that Spot did not follow, and then went up to the kitchen. He got a big mixing bowl out and filled it with water at the sink. He opened the refrigerator door and surveyed the shelves. A package of hamburger seemed like just the thing, and Jamie pulled a large wooden bowl out of a cabinet and plopped the ground beef into it. Then he made his way back down to the lower level, stepping carefully and spilling only a little of the water.

He brought the two bowls to the dog who observed his approach intently. He put the meat bowl down and held the water bowl under Spot's nose, so he could drink without getting up and moving. Spot drank and drank and drank, splashing water onto the rug and over them both. Finally he stopped, and Jamie put the water bowl down and picked up the wooden bowl. Again he held the bowl so Spot could get to it without moving. Spot went at the raw hamburger with a vengeance, knocking the bowl out of Jamie's hands. Clumps of hamburger fell on the rug, and Spot devoured them, almost in a frenzy.

"OK," said Jamie in a long, drawn out breath, his eyebrows raised.

Spot looked at him and the message was clear, "What else ya got?"

"I'll go check," said Jamie. Spot licked his snout and gave an impatient chuff. Jamie moved more quickly this time and returned with left over spaghetti and meatballs. Something prompted him to empty the beer bottle into the wooden bowl with the spaghetti. It'll help him sleep, he thought.

Spot didn't hesitate. He devoured the spaghetti and beer, licking the bowl clean. He panted when he had finished, licked his chops, grinned, and rolled over on his side, injured leg up. Jamie reached down and stroked the dog's head, smoothing the matted hair away from his eyes. Spot closed his eyes, and soon his paws were twitching. "Get those rabbits," said Jamie in a whisper. But his smiled faded as Spot growled and barred his teeth as if his dream was a nightmare and he was the pursued, not the pursuer.

* * *

They had parted down on Main Street, and it was such a small thing, the kiss. She had been aware of the possibility of that moment for weeks, had wondered if the time for it would come or not. She had pictured it differently, though, like at a dance or a movie. Jamie would turn to her and she would look up at him in a way that he could not resist. He would have a look of wonder as he gazed into her eyes and slowly, oh so slowly, he would bring his face close to hers, their breath mingling, and he would kiss her, gently on the lips. She would kiss back, of course. That was how it would happen, yes?

But, no. The evening doesn't quite go like that. First, those puffed up jerks Caleb and Dwight inject themselves into their evening. Then they almost freeze to death at the ball game and barely escape while all those inbred, up-river, small-town hicks tried to kill each other. And then, finally, standing on the corner of Main, spattered with beer and pop from all that stuff flying through the air, finally, she had kissed him. Oh, yeah. This was all going according to plan. Adele shook her head in disbelief. She would have to get this thing under control, pronto. At least he had kissed back. And he did have a look of wonder in his face, at least she thought it was wonder.

Adele crossed the tracks and walked out onto the bridge over the river. She put a hand on the guard rail and peered down at the water below. The river looked high here, dark and oily as it flowed through town. Bits and pieces of trees were swept along in the spring flood toward the Salish Sea. She imagined jumping off the bridge into the river and having it carry her down to the salt water, past the islands of the Puget Sound and on into the open ocean, next stop Hawaii. A gust of cold wind made her wince, and her boots sounded out on the old wooden bridge as she hurried on her way.

Her phone went vip-vip and she pulled it out. She had bars, now, and there was a message from her mother and a text from Rachel.

"Dwight ok ER total zoo U still virgin?"

Adele smiled and tucked the phone away.

The climb up the steep streets on the far side of the river warmed her. Everyone called this part of town The Far Side, a new subdivision of curving streets where commuters who had professional jobs down on the coast built their big, contemporary homes with big windows and big views up the valley to the snowy mountains beyond and down the valley to the distant glow of the city on the coast.

The streets here were hammered out of the bedrock of the steep hillside, carving a broad ledge to support the road and, on the downhill side, a pile of shattered rock, really just gravel, that they flattened out to create level building lots. Theirs had been one of the first houses built on the block, and when they were selecting the location, her father had tramped around the raw slopes with the developer and stopped on one particular oddly shaped lot. It was nestled in the elbow where the road made a sharp turn, and unlike the other lots, this one was dominated by a bare outcropping of solid bedrock with a small stand of old-growth Doug fir at one end. It had the least obstructed views, but the contractor told them it would be next to impossible to build on. What's more, this lot was the most expensive in the subdivision. Despite all this, her father had insisted on it, and the developer had given him an appraising look and treated him with a bit more respect after that.

That night, when they were driving back to their rental across the river, Adele asked her dad why that lot was his favorite. He said that piles of gravel liquefy during an earthquake and that all the houses built on the other lots would simply slide down the hill into the backyards of the houses below. Their house might shake, but even the most severe quake was not likely to destroy the house because it would be built on bedrock and bolted to it. Her mother had snorted and called him a survivalist. She said it would be better to go right away if the big one hit. Adele was silent in the backseat of the car, but on this one, she was with her dad.

Her father had designed the house himself, around a central courtyard where the exposed bedrock, a miniature Japanese maple and an expanding carpet of emerald green moss created a sense of space that reminded her of the mountain vistas visible from other parts of the house. Every room of the house had a view up or down the valley and a sliding glass door onto the inner courtyard. The house was beautiful, and when they finally moved into it, Adele's mom had kissed her dad and whispered something in his ear that made him smile. Adele had smiled, too.

A big, black SUV with tinted windows passed her going uphill and turned onto her street. Adele trudged up the hill and around the curve. Ahead was the main entrance to her house and their short, steep driveway. The lights were on in her house. Her mother was home. Adele felt a rush of gratitude for home and warmth and her mother, and then immediately a stab of grief as she remembered that her father was not here, but rather all alone, far up river in an empty house.

The black SUV was parked in their drive and a young man stood next to the driver-side door watching Adele as she approached. He was wearing a uniform of some kind. His big black belt had attachments of various sorts, including a holster and a sidearm.

"Hi! Are you Adele?" he asked as she went up the steps to the front door.

"Yep, that's me," she replied. "Who are you?"

"I'm Brandon from the CDC. I'm your mom's driver."

"Since when does my mom have a driver?"

Brandon paused a second. "She's inside. She'll explain," he said. He gave her a smile that was probably supposed to be reassuring.

Adele pushed through the door into the house.

The entryway led directly into a large room that was living room, dining room, and kitchen, all in one. Adele's mom was bent over the dining room table, writing on a piece of paper. An older man also in uniform stood next to her watching what she wrote. They both looked up when Adele walked in. Her mother threw down her pen and walked to meet Adele.

"Deli," she exclaimed. She threw her arms around her and pulled her into a hug. She held her for several seconds, squeezing tight, and then stepped back, holding her at arms-length. She looked Adele up and down. "Jesus, are you all right? I couldn't reach you. No one had any bars!"

"Yeah-yeah! I'm fine, mom. What's going on?"

"I was writing you a note. I've got to go in to work, sweetie. And I'm going to have to stay there for a while. There's an emergency. They're pulling in all the staff."

"Wow. For how long? What about me?" asked Adele.

"You have to go stay with your dad. I called him. He knows you're coming."

"OK," Adele nodded.

"Take the Prius and drive up first thing in the morning. OK?"

"OK." Adele kept nodding.

"Remember the emergency pack your dad put in the back of the Prius? Now's the time to use it. Got it?"

Adele stopped nodding and searched her mother's face. The emergency pack had food, water, blankets, a first-aid kit, a handheld shortwave transceiver, and a handgun.

"Got it?" her mother repeated.

"Got it," said Adele.

"OK. I'll call you in the morning."

"We should move right along, here, Dr. Prada," said the security guard. "We've got one more stop to make." The security guard stepped forward, carrying her mother's suitcase, and they all went to the front door. Adele walked down to the SUV with her mother, their arms around each other. Things were moving too fast, she thought. I don't get it.

The driver opened the back door while the other guard threw the suitcase into the back-back.

"What's going on, mom? Is this about that virus thing you've been working on?"

"We're not sure, sweetie. It might be, or it might not."

"So, how long will you be gone?" Adele asked again.

Her mother studied Adele's face for a few seconds. "Until we beat this thing. Could be a couple of days. Could be a couple of weeks."

Adele licked her lips. "Are we all going down, like the Middle East? Is that what's going to happen, mom?"

"Not if I can help it."

Adele's cheeks were damp and cool in the night air. "Do you have to go, mom? Can you take me with you? Or maybe stay? Can't you work from home?"

"I'm sorry, honey. They won't let the families come. You'll be safe with your dad."

"I'm scared, mom. It's like, will I ever see you again?"

"I will never leave you, Deli. Never." Her mother laid her hand on Adele's cheek. "I'm going only because I know that the absolute best thing I can possibly do right now for you and your dad is to go do my work."

Adele threw her arms around her mother and squeezed her tight. She drank in her mother's smell, tried to absorb every molecule and wisp of her. And her mother hugged her back.

"Here, sweetie. Blow your nose." Her mother pulled a wad of tissue out of her pocket and wiped Adele's upper lip.

"Dr. Prada..." called the driver.

"I love you," she said. "Tell your dad I send my love. Tell your dad that I love him." She kissed Adele full on the mouth, turned and climbed into the back of the SUV. She rolled down the window.

"I love you, mom," said Adele. She gripped her mother's hand.

"Make sure you lock all the doors and windows tonight," her mother said.

"Yes, mom."

The driver walked around and jumped in. The other guard looked up and down the street and then back up the street as if something might emerge from the dark at any moment, something that could move fast. He stepped to the front passenger's door, opened it and climbed in.

"Let's get the fuck out of here," he said to the driver, and slammed the door shut. The door locks clicked. They backed down the driveway and pulled away. Her mother waved out the window, and Adele waved back. The SUV disappeared around the curve.

Adele stood for a moment, looking down the hill at the empty street. Somewhere in the neighborhood, a dog barked desperately. Adele hugged herself against the cold and turned to look up the hill. There was one streetlight up that way before the cul-de-sac, and outside its pool of light the only illumination came from the exterior lights of a few houses. The street appeared deserted. Nothing moved.

Adele went back inside and locked the door behind her. She stood for a moment and listened to the silence in the house. The house seemed so empty now that both her mother and father were gone. She walked through all the rooms and checked that the windows were latched and that all the sliding glass doors were secured. Finally, she stepped into the garage, and checked the doors there. She popped the trunk of the Prius and pulled the box of survival supplies closer, opened it and made a quick, visual inventory. She picked up the radio and its wall charger and then hesitated before picking up the heavy zippered case with the handgun. Then she closed the hatch and went to her room.

She turned on the radio and checked that it was tuned to the frequency her dad described as the family emergency frequency. It was true, what her mother said. He was sort of a survivalist, but maybe not so dumb, after all. There was no chatter on the radio, just the wordless hiss left over from the Big Bang. She turned it off and plugged it into the charging cradle. She sat for a minute, looking at the radio, and then reached down and turned it back on. Better safe than sorry, she thought. It would still get fully charged by morning.

She unzipped the gun case and pulled out the revolver. Her dad had called it a reliable, light-weight .38. Light-weight for him, maybe, she thought. It was unloaded, of course, so she popped out the cylinder and inserted six rounds, clicked the cylinder closed and put the safety on. She set it down on the bedside table.

She stepped to her bedroom window and looked out. From this side of the house, she could look down the hill to town, mostly dark at this hour except for where streetlights traced the paved blocks of downtown. The hospital was easy to pick out, the biggest building, well-lit most of the time, and especially so tonight by the flashing lights of ambulances and police cars.

Adele thought of tuning the radio to the police frequency, but a wave of fatigue hit her. She checked her phone. Nothing new from anyone. She curled up on top of the bed and wrapped a little tattered quilt around her shoulders. She buried her face in the soft, well-worn fabric, and cried herself to sleep.

CHAPTER 7

Bonney's pickup turned into the driveway and the headlights flashed across the wall of the kitchen. Jamie looked up from the couch in the TV room and then returned his attention to the show. Zombies had overrun the camp and the small group of living humans were in great peril. Or was it the local news? The TV show made him feel afraid, more afraid than he had felt in the midst of the riot when he couldn't remember feeling anything other than the rush of adrenalin, a clarity without thought. He had just reacted.

"Jamie?" called Bonney as he came in the back door and through the kitchen.

"Here," replied Jamie. He muted the TV.

"Where have you been?" demanded Bonney. "Why aren't you answering your phone?"

Jamie looked up, surprised. "I was at the game. I got home about twenty minutes ago. I tried to call you, but my phone was dead." The phone was resting on the coffee table in front of Jamie, charging cable attached. He picked it up and showed Bonney. "Sorry," he said. "I should have checked for calls right away."

"Were you at the game?" asked Bonney. "Are you OK? Did you see the riot?"

"Boy, did we! Adele and I barely made it out. I'm OK, though. We're both OK."

Bonney took a deep breath and blew it out at the ceiling. "What happened? Tell me about it." He came around and sat down on the couch.

Jamie shook his head. "It was totally crazy, Bonney. It's like the fans were all pissed at each other, and then one old guy actually started a fight and the security guys came but he just kept on fighting." Jamie frowned at the wall above the TV. "Adele and I were, like, we gotta get outta here, but we didn't make it and the whole thing just blew up. It was all around us." Jamie looked over at Bonney. "We followed a couple of military guys and they were, like, clearing a path to the gate. And then we walked home."

"Wow," said Bonney. "And you're not hurt? Adele's OK?"

"We're fine, Bonney. Don't worry," said Jamie.

"I heard about the riot on the news. You didn't answer your phone, so I went looking for you."

"Oh, I'm sorry, Bonney. I didn't realize... Sorry about that. Is mom out looking for me, too?"

"No," said Bonney. He rubbed his eyes. "She got called in to work. Sounds like a bunch of people were injured. We should let her know you're OK."

"Can you text her?" asked Jamie. He held up his dark phone.

Bonney pulled out his cell and tapped and swiped. "I'll call. She's probably got her hands full, but she might pick up." He dialed her number and waited. "Oh, hi!" he said. "I didn't think you'd answer." Bonney listened for a few seconds. "He's right here. He's fine. Hang on, let me put you on speaker." Bonney pushed a button on the screen. "Can you hear me?" he asked.

"Yes, I can hear you," said Ellen.

"Hi, mom," called Jamie.

"Hi, sweetie! Are you OK? Did you get hurt?"

"No, mom, I'm fine! Deli and I are fine."

There was the slightest pause. "Is Adele there, too?"

"No, no. She was at the game with me."

"Oh... Well, you should have called to let us know where you were."

"Sorry! Just the flow of the evening, you know? And then things got kind of crazy. We didn't have any bars." Jamie saw a segue to a topic that didn't focus on his behavior. "So, what's up at work?"

"Cuts, bruises, blunt force injuries. A couple of stab wounds." Ellen's voice was business-like but fatigued. "We're really swamped. 27 admissions in the last 90 minutes. Three DOAs." In the background, a man's voice was raised, cursing. "It's really weird," said Ellen. "It's like some of these guys just won't stop fighting, like they're berserk." There was shouting in the background, multiple voices and a crash. "Gotta go," said Ellen. "I'll call." The phone went dead.

Bonney and Jamie looked at each other. "Jesus," said Jamie.

"Whoa," said Bonney, a long drawn out breath.

"Should we go check on her?" asked Jamie.

Bonney frowned and looked at the floor for a second before he shook his head. "I just drove by there on the way home. There were like three or four police cars there. We can't do anything. We'd just be in the way. Let's give it an hour. If we haven't heard anything, we can reconsider."

"Yeah, OK," said Jamie.

They both stared blankly at the TV, and then Jamie seemed to focus on the screen with its silent scenes of carnage. He reached out with the remote to turn it off.

"Let's see if there's anything on the local news," said Bonney, and Jamie switched the channel to the local 24-hour news station.

"... widespread rioting in the suburbs of Paris as frustration boils over in immigrant communities," said the newscaster. Jittery images of burning cars and running people filled the screen as a reporter spoke of joblessness and frustration. Jamie frowned. Something was odd about these images. The video showed a group attacking a police car, rocking it back and forth and finally rolling it over. The attackers danced around the car in jubilation, the ululations of the women almost drowning out the voice of the reporter.

"Wow," said Jamie. "Even women and old guys are getting into it." He looked at Bonney, who seemed frozen, his eyes riveted on the images flashing across the screen. "Bonney? What's the matter? What do you see?"

"In other news," the anchor continued, "the Vatican appears to have suffered a terrorist attack late yesterday afternoon. Doug Smetter, our chief European correspondent is on the scene. Doug?"

The image of a well-coiffed reporter in a black raincoat standing in front of the Vatican gates appeared. He paused, as if the audio feed from the newsroom was delayed by the satellite link, and then started speaking into the microphone in his hand.

"Well, Ken, information is coming from the Vatican very slowly. The attack took place almost twelve hours ago, as the College of Cardinals had gathered for an emergency consistory called by the Pope. Apparently, the attack started in that meeting and then spread through other parts of Vatican City from there. Units of the Vatican police - the famous Swiss Guards - responded initially but have requested help from the Carabinieri, the Italian national police force. These are the police personnel you see behind me." He turned and the camera focused on a checkpoint with concertina wire manned by heavily armed soldiers. "The police are still searching through the many buildings of the Vatican, Ken, and we continue to hear occasional gunfire."

"Doug, what news of the Pope? Do we know if he was harmed?"

"The Pope appears to have survived the attack, Ken, although he may be injured. Vatican TV has released a segment showing the Pope reading a prepared statement. The Pope is sitting in a chair and has a bandage on his left cheek. His voice sounds strong, but the paper he was reading from was visibly shaking." A clip of the Pope filled the TV screen as Doug spoke. Both newsmen were silent for a few seconds as the Pope spoke in his native language.

"Doug, has anyone claimed responsibility?" asked Ken, and the scene shifted back to Doug standing in front of the Vatican in a gray, morning rain.

"No one claims responsibility, yet, Ken. Suspicion immediately fell on radical elements from the Middle East, but the complete breakdown of communications with that part of the world has prevented us from contacting any of our sources there. There have been some reports, unconfirmed, that no outside attackers have been found by the Carabinieri during their search. This has led some to speculate that the attack might have been an inside job. The College of Cardinals has a reputation in some quarters for vicious factionalism and profound cynicism, but who might have mounted the attack against whom and for what purpose is completely unclear at this ti..."

A rapid series of pops interrupted Doug. He dropped to the ground and the camera swung wildly across the scene, showing Carabinieri crouched behind their barricades with their weapons trained on the façade of the Vatican. The camera came to rest, focused on the cobble stone street. At the edge of the image was an arm in a black raincoat lying slack in a pool of red-stained water.

The image of Ken sitting at the news desk reappeared. "We'll be right back," he said.

Jamie muted for the commercials and then unmuted when the news came back on. There followed reports of riots in depressed neighborhoods of American cities and a statement from the President that lawlessness would not be tolerated, and that the National Guard would be called out if necessary. The body count in Chicago was growing even faster than before, and now several other hopeless, rust belt cities were experiencing a similar upsurge in violent deaths. The report moved on to white water kayaking fun on the area rivers. There was no mention of a small riot at a podunk high school baseball game in Darnell, Washington. Jamie muted, again.

"What is happening, out there?" he asked. "Is it just the news, or what? It's like the whole world is reaching the boiling point, you know? Like it's a chain reaction or something."

Bonney was silent for a few seconds. "You know Adele's mom is a scientist at the CDC, right?"

Jamie nodded. "Yeah?"

"She's the one I've been doing all this work for. She hasn't told me exactly what she's trying to do, but she's had me create a database and a reporting engine that lets her analyze violence like an epidemic, you know, something that spreads like it's contagious."

"So the CDC thinks we're having an epidemic of violence?" asked Jamie. "Like...world-wide?"

Bonney made a face. "I don't know if the CDC thinks that. I get the impression that Rose is out on her own on this one. Like maybe her work on this is not an official, approved project." Bonney made air-quotes around official. "But if I understand the database correctly, that could be what she's researching." Bonney frowned at the wall.

"What?" asked Jamie.

"Oh, nothing," said Bonney. He glanced at Jamie and then looked away. "I'll have to ask Rose next time I talk with her." He got up and walked into the kitchen. "Hey, what happened to my beer?"

"Uh, the dog ate it," said Jamie.

"Uh, we don't have a dog," Bonney shot back. He came to the door of the kitchen and leaned against it, waiting.

"Well, define 'have'," said Jamie.

* * *

Bonney sat at his desk, a piece of leftover chicken on a plate and a fresh, cold beer in easy reach. He brought his laptop out of sleep and logged on to his home network. He clicked on an icon, and the custom reporting engine he had created for Rose started up, reaching out to the database on Bonney's server and loading up the statistical modules. Bonney took a swig of the beer, an IPA made by a local brew-pub, and smacked his lips.

He thought of the dog and Mr. Schultz walking down the street calling to Spot but carrying the baseball bat. The dog can stay for a while, he had told Jamie, until things settle down a bit. Ellen had called and said things were quieter in the ER. She expected to finish out the second shift and should be home around 7:00 AM. Jamie had started to play a first-person shooter video game but stopped after a couple of minutes.

"Just a bit too real," he said, and went up to his room.

Bonney looked at the bottle, but his eyes seemed focused on something much farther away.

He turned his attention to his screen, and brought up a list of the database columns, the different factors a user could feed to the statistical modules. He scrolled through: date fields of various sorts, location information, patient ID, patient age, sex, and so on. He paused on a set of fields that seemed to categorize an act of violence in various ways, and rubbed his eyes. Then he continued scrolling through the list until he came to the very end where there were three fields. The first was a yes-no-maybe-unknown variable labeled Virus Test. The second was a text field labeled Virus Name, and the third was a field that allowed entry of a number from zero to one hundred labeled Viral Load.

Bonney picked up the piece of chicken and took a bite. He wiped his hands carefully on his jeans and then began clicking and typing, selecting, dragging and dropping fields across his screen. He paused and reviewed what he had, and then clicked a button with a map icon. The progress bar appeared and pulsed. Bonney picked up the beer and sat back in his chair. He knew this would take a minute or so, even for his powerful system.

The sheer size of the database had surprised him, and at first he thought that Rose had done a really good job of getting him extensive test data that he could use as he developed the system. Good test data would allow him to make sure that the system he delivered to Rose was working as expected, but in his experience, few customers made the effort to generate an adequate test file. You could usually see patterns in the data that showed that it was artificially manufactured in some way, but no such patterns were visible in the CDC data Rose had given him. And now after Adele's comment, he was unsure of what he had in the database.

A map appeared on the screen showing a Mercator projection of the world. Bonney had coded the display so the map presented two buttons, one labeled "Actual" and a second labeled "Projected". He clicked on "Actual" and small red dots started appearing on the map. A date displayed at the top of the map changed rapidly, rolling forward through the last few years, day by day. The red dots clustered in the Middle East, slowly covering that section in a red wash. A second cluster appeared in North Africa and spread across the Sahara to Sudan and South Sudan. The animation stopped and the date displayed showed a day in the prior week. The Middle East was almost completely red, as was North Africa.

Bonney sat still for several seconds, looking at the screen. He moved the mouse pointer so it hovered over the "Projected" button, paused, and then clicked. The date rolled forward into the future, moving more slowly, now, as the statistical routines crunched through the existing data and tried to predict the most likely future trends. The red dots on the map started to scatter across the continents, small isolated points here and there, while the solid red blots of the Middle East and Africa grew, rolling through Iraq, Iran, Afghanistan and the republics on the southern border of Russia, and then up into Russia itself where it merged with a dense red stain expanding around Moscow which then merged with several blooming, red areas in Western Europe and the British Isles. China went from white to pink to deep red, as did South and North America. Finally, the entire world was covered, a flood of red washing across the map leaving just Antarctica and some areas far north of the Arctic Circle only lightly touched with a smattering of red. Bonney looked at the date displayed and frowned. He checked his watch and did a quick calculation. The final date on the map was just nine days away.

A few seconds passed and then Bonney took a breath. He clicked here and there and brought up a second screen with a graph. This screen showed the actual and the projected incidents of violence over time. The program started drawing a line across the graph, a line that started low, moving slowly upward. As the line approached the current date, it swung upward and then, a short time past the current date, shot up into a sharp peak before plunging back down and moving across the rest of the graph in a gentle downward slope, touching finally the zero point. Bonney exhaled and relaxed a bit. The statistical routines appeared to indicate that the violence would peak but then drop down to zero or close to it.

But then a second line appeared on the left and slowly moved across the graph. It started high and, when the first line peaked, the second line dropped precipitously almost to the zero level. Then it too leveled off and traced a slow slope across the screen dropping finally, also, to the zero point. Bonney checked the legend. The second line was world population. The end date on the graph was about six months away, in early fall.

Bonney sat without moving for several minutes. Then he pulled up the program he had written that powered the reporting system and generated the graphs and maps. He walked through the computer code, examining the arcane statements closely, his finger tracing each one on his screen. He stepped through the program modules in a special debug mode, watching each line of code execute in real time as it crunched through the data. When he finally reached the end of the program, he stared out the window of his office into the dark, starless night. Then he reached for his phone and punched in Rose Prada's personal cell number.

CHAPTER 8

Rose welcomed the dark in the backseat of the SUV. It hid her tears from the others, as grief and fear gripped her. Grief because she did not know if she would ever see Adele again, and fear for her daughter, for what she would face in the coming weeks and months. So great was the desire to protect Deli that when they pulled up to the stop sign at the bottom of the hill, she had almost jumped out of the door to run back up the hill. But that very desire to protect scorned the impulse. Adele's future depended on a cure for the contagion that was sweeping the world, spoke the fierce voice of the tiger mom in Rose. And that battle would be won in the CDC labs, not in the living room at home.

Her phone trilled, and Rose dug it out of her purse. Before she could answer, though, the older guard twisted around in the front seat and held out his hand.

"I'll take your cell, Doctor," he said.

"What do you mean, you'll take my cell?" said Rose. She glanced at the screen. Nate Bonney was calling. She was not ready for the CDC to know about the work Bonney was doing for her.

"Quarantine Protocol. All communications go through the CDC. You know the drill, Doctor. No one has a private line to the outside. Sorry." But he wasn't sorry, and his face was hard. The phone trilled again, and Rose held it out to him. He took it and answered. "This is the CDC, Dr. Rose Prada's phone."

There was a brief pause and then Bonney's voice came over the little speaker. From the backseat of the SUV, Rose could not make out his actual words.

"Dr. Prada is not available at the moment. Would you like to leave a message, or we can have her call you back?"

Pause.

"I'm sorry, sir. I don't know when she might call back. Would you like to leave a message?"

Pause.

"All right. We'll let her know." He pushed a button on the screen and ended the call.

"That was Nate Bonney. He said you had his number. You can call him back when we get to the CDC." He put the cell phone in the breast pocket of his shirt and buttoned the flap.

She glanced at the man sitting next to her, Ibrahim Zarruq, a slim, young statistician originally from Pakistan. He gave her a brief sympathetic smile. "I think the next couple of weeks will be interesting," he said. Typical bravado from a young man, she thought.

They continued on the two-lane state route that ran down the valley to the city and the coast. Their headlights illuminated patches of dense forest that crowded the road and other stretches of open fields bordered by old, barbed-wire fencing. They passed the occasional driveway and mailbox with a glimpse of a house or barn in the distance, each in a pool of light cast by the glare of outdoor floods. Once they passed a building engulfed in flames. Brandon lifted his foot off the gas and the SUV slowed.

"Step on it," said the older guard. "We don't need this shit. Not our problem."

Rose turned in her seat to look as Brandon accelerated away. She thought she saw the figure of a man, dancing around the flames.

They entered a small settlement, a cluster of buildings at an intersection, a few small houses, a gas station and a run-down bar. At the far end of the buildings a pickup truck and a car were parked nose-to-nose across the pavement forming a roadblock. Several men were standing with their backs to the SUV facing down the road toward the city. They turned around, shading their eyes from the headlights as the CDC vehicle approached. One of the men was holding a long gun, a shotgun, and motioned for the SUV to stop.

"What do I do, Carl?" asked Brandon.

"Stop here," said the older guard. Brandon pulled to a stop about a hundred feet from the roadblock.

Carl got out and walked up to the men. There was a little back and forth, one of the men pointing down the road and speaking. Carl made an impatient gesture, waving for the car and truck to get off the pavement, and said something emphatic. The men stepped closer, crowding him. Carl grabbed the long gun and slammed the butt into the face of the man who had been holding it. The man dropped to the ground and lay still. Then Carl turned the gun around and pointed it at the other two men who held up their hands and took a step back.

Carl said something, motioning toward the roadblock with the barrel of the gun. One of the men turned slowly, hands still up, and walked to the car and got in. Carl pointed the gun first at one man and then at the other, making sure both were covered. The man in the car started it up and put it in reverse, backing a bit so the nose of the car swung clear of the pickup and then pulled forward. He floored it and the screech of the tires was answered by the blast of the shotgun. The windshield disintegrated but the car plowed on hitting both Carl and the other man. It rolled over them, wheels bouncing over their bodies, and continued on across the road. It came to rest nose down in the ditch, the driver slumped across the steering wheel, the horn blaring.

"Holy shit," said Brandon.

Rose and Ibrahim were frozen in the back seat, staring at the motionless bodies on the pavement and the wrecked car in the ditch. A door in one of the buildings opened and a figure stepped out. He raised his arm toward the SUV and there was a flash and the bang of a handgun. Brandon crouched low over the steering wheel and the big SUV surged forward through the opening in the roadblock. There was another bang and something hit the back of the SUV.

"Down," yelled Brandon. He accelerated away from the scene. They went around a curve and the roadblock was no longer visible. For a few seconds, no one spoke.

"Should we go back and check on him?" asked Ibrahim. "I mean, maybe he's still alive. Maybe he needs help."

Brandon shook his head. "We can't go back. We don't know what's back there. Carl's dead. The car rolled right over his head."

"But..." started the Pakistani.

"That's not the mission," said Brandon. "My mission is to get you two to the CDC. And that's what I'm gonna do."

"What is happening to us?" asked Ibrahim, softly, shaking his head.

"You tell me," said Brandon. "What's happening? You know, don't you?" Rose met his eyes in the rear-view mirror. "What is this?"

Rose looked out the window. They were skirting the eastern edge of the city, now. In the distance, several large fires burned, painting the base of the clouds with a shifting red and orange.

"Don't take the route through town," she said.

"I'm not," said Brandon. "So?" he prompted.

"We're going to see a lot of violence, Brandon." She turned from the window and spoke directly to him. "I think everywhere is going to be like the Middle East. I don't know how many of us will survive. I don't know if any of us will survive. And I don't know how long it will go on." She paused, and then went on. "I know it sounds like nothing, but all I can say is stay aware. Everything around you is going to make you angry, but you must not give in to your anger. Everything around you is going to give you reason to despair, but you must not give in to your despair, either." She was quiet for a few seconds. "I'm sorry," she said. "That's all I've got."

Brandon was silent.

"Brandon," said Rose, "I need to call my daughter. I told her to drive up to her father's in the morning. I need to tell her to wait. The roads are too dangerous."

"Carl had your cell, Doctor. You can call from the CDC. We'll be there in fifteen minutes. Hopefully."

"Can I use your cell phone? Now?" The thought of Deli driving into a roadblock was unbearable.

"I'm sorry, ma'am. We'll be there soon. Don't worry."

Rose sat back in defeat. Something touched her leg and she looked down. Ibrahim had slid his cell phone across the seat. He leaned forward and spoke to Brandon.

"Perhaps she could just text her daughter, yes? That would not violate the protocol?"

"Sorry Doctor. That's the same thing."

"Oh... Of course," said Ibrahim, and he sat back, too.

Rose slid the cell onto her lap, keeping it low and out of Brandon's sight. She texted Adele, an urgent warning, an urgent message of love. The tears started again, and she pushed the phone back across the seat to Ibrahim. When he reached down to take the phone, she squeezed his hand in thanks.

I'm doing the right thing, she told herself. This is the best thing I can do for Deli right now. She's a smart girl. She's tough. She can take care of herself, now. And she'll have her father. He'll know what to do. But the thought of Deli's father brought its own sense of loss, grief for a chance for happiness wasted, a chance that, she feared, would now never come again.

Brandon reached up with one hand and pressed a button on the radio microphone clipped to his shoulder. "CDC, this is Brandon."

"Go ahead, Brandon," came the response.

"I'm coming in to the north gate in about fifteen minutes with Doctors Prada and...Zarruq."

"Roger that, Brandon. We'll notify the gate that you're coming," came the response.

They continued through the countryside around the edge of the city. The cloud cover above them appeared to glow brighter as they went, and each glimpse of the city in the distance seemed to reveal another fire. Once a naked man rushed out into their headlights and threw a rock at them. It smashed into their front grill and Brandon swerved barely avoiding the man. Rose twisted around to look out the back window. The man disappeared in the darkness behind them, still running and waving his arms.

They came around a curve and the CDC campus was ahead of them. It was brightly lit and there were two Humvees and soldiers around the gate. Rose sighed with relief, despite the knowledge that the soldiers were there to keep her in as much as to keep her safe.

* * *

The room was dim in the slow dawn of the early spring day. Jamie woke up and lay still, reluctant to push past the warmth of bed. He pulled the covers off his head and craned his neck to see the alarm clock. It was 7:15. He burrowed back into the pillows and blankets. Downstairs, Bonney was talking to someone or something. There was no back and forth, just Bonney speaking quickly and urgently.

Jamie threw back the covers and grabbed his jeans. He pulled on a long-sleeve T from the closet and a ratty sweater from the closet floor. He picked up his phone and stuffed it into his pocket. Then he went down the hallway, down the stairs and into the living room. Bonney stood at the window, looking out toward town.

"What's going on?" asked Jamie. "I smell smoke."

"Something's burning in town," said Bonney. "You can see the smoke."

Jamie stepped to the window and stood next to Bonney. The dark smoke rising from downtown was stark against the morning sky.

"Where's mom?" asked Jamie.

"Your mom isn't home yet." Bonney paused. "I just called but she doesn't pick up. I left a message."

"Maybe we should call the ER," said Jamie. "Hang on. I've got their number." He pulled his phone out and selected the work phone number under Mom. It started ringing, but no one answered. It rang and rang. Finally, Jamie ended the call.

"I'll call the police station," said Bonney. He thumbed through his contacts until he found the number and then pressed Call. They waited as it rang and then was picked up by the city voice mail. At the tone, Bonney started speaking. "I'm trying to reach..." but then the voice mail system cut him off and the line went dead.

Bonney stared at the phone in his hand and Jamie stared at him. Then Jamie went to the front door and pulled on shoes and jacket. He walked out into the middle of the street and stood looking down the hill. Houses and trees obscured his view of downtown but the oily, black smoke was now stark against the brightening sky. The fresh morning breeze pushed the plume up the valley.

The Far Side hill across the river was still in dark shadow, but here and there, a window was lit and shone out like a beacon. Jamie thought he knew where Adele's house would be, and he didn't know if he was troubled or relieved that no light marked its place.

Bonney came out of the side door and got into his pickup truck. He backed down the driveway into the street and came to a stop next to Jamie. He rolled down the window.

"I'm going to make a quick run down to the hospital to check on your mom. I should be back in half an hour."

"I'll come with."

"Yeah... Maybe you should stay here, in case she comes home or calls on the landline. This is where she would expect to find us."

"Well, OK," said Jamie.

"And could you clean up that dog? He's covered in mud."

"Sure," said Jamie, nodding. He stepped back from the truck and Bonney accelerated down the hill and out of sight. Jamie watched the smoke drifting through the air. The wind shifted and carried sounds from the valley, a low roar like distant ocean waves or a wordless chorus of voices. Something went pop-pop-pop. The smoke seemed darker.

Mr. Schultz stepped out his front door and looked toward town. He was even more disheveled than the day before but still clutched his baseball bat. He scanned the block and caught sight of Jamie, standing in the middle of the road. Their eyes met, and Mr. Schultz started down the steps. Jamie turned and made for home.

"Hey!" yelled Mr. Schultz.

Jamie took the porch steps three at a time and went through the door. He locked it behind him and then went into the living room and peeked out the window. Mr. Schultz was walking across the street toward the house.

"Where do you think you're going?" came a man's voice from a couple of doors down the block. Mr. Schultz turned and glared at someone Jamie could not see.

"What the fuck is it to you?" said Mr. Schultz. He shifted his grip on the bat and started toward the unknown speaker.

Jamie leaned closer to the glass and looked down the street. A man, a neighbor Jamie recognized but rarely spoke with, was walking on the sidewalk. He carried a military rifle and stood, aimed carefully and fired a single shot. Mr. Schultz' shirt flicked out in back with a faint spray of red, and he dropped to the ground, loose as clothes on a bedroom floor.

Jamie gaped, first at Mr. Schultz and then at the man with the gun. Had this neighbor been trying to help, he wondered. The man walked up to Mr. Schultz and prodded him with his foot. He glanced around at the houses on the street and, almost as an afterthought, raised his rifle and fired several shots. A bullet smacked into the side of Jamie's house, and he flattened himself on the floor.

There were no more shots, but the man started whistling tunelessly. Jamie lifted his head just above the window sill and watched him walk away. The man went up the steps to Mr. Schultz' house and went inside. Jamie stayed at the window, crouched low. After several minutes, the man came walking around the side of Mr. Schultz's house and crossed the street back to Jamie's side, several houses down. A door slammed.

Smoke escaped from an upstairs window of Mr. Schultz' house. Jamie pulled his phone from his pocket and pressed 911. There was a flicker of flame from another window, but no answer from 911. Plastic siding bubbled black and sagged in the heat before going up in flames. It seemed impossibly fast, and Jamie wondered if the man had found a gas can in the garage. Jamie ran to the kitchen and picked up the landline. There was a dial tone and he hit 911 again. Still no answer. He hung up and returned to the front room. Mr. Schultz' house was fully engulfed. Embers were falling on the roofs of the houses behind it.

A wet nose touched Jamie's hand. He snatched it away and turned. Spot stood next to him, looking out the window at the crumpled figure in the street and then at the fire. He whined. Jamie stroked his head.

"Good dog," he said. "It's OK," he said, but of course it wasn't.

No sirens approached. No concerned neighbors emerged from the surrounding houses to gather in the street at a safe distance. There is no safe distance, now, thought Jamie. Not anymore.

Jamie stood up and walked into the kitchen and down the stairs to the lower level. Spot limped after him. He pushed some boxes to the side and stood in front of Bonney's gun cabinet. He worked the combination lock and opened the doors. There was one gun, a single-shot bolt action hunting rifle that Bonney had used once to hunt deer when they first moved to Darnell. The hunting trip immediately preceded the family's vegetarian period, which lasted over a year. Bonney had allowed Jamie to use the gun to get his marksman patch when he was a Boy Scout, but no one had touched the rifle for at least a year.

Jamie breathed in the smell of gun oil and picked up the rifle. He worked the bolt which slid open smoothly. He found a box of cartridges, chambered one and slid the bolt home. He pushed the safety full on and pocketed the remaining shells. He looked down at the dog. "We're safe now," he said. But the dog looked doubtful, and Jamie realized that the rifle made him feel even less secure than before. He thought of Deli and reached for his phone.

CHAPTER 9

Adele's phone rang. It was somewhere on the coffee table, the ring muffled underneath a pile of magazines, a red hoodie, a map, and breakfast dishes. Across the room, the big screen TV sat dark and silent. Her mother had counseled her to leave it on at all times, tuned to the local news channel, but Adele could not stomach the stream of violent images served up. She had turned it off after five minutes.

Her alarm had gone off at six that morning, and Adele, groggy and unrested, snoozed it for fifteen. She had started awake repeatedly during the night, rising once with gun in hand to walk the dark house, her bare feet soundless on the cold floors. The house was empty, the doors all secure, and Adele, thoroughly chilled, had left her clothes in a heap by the bed and crawled under the covers.

Sleep would still not come, and Adele got up before the snooze alarm sounded. She reached for the switch on her bedside lamp but then stopped. Did she really want to advertise her presence by lighting up the house? She thought not, and picked up her phone from the bedside table. There were two unread texts, one from Rachel and one from an unknown number.

She read the one from the unknown number first: STAY OFF ROADS!! 2 DANGEROUS! CALL UR DAD IN MORNING. TELL HIM UR NOT COMING FOR A DAY OR 2. LOVE, LOVE, LOVE U!!!! MOM

She reread the message, taking in the awkward combination of abbreviations, sort of proper punctuation and all caps that so marked the sender's age, her mother's age. She cradled the phone in both hands, as if holding something precious.

She scrolled to Rachel's message: Riot downtown. Hiding @Guidos w Caleb Dwight. Where r u? Safe?

It had come in just before midnight. Adele texted: safe @home @far side. U? followed by 5 heart emoticons. She pressed send.

Adele got up and went to the window. A fire was burning furiously in downtown. A tall building – it must be the hospital – was engulfed in flames. She stood watching for a minute, but the chill of the morning finally drove her into the closet where she closed the door before she turned on the light. She dressed in tough, comfortable clothes, like she was going camping, and put her hand on the door handle before switching the light off and stepping back into her bedroom. She sat on her bed and dialed her mother's cell.

"CDC main switchboard." It was a woman's voice, country and a bit raspy. Adele could almost smell the cigarette smoke. "Dr. Prada is not available at the moment. Who is calling, please?"

Adele frowned at her phone. Had she selected one of her mom's work numbers? "This is Adele Prada, her daughter. How can I reach my mother? Why is the switchboard answering her personal cell phone?"

"Hi, Adele. Sorry to intercept your call. We're kind of in an emergency mode here and communications in and out are limited. Gotta keep those scientists focused on saving the world, now don't we? Do you want to leave a message or just have her call you back?"

The operator's manner had become informal, familiar, and Adele wondered if it was a technique to disarm callers or whether the staff was really giving family members special treatment.

"Yeah, I understand," said Adele. "Just have her call me as soon as she can, please. Tell her I'm at home in Darnell and that I'm safe."

"Great, glad to hear it, hon. I wish I'd hear that from my husband and son. They're in the city. I'll get your message to your mom and have her call you. You take care now." She ended the call.

Adele sat on her bed and stared at the wall. More than all the news reports with their urgent bulletins and images of mayhem, this short conversation with the switchboard operator brought it home. She pictured the woman, probably in her 40s, just starting to dye her hair to conceal a gray streak, struggling with her weight and worrying about how much she would gain if she quit smoking. She sits at her keyboard with her headset on, fielding calls from bigwigs in D.C. and daughters in Darnell, and calling out to her husband and son over and over, listening to the phone ring and ring. No one answers. Probably no one ever will. Sadness swept over Adele, and then a deep appreciation and respect for this woman who stayed at her desk at work while the world around her collapsed.

She stood and walked over to the window. The rising sun had crested the ridge behind her, illuminating downtown and the hill opposite. Smoke still rose from the hospital, but there were no longer flames. A wall collapsed as Adele watched, revealing that all the upper floors had already pancaked into a smoldering pile surrounded now on three sides by the empty, brick facade. It looked like the fire had spread to the roofs of some of the buildings in the next block.

Adele could make out figures in the streets. Some people were running, some walking. Some lay motionless, sprawled here and there, the pavement stained red around them.

An old, blue pickup truck came down the hill and pulled to a law-abiding stop at the intersection with First Street. It turned toward the hospital, passed behind some buildings and then came back into view. The street was blocked there by debris and the pickup could go no further. A tall, slim man got out and walked toward the rubble. He stood for a minute, surveying the scene.

A small group of men came running at the man from behind. They appeared to be carrying things, like clubs or guns, and the man seemed unaware of their approach. "Run," said Adele under her breath, "run!" The man looked over his shoulder. He must have realized that he could not make it back to the truck before they would be on him, and he wheeled around and sprinted in the opposite direction. Adele put her hand to her mouth. Something was familiar about the man. He was fast, and appeared to be out-distancing his pursuers, but Adele never saw the end of the race. They all ran out of sight and did not reappear.

Adele breathed out, a low moan. She scanned the town, looking for any sign of order or official presence. There was none, and she realized that the block that was now in flames included the city building and the police station. On the hillside across the valley, a house in one of the older neighborhoods was on fire, and it seemed impossible that the houses around it would not burn, too.

There was activity down by the bridge that crossed the river. Two cars blocked the side closest to Adele's subdivision, and several men milled around. A roadblock, thought Adele. Someone was trying to protect the Far Side from the violence that had overrun downtown. The morning light reflected vivid green off the emergency vests they wore. Were these the neighborhood watch or the community emergency response people, she wondered.

Adele picked up her binoculars and scanned the scene. She thought she recognized one or two of the men. Clearly not the police. She felt a touch of hope. The American citizenry was rising to the occasion. Light glinted off the barrels of the long guns some carried, and the hope dimmed a bit. Rachel lived a couple of blocks further up the hill from Adele. She would need to pass that roadblock if she was going to make it home. The same for Caleb. Would the men on the bridge let them through?

She slipped her phone into the pocket of her hoodie and gathered up the radio and a pair of hiking boots. She stepped out into the hall, clear now in the morning light, and walked to the kitchen. She sat at the kitchen table and put on her boots. They're not muddy, she thought. Might as well be ready for anything. It felt awkward to wear shoes in the house.

She considered calling her dad right away, but a grumbling stomach urged otherwise. She rummaged through the pantry and fridge and decided on cold cereal. She carried the bowl into the living room and settled on the couch. The bland food soothed her nervous stomach. When she was done, she put the dirty dishes down on one of the more stable piles of magazines, and made another quick tour of the house, peeking out windows. It was quiet outside. Everyone in the neighborhood seemed to be in hiding. She felt ready to talk with her father.

He answered before the first ring. "Deli? Is that you? Are you OK? Where are you?"

The sound of her father's voice was almost too much. She took a deep breath. "Deli? Are you there?" he asked.

"Yeah, yeah," she said. "I'm here. Everything's OK. Well, nothing's OK, but I'm OK."

"You're OK? You're safe?"

"Yeah. I'm at home. Mom is at the CDC. Things are quiet here."

There was a pause. She could hear him breathing.

"I heard there was rioting in Darnell last night. And fires in downtown?"

"Yeah. I can see it from the house. Looks like the hospital is gone."

"Has there been any trouble around the neighborhood?"

"No, nothing. It's so totally quiet it's creepy. Like no lawnmowers, no weed whackers, or anything. No one's walking the dog. There are some guys blockading the bridge. Like the neighborhood watch guys, except with guns."

"Yeah... It's a good idea to stay away from people. It's unpredictable. You don't know who to trust. Did you get into the emergency pack? In the back of the Prius?"

"I did. I brought the radio and the gun inside, like mom said."

"OK, good. Look, when I talked to your mom, she sounded funny. Like she couldn't speak freely, like someone was listening. So the radio is important. Keep it on. You should monitor the family emergency frequency. I think your mom might try to make contact with us that way."

"That's what I'm doing. It's on now."

"Can you hear me on the radio?" he asked. His voice came over both the phone in Adele's hand and over the radio sitting on the kitchen table.

"You're coming in loud and clear," she said.

"Talk to me on the radio. I want to make sure everything is working," he said.

"OK. Hang on…" Adele walked into the kitchen and picked up the little microphone attached to the transceiver. "Deli to dad. Over," she said. She had always felt slightly silly with all the over-and-out radio talk.

"Got you loud and clear," said her dad. His voice came over both phone and radio. "Let's stay with the phone, for now." This time, his voice came only from the phone, and Adele put it on speaker.

"I talked with your mom just a bit ago. She says they're locked down at the CDC. Probably for…" he paused. "Probably for days, maybe weeks."

"Yeah, I got a text."

"We need to get you up here to Power City as soon as we can. The National Guard is here. They're supposed to protect the dam and the power plant, but the company has cut a deal and they'll protect the town and families, too."

"Mom says the roads aren't safe."

"Yeah. I know. They're not." Adele wondered how he knew. His voice suggested more than a theoretical knowledge.

"Are you OK, dad?" she asked.

"Yeah, yeah. I'm fine. The National Guard is taking care of all that."

"So, what should I do?" she asked.

"You'll have to stay there for a day or so, until things settle down. Stay in the house. Keep the doors locked. Don't go wandering around town."

"OK. No bar-hopping tonight, then."

"Is the power still on?" Her dad was ignoring the lame humor. "Refrigerator works, TV, etc.?"

"Yeah, everything seems to be working. I'm not turning on lights, you know."

"That's good. Keep the house dark. You don't want to attract attention." This was dad-advice, par excellence, she thought.

"You loaded the Ruger? You have it close at hand?"

"Yes, dad. I loaded it. It's right here." She thought of the revolver on her bedside table at the other end of the house.

"OK… Look, sweetie, I'd come get you, but I'm classified as essential personnel, and I can't leave. We're required to stay on the job. Just lay low for a couple of days. I'll let you know when the roads are safe."

"OK, dad."

She heard someone speaking in the background, and her dad's voice, muffled, said "I'm on it."

"Deli, I have to go. The grid is kind of crazy, today."

"Sure. Of course. When can we talk again, dad?" asked Adele.

"Call me anytime," he said. "And I'll try to call you around lunchtime. You can reach me on the radio anytime, too, like if the cell phones go down. OK?"

"OK," she said.

"I love you, sweetie," he said.

"I love you, dad," she replied. He ended the call.

Adele sat for a minute, looking down at the phone in her hand. It showed seventy-five percent battery, and Adele went into the bedroom and pulled a charging cable from the drawer in the bedside table. She paused, considering the revolver, and then picked it up too and returned to the couch in the living room. She plugged in the cable and started recharging the phone.

Her father had asked whether she still had power at the house. Adele wondered what all depended on electricity. Their cable and internet, of course. The lights and refrigerator. The whole kitchen, really. The heat was gas, but would it still run if the electricity was off? What would happen to the smart thermostat? And how about the water? If the town lost power, how long would the faucets work? The shower? The toilet? There was a little solar charger for the radio in the emergency pack, and her dad had showed her how to plug the cell phone into it, too. And the Prius could charge small devices, until it ran out of juice. Adele tried to remember when they had last put gas in the Prius.

Adele thought of the National Guard and the news reports that she and her mother heard from the city in the Middle East, how the fighting seemed to be all-against-all. Did a hundred men with guns make Power City more or less safe, she wondered. She got up and walked to a window looking out on the valley. Black smoke poured from the roof of the city building, and now several houses on the hill across the valley were ablaze as the wind carried embers from house to house, across backyards and streets.

Her phone was ringing. She rushed to find it on the coffee table. It was Jamie calling.

"Jamie?" she said.

* * *

"Hey!" said Jamie. "How's it going? Are you OK?" He turned and leaned back against the arm of the living room sofa. From this angle, he could keep watch out the window and down the street. He tucked his stockinged feet under Spot, curled up next to him on the couch. The dog gave him a reproachful look but did not protest further. The hunting rifle lay on the carpet next to the couch, and Jamie put his hand down to touch it. He took some comfort from it and left his hand there.

"Yeah, I'm OK. It's pretty quiet up here," said Adele.

"Are you at home?" he asked.

"Yeah... Home alone! My mom and dad are both stuck at work. Essential personnel, or something. How are things around you? Are you OK? I can see a couple of houses on fire. Looks like that's in your neighborhood?"

"Yeah. On my street, just down the block. The wind is blowing it away from me, though. But there's been some shooting over here. There's actually a dead guy in the street."

"Oh, my god!" she said. "That's terrible! Are your folks home?"

"No. Neither one. My mom never came home from work. My dad's out looking for her now."

"Oh, Jamie. Your mom worked at the hospital?"

"Yeah. Why?"

"Jamie, I can see the hospital from my house. It was on fire."

Jamie frowned. "Is the fire out?" he asked.

"Yeah, but Jamie, there's not much left."

Jamie sat staring out the window, the phone in his hand forgotten.

"She's probably safe, Jamie." Adele rushed in. "She's on the first floor, right? So, it would be easy for her to get out. Right?"

Jamie looked around the room. He couldn't seem to settle on anything, nothing was quite in focus. He blinked.

"Jamie? Jamie? I'm sorry, Jamie. I shouldn't have said anything. I don't know what I'm talking about. You're mom's a smart woman. I'm sure she's safe. Jamie?"

"Yeah...yeah," said Jamie. He rubbed his eyes. "Sure. She'll be calling soon. She probably just lost her cell. She just needs to borrow someone's phone." He didn't really know who was speaking. He heard his voice saying things. Then it stopped. Neither spoke for several seconds.

"You can see downtown from your house?" he asked, finally.

"Yeah, and I've got binoculars."

"What do you see?"

"Hang on..." she said. "Let me get to a window." There was a pause. "OK...The fire's spreading. It looks like the city building is on fire. I see people moving around. There's a lot of stuff in the streets, trash and stuff. I think there's a wrecked pickup truck on Main. Looks like it was burned. A lot of broken windows... Oh! Oh, no. No, no!"

"What?" asked Jamie. "What's that?"

"I don't want to look out the window anymore, Jamie. I'm gonna go sit in the living room."

"Deli? Are you OK? Deli? What's the matter?"

"It's not good, Jamie, not good, not good..."

"Deli? Deli, can you hear me? Go sit in the living room. That's a good idea. Are you there, now? Deli?"

"Yeah... Yeah. I'm there now."

"OK. Just take a second, OK? Just breathe. Bonney says it helps to focus on the breath. All right?"

"OK. I'm OK, now. It's OK."

"What happened? What did you see?"

"People... They were chasing a man. And then they caught him."

"Ah," said Jamie. "Who was the man?" he asked. "Could you see who it was?"

"Couldn't tell. Too far away."

"I have to call Bonney, Deli. I'll call you back." He pressed End Call and entered Bonney's cell number. It rolled over immediately to voice mail.

"Bonney, this is Jamie. Call me as soon as you can. Thanks." He sat looking at the phone in his hand. Nothing definitive, he thought. Nothing for sure. He really didn't know anything about their situations, his mom and Bonney. He didn't know a thing. The earth seemed to be tilting, like everything was going to slide to one side of the room. He reached out and gripped the arm of the couch. He breathed through his mouth, measured breaths, and the world settled some.

"I love you, sweetie," said his mother's voice from the kitchen.

Jamie turned toward the sound. "Mom?" He got up and walked to the kitchen door. His legs were shaky and he leaned on the jamb. "Mom?" he repeated. He looked around, but there was no one there. He slid down in the doorway, drew his legs up and wrapped his arms around his knees. Sitting there on the floor, he felt utterly alone, with nothing and no one to turn to. He felt like his chest was open, and the chill of the empty house crept in. The cold seemed to penetrate his heart. He rested the back of his head on the door frame and closed his eyes.

He didn't know how much time passed. Perhaps he had slept. Something wet and warm touched his hand. Spot was standing there, looking at him. The dog whined softly. Jamie looked at the dog, who whined again. Jamie stroked Spot's head, tugged at his ears. "Good dog," it was barely a whisper. The dog took a step back, away from Jamie's hand and gave him a commanding look. "Ah," said Jamie. "I get it."

He pulled himself up and walked through the kitchen to the back door. He opened it a bit and scanned the yards and windows he could see. No one was about. There was no sound except the distant crackle and roar of the fires down the street and the sighing of the wind in the trees. He opened the door wider and Spot pushed past his legs, made his way down the steps and out into the yard. He sniffed the breeze and then sniffed the grass and then peed, awkward with his injured leg. He looked around, and then turned and looked back at Jamie. For a second, Jamie thought Spot was saying goodbye, and the thought of being alone in the house, finally and completely alone, was almost more than he could bear. But then the dog climbed back up the steps, carefully, one at a time, and came inside.

Jamie crouched down in front of the dog and scruffled his head with both hands. "Good dog," he said, and this time, Spot closed his eyes, and leaned into Jamie's hands. "It's OK. Everything is going to be OK," he said, but his voice caught, and a tear made a glistening track down his cheek. Spot licked his face, making an even bigger mess. Jamie wiped his cheek with his sleeve.

Jamie's cell buzzed against his leg and he dug it out of his jeans' pocket. It was Adele.

* * *

Jamie pressed Accept. "Hey," he said. His voice was soft. Spot lay down on the floor of the kitchen next to him.

"Hey. I just called to say hi. Hi. Hi? What am I talking about? I called to see if, if you're OK, if you're still alive, if you're still you."

"Still alive. Not OK. What do you mean, still you? Are you OK?"

"Yeah. It's still quiet up here. But I just talked with my mom, and I'm scared. Things are not looking good."

"How so?" Jamie walked back into the living room. He checked the street. The fire had definitely spread into the next block. Three or four houses appeared to be burning. There were still no fire trucks, no emergency vehicles. He sat on the couch so he could see out that way, and glanced at the rifle to make sure he knew where it was. Spot came in and curled up on the floor next to his feet.

"We have to be really careful, Jamie. People are becoming violent, like berserk violent. Crazy violent."

"No shit," he said, but immediately regretted his tone.

"She said she thinks it's a virus that makes people more sensitive to stress, and they can't control their emotions. They either get more and more violent or they go into a terminal state of despair, they just give up on everything."

"OK... So, how long is this going to go on? I mean, what do we do?"

"She said I should find a safe place and hide for a couple of weeks. She said younger people seem less susceptible, like they don't have as much of the virus in their system, or they haven't accumulated enough of the environmental stressors to trigger it. She said older people are dangerous, like anyone more than twenty-five could be a ticking time bomb."

"Yeah, that makes sense. I saw it on my street."

"She said that cynical or mean people are most susceptible. People who aren't that way seem to resist longer. But she said it looks like everyone goes, eventually."

Jamie was silent.

"What about a cure? Does everyone get it? Like, how do you avoid it?" Jamie waited.

"My mom is working on a cure, but she said it could be weeks or months before they have anything. If ever."

Jamie tried to wrap his head around this. "Well, how do you keep from getting it? I mean, do I stay out of public places, don't touch door knobs?"

"Well, they think it's airborne. If you breathe, you get it."

"So, we just stay away from people?"

"They've been doing tests. They've been testing people for the virus. Everyone they've ever tested has it. Everyone. They think everyone in the world has it."

"Everyone? Already?"

"Everyone. You. Me. Everyone."

CHAPTER 10

A roaring came and went in Jamie's ears. Everyone. Everywhere. It was like a bad storm approaching, or the sound of many voices. It came again, and several blocks down the hill, a man ran across the street. A distant boom. The man stumbled and fell. He did not get up.

Now more people appeared on the street, a mob, a riot. Like rising water, the crowd pressed forward. Streams of people branched off at each house, banging at doors and breaking windows. Screams. Shots. Smoke and flames. The roar.

"I have to go, Deli!" said Jamie. He ended the call before she could say goodbye. Spot was on his feet. He growled, low, teeth bared. Jamie picked up the rifle and worked the bolt partway to make sure a round was chambered. He flipped the safety off and checked down the hill again. The mob was one house closer, but still more than a block away.

"Oh, shit!" said Jamie. He grabbed his boots and headed for the kitchen. Spot followed. Jamie blew through the backdoor and into the backyard. Behind him, Spot barked, and Jamie turned. The backdoor had slammed shut before the dog could make it out. Jamie paused. The roar came again, closer.

"Fuck, fuck, fuck!" said Jamie, and ran back up the stairs and opened the backdoor. Spot came out like a shot, heading for the woods behind the house. Jamie ran after him, boots in one hand and rifle in the other.

He stepped on something sharp and hopped on one foot before falling over. "Fuck!" he barely breathed the word. He pulled on his boots without brushing the leaves and twigs off his socks, and got to his feet. He ran into the dense woods, following a path he had known since childhood, a path that wound up a slope past a hidden ledge where he could look back down without being seen. He pushed off the path through tangled bushes and lay down on the carpet of moss. He crawled forward and peered down at the path through a screen of brush.

For several seconds, nothing moved, then a sound, behind him. Jamie twisted around scrabbling to get the rifle pointed in that direction but the barrel caught in the dense brush. He struggled and almost had the gun free when Spot emerged. For a second they simply looked at each other, Jamie with his mouth open and Spot with a quizzical expression on his face. Jamie breathed out, and Spot came and lay down next to him. They both watched the path below.

They could still hear the riot, the roaring punctuated by shots. A slight change in the wind would bring the smell of the smoke, the rancid odor of burning houses and a yell, a shriek or a scream rising above the background. The cold penetrated Jamie's t-shirt and sweater: no time to grab a jacket when they ran. He shifted closer to Spot and the dog leaned against him.

A woman came running on the path, clutching the hand of a little girl who stumbled and struggled to keep up. She did not protest. Both were silent. Jamie thought he recognized the little girl from the stoop down the street he had passed the day before. He opened his mouth to call out, but did not.

A few seconds later, a man came along the path carrying a machete. He swung the machete at the brush on the side of the path, spewing a continuous stream of curses. He marched down the path after the woman and child, without haste but implacable. He will surely catch them, thought Jamie. He tightened his grip on the rifle and checked the safety, but the man was out of sight before Jamie could bring himself to act. He thought of going after him, trying to scare him off perhaps, but knew somehow that this man was not calculating, would not weigh his machete against Jamie's rifle and make the obvious choice.

Something in the sound of the mob had changed. Jamie listened intently. It was not that the sound was closer, but just louder, the voices harder. The shooting was continuous, punctuated by bigger explosions. Is it a battle, he thought? No longer simply a riot or a mob in search of victims, but a pitched battle? Had the National Guard arrived to take control? He searched the woods below. No one appeared, no one fled, no one pursued.

After fifteen minutes, the firing became sporadic, and the background mass of voices receded so the occasional shout or scream was distinct and individual. Jamie's phone buzzed, loud in the silence, and he pulled it out and declined the call. It was Adele. He thought of muting the phone or putting it in airplane mode, but then powered it down completely and put it back in his pocket.

Now the only sound was the distant roar and crackle of the fires. Jamie and Spot waited for another hour, huddled together under the bushes, thoroughly chilled. They shivered.

It was late afternoon when Jamie finally stirred. He flexed his fingers and rubbed his hands. He pushed himself up on hands and knees and backed out of the clump of bushes. He made as little noise as he could and held the rifle up in one hand so it would not drag along the damp forest floor. Spot followed.

Jamie crouched low and waited before he stepped out onto the path. He heard no one, saw no one. Spot sniffed the air, and then stepped past Jamie into the path. He turned back to Jamie and chuffed. Jamie rose, stiff and aching. "Good dog," he said and patted Spot with a cold, clumsy hand. They started back the way they had come. The light was fading.

Jamie approached the house through the woods. He stayed low and placed his feet carefully, making as little noise as he could. He stopped every few steps, looking and listening, turning his head slowly. Spot followed, moving when Jamie did and stopping when he stopped.

At the edge of his backyard, still in the shadow of the trees, he went down on one knee, and waited. The fires down the hill were still burning, but they did not appear to be moving up the hill toward his house. The house itself was dark. He had turned on no lights. Why attract attention? The houses on either side were dark, as well.

He remained in the trees for five minutes. Nothing moved. There were no lights in the windows other than the flickering reflections of the fires down the block. No sounds other than their crackling, and the wind in the branches above him. He rose slowly and gripped the rifle in both hands. Then he stepped out of the woods into the open and approached the backdoor. Spot came with him, head held low, setting his paws down carefully.

Jamie crept up the stairs and put his hand on the door knob. It should be unlocked, and he knew this door, how to open it so it did not creak, how to close it without a bang. The knob turned easily. The door swung open without a sound. Jamie stood and listened. The house was silent, with no sense of presence. Spot brushed by his legs and made for his water bowl. He drank with abandon. Jamie relaxed a little, and stepped in, but he closed the door silently.

The house was warm. The heat was still on, and Jamie took it in, breathing deep. He considered taking off his boots but decided against it, at least for now. He walked through the kitchen and visited each room on the first floor, then climbed the stairs and searched the second floor. He paused in his parents' bedroom and Bonney's study, looking for any sign that they or anyone had been there. There were no handwritten notes. The messages light on Bonney's office phone was not blinking.

He went back to his bedroom and sat on the bed. He took off his boots and socks, stripped off his jeans and underwear in one motion, and shrugged out of his layers of shirts. He pulled some flannel-lined jeans and wooly socks out of his dresser, put on multiple long-sleeve T's with his heaviest hoodie on top, and considered his boots. Better to be ready, he thought. He put them on and laced them up. Spot found him and pushed his nose into his hands.

He stood and walked down the hall to the window at the end. This window gave him the best view down the hill toward town and he stayed low as he drew near. It was darker inside the house than out, and he pulled the hoodie tight over his blond hair. He peeked over the sill.

The high-water mark of the riot was clear. Houses on either side of the street in the next block were either still burning or had collapsed into smoking ruins, but the violence had not crossed the street to Jamie's block.

There were piles of stuff strewn around the yards and in the street, wads of clothing, a big screen TV, a Lazy Boy recliner, extended and inviting. A car in front of one house had been rolled onto its side, and down a ways farther was the smoking skeleton of another. As he watched, the sun dropped below the layer of clouds and illuminated the scene. Jamie sucked in his breath. Some of the wads of clothing were revealed to be bodies, in fact many of them were. The rioters had not gone away, they were still there.

There was no movement in the scene. No one provided first aid or wailed over a loved one. No one scurried out to loot a body or carry off the TV. Jamie searched in vain for any sign of the police or military. The agents of order had left no signs of their presence. And then Jamie got it. The battle he had heard was no imposition of order by the government. It was simply the riot imploding on itself, in a final, furious battle of all against all until no one remained. Could it be? He watched and waited until the sun had set and only the fires remained visible, down the street and beyond in the valley.

The simple demands of the body finally moved him. His stomach growled, and he got wearily to his feet. A few steps down the hallway, a wave of dizziness hit, and he put out his hand to the wall. Then the world stopped spinning, and he made his way to the kitchen. He cringed when he opened the refrigerator door and the light came on, but his hands were weak and shaking, so he ignored it.

He made scrambled eggs with cheddar cheese and shared with Spot while sitting on the living room couch. He put his plate on the floor and Spot licked it across the room and returned to the couch. He jumped up and lay down next to Jamie with his head on Jamie's leg. The neighborhood was in flames, the world descending into violence, but he was warm, full, and even if just for now, safe. It was enough. For now, it was enough.

He needed something to wash down dinner. He got up and went to the kitchen. Shit, he thought. Enough of the apocalypse for today. It's Miller Time. He opened the refrigerator and found one of Bonney's IPAs in a dark corner. He went to a drawer to get an opener and stopped. He frowned. Something was wrong. He turned slowly and looked back at the refrigerator. He stepped over to it and opened the door. The light did not come on. He closed it and opened it again. Still no light.

He walked to the door of the kitchen and scanned what he could see of the house. Usually it looked like a city at night, twinkling, multicolored lights all over. The TV, the DVR, the cable modem, the wi-fi, a couple of tablets, all glowing and blinking. Now it was dark, except where the fires down the street cast a faint, red-orange glow across the far wall.

Jamie pulled out his phone and pressed a button. Nothing happened. "Shit," he said, and pressed and held the button until the phone booted up. He had one bar, less than normal. There were texts and phone calls from Adele, nothing from his mom or Bonney. The battery showed twenty-five percent.

He went upstairs to Bonney's study. Here he found the usual lights blinking on computers, printers and the wi-fi router. Jamie wasn't sure exactly how it worked, but Bonney had installed backup power for his office: he could function for several days, if the power went out. Jamie collected a laptop and carried it back to the living room. He set it up on the coffee table and plugged one end of a phone cable into the laptop and the other into the phone. The battery indicator on the phone showed it was charging.

He scrolled through the texts from Adele, which started off concerned, became alarmed, and then seemed on the edge of panic. The last was from fifteen minutes ago, and read simply "Jamie, Jamie, Jamie". He dialed her number. She answered before it rang.

* * *

"Jamie?" she said.

"Yeah, it's me," he said.

"Oh, god! I was so scared. I didn't know what happened, if you were OK. Are you OK?"

"Yeah, yeah. I'm OK. I just had to leave. There was a riot down the street. We had to run and hide in the woods."

"You turned off your phone?"

"Yeah. There were people in the woods. I didn't want the phone to ring while we were hiding."

"Right. Of course. Who's we?"

"Me and Spot, Mr. Schultz' dog. Actually, I guess he's my dog, now."

"Oh. Any word from your mom and dad?"

Jamie looked down at the floor, and then lifted his head and shut his eyes. "No. Nothing yet."

"I'm sorry, Jamie."

"Sorry? What are you sorry for? There's nothing to be sorry about. They just haven't called, yet."

Adele was silent. Jamie put a hand on his forehead.

"I... I'm sorry, Deli. I didn't mean to be like that."

"I get it, Jamie. We're all wound up."

Jamie sighed. "Have you heard from your folks?"

"Yeah. I talked with both of them. My dad says the power plant is still working but that some of the lines are down. Some places have power, but a lot don't. Do you have power?"

"No. It went out just a while ago. Bonney has emergency power in his office so I can keep my phone charged. At least for a while. You?"

"It's out here, too. My dad set up a solar system for the house, so basic things work. But it's not like I'm going to turn on lights or anything. Like, hello! Come shoot up my house!"

Jamie smiled in the dark. Her sass warmed him. He needed to be near her. It would be so much better if they were together. He wanted her, wanted to warm his hands at her fire, to warm her body with his hands.

"My dad says the cell towers might stop working," she said. "You know, power outages. And he said there's a lot of vandalism."

"I only have one bar, here." His voice had an odd, husky sound to it.

"Yeah, me, too." Adele cleared her throat. "I don't think we're hitting the usual tower. Like the closest tower isn't working anymore."

"We should get together," said Jamie. "Like maybe at your house. I can come over."

"Oh, yeah. That would be great! It's weird here, all alone all day. But how will you get here? The bridge is burned out."

"No shit? When did that happen?"

"This afternoon. I think the neighborhood watch guys burned it. There was a big confrontation with a mob from town, and I think they burned the bridge to protect Far Side."

"Wow! So, Far Side is still safe? You're still safe?" I should have asked this, first thing, he thought.

"So far, so good," said Adele. "I can see one fire on my side of the river. It's a house down by the bridge."

"There's the pipe. We used to crawl across the river on the pipe when we were kids. Like, on a dare."

"Yeah..." Adele sounded doubtful.

"I don't know," said Jamie. "Maybe I should just stick it out here. I mean, this is where my mom and Bonney would come looking for me."

"Makes sense," she said, but she sounded disappointed.

"Well, I'm not going to do anything tonight, anyway."

"No, no. Of course not," said Adele.

"So..."

"Yeah... So... Hey, look, I talked with my mom, too. She knows all sorts of things because of her job, and there's some really scary stuff happening out there."

"How so?"

"Well, it looks like they're having a hard time keeping control of the military. Like there are riots on the army bases. And she said that something went wrong on a nuclear sub and they actually launched a missile."

"Whoa! Did it hit anywhere?"

"I think she said North Korea. And then they fired back and some nukes hit South Korea and Japan."

"Wow!"

"She said it was amazing that more missiles haven't been fired. Apparently, there's no one in charge and no one's going to listen anyway because everyone is going crazy."

They were both silent for a minute. Jamie stared out the window without really seeing anything.

"She said they haven't been able to contact anyone in Washington D.C. all day. The phones are down and there's a bunch of interference so they can't get through with radio or satellite phones, or anything. She said they can't even contact Seattle."

"Jesus! I mean, what are we supposed to do?"

Adele sighed. "She said find a place and hide. She said it might be more than a few weeks. Like we should be ready to hole-up for months, maybe a year, even." She paused. "I don't know, Jamie. The way she said it... It was like she was afraid this was the last thing she would ever say to me. Almost like she was saying goodbye." Adele cried softly.

"Deli," said Jamie. "I'm sure she'll be OK." But he wasn't sure, and his voice sounded false even to himself. And all he could do was sit with the phone to his ear, repeating "I know. I know," to her softly. And he thought of his mom and Bonney and tears rolled down his own cheeks, and his voice caught. Spot jumped up on the couch and curled up next to him, with his head in his lap. Jamie put his hand down and rested it on the dog's warm, furry body.

They sat together on the phone, neither speaking. It was completely dark outside now, and the shape of the wingback chair across the living room was barely visible. There was a shot somewhere in the distance, but it was too far away, and Jamie didn't even blink at the sound.

"Deli?" he said. There was no response. "Deli?" He looked at his phone. No bars. "Shit," he said.

He went upstairs, and walked down the hall, pausing at several places to see if the phone would connect. Then he went into the bedrooms, standing near windows. Still no bars.

He punched in Adele's phone number just in case, but the phone remained dead. He tried to text, hoping that a simple message would make it through. "R u there?" It came back "SMS Error".

He went into Bonney's office and looked around. When they first moved into the house, Bonney had set up a cell phone amplifier because reception had been so poor. Things got better when they built more cell towers up and down the valley, and Bonney had disconnected the box. Various pieces of old electronic gear were stuffed here and there in the dark corners of the office along with coils of networking cable and mysterious things that looked like they would be dangerous to touch if the electricity had been on. Jamie frowned. He could barely see anything in the dim light of the LEDs. Even if he could find the amplifier, would he know how to set it up? And even if he could set it up, what good would it be if there was no signal to amplify? He threw up his hands.

He walked down the hall to the window at the end. The fires in the next block had burned themselves out, houses reduced to smoldering piles of rubble. A flickering glow from downtown illuminated the cloud of smoke that rose from the valley. He watched for several minutes. His street was dark, but there were hints of motion. A piece of newspaper blew down the gutter, catching on things that Jamie tried not to think about. The only sound now was the wind in the trees. Spot nosed his hand.

They walked down the stairs to the back door, and Jamie opened it a crack and studied the backyard. "OK," he said and let Spot out. The dog stood on the top step and tested the wind. He looked out across the yard at the shadowy line of trees that marked the beginning of the forest. Then he went down the stairs and over to some bushes. Jamie stared at the dark beneath the trees and remembered the rifle sitting in the living room. Stupid to be without it, he thought. Spot returned, and Jamie locked the door when they were inside.

He was tired, bone tired. The day was done, and so was he. He walked into the living room and picked up the rifle. He walked around the first floor, looking out windows and checking that everything was locked. Then they went upstairs and Jamie went into each room, again looking out the windows in all directions. All was quiet.

He returned to his bedroom and pulled a small backpack out of the closet. He put a change of socks and underwear in it and the box of cartridges for the rifle. He added a rain jacket, the camouflage one he despised, and a pocket tool he retrieved from the back of his desk drawer. He held a cell phone charging cable in his hand, considering, and then put it in an exterior pocket of the backpack. He would need it again, surely. I'll pack some cans of food in the morning, he thought. Just in case. This will be my go-pack, like, if I need to get out of here in a hurry.

He sat on the bed and pulled off his boots. He fell back and his head hit the pillow. "Ah," he said, a long exhale. Spot stood next to the bed and put his head on it. Jamie hesitated a second. His mother seemed to object to a lot of things, but for some reason she had never objected to Bodhi, their old black lab mix, sleeping on the bed with him.

"He's guarding you," she said. And when Bodhi was too old to guard anyone anymore, she said, "Now you're guarding him," and the old, smelly dog continued to sleep on the bed, to the very end.

Jamie made a clucking noise and patted the bed. Spot jumped up and lay down against Jamie's leg. Jamie reached down and pulled an old sleeping bag from under the bed and covered them both with it. Soon the dog was asleep, twitching and growling as he dreamed. Jamie laid awake for what seemed hours, exhausted but sleepless. Thoughts of his mom and Bonney crowded his mind, and then Adele, pale and luminous, came to him and somewhere in the early morning hours, he slept.

* * *

Jamie dreamed. He and Adele flew low over rolling, grassy dunes toward a windswept ocean. They lighted on the beach, the surf breaking and washing over their feet. The gray water stretched to the horizon and a setting sun. Waves and wind made a roaring sound, rising and falling.

Something solid hit Jamie's ankles. He looked down. A battered body of a man rolled in the surf and another wave shoved it against them again. The next wave brought more bodies, and the next yet more until the breakers were more flesh than water. A great wave rose, a vast tangle of arms and legs and slack faces, high above them, and came crashing down.

Jamie woke with a start. Spot looked at him in alarm and then at the window that let in morning light. Just a dream, thought Jamie. It was just a dream. And the relief washed over him, as forceful as the nightmare wave of bodies.

So powerful was the dream, though, that the roar of wave and wind was still in his ears. He waited for it to go away, but it did not, and now Spot growled at the window. Jamie looked from Spot to the window and back, and then leaped out of bed and crouched at the window. He peeked over the sill. There it was, the mob was back, and it had crossed the street into his own block. The neighbor who had shot Mr. Schultz started shooting into the mob from a second-floor window, and people down below were shooting back. Someone tossed a Molotov cocktail that broke against the side of the house, and the siding caught fire.

Jamie grabbed his boots and pulled them on. He picked up the backpack and the rifle and rushed out into the hall. "Spot! Come!" he yelled, and the dog passed him going down the stairs.

Jamie ran into the kitchen and paused with his hand on the refrigerator door. Something crashed through a window in the living room, and Jamie made for the back door. He glanced out the kitchen window as he went by. The backyard appeared empty. He opened the back door a crack and looked out. Then he threw open the door, jumped down the stairs, and sprinted for the trees, Spot just ahead. Someone behind him shouted.

He ran until he reached a large maple tree where the path curved around, and he leaned against the tree, panting. He tried to control his breathing but could not. He was sure his gasping would lead the mob right to him, but no one came after them. Up ahead, Spot turned and looked back at Jamie. He whined, and Jamie looked over his shoulder back the way they had come, and then started down the trail after Spot at a trot.

He took the path up to his lookout spot and settled down to wait. After a few minutes, he pulled the extra clothes from the backpack and put them on. The day was cool.

Jamie watched the path below for hours, but no one else came in sight. The sounds of the riot diminished, but the breeze brought whiffs of smoke that burned his eyes and made the dog sneeze. Somewhere around mid-day, Jamie crawled back out of his hiding place and made his way back towards his house. He stopped frequently, crouching down on one knee and holding very still. Spot stood next to him, and the two examined the way ahead.

As they neared his street, the smell of the fires became stronger, at times almost overpowering. And when his house came into view through the trees, Jamie could see that it was engulfed in flames. The roof had already collapsed. As he watched, something in the garage exploded, a gas can or a propane tank, and the back wall of the house slumped in a swirling cloud of sparks. Now the interior of the second floor was exposed to the open air, and the flames roared through his bedroom and exploded up the walls of Bonney's study. A few minutes later, the floor of his mom and dad's bedroom gave way, dropping flaming furniture and debris into the kitchen below.

The houses on either side were on fire, as well, and Jamie touched his face where he felt the heat. He scanned the backyards. No one rushed around with a garden hose or a fire extinguisher. At times, the flames parted to reveal the street. No one moved. The mob had left or perhaps just devoured itself. Jamie shifted, standing straight to stretch, and then sat on the trunk of a fallen tree. He looked around, checking to both sides and behind. He reached out and touched Spot who had settled next to him, alert but not alarmed.

Jamie watched. The light from the fires flickered across his face. The taste of the smoke was acrid, and he breathed through the fabric of the hoodie. Finally, hunger and thirst won out. He stood and approached the smoldering remains of his home. A few feet back from the edge of the trees, he stopped. The brick chimney rose stark from the blackened pile of rubble. He looked right and left. An unburned house a few doors farther up the hill looked possible, and Jamie retreated into the trees out of sight from the houses and started working his way toward it.

When he figured he was even with the back of the house, he turned and approached it, placing his feet carefully. He watched the house through the trees for several minutes. There was no movement, and all seemed in order, except the back door stood open. He looked at Spot, who sniffed the air.

Jamie moved out from the tree-line, staying close to a tall fence that ran along one side of the backyard. He kept his eyes on the house, watching the windows for any sign of movement. When he reached the house, he walked along the back wall toward the open door, checking each window as he passed. The interior seemed untouched by the violence in the street. The house appeared empty.

At the door, he listened. Somewhere in the house, a clock ticked. He debated calling out but didn't. He glanced down at Spot, who sniffed the air. Jamie pushed open the door, and stepped in. To his right was the kitchen. To his left, a sitting room with a dark TV and a doorway into the rest of the house.

Jamie checked the kitchen first. A bowl of fruit sat on a doily on the kitchen table, and he couldn't resist the impulse to grab an apple and chomp it down. It was crisp and juicy, and made a lot of noise when he bit into it. He froze, afraid he had betrayed his presence, but there was only the clock ticking. He continued chewing as softly as he could. Spot sat at attention, and Jamie gave him the last chunk.

He wiped his hands on his jeans and turned to the TV room. It was empty. He stepped over to the doorway at the far end of the room and listened. There was no sound. He leaned into the doorway and glanced around the room. This was a formal living room with windows that looked out onto the street. The houses across the way were burned, and the road was littered with debris.

Jamie stepped into the living room and went over to a window. He scanned the street. Nothing moved except a family of crows that pecked and pulled at things lying on the pavement. Jamie tried not to think about what they had found.

"You're Jamie, Ellen's boy, aren't you?" said a voice behind him.

Jamie spun around and pointed the rifle at a figure sitting in a chair in a shadowed corner. It was an older woman, wearing a bulky winter coat and winter boots. Her hands were pushed deep into her pockets. Gray hair peeked out from beneath a knit cap.

For a second, they looked at each other without speaking. "Yeah, I'm Jamie Montane," he said finally. "I live just down the street. Sorry. I should have knocked. The door was open."

"Not a problem. Things are getting pretty informal around here, aren't they? I'm Mrs. Yates. Take whatever you want," she said. "There're more apples in the fridge."

Jamie considered refusing the offer, but he was too hungry. "Thanks," he said. "It's just... You know... I haven't eaten all day."

"There's bread and peanut butter in the pantry. Cheese in the fridge, too. Should still be good. Someone should eat it before it goes bad."

"Well, maybe you should eat it."

"No. You take it. I'm done with eating."

"What do you mean?"

"I'm just done. You looked out the window. Everything is done. I'm not interested in hanging around, anymore."

"You could come with us," said Jamie.

"Who's us? Are your mom and dad with you?"

Jamie looked away and blinked. "Me and Spot," he said. "It's just me and the dog."

Mrs. Yates smiled. "No thanks," she said, a bitter note in her voice. Then, as if regretting her tone, "I'd just slow you down."

"You can't stay here." Jamie looked out the window. "They might come back."

"They will certainly come back," she said.

"But what will you do? Can you fight them off?"

She smiled and patted a small, silver handgun sitting on the side table. It was an old-fashioned, pearl-handled derringer, that had one - maybe two - shots. "Don't worry. They don't stand a chance." She stood up and pocketed the gun. "Let's get you some supplies."

Jamie followed her into the kitchen. She handed him plastic jars of peanut butter, cans of soup ("They're fully cooked. You can eat these without cooking them."), a loaf of sliced bread, a bag of apples. She held out a two-liter bottle of sparkling water and Jamie opened it and drank. The carbonation burned, but he gulped it down.

Mrs. Yates poured out a big bowl of cat food for Spot. He devoured it.

The backpack was full, now. Jamie shrugged into the straps. It was heavy.

"Where are you headed from here?" she asked.

"I'm going to a friend's house. She lives over in Far Side."

She frowned. "You going through town?"

Jamie looked out the back window. The sun was low in the sky. "My mom is somewhere in town. She was at work. I'm going to look around for her."

"Going through town is a very bad idea, Jamie." She shook her head. "Your mom would not want you to put yourself in danger looking for her. She's a smart cookie. She can take care of herself."

Jamie was silent.

"Your job is to keep yourself safe, Jamie. She'll find you when things settle down."

Jamie nodded. "Sure," he said. He picked up the rifle and looked at Mrs. Yates. "You sure you don't want to come with us?" he said, but the offer sounded half-hearted, even to him.

"Don't worry. You go on. I've got this." She smiled, and her eyes crinkled.

"Yeah. OK. Take care." He stepped to the door and held Spot back while he scanned the backyards. He looked back at Mrs. Yates, and then he recognized her. "You're the music teacher, at the grade school."

"That was me. I'm retired, now."

He remembered a younger Mrs. Yates, full of energy and fun. He had loved singing as she played the piano, the entire class wailing away on "Let It Be", or almost achieving harmony on a Christmas carol. The PTA had grumbled about the inclusion of "Stand By Me" by Ben E. King in the Winter Solstice Concert, but it was the favorite of the 4th grade chorus.

"When the night has come, and the land is dark," said Jamie, quoting the first line of the song. He grinned.

Mrs. Yates smiled. "That was a good one, wasn't it?" Her eyes were moist.

Jamie looked out at the backyard once more, and then turned to her. "Take care," he said, again, and went out the door and made for the woods. Just as he reached the trees, the sound of a single shot came from the house. He stopped and turned, listening. There was only the low moan of the wind in the trees. He went on, with Spot trotting ahead, into the dark land.

CHAPTER 11

The rifle stock was slick where he gripped it, his hands nervous and sweaty despite the cool afternoon. Bushes along the overgrown path slapped at his legs as he hurried along. He held the rifle in both hands, in front of himself, more a shield than a weapon. Spot ran ahead on the path and then back to Jamie, scouting their way but never letting Jamie out of his sight. On a normal day, it might take ninety minutes to walk down the hill, across town and up the other side to Adele's house, but Jamie doubted they would make it all the way today. The sun had started its long slide down to the horizon, and their route through the late-day gloom of the woods was anything but direct. Through downtown was shorter, and Jamie ached to search for his mother and Bonney, but he knew Mrs. Yates was right: the town was a dead zone. And Adele said the bridge had burned. He would have to cross on the pipe that spanned the river downstream from town.

Spot ran ahead to a curve in the path and stopped. He stood looking at something for a second and then looked back at Jamie. Jamie put his feet down carefully, making no sound as he approached. He crouched and listened. Then he leaned out and looked past Spot. A woman lay half on and half off the path. Jamie put his hand out and rested it on Spot's shoulder.

Several seconds passed. Jamie remembered the woman and little girl who had run down the path the day before, pursued by the man with the machete. He had caught them here, and the trampled brush around the woman's body suggested a struggle.

Jamie checked that the safety on the rifle was off, and then stepped down the path toward the woman, staying low and scanning the trees and brush. The path was damp here, and the mud had a rusty tinge. Jamie stopped, and then moved to the far edge of the path where it was dry. Spot followed.

The woman was clearly dead. The machete had bit into her body repeatedly. It looked like the man had stood over the fallen body and hacked at it as it lay. Spot growled low and Jamie looked at the dog. His gaze was fixed on something in the bushes and Jamie put the rifle to his shoulder and pointed it that way. Jamie's eyes were open wide, and his breath was ragged. He edged toward something lying still in a bramble thicket. First there were legs, clad in worn jeans, and then a blood-soaked torso and a face, the man's face. The handle of a small kitchen knife protruded from the man's chest. He was not breathing.

Jamie imagined the scene, the desperate woman defending herself and the child with the small knife she had grabbed as she fled the house. The man with the machete closing in and the woman making a lunge with the knife, a strike that should have stopped him cold but did not. The man collapsing finally from loss of blood, just steps away.

Spot growled again, facing back toward the bushes beyond the dead woman. Jamie frowned, then understood. Spot was not growling at the woman, but at something else. Again, he moved in that direction with the rifle held ready. Spot pushed into the bushes, which rustled as he passed. The rustling stopped. "Spot," Jamie called, a hoarse whisper. He hesitated and then went into the bushes after the dog.

He found them in a small clearing. The little girl sat on the ground, her back to a fallen tree. Spot stood a few feet away, facing her. She was alone. Jamie lowered the rifle. His breathing eased. Her gaze was fixed on the ground in front of her, and she seemed unaware of the dog and Jamie.

Her clothing was crusted with dried blood and there were smudges of dark red on her hands and face. Other than her eyes, her face was still. She did not appear to be in pain, perhaps just in shock. Jamie knelt in front of her and put a hand out. He touched her tangled hair, brushing a dark strand from her face. He guessed she might be about four.

"Are you hurt?" he asked. She did not respond. Jamie touched her clothing. It was stiff with dried blood, but there were no cuts in the fabric. She didn't appear to be injured. Jamie imagined her trying to rouse her mother. It must be her mother's blood.

"What's your name?" Jamie tried again. No answer.

"Are you hungry? Do you want an apple? Some water?" She blinked.

Jamie pulled off his backpack and dug around for the water bottle. He opened it and realized he didn't have a cup, so he simply held the big plastic bottle to her lips and tipped it so a little liquid dribbled down her chin. She licked her lips, and then put both hands to the bottle and drank. She gulped it down.

She took a deep breath when she was finished. Jamie smiled and screwed the cap back on. "Here... I've got an apple for you." He pulled one out of the pack and held it out to the girl. She looked up at him now, in the eye. Then she reached out and took the apple and bit into it. Juice ran down her chin, and she wiped her mouth with her sleeve, leaving a bloody smear across her face. At first Jamie was alarmed, but the smear was not fresh blood. She ate the entire apple, seeds and all.

"I've got some cheese, too. Do you want some cheese?" Jamie broke a piece off the block of cheddar Mrs. Yates had given him and held it out to the girl. She took it without hesitation and devoured it. Jamie gave her another.

Spot moved closer to them and sat. He watched the girl eat the cheese and followed Jamie's hand as he gave her more. Jamie broke off a piece for Spot and held it out to him. Spot took it and swallowed it without chewing. The girl watched. Jamie wiped his fingers on his jeans.

"Would you like to give Spot some cheese? He'd be your friend for life." The girl looked at Jamie but did not speak. Jamie broke off another piece. "Here, let me show you how." He reached out and took the girl's hand. She let him place the cheese on her palm, and then Jamie held her hand in both of his, so that only the piece of cheese was exposed. He moved her hand slightly toward Spot and called wordlessly "Tsk, tsk". The dog approached and took the cheese from her with the most delicate touch of lips and whiskers. She jerked her hand back from Jamie's and held her fist tight against her chest. Jamie reached out and laid his finger on the little fist.

"Did that hurt?" he asked. She looked at Jamie for several seconds, and then gave the slightest shake of her head. A response! Jamie grinned a big, foolish grin. He blinked. "There," he said, "friends for life." He looked at Spot. "His name is Spot. You should tell him your name." He looked back at the little girl, but her eyes were unfocused again, and fixed on the ground to Jamie's right. He waited, but she did not move.

Jamie looked up at the sky through the tangled branches. It was getting dark. He looked back at the girl. Could he just leave her here, he wondered? Did she have people? Maybe someone would come looking for her? But as soon as the thought occurred to him, he dismissed it. No one would come looking. There was no one left. Even if there was, you probably wouldn't want them to find you.

"Do you want to come with me and Spot?" he asked. She was silent. Jamie swallowed, and glanced at Spot. "You know, you can't stay here. Your mom is... She can't take care of you anymore. And that man... Is he your dad?" She was looking at him now, her face expressionless. Jamie reached out, took her hand, and started to stand. She jerked her hand back and crossed her arms over her chest. Spot stood and looked from Jamie to the girl and back. Jamie settled back in front of her on his knees.

"You probably don't want to leave your mom and dad, huh?" he said. "And they're right over there." Jamie motioned with his head. "So you want to stay here, with them, don't you?" He paused. "But they aren't really over there, anymore, are they? What's over there is something else. Your mom and dad are gone. And they wouldn't want you to stay here, all alone, either. They would say 'Go with Jamie and Spot.'" He held out his hand to the little girl, but she didn't take it. A single tear followed a well-worn path through the blood and dirt on her face. Jamie reached out and wiped it away. She looked up at him.

"I lost my mom and dad, too," he said. "They're gone, and I don't know where they are. I'm afraid I'll never see them again." He swallowed, and his eyes stung. He blinked back tears, but one escaped and rolled down his cheek. She watched it, and then put out her hand and touched the wet streak on his face.

He remembered something Bonney had said once, about the power of ritual. "I know how to say goodbye. Let's go say goodbye." He held out his hand again, and this time she took it but with her left hand, and Jamie saw the bandage on her other wrist. He helped her up, and they made their way through the bushes back to the path and the two bodies. Jamie reached in his pocket and found some coins. "Put one coin on each eye, like this." He bent over the body of her father and placed a coin on each eyelid. He gave her two pennies and she squatted down beside her mother and placed the coins on her eyes.

"Now you say, 'Goodbye, mommy. I will love you and remember you forever.'" Jamie felt like a fraud. All memory of her mother would surely fade away. She would remember nothing of this day. And it would be a blessing. The little girl looked up at him and then back to her mother.

"Te amo, Mami," she whispered. Then she stood up and turned to Jamie. Jamie held out his hand and she took it. They walked down the path. Spot led the way.

* * *

Rose walked down the hallway from the lab back to her office. She nodded as she passed a young soldier sitting at a desk, his hands folded in front of him. He responded with a big smile.

"How are you today, Dr. Prada?"

What a phony smile, she thought, but she gave him a big smile back. "Hanging in there, Brandon. Keeping busy?"

She kicked herself for that last. The job of the security detail was exactly to just sit there, just watching. Busyness was a distraction that would keep him from doing his job. Her sarcasm was unhelpful. And a symptom, she thought, with a touch of anxiety. She frowned. Anxiety was a symptom, too. Her frown deepened. Then she almost laughed at her own train of thought, how quickly it fed on itself, spiraling down. Then she frowned again. The spiraling was part of the syndrome, too, and she was glad Brandon couldn't see her face as she walked away.

She was tired, dead tired. The last twenty-four hours had been everything she had ever feared, quarantined inside the locked-down CDC facility while an epidemic raged outside. Her access to data, the number dead, age, sex, symptomology, had become a curse, haunting her sleep when she caught the odd catnap. Now she had six full hours off. The cot set up in her office called to her.

She stepped through her office doorway, glancing down the hall at Brandon sitting at his desk. He was watching her. What did he see, she wondered? We're all tired and on edge. Would Brandon see normal fatigue and irritability, or would he sound the alarm, that yet another of the older staff was showing symptoms, was succumbing? She closed the door behind her and sat at her desk.

She checked her watch, picked up a report and tried to read. She would give it five minutes. If security was going to object to a closed door, they would do it quickly. But she was betting they wouldn't. The offices were bedrooms now, and she thought the young man would be reluctant to intrude on the privacy of a woman almost old enough to be his mother. She was right.

She unlocked the bottom drawer of her desk and pulled out the small handheld radio. She extended the antenna and turned it on. She keyed the mike. "Deli, are you there?" No fancy radio talk, no call signs to identify herself as required by the FCC. There was no FCC, anymore, she thought.

"Mom?" came the voice on the radio, a bit faint and crackling with static but still clearly and joyously Deli's voice.

Rose keyed the mike and spoke. "Yes, it's me, sweetie. How are you? Are you OK?"

"I'm fine, Mom. I'm at home. How are you? Where are you?"

"I'm safe. We're all locked up here at work." She had meant to say "locked-down" but didn't correct herself. "There's a big security detail of soldiers or national guard or whatever. This is probably the safest place in the country, right now. Are you hanging in there? What's going on in Darnell?"

"I'm hanging in. Getting restless, bored. The town is pretty much wrecked. Fires still burning. The hospital and city building are gone. It's, like random. People are moving around and then all of a sudden there's a bunch all together and they're just a mob, you know? And they go marching off and there are more fires and I can hear shots and then there are more shots and then it gets all quiet. And then it starts again. Hang on. I'll look out the window." There was a pause, then, "Looks quiet, now."

"How's the neighborhood? How's Far Side?"

"All quiet around here... The bridge is burned out, so nobody can get across. Looks like all the rioting is on the other side. We're pretty safe here, mom."

Rose had a sense that something was not being said. The reports from the field were clear. No place was safe. It wasn't a matter of keeping dangerous people out. Everyone was potentially dangerous, your neighbors, your friends, your family, your co-workers. Who needs reports from the field, anyway, she thought. The hallway I walk down is the field, as much as Beirut or Seattle. As much as my own mind. The anxiety returned.

"Deli, don't depend too much on that bridge. Remember, everyone's probably infected. Far Side isn't... It's like you said. It's random. It could break out in Far Side at any time." Rose licked her lips. "Just stay aware. Make sure you know what's happening around you. And don't attract attention."

She stopped herself. It was too much. She had unloaded too much on Deli, too much fear and anxiety. But how else could she keep her daughter safe? She had to understand what was happening, what could happen, what would almost certainly happen in Far Side, if not today then tomorrow or the next day.

"Don't worry, mom. No one knows I'm here, except Jamie and Rachel. I haven't been outside for, like, days."

"Look, Deli. Here's what we know so far. Older people are definitely more susceptible. It's like it started with the oldest cohort and is working its way down progressively through younger and younger people. I think it's a combination of how the immune system weakens as people age and how much cumulative stress people are exposed to. It looks like it's rare for people below twenty-five to succumb. At least for now, but who knows whether even young immune systems can resist the end of the world. That's a big fucking load of stress."

What am I saying, she thought? Jesus, this is my daughter. But she has to know. Not telling her leaves her ignorant, unprepared, vulnerable. The only protection I can give her is knowledge.

"Mom? Are you OK? Are you safe?"

"Yeah, yeah, Deli. I'm fine. I'm just over-tired. Sorry about the language. Don't want to piss off the FCC, huh?" Rose shook her head. Stop, she thought. She hit her forehead with the palm of her hand, hard.

"There's one more thing, Deli. No one else agrees with me, but I think that mood or mindset or something can make a difference. Most of the older staff here have succumbed, but not all of them. There are a few who seem to be hanging on." Like me, she thought. "The ones who have remained healthy seem to be people with a strong sense of purpose or mission. Like they aren't the cynical, power-hungry ones. Or the depressed, just-working-until-they-can-retire ones."

"What's going on there, Mom? Is there something you're not telling me?"

Rose closed her eyes and took a deep breath. "OK...I'm going to tell you everything, sweetie. It's not a pretty picture, but I think time is short. It's time to talk frankly." She rubbed her eyes. "I'm not sure we're going to make it, that the CDC facility here is going to survive. And I don't know if we'll be able to find a cure or a vaccine in time. In fact, I think the chances are zero that we're going to."

"You don't know that, mom. You've still got the National Guard protecting you, right? Aren't they mostly young guys?"

"It's not that, Deli. It's the scientific staff, the researchers. We're an older bunch. The youngest is Zarruq, and he's just a statistician. He doesn't know how to do the lab work."

"You can do it, mom. You're close, right? You've identified the virus, and all those factors, stress and everything? It's like you said, maybe just a couple of weeks."

"I don't think we've got a couple of weeks, sweetie. I don't think we've got a week. I can feel it in myself, Deli, the emotions, the anger and despair. It's like it's sucking me down and down and down. I can pull myself out of it, you know, distract myself with the work. But it's getting harder and harder."

"Oh, mom. Don't talk like that. You're just tired, that's all. You just need a good night's rest and you'll be good again."

Rose sat silent for a few seconds. "Sure. Sure," she said. "It's easy to get depressed. I feel so far away from you and your dad. It feels like people are watching you all the time around here, like you're never really alone. But I'm lonely. I miss you, honey. I love you, Deli. No matter what, remember that. I love you, always. You're my sweet baby."

"And I love you, mom. Don't worry. Everything will be all right. It's going to be OK."

"I know. Somehow, I know it's going to be OK." She sniffed. "OK... I've got to get some rest, sweetie. I'm going to take a nap for a couple of hours. Then it's dinner and back to the lab."

"OK, mom. Sleep well. I love you."

"Take care, Deli. Tell your dad I love him. And I love you. Signing off." Rose put down the mike and stared at the desk. She fought back tears and pushed herself up from the chair. The cot was just a step away on the other side of the small office. She sat on it and then fell sideways, her head on the pillow. She pulled her feet up without taking off her shoes, curling in a fetal position. She closed her eyes, and tried not to think, tried just to sink into the darkness of sleep. But her thoughts would not let her, and the sense of loss overwhelmed her. Loss and regret and bitter anger at herself that she had failed to find a cure or a vaccine. Failed to love her husband and daughter as she should have. And she sank into a different darkness, a darkness so deep that she knew she would never surface again. I'm done, she thought. The human race is done, and we deserve it.

* * *

Adele examined her hands, first the palms and then the backs. Her fingers were long and thin, the nails last done over a week ago. She picked at a spot of something on the heel of her left hand.

That language... Her mother must have been exhausted. She would let slip the occasional "shit" or "hell," but the f-bomb? Exhausted or overwhelmed or both.

An old fear came back and settled in Adele's stomach. She remembered her mother, lying in bed, staring at the ceiling, and little Adele, climbing up into bed next to her, wrapping her arms around the still, unresponsive woman. Her father had called to Adele, come looking for her, and when he found her, he lifted her gently from her mother's side and carried Adele back to her own bed. Mom needed rest and quiet, he explained, but understanding had come only later, when adolescence brought her her own storms and periods of desperate quiet.

Adele stood up. The little radio slid off her lap and fell onto the rug at her feet. She turned toward the kitchen and stood still for a moment, but then turned back and sat down on the couch again. She stared at a shadowy corner of the room for a second, and then reached down and retrieved the radio. She put it on top of a thick, glossy magazine on the coffee table, and stood up. She glanced around the great room, its muted tones even more so in the dusky light, and then gathered up the radio and mike in one hand, the revolver in the other, and set off on an inspection tour of the house.

She paused at each window and looked out. Her eyes were adjusted to the dark since the interior of the house was as dark if not darker than the evening outside. She saw that the fires across the way had mostly burned down, leaving dots of glowing orange that flickered as the neighborhood trees swayed in the breeze. Below her on this side of the river, the fires still burned bright and appeared to have continued their advance up the hill. She could smell smoke, now, but the flames seemed distant. How did they spread, she wondered. This side of the valley was relatively sheltered from the winds that blew the sparks and embers from one house to the next in Jamie's neighborhood. Somewhere a door slammed, or it was a firecracker, or a gunshot. Who would mourn her, she wondered. Was Jamie still out there on the hillside in the woods? Would he come? Had Rachel, Caleb and Dwight survived the day? She walked back to the living room and sat on the couch. She checked the revolver. Yes, it was still loaded, six shells in the cylinder. How many would she need?

The room was chilly. She got up and went over to the wood-burning stove, loaded kindling and a couple of logs, stuffed a few pages from the Sunday paper in the gaps, and lit them. She closed the door and stood there until the fire was blazing and the heat poured off it. The room was visible now in the flickering light that came through the glass in the stove door. She looked around. Her gaze rested on the windows looking out over the valley. The windows reflected her shifting image, a girl surrounded by a room full of dark corners. For a second she stood still, and then she rushed around the room, pulling drapes and closing blinds. She returned to the couch and sat watching the fire. She did not look around the room, full now of moving shadows.

Someone knocked on the front door. Her head jerked up and she stared at it, frozen. The knocking came again, insistent.

"Deli? Deli, are you there? It's Rachel. Let us in!"

CHAPTER 12

The powerhouse was three stories high, with a red brick façade in the neo-classical style popular a hundred years ago. Beyond, farther up the forested valley, the dam itself was visible, a high, delicate, curved expanse of reinforced concrete that held back a billion tons of springtime glacial runoff. The spillways were wide open, and the roar of the gushing water could be heard all the way down in the little town of Power City.

Adele's father looked up as he approached the main entrance to the powerhouse. Most of the windows were gone now, boarded up with plywood or covered by sheets of cardboard. The bricks were chipped and blasted from the spasms of violence that had wracked the area. The good news was that they were protected by a company of Army National Guard. The bad news was that the average age of the guard was just about thirty, and the virus was taking its toll. A few days ago, the power plant and the little town might have held seven hundred people, employees, families, and the military. Today, there were maybe one hundred or one-twenty, the rest had fled back down river to civilization and safety. Or they had died.

He paused at the door and held out the identification card that hung from a lanyard around his neck. A young soldier stepped forward, her face severe and watchful.

"Morning, Private...Leung," he said, reading the name tag on her fatigues.

The young woman ignored the pleasantry. She took the card from his hand and examined it, comparing the photo to his face. Then she stepped back and examined him. He kept his expression neutral, knowing the soldiers had been briefed to suspect an overly friendly expression even more than one of hostility or irritation. She looked him up and down, and he felt a touch of anxiety, wondering if she would misinterpret the slightly disheveled dress of a man away from home and living out of a suitcase for that of a man coming unhinged. It had been too much for him to bother to shave, that morning. She looked him in the eye and held his gaze for several seconds. Satisfied, she waved him on. "Morning, sir," she said, but she was already looking beyond him, scanning the activity around the building.

He stepped into the powerhouse. It had only one floor, the ceiling high above. To the left were the three generators, each the size of a small house. They were quiet now. The demand for electricity had dropped to near zero yesterday afternoon, when the transmission lines down the valley had been burned. To the right were the offices and workshops.

An older man in greasy work clothes walked up to him. "Hey, Mike," he said.

"Hey, Connor," responded Mike.

"How was lunch?" asked Connor.

Mike just smiled. He'd been eating ramen several times a day since he moved in to the little bungalow. Somehow everyone on his crew knew this. He turned to the generators. "How's it coming?" he asked.

"Fine. We're lubricating bearings on Number Two. Number One is done. The evening shift will probably finish Number Three."

"How's that lubricant?" asked Mike.

"Yeah, well... Not the best, but it's what we've got, right? I mean, it buys us some time. When's the next shipment expected?"

Mike twisted his lips and shook his head. "Beats me. But I don't think it's going to be an issue. If someone needs electricity, then the roads are probably passable. When they need the power, they'll ship us the lubricant."

"Sure," said Connor, but he looked unconvinced.

There was a loud bang outside the building, and shouting. All heads turned. Several people moved to the tall windows and looked out. Two soldiers from the guard detail rushed inside, closed and bolted the front doors. Mike looked over his shoulder at the back doors. They appeared to be open. He started toward them.

There was a thumping roar from the front of the building and the inside of the powerhouse seemed to be filled with dust and splinters. Mike found himself face down on the floor. Jesus, not again, he thought. There were more shots, and screams, then a brief silence. Someone was shouting orders. Mike could not make out the words.

He coughed and rolled over. Everything seemed to work. He wiggled his toes and held his hands up in front of his face. The palms were scraped but the fingers were all there. He sat up and touched his chest: no blood.

He looked up. The front doors were shredded. The remains of one hung from a single hinge. He thought he could make out figures in camouflage lying still, but he couldn't determine how many. Would all those parts combine into two soldiers?

"Connor?" he said. He looked where he had last seen the man. There was something there, on the floor. It was splashed in red and he could make out an arm, then legs, but they weren't in the right configuration, the right relationship with each other. Connor's head was there, so those must be his neck and shoulders. Mike rolled over and got his hands and feet underneath him. He pushed up into a standing position and started toward what was left of Connor.

He stumbled and almost fell to the floor, but an army medic caught him. "Easy, there," the soldier said, and helped him down into a sitting position. "Are you hurt?"

"I don't think so," said Mike. "What happened?"

"Our NCO... He lost it, got a hold of a big gun."

"An older guy?" asked Mike.

"Yeah." The medic looked at Mike and then over at Connor. "The company's down to about fifty personnel now. I don't think we've got anyone with a rank higher than Corporal. That's Jose Garcia. He just started shaving." He turned back to Mike. "Why don't you stay put for a while? Don't get up until you feel like it." He patted Mike on the shoulder and moved on to another man struggling to get up.

Mike tried to feel grief. So many dead and injured! But all he could feel was relief. It sounded like the only military personnel left were younger, unlikely to go berserk and start shooting people. What am I coming to, he thought? His face hardened, he forced himself up, and went over to Connor. He looked down at the mess of him, and then knelt. He reached out and closed Connor's eyes, and for a second rested his hand on Connor's cheek. Then he looked up again, over at the generators. The one closest to the windows had taken a hit. How bad, he wondered? Mike started over. This is my job, he thought. Focus on what you can control. Just do the next thing. A fierce joy swept over him. I'm still alive, he thought.

* * *

It wasn't what he had expected, although he really didn't know what he had expected. Just that this wasn't it. Sometimes the path was too narrow, so she followed along behind, hanging on to one of his hands twisting him into an awkward sideways walk. When the path was wide enough for them to walk side-by-side, it was more comfortable, but incredibly slow.

"Here," Jamie said, finally. And he turned to her and picked her up. "Let's try this." He settled her on his shoulders, and she wrapped her arms around his head, covering his eyes and almost knocking his cap off. It was a grim smile, but he did, indeed, smile. "Oops, careful there," he said, and rearranged her grip and resettled his cap. They made better time.

Jamie held her right ankle with his left hand and she rested her chin on top of his hat. She was silent as he walked, no whining or complaints. He carried the rifle in his free hand, and worried that he would not be able to move quickly if they had to run or hide or fight. He listened and watched, stopping occasionally to check the path behind, holding his breath to hear better.

Once he thought he heard something moving in the woods and he crouched down, shrugging the girl off his shoulders. He held the rifle with both hands and watched the bushes in that direction. The sound came again, something small, scuttling through the underbrush. Then it stopped, and there was nothing but the breeze in the trees and Jamie's pounding heart. He helped the girl back up on his shoulders, and they turned and went on. Spot took up the lead again, ranging up and back.

The path led away from his subdivision, running level along the shoulder of a forested hill and then down into a valley to cross Miller Creek and climb again. Eventually the trail would turn to the left and begin a long stretch downhill to the Darnell River and the pipe. Jamie knew the trail well. A childhood in Darnell was a throwback to a simpler time when kids ran out the door Saturday morning and called out that they were going to play in the woods and would be home for dinner, and all the adults were good with that. Jamie was sure-footed as he moved through the gloom, despite rifle, pack, and the nameless little girl.

Then it was too dark, and he was too tired. There was a small side path, just a game trail, and he pushed through the brush until the trail skirted the base of a large rock. Jamie helped the girl down and they made their way around the boulder to a little mossy area. It was not visible from the main path, and Jamie dropped his pack. "We're going to sleep here tonight," he said. She simply looked at him, still without speaking. "Are you OK?" he asked. He brushed her hair back away from her face. "How about something to eat?"

He didn't wait for a response, but opened the pack and brought out water, apples and cheese. All three shared the meal, and when they were done, Jamie wrapped the little girl in his jacket. "Time for bed, eh?" he said, but she was already curled up with her eyes closed. Spot came and circled and then settled on the moss right next to her, and a small hand emerged from the jacket and clutched a handful of fur. Jamie sat on the other side of her, his back to the rock, straining to hear and see in the dark wood. He slept.

Her cries woke him. It was pitch black under the trees, and cold. His neck hurt when he lifted his head. "Shhhh," he said, and patted her, but to no effect.

"Mami," she called, and the forest seemed to still, her call going out into that dark night, unanswered.

Jamie scooted down, rolled onto his side and wrapped himself around the little body. He put his arm over her and found the dog on the other side. He rested his hand on Spot, thankful for the warmth. "Shhhh," he said. "Shhhh."

After a while, the sobs subsided. She seemed asleep, again, but Jamie laid awake, cold and uncomfortable, until the black shapes of trees and bare branches showed faintly against a gray dawn.

CHAPTER 13

Adele threw the door open and Rachel rushed into her arms. They hugged and cried, and Adele almost jumped up and down but stopped herself just in time. Caleb and Dwight hugged her too.

"Oh my god, I am so happy to see you!" Adele said.

"Oh, god, Deli! I never thought we'd make it!" said Rachel. "Jesus! It's crazy out there!" And they cried and hugged again.

"Come in, come in," said Adele, and they trooped into the living room, shedding coats and hats as they went. They gathered around the wood-burning stove, holding out their hands to its warmth.

"Ahh," said Rachel. "Oh, shit! I'm so cold. Have you got anything to eat?"

Adele thought for a second. "Soup," she said. "I've got canned soup."

Everyone went out to the kitchen, and Adele pulled a half-dozen cans of Progresso soup from the pantry. They ate directly from the cans without heating them up and finished off a partial loaf of sourdough bread along with a nearly full jar of peanut butter. Caleb sniffed a carton of Greek yogurt and made a face. "Whoa," he said. "Not that desperate yet." He tossed it into the garbage.

"We haven't eaten all day," explained Rachel. She scraped the last of the peanut butter from the jar and licked the knife clean. She went back into the pantry. "Chips!" she crowed and emerged holding up a large bag of potato chips, triumphant. They retired to the living room and crowded onto the couch. They passed the bag back and forth and for a few minutes, the only sound was the crunching of their chewing and the crackling of the fire in the stove.

Rachel waved her hand. "Here," she said. Dwight handed the bag to Caleb who handed it to Rachel. She shook the bag which made a slight rattling sound, and then tilted her head back and poured the last bits into her open mouth. She shook the bag again. It did not rattle, and she crumpled it up and tossed it on the coffee table, where it bounced off of Dwight's feet and landed on the floor.

They sat on the couch, resting against each other without speaking. Rachel held Adele's hand and stared at the flickering light of the stove.

"What happened out there?" asked Adele.

Caleb blew out a long, slow breath, as if preparing to speak, but Rachel started in.

"I don't know what's happening, Deli. Everyone is crazy. It's like the baseball game, only without the cops and the ambulances. Just the riot." She shook her head.

"You guys were at Guido's?" Adele prompted.

"Yeah. There were a bunch of us. You know, customers and employees. And Juan turned off all the lights and made us get in the back and stay quiet, because of the fighting in the street. He didn't want anyone to know we were there. And that worked for a while. But then some old guys started complaining, said Juan couldn't tell them what to do. And they started pushing him around and hitting him. And they wouldn't stop. And then Dwight and Caleb grabbed Juan and pulled him away and we all went out a back door into the alley. I think they would have beat him to death if Dwight and Caleb hadn't saved him."

Caleb offered Dwight a fist bump. Dwight turned his face from the fire and looked down at the fist. He hesitated, then bumped him, but barely. He let his fist fall back into his lap and returned his gaze to the fire, as if the flames held a mystery.

Rachel went on. "We wanted to run away, but Juan said he couldn't leave his family. Like, they live above the restaurant, right? So, we left him there."

"What else could we do?" said Dwight, but he seemed to be speaking to someone no one else could see.

"How'd you guys make it across the river?" asked Adele. "I mean... the bridge and all."

"There was one beam that was not like completely burned through," said Rachel, "and someone strung a rope to hang on to, and if you go one-at-a-time, you can make it."

"Except for when the beam breaks," said Caleb. "Then you have to hang from the rope and go hand-over-hand."

"Yeah," said Rachel. "Dwight was the last one over. And we were being chased, and Dwight got halfway and then one of the crazy guys started across. So Dwight jumped up and down and broke the beam, and he was just hanging there, you know, hanging from the rope. I thought he was going to fall in, like the crazy guy on the beam. But he made it."

"Then, we cut the rope," said Caleb.

"They started coming across on the rope, and two of them were already halfway across," said Rachel. "We had to do it. They had knives and stuff. It was them or us."

The room was silent for a few seconds. Adele watched her friend's face.

"It was," said Dwight, his eyes fixed on the fire. He nodded to himself. "Them or us."

"And we thought we were protecting Far Side," said Caleb. He frowned and shook his head. "But it was too late."

"What do you mean?" asked Adele.

"The neighborhood watch guys?" said Rachel. "We found them when we got off the bridge."

"They didn't recognize you?" asked Adele.

"They were all dead," said Rachel. "And you could tell, they had been fighting each other."

"And all the fires," said Caleb. "They're being set by someone on this side of the river."

"And then we heard shooting," said Rachel, "and it was like, they're shooting at us. So we ran and hid, and we waited until it was dark and then we had to sneak through backyards all the way here."

The room was silent. In the distance, there were several shots. All heads turned toward the sound.

"It's getting closer," said Adele.

"I have to go home," said Rachel. She stood up.

"Me too," said Caleb.

"Tonight?" asked Adele.

"I have to check on Stevie and my parents," said Rachel.

"Maybe better to move at night, while it's dark," said Caleb.

"Rache, your place is closest, right?" said Adele. "Maybe Caleb and Dwight could go with you? Like drop you off?"

"Yeah, we could do that," said Dwight.

"I'm just a couple of blocks up the hill," said Rachel. "Caleb, you're on Eagle Ridge, right? So you're just a couple of blocks beyond me."

"Yeah, that'll work. Dwight, you can stay at my place tonight. My folks won't mind."

"Dwight, where do you live?" asked Adele.

"Downtown," said Dwight. "I live with my dad in an apartment above the cafe."

"Oh," said Adele. "Is your dad OK?"

"He got a DUI, like his fourth," said Dwight. "He was on a thirty-day work-release."

"Oh," said Adele, again. She frowned, puzzled.

"Work-release means you live in the city jail and get out just to work," said Caleb. "He had to return to the jail every day after work."

"But the city building burned down," said Adele. No one spoke. No one looked at Dwight. "Oh," said Adele. "I'm sorry, Dwight. I... I wasn't thinking."

"It's OK," said Dwight. "They probably let everyone out when the fire started. And anyway, he was a mean son-of-a-bitch." He blinked. "Every time I visited, he was worse."

There was a shot, a hard crack that echoed off the hillside, and then three shots that sounded like they came from a smaller gun, in response.

"That sounded close," said Rachel. "Deli, why don't you come stay at my place?"

Adele considered. "I'm not ready. All my stuff is here. This is where my parents think I am. Jamie is coming. I want to make sure I'm here when he gets here." Her eye fell on the revolver sitting on the coffee table. "And anyway..." she leaned forward and patted the gun, "I've got Mr. Ruger here in case there's trouble." She put a big, can-do grin on her face and looked around at her three friends. The doubt was clear on their faces.

"I don't think a couple of blocks makes you safer," said Adele, her face sober, now. "I talked with my mom. She's a scientist at the CDC and they're studying what's happening. She sees a lot of data. And she says it isn't like limited or localized anymore. It's all over. She says just stay away from people, especially older people, people above like twenty-five."

It took a few seconds to sink in.

"Older people..." said Caleb.

"That explains a lot," said Dwight.

"I've gotta go check on Stevie," said Rachel.

All four walked to the door. They gathered up hats and coats as they went.

"Hang on," said Adele when they reached the door. She put her eye to the peephole and studied the dark street. Then she stood back. "Looks OK." She opened the door just wide enough to let them slip out, afraid that the faint glow of the stove might show like a beacon in the otherwise lightless night.

Rachel hugged her tight. "We'll talk in the morning," she said, and joined Caleb and Dwight.

They moved off, quiet, pausing to check around corners, and then hustled across the street in a tight, little group. Adele thought she heard someone get shushed, and she couldn't help but smile. She closed the door and went back to the couch, which seemed now large and empty. She sat in the middle, and felt like a little child in a big, grownup chair. She already missed her friends. What's taking Jamie so long, she thought. She sat back on the couch and hugged herself.

* * *

The NCO had swept the big gun back and forth across the face of the power house, just once to the left and once back to the right, before he was brought down by a motor pool guard. The front of the building, already scarred and pock-marked from the day before, was even more chewed up now. The plywood over the windows had disintegrated. In places, the rounds had penetrated all the way through the old brick facade.

Generator Number One, closest to the windows, had taken multiple hits. Mike and a couple of his junior engineers moved along the catwalk of the hulking machine. They counted eight neat round holes in the generator's outer housing. The gun (an auto-cannon, M-something-or-other, Private Leung had explained) fired five hundred rounds a minute, and three had come through the north window, four through the center window, and one through the south window to strike the generator. Mike could fit his thumb in the holes, with room to spare. He sighed.

"OK," he said. "Let's get the housing off."

The outer housing would be easy to patch, an afternoon of welding and grinding. The real damage was visible when they removed the housing and saw that the armor piercing projectiles had shredded the copper wire windings. Who knew what other damage they would find when they dug farther in. The generator required more than a repair. It needed a major rebuild.

Mike knew how to do that, but he doubted that anyone else on his engineering team had the knowledge or experience to pull it off. He wasn't sure it was really necessary right now, anyway. They still had two functional generators, assuming the lubricant held up, and there was no demand for electricity from whatever remained of civilization down the valley and along the coast. The power plant itself and Power City were still consuming electricity, but they could service that need with a single generator on-line running at minimum capacity. It could be months or years before they would need a third generator, he thought. Before that, they would need spare parts. And then it hit him. It almost made him feel cheerful. Generator Number One was now a parts machine.

"How's it look?" Mike stepped to the railing of the catwalk and looked down at the speaker. Private Leung stood below him, an assault rifle slung over her shoulder. Her voice had been pitched low, and Mike noted the absence of the "sir". The title had amused him at first, then made him feel old. He didn't miss it. He didn't need to be reminded that now he was the oldest guy around.

"Come on up and take a look," he said. Mike watched her come up the stairs. She moved easily, her eyes on the steps until the last few when she looked up and met his gaze. Her eyes were very dark. "Tell me what that gun can do," he said.

She turned toward the exposed innards of the generator and raised her hand to a tangled mess of copper wire. "Can I touch that?" she asked.

"Yeah. All three are shut down until we can do a safety inspection. There's no current."

She pushed and pulled the severed end of a piece of wire, testing its give. "How thick is the wire wrapping?" she asked.

"It's about six feet."

"Huh," she said, with a nod. "He was firing depleted uranium rounds. They're designed to penetrate armor, but six feet of copper is a lot of armor." She went up on her toes and leaned forward to get a better view. Mike kept his eyes on the damaged area. "The copper wire would have dissipated the impact better than solid metal, actually," she went on. "I doubt if it penetrated through the wire. And whatever's under the copper is probably fine." She turned back and looked up at him.

Mike swallowed. "Great. I'm thinking this generator is our source of spare parts, for now." He reached out a hand and leaned on it, trying for casual.

Private Leung smiled, just a little. "How do the other two look?"

Mike straightened up and frowned, thoughtful. "No visible damage," he said, "We won't restart any of them until we know for sure. Our only real concern is the lubricant. We're re-purposing some stuff. Not up to spec."

"I'll talk to our quartermaster, have him contact you. We might have something."

"Oh, yeah," said Mike. "That would be great."

"The company still has an electronics specialist and a vehicle mechanic. I know your team suffered some casualties." Mike looked over her head at a distant wall. "I'm sorry about Connor," she said.

"Thanks," said Mike.

"Let me know if you need more people. Maybe just muscle?"

Mike nodded. "Sure, thanks. I'll keep that in mind."

She stood for a minute without speaking. "Anything else you need?" she asked.

Mike considered. "I'm about done here. You want to go grab a beer, or something? The Tap still has cold ones. I mean, if you're not on duty, you know, still, or anything."

She studied his face for a second. Then she smiled and shook her head. "Duty calls," she said, and turned and went down the stairs.

Mike watched her go across the big room and out the front door into the night. She did not look back.

What am I doing? he thought. I'm tired. I'm really, really tired. I'm a really tired man who loves his wife, even if she kicked me out.

He made some notes in the logbook, underlining the words "depleted uranium" twice. He left the log open to that page and started the ten-minute walk back to his house in Power City. There were checkpoints now along the road, and groups of nervous, young soldiers demanded his ID twice. He was well-known and could call several of them by name, too, but did that just make things worse, he wondered? Did they know him as the affable, chief engineer? Or as the last old-guy who hadn't gone crazy?

The house was almost as empty as when he had first moved in. A couch and TV in the living room, his futon on the floor of the smaller bedroom. No table in the kitchen. He ate meals - if you could call them that - on the couch watching news or streaming something. The only additions were the bed, dresser and a chair in the master bedroom, preparations for Deli's arrival.

He tossed his coat on the couch and went into the kitchen, opened the refrigerator door, and leaned on it for a few seconds. The fridge had a carton of half-and-half, a couple of apples, something leafy, slick and brown - it might have been romaine lettuce, once - and the remains of a case of Deschutes Black Butte Porter. The freezer had a couple of Stouffer's microwave entrees, but even that effort was beyond him. He plopped down on the couch with a porter.

Somewhere around the fifth bottle, he fumbled in his coat pocket and pulled out his handheld radio. It was on, so he hadn't missed any calls over the last couple of hours. It was late. Everyone was probably in bed, and he didn't want to wake anyone up.

He keyed the mike, on and off. Anyone monitoring that frequency would have heard the static ker-chunk and known that someone, somewhere was on the air, listening, sending a wordless signal of their human presence. Mike listened for a minute. There was no response.

He pushed himself up and draped his coat over his shoulders, picked up the radio and the beer, and lurched out onto the front stoop. He sat on the cold, cement steps with the bottle on one side and the radio in his lap. He shifted to get comfortable and knocked over the bottle. It didn't break but was loud in the quiet night as it hit the cement and rolled off into the lawn. Mike blew out a breath and swallowed something that tried to come up.

Out here, the radio would work better. No walls interfered with the signal. He keyed the mike again and waited. Nothing but the usual faint, distant, hiss that was the senseless echo of the Big Bang. Mike looked up at the night sky. It was a moonless night, and stars faded in and out as clouds passed by.

He put the mike to his mouth and pressed the key. "Rose? Are you there, Rose? This is Mike." He let his hand fall to his lap and leaned back. He watched a star as it brightened and then faded again behind a passing cloud. I love you. He barely breathed the words, sending the thought into the dark, down the valley to

Darnell and beyond to the coast. His engineer's mind knew that this thought went nowhere, but it also knew that nothing else was getting through.

He had no more thoughts. No more words formed in his mind. He leaned back against the stairs and his coat fell open. The night air was cold on his neck and chest. He spread his arms out wide to that freezing dark sky and the whispering, indifferent universe. The image of Rose and Deli came to him, a picnic once when they were all three young, on a high grassy bluff above the sun-drenched, wind-swept waters of the Puget Sound. They spread a blanket in the shelter of a big leaf maple and ate sandwiches and chips. Lying now on the stairs, Mike was filled with gratitude. It is enough, he thought. No matter what, now. It is enough.

* * *

The pounding on the door jerked Adele awake. She sat up, still on the couch where she had fallen asleep, the fire in the stove now just a bed of coals, a distant glow across the cold, dark room.

"Deli, let us in!" called Rachel. There was a touch of panic in her voice. Adele ran to the door and threw it open. Rachel and Stevie rushed in. Rachel turned and slammed the door shut behind her.

"Is it locked?" she asked. She braced the door shut with both hands.

"It's locked," said Adele. Rachel exhaled and stepped back from the door.

"Someone's out there. I think they were following us."

"Who?" asked Adele.

"Some man. I couldn't see." Rachel wouldn't look at Adele.

She knows, thought Adele. She knows who it was, and she doesn't want to say.

She looked at Stevie. He was clinging to his sister, his arms wrapped around her waist. His gaze rested on the floor of the entryway, averted from the world around him. She looked back at Rachel.

"Did the man see you at my door?" asked Adele. She put her eye to the peephole. No one stood at the door. There was no movement in the night scene other than the breeze in the trees.

"I don't know, Deli. We ran. I don't know what he saw."

Adele thought of the gun on the coffee table. "Come on," she said, and led them to the couch. She touched the revolver with her hand, pulling it out from under a magazine that had slid over it. She looked around the room. All the shades and drapes were drawn. Rachel settled on the couch and Stevie curled up next to her. He leaned on her, and Rachel put her arm around his shoulders.

Adele went to the stove and set a couple of logs on the coals. They caught quickly. She returned to the couch and sat next to them.

"Are you OK? What do you need?" she asked.

"He's shivering," said Rachel. "Do you have a blanket?"

"Sure." Adele got up and went into her parents' room. She gathered up a big down comforter that was folded at the foot of the bed and carried it back to the couch. Rachel pulled it close around herself and Stevie. Only his nose stuck out. Adele sat next to Rachel and tucked her legs under a corner.

They sat in silence. Adele listened for any sounds around the house, any hints that someone might be trying a door or prowling beneath a window. The house creaked in the wind, and Adele leaned over and picked up the revolver. She rested it in her lap, the muzzle pointing at a dark corner of the living room, away from Rachel and Stevie.

After a while, Stevie's breathing became deep and regular. Rachel remained awake, upright on the couch, her eyes fixed on the fire in the stove. There was a sound outside the house, perhaps a small branch falling in the wind, or a piece of newspaper blowing down the street. Both girls held their breath. Adele gripped the gun and slipped her finger onto the trigger. The wind sighed. They breathed, again.

"My mom is dead," said Rachel. She spoke in a murmur, turning her head toward Adele and away from the sleeping Stevie. Adele sat, her mouth open, staring at Rachel.

"Oh, Rache," she said.

"I couldn't find Stevie. He was in a closet."

Adele did not speak. I don't want to hear this, she thought.

"It was my dad," said Rachel, now just a whisper. "It was my dad following us."

Adele looked away from Rachel's face, looked down at the gun in her lap. The impossibility of their situation overwhelmed her. She was going to shoot Rachel's dad? Was every adult curled up in the fetal position or out roaming the streets, crazy vicious? How were they going to survive? What's going to happen to me when I get older, she thought? If I get older? Am I going to go down some black hole of despair? Or explode in bloody fury?

Neither spoke for the rest of the night. Eventually, they all slept. Once, Stevie cried out, and Rachel pulled the comforter close around them both. The fire died down, and the room was given over to deep shadow. No one stirred when the radio, buried beneath magazines and dishes, made sounds and a muffled voice called out.

CHAPTER 14

They hit the clearcut about midmorning. The path disappeared beneath a wild tangle of slag and tree stumps. Jamie stopped just inside the tree-line and went down on one knee so the girl could slip off his shoulders. He stood and shrugged off the ache and studied the way ahead.

It was a rare, sunny day for spring in the foothills, and Jamie shaded his eyes. The only movement in the cut was a group of little birds that flitted from limb to limb. The only sound, their high-pitched cheeping. A week ago, the scene would have been peaceful, the open sky inviting, but today Jamie hesitated to step out into that exposed expanse. The little girl stood next to him with her hand on his leg. A squirrel perched on a stump and eyed them suspiciously.

"Do you want some water?" Jamie asked.

She looked up at him and nodded. Jamie pulled the water bottle out of the pack and unscrewed the top. The bottle was nearly empty, but he let the girl drink her fill.

"Done?" She nodded again, and Jamie finished the last of it. He looked at the empty bottle for a few seconds and then put it back in the pack.

Spot followed all this with interest. "Sorry," said Jamie, and gave him a scratch behind the ears. The girl held out her fingers to Spot and he licked a few drops of water off them.

Jamie put the pack on and then helped the girl climb up onto his shoulders. They were getting good at this after a morning of frequent stops. Jamie squatted down and steadied himself with the rifle in one hand. She stepped into his other hand and he lifted her up. The girl had not spoken since the night before when she put the pennies on her mother's eyes, and Jamie did not press her.

He pushed himself up with the rifle and then stepped out into the cut. The path was impassable. The wrack and ruin left by the loggers was dense, and the heaps of debris rose in places above his head. Jamie looked to the right and left and started picking his way along the edge of the trees uphill to the right, where the beginnings of a game trail wound along. It was slow going, and Jamie was soon sweating as he pushed up the slope.

He paused when he reached the upper edge of the clearcut and wiped the sweat off his face with his sleeve. The air in the valley was hazy, smoky, but from here he could see the river and the slim, dark line of the pipe running across. The water below the pipe was moving fast, the rapids glinting frothy white. It would be easy for him to cross, not so easy for the girl and the dog.

That morning, he had risen while the girl still slept and moved off into the forest to pee. He made his way quietly, stepping carefully as he returned, but when the girl and the dog came back into view, something stopped him. She was awake, now, and sat with her back to the rock. Spot sat next to her. They were waiting, waiting for him, and it pissed him off. He would already be at Adele's house, if it wasn't for them.

The dog saw him first and grinned. Then the girl saw him standing there, back in the woods. Her face was expressionless as she watched him. For a second, Jamie simply looked back, and then he was overcome by shame, and pushed into the little clearing. He gave her a big smile, but she did not smile back.

He laid out a breakfast of bread and cheese. "How's that?" he asked. She just looked at him. "Go ahead. That's for you," he said, and she took a piece of cheese and devoured it.

She doesn't expect much, he thought, and no wonder. But the worst of it was the part he had played in teaching her that lesson just now when he considered leaving the girl and the dog, so he could go on alone. She had seen him standing there and understood immediately what was in his mind. Resting now in the clearcut and looking down at the river with the pipe running across it, he turned away from these thoughts. "Ready?" he asked. She stood and he helped her up onto his shoulders.

When they reached the other side of the clearing, he stopped and leaned against a tree stump. The girl climbed down from his shoulders and stood on the flat surface of the stump. From this vantage point, the town of Darnell and the blackened remains of the bridge were visible. The fires across the river at the base of the Far Side hill had spread halfway up. Jamie squinted. The flames had not reached Adele's house, yet, but there was no way Jamie could reach her street from down below. Maybe they could make it through the firestorm, but what if they met those who had started the fires? Instead, they would have to hike through the woods and approach her house from above. Another delay. Jamie took off his hat and wiped his forehead. He pushed his hair back from his face with both hands, and they came away slick with sweat and grease. He rubbed his palms on his jeans.

He dug his phone out of his pocket and powered it on. No bars, of course, and only ten percent charge left. He stared at the screen for a moment, willing a connection, some message, any hint that his mom or Bonney were still alive. He looked away from the phone, off across the valley to the distant hills, and then back down again to the screen. It had already blanked out. He shut the phone all the way down and pushed it back into his pocket. He figured they could reach the pipe by noon. "We gotta get going, here," he said. He bent his knees, and the girl hopped back on his shoulders.

It was mostly downhill from here. Downhill had its own challenges, he knew, with pack, rifle and the girl. She might have to walk. That would slow them down even more. How long could Adele stay in her house? Would the fires or whoever was setting them force her to run? Would she still be there when he arrived? Would her house? Jamie picked up the pace.

* * *

The pipe ran straight and level across the river at a narrow point a mile downstream around a bend from the town. The rushing, white water was more than forty feet below. Two piers rose from the water to support the tube, and an arch of rusted metal girders spanned the hundred feet between them. The pipe itself was about three feet in diameter. Patches of black paint showed that it had once been maintained, but it was no longer in use and was now neglected. Jamie had never known what the pipe was for. It just emerged from the ground on one bank and disappeared into the ground on the other.

Jamie, the girl and the dog stood next to the pipe where it first emerged on this side. Here it was mostly buried in the dirt and a boy exploring the riverbank might step over it without noticing. Farther on, the ground dropped away down to the river and the pipe was unmistakable.

The summer before fifth grade, walking across had been the ultimate dare issued among Jamie and his friends. Two boys had made it, but a third had not. His body was never found, presumably washed down to the Sound and out to sea. The county had erected a chain-link barrier at both ends of the pipe after that, but vandals had pulled the fencing away on this side and access was no longer blocked. It looked like the same was true on the far bank. Either way, Jamie was confident he could make it. He was not so sure about the girl and the dog.

"OK, you ready for this?" he asked. The girl stared at the pipe and did not respond. "Here's what we'll do," he went on. "I'll take the lead, and you come behind me. You can hold on to my belt with both hands, see?" He lifted up his hoodie in back so she could see his belt. She looked at his belt and then back at the rapids below.

He walked over to the pipe where they could step up on it easily. He held the rifle in one hand and beckoned with the other. "OK, let's go," he said. She did not move. "Are you coming?" he asked, as if she might choose not to. He took a few steps along the pipe and tried to give her an encouraging smile. She looked at him. Tears were running down her cheeks.

Jamie sighed. He looked across the river to the other side, considering, and then back at her. "Well, OK," said Jamie. "Maybe that's not the best way. So, I'll carry you across, OK? But you have to stay very, very still and keep your eyes closed until I tell you. Can you do that?" She nodded. "OK. Come on over here," he said.

He positioned the rifle on its sling on one shoulder across his back. Having both pack and rifle on his back was awkward, but now both hands were free. He held them out to her and she raised her arms to him and let him lift her up. She wrapped her arms around his neck and her legs were tight around his ribs. He started out along the pipe.

When he reached the remains of the chain-link fence, he reached out with one hand and steadied himself. He turned a bit and looked back. Spot was standing on the bank, his front feet on the pipe but his hind legs still on the dirt. He whined, the distress clear on his face.

"Come on, Spot! Come on, boy. Good dog! Come," Jamie called. Spot climbed up onto the pipe and took a few steps but then stopped. He looked at the ground on either side of the pipe, now a couple of feet below, and almost jumped down but did not. He tried to turn but a foot slipped off the pipe and he scrambled to regain his footing. He looked at Jamie and barked, a single note of fear.

"Come on, Spot! Come on! Good dog! You can do it! Here, Spot! Come!" he called. Spot shifted his feet but could not bring himself to continue out on the high, narrow path.

Then a high, little voice sounded, loud and clear. "Ven, Spot! Ven!"

Jamie joined in, and the combined force of their two voices calling together moved the dog. He came slowly along the pipe, his body low, and Jamie stepped past the fence out over the water. He fixed his eyes on the pipe about ten feet ahead. The sound of the rushing water rose all around them. Jamie was afraid to turn, to look back to make sure the dog was following, and simply went forward. The breeze blew up the valley from the coast and brought the stink of smoke.

He took it one step at a time, careful not to set his boots down on the joint ridges between the sections of pipe. Once he had to throw out an arm to balance himself, and the girl clutched him even tighter, her heart beating against his chest, racing. He fought down fear and focused on the way ahead. No water below, no empty space beneath them, just the pipe and his next step.

His arms were aching, but finally the sound of the water receded, and tree limbs appeared around them. He reached out and gripped a pole that was part of the chain-link barrier and had to step over a twisted piece of the fencing that was draped over the pipe, dangling still twenty feet above the bank. Then the ground rose up to envelop the pipe and Jamie stepped off onto the dirt.

"We're here. You can open your eyes, now," he said. He lowered the girl to the ground and at first she would not let him go. He did not pull away. "You're the bravest girl I know," he said, and gave her a hug. She released him then, and he straightened up. He turned and looked for Spot. The dog was stalled at the chain-link fence, unable to step over it. He lifted a paw and tried to put it down but something about the fragment of fence spooked him. He looked up at Jamie and whined.

Jamie unslung the rifle and leaned it against a rock. He shucked off the pack. "You stay here," he said to the girl, and stepped back onto the pipe. He walked rapidly out to the barrier, his arms held out for balance. When he got close to Spot, the dog whined again and started to jump over the piece of fence but lost his footing and nearly fell.

"Easy there, easy boy," said Jamie. He held up his hand, palm out, telling Spot to stay.

Jamie lowered himself and sat straddling the pipe. Then he scooted forward until he was at the fence. He gripped the chain-link and tested it, pushing it first to one side and then the other, but it would not move. Spot whined and danced on his paws. Jamie reached out and stroked the dog's head. "There ya go. Good dog," he said.

Jamie studied the fence. He pulled up on it but managed to lift it only a few inches off the pipe. He let it drop back. He wrapped his fingers around the top strands of the fence and pulled it toward himself. He leaned forward to put some weight on it and pushed the fence almost flat on the pipe. The dog could get by it, but Jamie's head and shoulders now blocked the way.

Jamie shifted so both legs were on one side of the pipe. He pulled the fence down as flat as he could, and then edged over until he was sitting on it. His weight kept it down.

Spot could reach him now and leaned forward to lick his face in greeting. Jamie twisted his upper body toward the dog, reached around him, picked him up and then set him down astride his lap. Spot's hind paws were still on the flattened fence but his forepaws were on the other side of Jamie's legs on the pipe and his nose was pointed at the girl. "Ven, Spot!" she called, and Spot, seeing the way to terrafirma clear before him, made for her, stomping on Jamie's crotch and scrambling along the pipe. When he reached her, the girl threw her arms around his furry neck, and the two tumbled on the ground. Spot leaped up and rushed around her, all frenzied joy.

Jamie grinned, but rested a bit before he started back. When he finally stepped off the pipe, he got a warm welcome. Spot jumped up on him licking his face, and the girl - seeming to forget for a moment the darkness of the past few days - hugged him around the knees, turned her dirty, blood-smeared face up to him, and stunned him with her beautiful laughter.

CHAPTER 15

Adele walked to a back window and put a hand on the mini-blinds. She bent a slat the least bit and put her eye to the opening. She blinked at the bright light.

A bunch of men and women milled around a house on the far side of the next street down the hill, trampling flowerbeds and breaking windows. A couple of men ran up with a battering ram, the kind the police use to break down the door during a drug bust. They smashed the ram into the front door once, twice, and it flew open. The mob poured into the house.

"What are they doing?" asked Rachel. Adele started at the sound of her friend's voice. "Sorry," said Rachel. "Didn't mean to sneak up on you." She leaned over Adele's shoulder, and frowned. "Are they looting?"

Adele watched in silence. A chair came flying through the picture window of the house and landed on the front lawn. A man appeared at the window, fists raised high above his head in triumph, and a cheer went up from those who remained outside.

A man in the street ran toward the house. In his hand, he had a bottle with a strip of cloth stuffed in the neck. He paused, lit the cloth and threw the bottle hard against the house. The Molotov cocktail exploded, splashing flaming liquid across the siding. Another cheer. Now some people inside the house rushed out.

Another Molotov cocktail arced through the air. This one went through the front window and shattered on the floor inside. For a second nothing happened, and then the room was engulfed in flame. A figure inside staggered by the window, fully aflame, arms flailing. The mob whooped and clapped. Rachel let out a long breath, a moan, and gripped Adele's arm with both hands.

Adele straightened up and let the blinds snap back into place. "We can't stay here," she said. "We've gotta go, Rachel. Get Stevie and pack up. Let's go."

Rachel rushed into the living room where Stevie was reading an old Tintin book. "Shoes, quick!" she said. Stevie looked at her for a second and then jumped up, ran to the front entryway and pulled on his shoes.

"Hang on," said Adele. She went back to her bedroom and grabbed a book bag. She dumped out books and papers on the floor and stuffed in the solar charger for the radio. She ran down the hall back to the living room. She picked up the gun and radio from the coffee table and shoved them into the bag.

"Kitchen," she said, and Rachel and Stevie followed her in. "Stuff your pockets! Anything you can find." She stepped into the pantry and added two full plastic bottles of sparkling water to her pack and a couple of unopened jars of peanut butter. When she returned to the kitchen, Rachel and Stevie were waiting, already in their jackets, pockets bulging.

Adele paused and looked around the room. She stepped over to a drawer and jerked it open. She searched for a second and then pulled the drawer completely out and dumped its contents onto the kitchen floor. She put a box of kitchen matches into an outer pocket of her book bag and a swiss army knife in the pocket of her pants.

"Let's go," she said. They went to the front door. Adele pulled on a down jacket and slung the backpack over one shoulder. She put a hand on the door knob and leaned in to the peephole. She was still for a second. The distant growl of the mob and the crackling of fire were the only sounds.

She opened the door and stuck her head out, looked up and down the street.

"OK," she said, and they stepped out. Adele turned back to the door and tested it to make sure it was locked.

"Where do we go?" asked Rachel.

"Up hill," said Adele.

"We should go to Caleb's. We should warn him," said Rachel.

"Right."

They crossed the street and started up the sidewalk. Rachel held Stevie's hand. Adele looked over her shoulder. Smoke from the burning house rose above her roof and drifted up the valley. The mob seemed to be on the move. Some people rounded a corner down the hill and paused. They looked up the hill and one person pointed at Adele, Stevie and Rachel. Another pointed at the next house on the street, and the group started for it.

Adele grabbed Stevie's free hand. "Let's move it," she said, and pulled him along.

The streets were steep in this section of Far Side, and they were breathing hard when they reached Caleb's house. Adele turned and looked back down the street. A second plume of black smoke rose in the air and merged with the first in the breeze.

Rachel knocked on the door. “Caleb! Dwight! It’s us. Let us in.” There was a pause, and then the door opened. “Come on,” said Caleb. He leaned out of the doorway and scanned the street. He looked up at the black smoke in the sky, then he pulled back in, shut the door, and locked it. Dwight joined them from the kitchen.

“They’re burning all the houses, and they’re coming this way,” said Rachel. She did not say who ‘they’ were, and no one asked.

“We’ve got to get out of here,” said Adele. “We can’t stay here.”

Caleb blew out a breath and frowned at the floor. He shook his head.

“What’s the matter?” asked Rachel. “You can’t stay here. They burned a man.”

Caleb looked over his shoulder at something on the living room floor. Rachel and Adele stepped forward to see. A woman lay bound hand and foot, gagged with a red bandanna. She looked at the young people and her face contorted in fury. For a second, she thrashed, as if she were trying to reach them. Muffled screams escaped the gag.

“Jesus, Caleb! What is this?” said Adele. Stevie shrank back and wrapped his arms around his sister.

“It’s my mom,” said Caleb. He raised his hands in a gesture of helplessness and then let them fall. “It’s like she’s crazy. She attacked us. She tried to stab me.”

The bound woman lay still, panting. Adele looked at Caleb and saw now the dark rings under his eyes, the exhaustion clear on his face.

“She’s been like this all night,” he said. “She just won’t stop. If you get near her, she tries to kick you.” Caleb’s eyes glistened. He shook his head again. “I can’t talk with her. It’s like she doesn’t know who I am.”

Adele covered her mouth with her hand. She looked from Dwight to Caleb. “She’s turned,” she said. “I’m sorry, Caleb. We have to go, and she can’t come.”

“Bullshit,” said Caleb. “She’s going to get better. Sometimes she knows it’s me, I’m sure.”

“People don’t get better, Caleb. My mom says no one’s ever come back.” Caleb looked at Adele and she met his gaze. “It’s not your mom, anymore, Caleb.” There was the sound of the mob in the distance, a roar, a gunshot. “We have to get out of here,” she said.

Caleb stood for a second, and then turned to the hall closet. He pulled their jackets out, put his on and handed the other to Dwight. Then he rushed off down the hall. He returned with a pillow slip and approached the bound woman. She glared at him but seemed too exhausted to resume her attack. Caleb put the pillow slip over her head and tied it loosely. “Help me,” he said to Dwight. The two of them hoisted the woman up over Caleb’s shoulder. She resisted, briefly, weakly, and then lay still draped over Caleb’s shoulder. “OK. Let’s go,” he said.

“This isn’t going to work,” said Adele.

"I'm not leaving her," said Caleb.

"It'll work," said Dwight. "Caleb and I can trade off."

Adele looked from one to the other.

"I'm not leaving her," said Caleb.

"OK," said Adele. She turned to the door, opened it a crack, and looked out. Then she opened it farther and stuck her head out. She turned back to the group, gave a quick nod and was out the door. The rest followed.

They pushed on up the hill, past houses, shuttered and quiet. Once a face appeared in a window, watching the young people and their strange burden. Adele looked at the window and the face disappeared.

The newest houses were at the top of the hill and beyond that was new construction. They hurried past foundations and frames of studs, bare, bulldozed lots, and finally the end of the pavement.

"I've got to stop," said Caleb. He was gasping for breath and sweat ran down his face.

"Here," said Dwight. "I'll take her for a while."

They transferred the bound figure from Caleb's shoulder to Dwight's, without putting her down. Caleb put his hands on his hips, stretched his back and neck.

Adele looked back the way they had come. "Oh, shit," she said.

Everyone turned and looked down the hill. Three men were coming up toward them. One man carried a bright red baseball bat, another a long stick, a weed digging tool with a sharp metal tip. The third was empty-handed. They were still two blocks away, but they were coming fast.

"Go!" yelled Adele. "Go, go, go!"

They turned and ran to the end of the dirt and into the trees. A path led them on and they were running single file, branches slapping at their faces. Stevie stumbled on the uneven ground, and Rachel dragged him along several steps before he could get to his feet again. The trees thinned out a bit and thick undergrowth filled the space, tearing at their legs as they passed.

Adele looked over her shoulder and saw that the three men were close behind them and gaining. She pulled her book bag around in front of her and unzipped it. She pushed her hand in, wriggling around the water bottles. She felt the pistol grip and managed to wrap her fingers around it, and pulled, but the revolver caught and would not come free. She stumbled and went down on her knees. Rachel and Stevie sprawled over her. Dwight managed to stop before he hit them but fell to his knees. Caleb's mother slid off his shoulder and Caleb reached out to ease her to the ground.

The man with no weapon hit them first. He launched himself at Caleb and hit him hard, taking him down into the dense brush on the side of the path. Dwight grabbed the man from behind, leaving Caleb's mother where she lay. The second man had the weed digger, and he lifted it high above his head and stabbed down at the bound and hooded figure, again and again. The man with the baseball bat rushed by him and knocked him down. He stood over Stevie and the two girls and raised the bat high over his head. Adele lifted the heavy book bag out toward the man and pulled the trigger. The bag exploded. The bullet hit the man in the stomach. He dropped the bat and collapsed on the path in a tight ball.

Stevie got up and turned to run. The man with the weed digger was on his feet now and rushed toward him. Adele couldn't shoot the man because Stevie was in the way. "Down!" she yelled, but Stevie tried to scramble over her and she couldn't get a clear shot. The man stood over Rachel. He raised the sharp tool, holding it in both hands. Rachel screamed, and put up her hands to ward off the blow, but before he could stab her, there was a sharp report and something hit the man in the side. He staggered, and the weed digger slipped out of his hands. Then he dropped to his knees and fell over sideways into the brush beside the path. His legs twitched, and then they were still.

Adele wrenched the revolver out of the ragged book bag and ran to Caleb and Dwight. There was a tangle of arms and legs, bodies thrashing in the dense undergrowth, but no clear target. Then the thrashing stopped. "Hold him, hold him!" yelled Caleb. Dwight had an arm hooked around the man's neck from behind, choking. The man's face turned beet red, his eyes rolled up and his body went limp. Dwight relaxed. "Don't stop," said Caleb, and Dwight tightened his grip.

Caleb struggled to his feet and rushed to his mother. She was bloodied and motionless. He dropped to his knees and pulled the pillow slip off her head. Her eyes were closed, her face peaceful. Caleb looked down at the stab wounds across her chest and stomach. She was not breathing. He bent down and gathered her up in his arms. Her head rested on his chest. He laid his cheek on top of her head and rocked back and forth.

Adele held the gun in both hands, pointing it at the ground. She looked from Dwight to Caleb and back again. She took a step toward Caleb but then stopped. She went back to where Dwight had the man in a choke hold. "I think he's dead," she said.

Dwight slowly loosened his hold. The man did not move, and Dwight rolled the body off him and stood up. Dwight looked at Caleb and his mother and then down the path to where Rachel held a sobbing Stevie. Somewhere a dog barked, and Adele looked up past Rachel. Jamie came running down the path from the woods, a rifle in his hands, a filthy golden retriever and a little, dark-haired girl behind him.

* * *

Spot had the lead and Jamie tramped along behind with the girl on his shoulders. The rifle was heavy in his right hand, slick with sweat despite the cool, late morning air. Somewhere along here, the smaller trail that led down to Far Side and Adele's house branched off to the left. It would be easy to miss. The trails were overgrown after a long winter of neglect.

Spot froze, a paw in mid-air, and gave a low growl. Jamie looked. He saw nothing, but then he heard them: people running off to their left, coming up the path from Far Side. He crouched down and the girl slid off his shoulders. He stood and flicked the rifle's safety off. Jamie gripped the gun in both hands and held his breath.

They came into view, and Jamie recognized them immediately. It was Adele, Rachel and a boy, Caleb, and Dwight with what looked like a woman thrown over his shoulder. Jamie opened his mouth to call out to them, a joyous greeting, but then stopped. They're being chased, he thought, and the three pursuers burst into view, just steps behind. The first man was unarmed, the second carried a garden tool, a harpoon-like thing, and the third a bright red baseball bat. Caleb and Dwight went down first in a desperate battle with the unarmed man, and a man was standing over Adele and Rachel with the bat held high and Adele held up her book bag and there was a loud bang and the man with the bat doubled over and went down but then the man with the harpoon-like thing was there and he raised it high above his head with both hands and Jamie heard the rifle go off and felt the kick against his shoulder. The bullet hit the man in the side, chest-high, and he went down. Adele jumped to her feet and ran past Rachel and Stevie to Caleb and Dwight where they were still struggling with the unarmed man.

"Stay here," said Jamie to the little girl, and sprinted past Spot, up the trail and down the path to Far Side. He worked the bolt of the rifle as he ran, ejecting the spent cartridge, and slipping a fresh one in, slamming the bolt shut. Spot barked, close behind.

Jamie jumped over the two men who had been shot. They sprawled across the path, bloodied and unmoving. He rushed past Caleb and Adele to where Dwight was getting to his feet. Jamie stood over the man who lay still and tangled in the bushes by the path, the rifle pointed down at his chest.

"I think he's dead," said Dwight. He took a few steps toward Caleb and then his legs folded up underneath him and he sat straight down in the path.

Adele put a hand on Dwight's shoulder. "Are you hurt?" she asked.

Dwight stared down the path at Caleb and his mother. He shook his head and crawled to Caleb. He sat next to him and wrapped his arms around both Caleb and his mother. "I'm sorry, Caleb. I'm sorry, bro," he said.

Jamie looked at Adele. She was wearing baggy, outdoors clothes, dirty and scuffed. Her hair had twigs and leaves in it. She was breathing hard and had a gun in her hand. He walked up to her. Something red, blood, was spattered across her face, and she had a wild look in her eyes. He wanted to ask her if she was all right, if she was hurt, but the words died the moment he opened his mouth. He just stood there, looking down into her eyes, and then he smiled. Adele threw the arm with the pistol around his neck, pulled him down, and kissed him hard on the lips. He kissed her back.

CHAPTER 16

"Get a grip, everybody! We've gotta go!" Rachel's voice was strained, and Jamie turned away from Adele to look at her. She stood a little way down the path, several steps beyond the two bodies, her arms wrapped around her little brother.

The riot down in Far Side sounded louder, closer. It had a particular sound, one that Jamie remembered from the destruction of his own neighborhood when the mob turned on itself in the final viral frenzy of self-annihilation, all against all. There were screams and gunshots.

"Yeah. Let's go," said Jamie. "Get your stuff."

He walked over to the little girl. She stood next to Spot, one hand gripping his fur, and looked up at Jamie as he approached. He squatted down next to her and she tried to climb up on his shoulders over the backpack.

"Who's this?" asked Adele. She lifted the girl and settled her on Jamie's shoulders.

"She's from my neighborhood," said Jamie.

"Ah," said Adele. She tucked a strand of the girl's dark hair behind her ear.

"Come on, everybody! It's getting closer," said Rachel. Adele picked up her book bag. It was sopping wet from an exploded two-liter, and had a hole in one side, but still held together.

Jamie turned to Caleb and Dwight. "We've gotta go," he said. "Time to go."

Caleb seemed not to hear. He rocked his mother's body. Dwight looked up. "Time to go, Caleb," he said, gently.

Caleb looked up at him and then at Jamie and Adele. His face was scratched and red from the fight, and wet from his tears. His mouth worked. "I can't leave her. I'm not ready," he said.

Adele walked over to him and crouched down in front of him, eye-to-eye. She was silent for a second.

"It's time to go," she said. "We have to go. We can't stay here any longer."

Caleb simply looked at her.

"If you stay here, the mob will find you. If not today, then tomorrow." She put a hand on his cheek. "Your mom would want you to go," she said. "She wouldn't want you to stay."

Caleb lowered his mother's body to the path. He knelt by her and undid the ropes around her wrists and legs. Then he kissed her on the forehead, rested his hand briefly on her face, stood, and started down the path. They all followed.

When he reached the juncture with the main trail, he stopped. "Which way?" he said. He looked down the path that Jamie had come up and then the other way. Everyone just stood there, looking at the path and at each other.

"Which way is Power City?" asked Adele.

"This path runs all the way up the valley," said Jamie. "It joins the Pacific Crest Trail above the dam." He pointed. "Power City is that way."

"That's where I'm going," said Adele. "My dad is there. The army is there. We should go there."

"It'll take us, like, a week to walk there," said Rachel. "Where are we going to sleep? What are we going to eat?"

"There are cabins along the way," said Jamie. "You know, vacation places and hunting cabins. We'll have to break in..."

"What's this way?" asked Dwight. He looked back down the path that Jamie, the girl and Spot had come up.

"Well, that way is the coast and the city," said Jamie.

"The city isn't safe," said Adele. "My mom is down there. She says don't come here."

"OK... I'm with Deli," said Jamie.

"Yeah. So are we," said Rachel.

"Whatever," said Caleb, and they all turned up the path. Adele was in the lead, followed by Jamie, Rachel and Stevie. Caleb and Dwight brought up the rear. Spot ran ahead and then back again, patrolling but never out of sight, and the sounds from Far Side grew fainter as they went.

* * *

Mike stood at his desk and pointed at the large diagram spread out across it. The safety inspection team, which included all his surviving engineers, leaned in for a closer look.

"We'll hook the crane here and here to lift off the housing..." he said. A hum went through the building, starting low and accelerating. Mike stopped speaking and looked up. He frowned. "What's that?" he asked.

He didn't really need an answer. The sound was unmistakable. Someone was cranking up a generator.

"What the hell's going on?" he asked. He turned to the inside windows and looked out across the cavernous interior of the powerhouse. The door to the hydraulic control room on the far wall was open. Mike looked at the group around him, wondering for a moment who of his staff was not present, who might be operating the valves that allowed the water from the dam to spin the generators. But, of course, the only engineers not there were dead. Someone, who almost certainly didn't know what they were doing, was trying to start the system.

A second tone joined the first, climbing slowly as another generator came online.

"What if they try to start the damaged one?" someone asked.

"Oh, shit," said Mike. He charged out the door and sprinted across the powerhouse. His team followed.

Mike came through the doorway of the hydraulic control room at full speed and crashed into a young soldier. They both tumbled onto the concrete floor. Mike tried to scramble to his feet, but the soldier hung on to him.

"What the hell?" yelled Mike, and broke free. He pushed up on one knee and reached out to grab another soldier who was standing at the control panel, his hand on the switch that would start up the damaged generator Number One. Mike managed to get a grip on the soldier's tunic and jerked hard. The man stumbled backwards, his flailing hand flipping the switch as he staggered. Mike did not notice the third soldier in the room. This man pulled his service pistol, aimed carefully, and shot Mike in the chest.

Mike collapsed on the floor. The pain was crushing, so great that no moan or cry could express it, and he was silent except for the shallow, panting breaths he took, each a new stab of pain.

Private Leung rushed into the room. "Cease fire! Cease fire!" she shouted, and she knelt down putting herself between Mike and the shooter.

"He turned," said the shooter. "The old guy was crazy."

"Turn him over," she commanded. "Easy." One of the soldiers got next to her and together they rolled Mike over onto his back, revealing a pool of bright red blood on the concrete. "Oh, Jesus," said Leung. "Medic! Medic!" she yelled over her shoulder.

"Stay with me, Mike! Stay with me," she commanded. She bent over him and held her face close to his, her gaze fierce and demanding.

Mike looked down at himself and Private Leung. He seemed to be somewhere near the ceiling of the room, floating above the chaotic scene on the floor below. The pain was gone. Private Leung had one hand under his head, holding it up above the level of his chest like she was trying to keep his face above the spreading pool of red as if he might drown in it, while she fumbled with some sort of pressure bandage on his chest with the other hand.

Everyone seemed so frantic. A wave of compassion for them all swept over him, compassion for himself, for the shooter, for Private Leung. He wanted to smile at her, give her some reassurance. He willed it, with all his strength, a clear, pure, wish. And there on the floor, his mouth twitched. His mouth twitched, and he winked at Private Leung, one, slow, unambiguous wink. She stopped for a second. She had seen. She had understood.

Now a wind blew through the control room, and with it came the sound the breeze made in the evening when it blew through the fir trees around their house in Far Side. He thought of Adele and Rose. Thank you, my dear, sweet ones, he thought. It's all good! And the wind carried him off.

* * *

Jamie held his hands out to the fire. The warmth and light seemed a great luxury after his last night on the trail, curled up outside on the moss next to a rock, a dog and a little girl. Tonight, they were sitting in a semi-circle around the stone fireplace of a dilapidated cabin, under a section of roof that hadn't fallen in yet and that almost kept out the rain. They huddled together, Adele on Jamie's one side and Rachel, Caleb and Dwight on the other. The little girl was sprawled on Adele's lap, sleeping. Stevie sat on his sister's lap. Spot had curled up in front of Jamie and gave him a guilty glance as if he wasn't sure he was allowed to occupy such prime real-estate so close to the warmth of the flames. Now he snoozed, his paws twitching as he ran in his dreams.

Jamie scooted a bit to the side, closer to Adele. "Damn roof leaks," he said. Adele laughed and hooked an arm through Jamie's, pulling him closer. Dwight picked up a piece of wood from their pile and added it to the fire. It cracked and sizzled.

They had pushed hard all day, looking over their shoulders, continuously checking the trail behind them. More than once, one of them had stopped and held up a hand with a furious "Shh!" Everyone would turn and face back the way they had come, listening, breathing silently through their mouths, straining to detect approaching danger. The nightmare of the three crazed attackers was never repeated, though, and when they came on a small lake of pristine, crystal clear water, they all stopped, dropped their packs and splashed the cold water on their faces.

Stevie knelt down by the water. "Can we drink it?" he asked.

Rachel turned to Adele. "Do you have any bottled water left?"

Adele picked up her book bag and unzipped it. She pulled out shreds of clear plastic, all that remained of the two-liter bottles after she had fired the gun from inside the bag. She looked up at Rachel and shook her head.

Jamie stood and looked around the shore of the lake. "Here," he said, and pointed to a small stream that entered the lake a bit beyond where they were. "Running water might be OK." He walked over to the stream. It rushed clear and cold, almost numbing his fingers. He washed his hands and then lifted them up to his mouth, tasting the water. "Let me check upstream."

Bushes crowded the stream bank, and it was tough going to push up the gentle slope. Jamie watched for animal tracks and other signs that the water might be contaminated. After a hundred feet or so, he broke out into a clearing and there was the cabin. He stopped, his empty hands instinctively gripping the rifle that he had left back at the lake. Then he realized that this cabin had been abandoned, and that no one had lived there, probably for years. The walls slumped, and the roof was completely gone at one end. At the other end, a stone chimney supported the remaining roof. All the windows were broken out, and no door hung in the entrance. He walked around the cabin and peered in through the windows. It was all one room, and empty except for drifts of dirt, leaves and pine needles.

A faint trail led from the clearing down to the lake and Jamie followed it back to the group. "The stream is our best bet for water. I wouldn't drink from the lake, and," he paused for effect, "I found an old cabin." Everyone looked up at him, and the first drops of rain fell, stippling the surface of the lake.

"Awesome!" said Dwight. They gathered their things and trudged up the trail to the clearing.

"Oh, this is great," said Rachel. She stepped into the cabin and looked around, hands on her hips. "A little dusting, a little mopping and you'd never guess the place was an ancient, diseased dump."

Jamie stepped by her and looked around. He could see her point, but it was raining harder, now.

Adele pushed in and walked over to the fireplace. "We need a fire. Somebody go gather some wood." She rummaged around in her bag and pulled out the box of matches. It was wet, but not all the matches were soaked. She selected a couple of the drier ones.

Dwight, Caleb and Jamie moved to the door. Stevie and the little girl made to follow but Rachel snagged Stevie.

"Hey, you," said Adele. The little girl stopped and looked at her. "You stay with us. Come here."

Jamie paused in the doorway and looked back at Adele and the little girl.

"What's your name?" Adele asked her.

"She won't say," said Jamie. "She doesn't talk."

"Maria," said the little girl.

"Well, Maria," said Adele. "Let's get you cleaned up." She wet the sleeve of her shirt and started scrubbing Maria's face.

Jamie caught Adele's eye and gave her a well-aren't-you-special look.

And Spot, who had been sniffing around the cabin had apparently decided that a dry place near the hearth was his. He laid down and looked at Jamie as if to say hurry up with that firewood, boy. Jamie turned and went out into the dim, rainy afternoon.

Now it was night, after their spartan dinner of cheese, apples, and some canned soup that Adele had warmed by the fire. Jamie looked around at the group. Everyone appeared to be sleeping, bundled in all their clothes and snuggled up close to each other. They seemed almost to cling to one another, barely sheltered from rain and wind by the collapsed roof and walls of the cabin, and dimly lit by the glowing coals. The corners of the cabin were dark, the night beyond inky black.

He thought of his mother, and grief came as hard and physical as if someone had punched him in the chest. Was she alive? Had she suffered? The sense of possibility and openness that had filled him the night of the baseball game, when he and Adele had first kissed down by the bridge, seemed now to show its true face. Possibility was nothing but threat, and the openness had become a vast and bottomless darkness through which he fell.

He thought of Bonney and longed for his presence. If only he could talk with him, touch him. Bonney would know what to do, how to deal with it all. Anger and self-pity flared up. How am I supposed to know what to do, he thought? I'm not an adult. I'm just seventeen! And he pushed away the thought that now they were the grownups, and that this was what adulthood was like.

Jamie threw another piece of wood on the fire. Adele murmured in her sleep and clutched him closer. The wind whispered through the night forest and brushed his cheek. We should set a guard, or something, he thought. And then he slept.

CHAPTER 17

Someone was crying. Maria was crying. Jamie struggled up out of sleep, groggy, damp, stiff. Adele held Maria and spoke softly to her, but she just kept on crying. The little girl pushed her way out of Adele's arms.

Jamie blinked. "What's the matter with her? Can't you keep her quiet?"

Adele eye's flashed. "Since when is she my job? You're the one who brought her."

Maria looked from Adele to Jamie and cried louder. Jamie suspected that this bickering was familiar to the little girl. He felt ashamed.

"Hey there, sweetie. What's the matter?" he asked.

Marie stopped crying and looked at Jamie. "I'm hungry," she said.

"Well, let's see what we can do about that. What do we have left for breakfast?"

Everyone was stirring now. Dwight re-lit the fire. Rachel and Caleb went to get water, and Adele rummaged through packs and pockets. Jamie stood where he could look out at the surrounding forest. He rested the rifle in the crook of his left arm. No one complained that he was just standing around.

Adele stepped past him with the handheld radio and stood in the clearing. She held the microphone to her mouth and spoke briefly and then paused, listening. She did this several times and then she turned back to the cabin. She looked at Jamie. Her face was full of sadness, her shoulders slumped in dejection.

"No luck?" asked Jamie when she stepped back into the cabin.

Adele shook her head. "No. It got wet." She held up the little radio. "I thought it was dry but maybe not yet. Or the hills are blocking the signal." She shrugged. "I don't know."

"Well, you can try again later." It was all he could think of to say. Adele went by him and busied herself with something inside.

Breakfast took hardly any time at all. No one was satisfied, and Maria was persuaded not to cry only because there was obviously no food left. Jamie gave her his last slice of apple.

"We'll get more, soon," Jamie told her.

"How are we going to do that?" asked Caleb.

"We'll have to find a house or a store or something," said Jamie.

"Yeah? Like where? Do you know where the closest store is?" said Caleb.

"We haven't crossed County Road 35, yet. This path has to cross 35. And there's a convenience store at the intersection of 35 and 18" said Jamie.

"So, how far is that?" asked Rachel.

"I'm guessing something like three, four, maybe five miles," said Jamie.

"In other words, you've got no fucking idea," said Caleb.

"Jesus, Caleb," said Adele. "What's your plan? Order a pizza?"

Caleb made a face and looked out a window.

"Wouldn't that be dangerous?" said Rachel.

"We don't know," said Jamie. "We just don't know what's going on down there."

"What's today? How long has it been?" asked Adele.

Jamie looked at her. "Why do you ask?"

"It might be over, the first wave," she said.

"What do you mean?"

"Well, the virus triggers older people, right? Like anyone in their mid-twenties or older. And once they start showing symptoms, they progress to the end-stage fast. A couple of days, and bang, they're there." Adele looked around at the group. "That's what my mom says."

"So?" prompted Dwight.

"So, the end-stage is all-against-all." Adele paused. "All-against-all..." she repeated. She looked around at the blank faces. "There's no one left, Dwight."

"What?" said Dwight. He looked incredulous.

Jamie studied Adele's face. "I get it," he said. He turned to Dwight. "I saw it. In my neighborhood. Think about it. All those rioters... They get more and more violent until they turn on each other. It's like they're rabid. They can't really think anymore. They just want to destroy. If there are two of them left, then they fight until there's only one left."

"What about us?" said Caleb. "We're left."

"Yeah, well, we're still young, right?" said Adele. "The virus hasn't had enough time to grow in us. Or our immune systems are still strong enough to fight it off." She paused and frowned, as if trying to recall something. "Look, stress affects our immune systems. OK? It looks like the virus has grown enough and people have accumulated enough just normal life stress by the time they're in their mid-twenties to trigger the symptoms. We," Adele gestured to the group, "just haven't reached that point, yet."

"Speak for yourself," said Rachel. "Give it a couple more days. I'm thinking I could go off anytime." She looked around at the alarmed faces of her friends. She threw up her hands. "Hey, come on! I'm just kidding! It was a joke, for Christ's sake!" And then, for some reason, it was funny. It was really funny. And they laughed. They laughed until they cried.

* * *

They reached the road mid-morning. The path descended into a small valley, followed a meandering stream and then met the road where it crossed the stream on a bridge. Adele was in the lead. She climbed a rain-slick embankment up to the shoulder and lifted her head slowly to scan the scene. The others followed and gathered around her. Caleb walked out onto the pavement to get a better view.

"Caleb! Someone might see you," said Jamie.

Caleb looked down at Jamie. "I thought no one was left?" he said.

"You want to bet your life on it?"

Caleb frowned and shook his head in irritation but retreated to the side of the pavement and took a couple of steps down the embankment.

The valley across the road was open and broad. It was cultivated, the first green shoots of something showing in neat rows extending to the far tree-line. Off to their left was a charred pile of rubble, the remains of the farmhouse.

"Anyone moving around?" asked Jamie. He squinted at the ruin and turned slowly until he was looking down the road in the other direction.

"I don't see anyone," said Adele.

"Let's go," said Caleb. "I'm hungry."

"We should wait a bit," said Adele.

"Screw it. I'm going," said Caleb and started off down the road. For a second, no one moved. Then Dwight, Rachel and Stevie followed.

"Looks OK," said Rachel as she stepped past Adele.

Jamie looked at Adele and blew out a breath. Disgust was plain on her face.

"We could let them go ahead and smoke out any trouble," suggested Jamie, only partly in jest.

Adele gave him a look, and then stood and followed the others. Maria stepped out onto the pavement but turned and waited for Jamie when she realized he was not right behind her. Jamie straightened and checked up and down the road one more time. He joined Maria and held out his hand to her. She took it, and they hurried after Adele.

Adele stopped and watched Jamie and Maria as they came up, and then all three walked along together about thirty feet back from the others. No one spoke as they went past what was once the farmhouse. A family of crows took wing at their approach, rising from something lying in the grass, and perched on a brightly colored swingset in the side yard. The young people quickened their pace, pursued by the birds' raucous calls. The acrid smell of the burnt house seemed to follow them.

They passed through a landscape both familiar and strange. On one stretch of road, only the tidy fields and orchards were visible, and the world looked normal, safe. But the sun was filtered through a haze of smoke that blew up the valley from burning farms and towns, and the light touched everything with a reddish tinge.

Every twenty feet or so, their feet scuffed through a tiny hedgerow of weeds that flourished in the expansion joints of the pavement. Jamie was surprised to see how quickly the dandelions and plantain rose up and spilled out over the concrete after just a few days of little traffic. How long had it been since cars and trucks had come this way, he wondered?

They passed several more houses, most piles of smoking rubble or substantially burned. One small house, up a hill from the road, seemed undamaged. They paused at the driveway and a dog, a pit bull-mix, launched itself from the front porch, barking ferociously. It rushed across the front yard and everyone turned to run but then the dog was brought up short by a chain. It strained against the chain and continued to bark. Spot barked back, and Jamie was shocked by how vicious he sounded. He shushed Spot, and the dog stopped barking but growled low in his throat, hackles raised.

"Should we check it out?" asked Dwight. "There might be food and stuff up there."

"I don't know about that dog," said Jamie. "And what about the owner? He might still be there."

"We've got guns. Shoot the dog," said Caleb.

"I'm not shooting the dog," said Jamie. "And what if the owner's still there? Do we shoot him, too?"

Caleb gave Jamie a contemptuous look. "Give me the gun. I'll shoot the dog." He held out his hand.

Jamie looked at the hand and then up at Caleb's face. "I don't think so," he said. "Have you ever shot a gun before?"

"What good is a gun if you never use it?" said Caleb. "Here, give me the gun." He took a step toward Jamie.

"The rifle is mine, Caleb. It stays with me." Caleb stared at Jamie, his hand still held out. Jamie looked back without blinking. "I know how to use it, Caleb. And I will use it, whenever I have to."

For a second, no one moved, and then Rachel stepped up to Jamie. "You saved my life yesterday," she said. "I never said thanks." And she kissed him on the cheek. She linked an arm through Jamie's. "Let's go," she said, and pulled him on down the road, away from Caleb.

"Yeah. Let's go," said Dwight, and everyone fell in behind, even Caleb who brought up the rear.

Jamie felt a rush of relief and gratitude. He turned to Rachel as they walked. "Thanks, Rache," he said.

"No problem," she said, and smiled up at him. "I owe you."

And another moment from the confrontation at the foot of the driveway came to Jamie, an image of Adele that he had caught out of the corner of his eye. When Caleb had taken a step toward Jamie with his hand held out, Adele had laid her hand, most casually, on the grip of the revolver tucked in her belt. A small move, but Jamie wondered what had actually stopped Caleb. The rifle was slung over Jamie's shoulder. Caleb would have been on him before Jamie could bring the gun into play. And for all that Rachel could do with her force of nature act, it probably was not enough by itself to avert Caleb's aggression. Jamie looked over his shoulder and caught Adele's eye. He didn't smile, but simply looked at her, as if seeing her was something new. And she looked back, a level look with nothing flirtatious or contrived in it. Her look held nothing back.

CHAPTER 18

They came around a curve in the road and ahead was the convenience store, a low building with gas pumps out front. The pavement around the pumps and the building was charred, and Adele imagined the pumps burning and a fireball rising from the underground gas tanks, engulfing the store and the cars around it and anyone nearby.

The road in each direction was blocked by cars parked across both lanes. It looked like someone had attempted to build barricades around the store, and the burned-out cars told a story of a furious assault and a desperate defense. Several bodies were scattered about, lying on the road.

The group stood together, close, taking comfort from each other.

"Well... That's that," she said.

"There's another building, isn't there?" said Jamie. "Behind the store. Maybe a warehouse?"

They walked on, and as they got closer, the building behind the store came into view. The wall facing the store was damaged, the paint blistered and dark, but the wall itself was made of cinder blocks and the building seemed intact. There was a small loading dock on the side. Its overhead door was buckled and folded on itself, revealing a shadowed interior.

They skirted the main structure, keeping their distance from the charred remains of a pickup truck that looked like it had run over the gas pumps and then rammed through the front window of the store. Rachel put her hand on the side of Stevie's face and turned him away from a blackened figure lying on the concrete. They approached the loading dock door and stopped.

"How do we do this?" asked Adele. "Send someone in to scout?"

"I'll go," said Dwight.

"Me, too," said Jamie. He unslung the rifle and checked that it was loaded.

The two walked up to the doorway and Spot trotted along with them. They peered in, and then Dwight ducked inside, followed by Jamie and Spot.

Adele looked at the others. They were focused on the doorway where Jamie and Dwight had disappeared. Adele felt how exposed they were, standing in the open in a tight little group. She glanced around, looking for any movement or signs of danger. The only movement was in the branches of the trees, nodding in the breeze coming up the valley. She looked back to the doorway just as Jamie emerged. He waved them in.

"Looks OK," he said. "It's been looted, but there's some stuff left." He moved aside, and the others stepped in. He smiled at Adele as she went by, and she smiled back. She paused to let her eyes adjust to the dim interior. It was one large room, with an open area just inside the doorway where a small truck could park while being unloaded. Against the walls were shelves. They were in disarray, some with boxes still on them but others bare with a jumbled pile of cartons on the floor below.

"What are we looking for?" asked Adele.

"Uh..." Jamie furrowed his brow. "Beef jerky...bottled water... Candy. Candy would be good. Energy bars. That kind of stuff." He looked around. "I think they sold camping gear, too. We need tents, sleeping bags, rain gear, big backpacks." The group split up and they started poking through the mess.

Adele looked to where Rachel and Stevie were rummaging around. She walked over to them, Maria in tow. "Let me know if you find lotion, soap, tampons and stuff," she said. Stevie made a face and moved off down the aisle.

"You got it," said Rachel.

Adele started searching through the piles of cartons down the next aisle. She found a backpack and transferred the contents from her old pack to the new. Maria found a box of Snickers bars and managed to get two down before Adele intervened.

"We'll save the rest for later," she said. Maria looked outraged, but let Adele put the remaining chocolate bars in the pocket of her new backpack.

They scavenged for another half-hour and then Adele noticed that Jamie was standing just inside the doorway, looking out. She walked over to him and put her hand on the small of his back. She leaned in close and put her head next to his, following his gaze.

"What do you see?" she asked.

"Nothing," he said. "I just suddenly felt like we weren't paying attention, you know, to what was happening around us. We need to be watching all the time. What's out there? We don't know."

Adele rubbed his back and leaned into him. Jamie's posture didn't change in any obvious way, but she felt his body receive hers.

"I think we're done, here," said Rachel.

Adele and Jamie turned. Rachel and the rest of the group were gathered a few steps away, piles of loot at their feet. Stevie had found jerky, and everyone was chewing away. Caleb held up a plastic liter bottle of Wild Turkey bourbon and grinned.

"How are we going to transport all this stuff?" asked Adele. She looked at the four sleeping bags and two family-sized tents. "We can't carry these tents."

"We need to find a car," said Caleb. "I'm tired of walking, anyway."

"We don't know if the road is safe," said Jamie. "And it might be blocked, anyway."

"Yeah, well, we've been walking on a road all morning and haven't seen anyone. And yeah, the road might be blocked, but it might not. Anyway, even if we get to ride for just a couple of miles, that's better than walking it."

"It's worth a try," said Adele. "Maybe the army is patrolling the road, keeping it safe." She thought of seeing her dad in a couple of hours rather than a couple of days, of a house and a real bed and not needing to make sure your gun was loaded every time you stepped outside.

Jamie looked at her and around at the others. "OK." He shrugged. "Works for me. Let's find a car."

* * *

Caleb ignored the lane markings. He drove fast up the center of the county road, and Jamie had to admit that this was way better than schlepping their packs on a trail in the back country. Dwight sat shotgun next to Caleb, Rachel and Stevie were in the next seats, and Jamie and Adele sat in the third seat of the SUV with Maria sandwiched between them.

They had been driving for fifteen minutes and had covered more miles than they had all morning on foot. Just the warmth was heavenly. Dwight had cranked up the heat to max and everyone unzipped their fleece and down. A stream of cold air came through a small, neat bullet hole in the windshield low on the passenger's side until Dwight plugged it with a wad of well-chewed gum supplied by Stevie. Maria had responded to the swoosh of wind and tires as if she had been shot with a tranquilizer gun. She slumped against Jamie, snoring, a stick of half-eaten turkey jerky hanging out of her mouth.

This far up the valley, away from the coast, the forest crowded the road and the tree limbs from either side almost met above it. The rainstorm of the previous night had blown twigs and leaves onto the roadway, and the carpet lay undisturbed by a county cleaning crew or passing vehicles. Jamie twisted in his seat and looked back the way they had come. Their tracks were plain to see in the debris, and they were clearly the only vehicle to have passed this way today. How long until the road was just a strip of leaf and twig covered ground that ran through the trees, he wondered. He remembered a bumper sticker he had seen once protesting suburban sprawl. "Pavement is forever!" it warned. Apparently, the forest had not gotten the memo.

Buildings were few and far between. They passed the entrance to a state park, and every couple of miles a dirt driveway wound back into the woods to isolated, invisible houses. Some were marked with cheerful, rustic signs announcing, "The Smiths" or "Shangri-La". Others had only a mailbox on a post or just a chain stretched across the foot of the driveway.

Caleb let up on the gas when they approached a single-wide trailer on a small lot close by the pavement. Jamie tensed and shifted his grip on the rifle but relaxed when he saw that the trailer was caved in and overgrown with blackberry bushes. This dwelling was an old story of defeat and abandonment, not a clear and present danger. Caleb accelerated by.

The road followed along the Darnell River and crossed it several times on sturdy bridges. The water ran high, and tangles of fallen trees and branches created white water rapids in the spring melt. At one point, a large tree had failed to pass underneath a bridge and its branches hung over the guardrail, completely blocking one lane. Caleb squeezed over to the right but barely slowed. Branches slapped the SUV as they went by.

"I need to pee," said Maria.

Adele leaned forward. "We need to make a pit-stop," she said.

"How soon?" asked Caleb.

"Right now," said Maria.

"Right now," Adele relayed.

"OK," said Caleb.

They passed a sign that said "Roadside Park" and up ahead was a small, gravel parking lot and some picnic tables overlooking the river. Two big blue porta-potties stood at the far end of the parking lot. Caleb pulled in.

"You remember how to use a toilet?" asked Jamie. Maria gave him a disgusted look.

Jamie and Adele got out with Maria. She climbed up into the porta-potty, protesting at the smell. Adele and Jamie stood a few steps away and watched the water rush by.

"I'm going to try the radio again," said Adele. She walked back to the SUV and extracted the radio from her pack. She came back to Jamie and switched it on. She waited as it made various noises and examined the little LCD readout that displayed numbers and symbols. Satisfied, she started calling.

"This is Deli, calling dad. Come in dad." She repeated this several times and then stopped to listen. The only response was the low hiss of static. She called out again with the same result.

"This is Deli, calling mom. Come in mom." She tried, but again with no success.

Finally, in desperation she sent out a general call. "This is Adele Prada. Is anyone out there? Come in, anyone who is monitoring this frequency." And then the answer came, an odd, foreign voice speaking precise, lilting English, a man, fading in and out.

"This is Ibrahim Zarruq. Can you hear me? Am I doing this right?" The transmission was faint and full of static.

"Yes!" said Adele. "Yes, I can hear you. Where are you?"

"I am just north of the city. Are you related to Dr. Rose Prada of the CDC?"

Adele looked at Jamie, her eyes wide and her mouth open. "Yes. Yes, I am. I'm her daughter. Is she there?"

There was no answer for several seconds. Then Ibrahim came on. "She is here, but she is sleeping, now."

"Wake her up, please. I have to talk with her."

There was the sound of Ibrahim keying the mike, but at first he did not speak.

"I'm sorry Adele. Your mother cannot speak with you right now. She is exhausted and must not be disturbed."

Adele stared at the radio in disbelief. "What do you mean, must not be disturbed? Is she all right? Is she hurt?"

"She is sleeping, Adele. She..." There was a pause, and then Ibrahim went on, his voice different. "She has become depressed, Adele. She may have succumbed to the virus. She took to her bed several days ago. She won't eat or drink. It is not good. I don't know how much longer she will last."

Adele put her hand to her mouth. Tears filled her eyes.

"Are you with her?" she asked. "Can I talk to her?"

"Yes. I'm sitting with her now. The radio is near her ear. Go ahead."

"Mom? Mom, this is Deli. Mom, I love you. Listen, Mom. You have to eat something. Or you'll die. Ibrahim will give you something to eat and drink, Mom. You must take it! Ibrahim, is she listening?"

"I'm sorry, Adele. Your mother gives no sign of hearing you. I am not sure she is conscious, at all."

"I love you, Mom. I love you. Dad loves you. I'm going to Power City. I'll be with Dad, there. Don't give up, Mom! Please don't give up. We'll come for you, soon. Dad and I are going to come get you. You have to stay with us, Mom. We're coming for you. We love you." Adele put a hand over her eyes and sobbed.

Ibrahim's voice came over the radio. "We've seen many cases, now, Adele. I've seen many. I'm sorry, I don't think she has long..." His transmission was lost in a storm of static.

"Ibrahim? Ibrahim, are you there? Come in Ibrahim."

They waited, but there was no response.

"This is Adele Prada calling Ibrahim at the CDC. Come in, Ibrahim." But still, nothing.

A horn blew, and Jamie looked over to the SUV.

"Let's go!" called Caleb.

Jamie turned to the porta-potties and almost tripped over Maria, who was standing by his leg gripping the cloth of his jeans in a little fist. The horn blew again.

"We should go, Deli," said Jamie. He touched her arm and she looked down at his hand and then up at his face. Tears flowed down her cheeks and there was something empty and hopeless in her eyes.

"We have to go," said Jamie. "You can monitor the radio in the car, right? Let's go find your dad."

Adele let herself be led to the SUV. They sat in the back, and Maria rested against Adele and hugged her. Jamie stretched his arm along the back of the seat and held his palm on her shoulder. Adele cradled the radio on her lap, where it hissed and crackled, but did not speak.

CHAPTER 19

Caleb came around a curve and slammed on the brakes. The ABS chattered on the leaf-slick pavement and they slid to a stop half on the road and half on the shoulder. Ahead was a semi-truck and in front of that a line of cars, pickups and SUVs that stopped at a fallen tree that blocked both lanes. All the vehicles were burned.

"Holy shit," said Caleb. They stared, mouths open.

"Heads up! What's around us?" said Jamie. He twisted around in his seat, trying to see what was behind them. Adele looked up.

"What's happening?" she asked, then she screamed as several figures in camouflage uniforms closed in on the SUV, pointing assault rifles at the windows.

"Don't move! Hands up!" they shouted, their voices hard.

Stevie and Maria wailed. Everyone put their hands up.

One man pulled open the driver's door and dragged Caleb out. "Down," he shouted.

"I'm down! I'm down!" Caleb said and laid flat on his face on the road.

Dwight was pulled out his door, and Rachel and Stevie, only slightly less roughly, out of theirs. They were also forced to lay on their stomachs on the road. Several soldiers stood over them, guns pointed at their backs.

A young oriental woman flipped the back seat forward so Jamie, Maria, and Adele could climb out. "Gun!" she shouted and shoved her rifle in Jamie's face. Now their SUV was surrounded by even more camouflage-wearing figures, all with assault rifles aimed, fingers on the triggers.

Jamie held his hands out to her, fingers spread. The butt of his hunting rifle was resting on the floor between his feet, and the barrel stuck up in plain sight, leaning on his shoulder.

This is going wrong, thought Adele. This is all wrong.

Jamie looked directly in the eyes of the soldier. "Are you military?" he asked. "We're trying to get to Power City." He licked his lips. "We have family there."

The soldier blinked, but the barrel of her rifle did not waver. "Hand me the rifle," she ordered. "Left hand!" she shouted when Jamie reached for it with his right hand. He complied. A uniformed figure took the rifle from him, careful not to stand in the way of the young woman covering Jamie.

"Gun!" she shouted again, as Adele struggled out of the back seat. Adele froze, and the soldiers pulled the revolver from her belt. They shoved her down on the pavement next to Jamie and Maria.

Maria jumped up and made for the trees on the side of the road. A soldier snapped around and aimed his rifle at her. "Halt!" he shouted.

"Jesus Christ! Don't shoot!" yelled Jamie and half rose. A soldier smashed him in the back of the head with the butt of his rifle and Jamie collapsed.

"Jamie!" cried Adele. She scrambled over to him and cradled his head in her lap. Her hands were bloody, and Jamie's eyes were closed. The nearest soldier took aim at them both and his finger tensed on the trigger.

"Hold your fire!" ordered the woman soldier. The young man covering Adele and Jamie lowered his gun slightly and took a step back. "Are they armed?" she called to the men searching Caleb, Dwight and the others.

"They're clean," came the response.

"Johnson, Harris. Search the vehicle," she ordered. Two soldiers started pulling things out of the SUV, throwing stuff on the pavement.

"Rodriguez, search them," she nodded at Adele and Jamie, "then patch him up. Yasutani!" The soldier who had taken aim at Maria straightened up. "Go get the little girl. Try not to shoot her. Yell if she's too much for you." The soldier trotted off to the trees where Maria had disappeared.

"They're clean," said Rodriguez. He rolled Jamie over and started cleaning the gash in the back of his head.

The young woman squatted down in front of Adele. "What's your name?" she asked.

Adele studied the soldier's face. "Adele Prada," she said.

The young woman soldier looked at Adele for a few seconds. She seemed to be considering her next words. "Do you have family in Power City?"

"Yes," said Adele. "My father. He's an engineer at the generating plant. His name's Mike Prada."

The soldier and Rodriguez exchanged glances. "I'm Private...Sergeant Leung," she said, correcting herself. She stood up. "You look like your father."

Yasutani came back carrying a struggling Maria under his arm. He had fresh scratch marks on his cheek and looked put out. "What should I do with her?" he asked Leung.

Adele stood up and held out her hands. "I'll take her."

Yasutani looked at Leung, who nodded. He put Maria down and she rushed to Adele and threw her arms around Adele's legs. Adele knelt and put her arms around the little girl.

One of the soldiers who had been searching the SUV came up to Leung. "Nothing there," he reported.

Adele looked over the mess on the road where clothing, sleeping bags, and food were strewn around the vehicle. She looked over at Jamie, who was making weak movements with his arms. He moaned, and Adele and Maria went to him. Adele turned her head to Sergeant Leung. "Was all this necessary?" she asked, the anger clear in her voice.

The sergeant looked at Adele, her expression unreadable. "You know what it's been like," she said. "We've lost a lot of good people because we hesitated." She looked at the things scattered on the pavement as if noticing for the first time that a search was an act of vandalism. It began to drizzle. "Listen up, kids," Leung addressed the young people. "Pack up your personal belongings," she ordered. "You'll have to schlep your packs about a klick down the road. They're going to send a vehicle to meet us. You can ride the rest of the way to Power City."

Relief rolled over Adele. Something inside her relaxed, something that had been taut for so long that she had forgotten it could be any other way, let go. She wiped her eyes. "Can you let my father know I'm coming?" she asked.

Leung studied the road back the way they had come. "We'll radio ahead," she said, without meeting Adele's eyes.

* * *

Jamie had a splitting headache. The road to Power City was the major artery into the mountains and was well-maintained, but he winced as every little bump the bus hit had an echoing throb of pain at the base of his skull. They were riding in a small, yellow school bus. Jamie and Adele sat together. Adele held Maria on her lap.

Two of the soldiers rode with them, Sergeant Leung and Rodriguez. They sat up front in the row of seats behind the civilian driver. Leung faced forward, watching the road through the front windshield, holding her weapon carefully. Rodriguez sat half turned toward the back, boots in the aisle. His rifle was across his knees, the muzzle pointing down the aisle to the emergency exit, not at the young people but in their direction. His hand rested casually on the gun's grip, his finger on the trigger guard. His eyes moved constantly, checking the woods along the road and the young people in the back.

Jamie knew he should feel relief, that the soldiers were order and discipline, safety in a world gone mad. The rough treatment of the first minutes was just how things were, now. You never knew who was standing there until you had a chance to talk with them, see them in action. Jamie shifted uneasily, trying to get comfortable. Rodriguez stared at him.

Jamie turned his head carefully, looking out the rain streaked windows. He thought of how they had packed up, how a soldier had picked up Caleb's bottle of bourbon and slipped it into his own pack. And something about their faces... Some of the men were unshaven, almost scruffy. Leung was clearly in command while they were in the field, but Jamie sensed that there might be less discipline than the uniforms implied.

The sergeant had taken down everyone's name and age. Maria was just "Maria", and she held up four fingers when asked for her age. Leung relayed these over the radio as they approached a couple of Humvees blocking the road at the edge of Power City. They slowed to a stop and a soldier pulled himself up the steps into the bus.

"Sergeant," he nodded to Leung. She nodded back.

The soldier turned to the group in the back and counted. He checked a clipboard and started calling off names. When he called "Maria", Adele whispered in Maria's ear and she gave a shy wave. Leung gave her an encouraging smile. The soldier with the clipboard did not smile. He jumped down from the bus and waved to a soldier in one of the Humvees who backed the vehicle out of the way, so the bus could continue.

Power City was a tiny place. The original houses and offices were built around an open, grassy park, and the newer residences extended just a few blocks on one side along the river. The massive powerhouse loomed above a line of trees upstream from the town. Jamie frowned at the smoke from multiple small fires that rose into the gray sky just to the south of the powerhouse. "What's that?" he said in a low voice. Adele looked where he nodded.

"That's where the army base is. Must be campfires."

"Don't they believe in electricity?" he asked.

Now they both frowned and craned their necks to look around as the bus drove through town. It wasn't dark, yet, but the spring afternoon light had dimmed. Perhaps it was too early for streetlights, but not a single porch light was lit, and no window showed the glow of a table lamp or a kitchen light.

"I'll ask my dad," said Adele. "It's like they aren't running the generators."

The bus parked on the street next to the open area. "I think that's my dad's," said Adele. She inclined her head toward one of the smaller houses just across the street, painted a cheerful yellow.

Leung stood up. "OK, everybody. Listen up. You'll be staying here for the night, in Adele's dad's house. We've moved in some spare cots, so everyone has their own bed. The toilets are still working, and you've got drinkable water, but showers and baths are forbidden. Don't...waste...water." She spoke slowly and paused to look at each of the young people. Then she went on. "I think you've got a Coleman camp stove and some canned goods. You'll have to cook your own dinner, tonight."

"What about the food in the SUV? Where is it?" asked Jamie.

"All supplies are under the control of our quartermaster. Tomorrow you will be issued a ration card and you can pick up more food."

"That was our food," said Jamie. "We collected it."

Leung studied his face for a second, as if his angry words might reveal something deeper than a passing irritation. "The dam and Power City are under martial law, kid. That's just the way it is." Her tone was tough, provocative.

Jamie pursed his lips and sat back in his seat. He blinked and looked away from Leung. She watched him for a few seconds longer. She appeared satisfied. "One more thing... There's a curfew in effect. No civilians are allowed out of their quarters after three P.M. unless they're escorted by army personnel." She looked at her watch. "That means you can't leave the house until tomorrow morning. Any questions?"

"Where can I find my dad? Is he in the house?" asked Adele.

Something flickered in Leung's eyes. "Everyone off the bus. Follow Private Rodriguez," she said. "Adele, you stay here with me for a minute." She stood aside, and they started filing off the bus. Jamie didn't move from his seat next to Adele. Leung looked at him and then at Adele and Maria. "Jamie, you should take Maria and wait for Adele in the house." She spoke gently. "This is just for Adele."

Jamie hesitated, and looked at Adele. She was silent and still, her eyes fixed on Leung. A tear rolled down her cheek and touched the corner of her mouth. She took shallow breaths through parted lips.

"Here. Take Maria," she said, and set the little girl on Jamie's lap.

"I'll... I'll be on the porch." He put Maria down in the aisle and shouldered his pack. He held Maria's hand as they moved to the door. Jamie looked at Leung as they passed, but she did not meet his eyes. Rodriguez helped Maria down the steps and they walked to the house through the afternoon rain. Jamie dropped his pack on the porch next to the front door. He opened it for Maria. She turned to him.

"What are they going to do to Deli?" she asked.

"Nothing, sweetie," said Jamie. "They just need to talk with her. She'll be with us in just a sec."

Maria looked up at Jamie, her face full of doubt, and Jamie bent down and kissed her on the forehead. "Don't worry," he said, and pushed her hair out of her face. "It'll be OK." Maria turned and went through the door. Jamie turned back to the bus and sat on his pack with his back to the wall under the porch roof.

The interior of the bus was illuminated. Adele sat in her seat. Leung stood in the aisle leaning against the back of the seat in front of her. Adele was looking up at the sergeant, who was speaking. She stopped speaking, and Adele lowered her face into her hands. Her shoulders shook.

Jamie was at the door of the bus before he realized he was moving. He pushed it open and rushed up the stairs. Leung swung around but did not try to stop him as he pushed by her and sat next to Adele. He wrapped his arms around her and held her. He had no words to offer. He just held the sobbing girl and rocked her.

CHAPTER 20

The spade bit into the turf and Ibrahim felt the shock of it up the handle to his shoulders. He put his foot on the blade and leaned on it. His weight pushed it only a bit deeper into the soil. He lifted and turned it over. The grave was now a small black divot in the spring grass.

He worked methodically, digging the outline of the hole first, measuring it against the sheet-shrouded body of Rose lying beside it. He sang as he dug, Sufi hymns, Rumi's poetry set to ancient Persian tunes, all under his breath. Beneath the turf was a thin layer of dirt and then below that the hard pan. He chipped away at the hard pan for most of the morning. He rested frequently.

He wiped the sweat off his face and blinked up at the patio and windows of the CDC cafeteria. This is where he met Rose to talk about her project when it was still unofficial, before the small group of surviving senior scientists were finally convinced. She had outlined a series of statistical tests she wanted done and he had agreed to do the work. She was convincing and passionate. He was young and believed in science with the fervor of one who had seen a society where a scientific theory could be blasphemy and blasphemy carried the death penalty. He thought he was betting his career on her theory, but her theory was correct. Now, he was the senior scientist at the facility. He grinned. He was of course the only scientist and, in fact, the only living person now in the complex. Everyone else had succumbed, taken by fury or despair. Rose had mentioned that the patio where you could sit on a sunny day and sip coffee in the lacy shade under the locust trees, was her favorite place on the CDC campus.

He looked at his hands. The palms had been smooth and uncalloused, but now blisters were forming. He picked up the spade and began to trim the sides of the hole.

After he had lowered her body into the grave and turned her toward Mecca, he dropped three handfuls of dirt over the shrouded figure and filled the grave back in. She was not a Muslim, of course, but these were extreme circumstances. Allah loved her, and Ibrahim did not hesitate. He prayed over the grave. "Save me, my Lord, from the earthly passions..." Who would pray over my grave, he wondered.

The evening was cool, and he was hungry, shaky. He went back to his room and ate a cold can of soup. Just one. Rioters had looted the kitchen and not much food remained. Anyway, his appetite was spoiled by the smell of decay. He had dragged all the bodies he could find into the biosafety wing of the lab and sealed it shut, but it wasn't working.

He looked out the window toward the city. How much of it had burned! The fires glowed in the dark. His reflection looked back at him, dark hair framing a thin, unshaven face. He thought of Rose. He had done all he could for his friend in her final days and after she died. He was finished, here. It was time to go.

"Allahu Akbar," he murmured, a benediction, a farewell.

CHAPTER 21

Adele sat slumped in the middle of the couch in the living room, a coffee mug full of lukewarm chili cupped in both hands in her lap. Her knees were drawn up, and the soles of her boots were propped on the edge of the coffee table. She stared at the opposite wall, indifferent.

Jamie sat next to her on one side with Maria on his lap. Rachel was on the other side of Adele, and Spot was curled up on the floor at Jamie's feet. Caleb had brought in one of the kitchen chairs and sat with his legs stretched out, crossed at the ankles. Dwight and Stevie had settled on the floor, backs against the wall. A kerosene lantern illuminated a scattering of dirty spoons, bowls, and cups from dinner, and an old wood-burning stove was finally generating some heat.

"What a shit-hole," said Caleb.

Jamie looked over at him. "Yeah. We should have stayed at that neat cabin by the lake."

Irritation flitted across Caleb's face, and he turned to Jamie. They locked gazes for several seconds until Jamie blinked and looked away. "They took away your gun, Jamie," he said. "You think that's a good thing?"

Jamie swallowed, and did not answer.

"I thought everything would be under control, here, you know?" said Rachel. "I thought I'd feel safer."

"Yeah. Me, too," said Dwight. He looked at Adele. "Any idea what they're going to do with us?"

Adele shrugged without shifting her eyes from the wall. She lifted one hand, and then let it fall.

"You're the one who convinced us to come here. What were you expecting?" said Caleb.

Jamie started to say something, but Dwight spoke first. "Hey, back off, dude. How was she supposed to know they'd lock us up?"

"She doesn't need this right now," said Jamie. "She lost both her parents in one day. Give her some time."

For a moment, no one spoke. "Like that makes her different from the rest of us?" said Caleb. "You know, is there anyone left alive in the world at all who hasn't lost someone? Or everyone?"

They considered this in silence.

"We all need some time," said Rachel, finally.

"Yeah, but do we have time?" said Caleb, all anger gone from his voice. "Do we have a day? A week? A year?"

Stevie was looking at his sister, his face filled with fear.

"We have all the time we need," said Rachel. She got up with her spoon and cup. "Come on, Stevie. Help me in the kitchen. Bring your stuff." She nodded at the bowl and spoon in his hands. They went out into the kitchen. The others followed, one by one.

Jamie looked at Adele and her untouched food. "You should eat. You'll need it," he said. Then he turned and carried his dishes into the kitchen.

* * *

Jamie leaned against the doorjamb of Adele's bedroom and looked in. It was Adele's room, even though her dad was dead and she had never slept there. It was her room still, and no one had objected when she claimed it, dropping her backpack on the floor next to the battered, thrift store dresser. She sat on the narrow twin bed, prim as a little girl with her hands clasped in her lap. She stared off into an empty corner.

She didn't look up at him, and Jamie walked over to the bed and sat beside her. Caleb walked by in the hall, glancing in with a smirk. Adele got up and closed the door and, without looking at Jamie, sat back down next to him, closer, her thigh warm against his.

Jamie didn't know what to say or what to do. The moment for "I'm sorry," had passed: he had spoken the words on the bus earlier. Where does one go from here?

Adele stretched out on the bed. "You can sleep here. If you want..."

Jamie turned his head and looked down at her. She met his gaze, and he pulled a blanket folded at the foot of the bed up over them both and laid down facing her. Their noses almost touched. Adele kissed him on the lips, and Jamie moved his hand down, following the curve of her body until it rested on her hip, full of warmth.

Adele moved her leg over him and rolled onto her back pulling him on top of her. She dragged his shirts and hoodie off as one and her shirt lost a button on its way to the floor. She fumbled with his belt and he helped her. And then it was just skin against skin.

Afterward, they crawled under the sheets and piled up more blankets against the cold. They spooned and Jamie laid awake for what seemed to be hours feeling her body against his. He slept, but she woke him and again their heat drove the cold dark outside from their minds for a few more minutes. Finally, spent, they fell into a sleep untroubled by dreams and did not wake until the hard, bright morning light came through the window.

* * *

Sergeant Leung collected them all the next morning after breakfast and walked them up to the camp commandant's office. They passed two checkpoints, one on either end of the paved walkway that connected the houses of Power City to the industrial complex around the powerhouse. The soldiers at the checkpoints were sitting around and didn't bother to stand as Leung approached. Their uniforms appeared haphazard, with bandannas replacing regulation field caps, and one soldier sporting a Hawaiian shirt. It was a warm spring day.

They waved Leung and the group through, but one young soldier elbowed his buddy and then stood up and blocked Rachel's way. He smiled down at her. "Got ID?" he asked. His breath smelled of beer.

"Well... No," said Rachel.

His smile broadened. "Well, miss, I'm afraid I'm gonna have to check you out, then." He took her arm. "Come with me, please." Rachel tried to pull away, but he held her fast.

"Walker." Leung's voice came soft but hard. The smile faded from the soldier's face. "They are with me. Let her go," she said.

He turned and looked at Leung. She stood facing him squarely. She had unbuttoned her field jacket and her hand rested on the butt of a handgun on her hip. The other soldiers edged away from Walker, who shifted uneasily. Then he let Rachel go and put up his hands. "Easy there, Sarge," he said and smiled. "Just being careful."

Rachel walked away from the soldier, making a wide circle around Leung as she joined the others, staying out of the line of fire. When everyone was safely by, Leung took a couple of steps backwards, and then turned and walked with the young people.

"Just keep moving," she said.

The walkway curved around a grove of trees and the checkpoint was out of sight. Adele let out a breath and turned to Rachel, who was gripping her arm with both hands. "I'm sorry, Rache. I didn't know it would be like this." Rachel gave her a tight smile.

The walkway joined the parking lot in front of the powerhouse. Adele stopped and looked at the building. The front was blackened, the darkest stains rising up the bricks above the windows. The roof had collapsed, and some parts of the outer wall lay in charred piles of rubble.

"Oh, my god," said Adele. "What happened?"

Sergeant Leung stood next to her. "One of the generators was damaged. It caught fire when we tried to start it."

"How did it get so bad? It burned the whole building?"

Leung sighed. "The lubricating oil for the generators caught. The fire crews... None of them were left. We didn't know how to fight it."

"It looks like it might be a while before you're generating electricity again," said Jamie.

"It looks like it might be forever," said Dwight.

"No shit," said Caleb.

They stood silently for a minute, letting the implications sink in.

Adele looked at the sergeant. "There's nothing left to guard, is there?"

"Let's go," said Leung. She led the group toward a low building on one side of the powerhouse. Two soldiers lounged around smoking on the steps leading up to the front door. It didn't smell like tobacco. They shifted a bit to let the group pass, single file. They looked the two girls up and down as they climbed the stairs and went inside. The young people followed Leung down a dim corridor to a large office at the end. She stepped through the door and snapped to attention.

"At ease, Sergeant," said the soldier behind the desk. He seemed busy with some papers that he held in one hand. He put them down, straightened the pile and looked up. He was young, as was almost everyone, now. He had a pale, fleshy face and a carefully trimmed, sandy-colored mustache. Another soldier leaned against the wall behind him.

"So," he said, and smiled. "What have we here?"

A frown touched Leung's face, as if she was biting back a sharp reply. "This is the group that came in yesterday afternoon, colonel. We have an appointment."

"Ah, yes." The colonel sat back in his chair and surveyed the group. "I'm Colonel Wilson. This is Lieutenant Novak," he nodded toward the soldier leaning against the wall. "Welcome to Power City. I hope we've made you comfortable. We have lots of room, at the moment." Something flitted across his face - dismay, fear - but he got it under control and smiled again. "Enjoy the running water," he said, and smiled more broadly like this was a joke.

The young people smiled back. It seemed the thing to do.

The colonel looked down at his desk. "Here's what we have to offer," he went on, before anyone could ask a question. "Power City is under martial law. The whole thing is really a military base, now, and I'm the commanding officer." He looked up, and the smile was gone. His face was set. He paused a second, a challenge, but no one spoke. "Our original mission was to protect the dam and the generators. Our mission is... different, now. We're simply trying to stay alive. But not just that," he went on quickly, raising a hand as if to forestall objection. "We are an island of order and safety in a crazy world. More than an island. We are the start of a new order, the seeds of a new civilization." He seemed pleased by his own words.

Jamie looked out the window, at the blackened remains of the powerhouse. "Are we all that's left?" he asked. "I mean, where's the government?"

"Well, our contact with the outside world is limited," said the colonel. "Seattle isn't responding to radio transmissions. We were in contact with Spokane for a while, but we haven't heard anything from them in about forty-eight hours."

"What about Washington, the national government?"

"Oh, shit. They were the first to go." Novak spoke for the first time. The colonel gave him an irritated look, but the lieutenant went on. "No one is responding. If anyone is alive out there, they're just hiding out. Like you kids."

"We are the government, now," said the colonel. He looked at the young people and waited.

"So, what about us?" asked Adele.

The colonel straightened up in his chair. He rested his elbows on the desktop and fiddled with a fancy pen. "We are happy to have you here," he said. "And you have a couple of choices." He looked up. "We've lost a fair number of people recently. Good people," he added. The lieutenant rolled his eyes. "But we need to rebuild the ranks. We're accepting new recruits, and we're hoping you older kids will enlist. We can provide food, shelter, training. And you'll be part of rebuilding America." Now the lieutenant snorted. The colonel ignored him. "If you choose not to enlist, there is still an important role for you to play. We need cooks, laborers, what have you. Everyone has to pitch in."

"I need time to think about this," said Adele. "I don't know about anyone else, but so much has happened. You know, we've lost so much. I just need a couple of weeks to let it all settle down. I mean," she shook her head slowly, "I might just head out. See what else is out there. We can't be the only ones."

The colonel just looked at Adele. She shifted uneasily. He cleared his throat.

"Our need for replacements and support personnel is... extreme. 'Heading out' may not be an option. We don't have the luxury to lose any more people."

"So, you're saying we can't leave?" said Jamie. "You're going to keep us here?"

"It's for your own good," said the colonel. "It's a dangerous world out there."

"You can't hold us here," said Rachel.

"Wanna bet?" asked Novak. "Look, be sensible. You think you can take care of yourselves out there? What about the little kids? Can you take care of them?"

"What about the powerhouse? What about my dad?" said Adele. "You're just a bunch of guys with guns. And that guy at the checkpoint, he grabbed Rachel. We're supposed to feel safe here?"

The colonel looked at Leung. "Walker was out-of-line with one of the young women, sir," she said.

The colonel frowned. He turned to Novak. "Have a talk with him. Get him squared away."

"Will do," said the lieutenant.

Wilson looked down at his desk and picked up a sheaf of papers. "I want your decisions by tomorrow morning. You're either in uniform or a civilian, but either way you're here and under my command." He turned to Leung. "Sergeant, escort them back to the house. And put a guard on the house. Dismissed."

Leung held up a warning hand before anyone could object. "Let's go, kids," she said. She led them down the hall and out the front door. "Rodriguez," she called to one of the soldiers lounging on the stairs. "You're on guard duty. Move it."

Rodriguez muttered something to his buddy and got slowly to his feet. They all walked back to the house in Power City, silent, Leung leading the way and Rodriguez bringing up the rear. The soldiers at the checkpoints snickered as the group passed but did not challenge them.

CHAPTER 22

Life was simple now. The power was off, the halls dark and deserted. Ibrahim performed the morning prayer to candle light and finished meditation as the first light of dawn showed in the east. He chanted silently as he prepared a breakfast of dried fruit, salted peanuts, and very strong coffee. He stepped to the door of his room and paused, his head cocked to one side, listening. Something small scurried down the hallway away from his room, and then silence. He started his rounds.

His running shoes made no sound as he moved through the CDC campus. He checked the rooms on his floor, standing at the windows as he scanned the grounds outside. There was no movement other than the long, unmown grass bending in the wind and trees swaying. It looked like rain. What a surprise, he thought, but then turned away from the spirit of discontent in the thought.

He picked up the chant and looked out toward the city. The sun had crested the mountains, a red circle in the clouds that illuminated the smoke and ruins. The distant skyline was changing. Several tall buildings had disappeared, collapsing as days of fire weakened them and finally took them down. Some remained, at least for now. A new fire was burning in the PNW Insurance tower. Black smoke mixed with the gray sky above the city.

Something caught Ibrahim's eye, movement out beyond the chain-link fence that surrounded the campus. A block away, figures slipped into the dim interior of a grocery store through the shattered glass of its doors. Scavengers, he thought. Good luck. In the first, chaotic days, the store had been looted repeatedly by waves of rioters, each more frenzied than the last. These scavengers moved cautiously. They were survivors. But for how long, he wondered. How long until the virus took another one and another, until all had been gathered? How long until his own time would come? It is not your concern, came the thought. He let it go. "Inshallah." He spoke the words in a whisper.

He walked back to his small suite in the dormitory wing. He pulled on his Gortex jacket and shouldered the knapsack he had packed the night before, and then turned and surveyed the room. The suite had been his for the year since he had left Harvard to take the job at the CDC. It held no decoration, no pictures or personal touches, but still it had seemed like home, a refuge. Now, surrounded by the burning city and looted towns, all littered with the mortal remains of violence and despair, it felt like a trap. Everything in him said get out, get away. He took the back stairs to the first floor, pausing to listen at each turn in the corridor and each intersection before going on.

He had selected an unobtrusive delivery door for his escape. It had a window next to it so he could survey the area without exposing himself, and it gave out onto a small parking lot on the back of the building above a tree-lined creek. He followed the creek upstream, keeping to the cover provided by the springtime foliage.

There was a gap in the chain-link fence where it crossed the stream, and this is where Ibrahim left the CDC grounds. Ahead, farm fields ran along the creek on either side, the dirt turned but not yet planted. Beyond lay the foothills and the high mountains. Ibrahim stopped to rest and shrugged his shoulders. He looked up at the snowy peaks and a beam of sunlight broke through the clouds. The heights sang in the morning light, shining, white, pure, and brilliant above the grim valley. Ibrahim felt his heart open up. It is a call, he thought. This is the way to go. Whether he lived or died, he would do it far above the valley with its fires and decay. He walked all day, chanting and singing under his breath, sure of his direction and trusting what lay ahead.

* * *

"It might not be so bad," said Caleb. He studied the wall above the wood stove. "You know, at least there are some grownups around."

Jamie snorted. "Leung might be a grownup. The rest are just assholes."

"Assholes with guns," said Rachel. "I don't think I want to go where they want to take us."

"Yeah, I just don't see it," said Dwight. He licked a spoon and stuck it in an empty can of lentil soup.

"Salt? Who's got the salt?" said Rachel.

"Everyone smells like beer or pot," said Dwight. "Reminds me of my old man." He frowned and touched a spot on his cheek.

Adele was sitting on the floor with her back against the couch. She rested her elbows on her knees and covered her eyes with her hands. She breathed carefully.

"So what choice do we have?" asked Caleb. "How could we survive out there?" He turned to Adele. "You said the worst of it might be over, all the crazies might be dead, now. Like all the old people are dead. But we're not getting any younger. What happens when we turn twenty-five, or whatever it is? We're going to go nuts, too, right? It'll never stop."

Everyone was silent. There was the sound of a gunshot in the distance and its echo off the hills. Then more shots, and the ripping sound of automatic fire.

"That does not sound like target practice," said Jamie.

"Shit," said Dwight. He jumped up and rushed to the front door. He threw it open and found Rodriguez standing on the porch.

Rodriguez pushed him back into the house and blocked the doorway. "Everyone stay put," he said. The firing was louder now, coming through the open door, or perhaps closer. Rodriguez looked over his shoulder. "Y'all are safer here." He backed out of the door and turned toward the sounds. Someone shouted, and Rodriguez disappeared.

Jamie went to the front door and looked out. "There's smoke," he said. Now all of the young people were at the door. Jamie stepped out onto the front porch and looked toward the powerhouse. A black plume rose next to it, where the colonel's office would have been. The sound of firing was continuous.

A uniformed figure ran toward them. Sergeant Leung jumped up on the porch. She was carrying Jamie's rifle and his backpack in one hand and her M-16 in the other. She shoved the rifle and backpack at Jamie.

"Time to go," she said. "Grab your stuff. Quick!" She turned to Adele. "Your gun's in the pack." She faced back toward the powerhouse and knelt on the porch behind a post. She scanned the scene and then looked over her shoulder. Everyone still stood in the doorway, their mouths hanging open.

"Move it!" yelled Leung. They scattered through the little house, stuffing clothing and food into their backpacks, rolling up sleeping bags and bouncing off each other as they collided in doorways. The gunfire was louder, and the crackle of small arms was joined now by the deep pounding of a big gun.

"Let's go, people, now!" shouted Leung from the porch.

They poured through the front door and followed Leung across the lawn to the side yard, putting the house between them and whatever was happening back around the powerhouse.

"Wait a minute! Where's Maria? Where's Spot?" said Jamie. He stopped and looked around. "Shit," he said and ran back to the house. "Maria!" he called as he charged through the empty living room. He stuck his head in each of the bedrooms, but she was not there. Spot barked from another room, and Jamie found him in the bathroom, facing the tub. He rushed in and swept the shower curtain aside. Maria was huddled down against the old porcelain, covering her face with her arms.

"Hey, sweetie," said Jamie. "We've gotta go." He leaned down to lift her out, but she pulled away.

"No!" she yelled.

Adele came through the door and jumped into the tub. She crouched down and put her face close to Maria's. "You're with us, little one." She spoke gently and put her hand on Maria's shoulder.

"No!" the little girl insisted and pulled her arms and legs even tighter.

The sound of gunfire was louder.

Adele gathered Maria up and stood. Jamie reached out. Adele handed the girl to him and they started for the front door. Maria wrapped her arms and legs around Jamie and did not resist. As they entered the living room, an explosion rattled the glass in the old windows. A military vehicle rolled across the street a couple of blocks down, flames pouring from its undercarriage, and then disappeared from view behind a building.

Adele leaned out the front door and checked the street. "Now," she said. They jumped off the porch and darted around the corner. The others were waiting, crouched low against the side of the house in the shelter of the brick foundation.

Leung took a quick look at the backyards up and down the block. "Let's go," she said, and started off, keeping low, staying close to the walls of each house. She paused before crossing the side yards, sticking her head out to see around the corner and pulling it back quickly. They crossed the open spaces at a run.

As they passed one house, the back door swung open with a bang like a shot. Leung spun around and aimed at the door but did not fire when two teenage girls ran out.

"Take us with you," said the older, who looked to be about sixteen. The younger clung to the older girl, her face streaked with tears.

"Where the hell do you think you're going?" A soldier lurched out onto the small back porch, a can of beer in one hand and a handgun in the other. "Get back in here before I blow your sweet, little asses away." He pointed his gun at the girls.

Leung shot him in the chest. He fell back into the house. "Stay close," she said to the girls, and they all ran across to the next backyard.

When they reached the last house on the block, Leung stopped and studied the terrain. Ahead of them across an expanse of lawn was the main two-lane that ran up the valley from the coast. On the far side of the road was a parking lot, and beyond that a heavily wooded slope. A figure in camouflage lay still in the road in a pool of blood.

The young people were hunkered down and bunched up behind Leung, as if taking shelter in her shadow. She turned. "Listen up. We've got to cross that open area to the trees on the other side. There's a trailhead there, by that sign." She pointed. "Everyone who makes it across the road, keep going up the trail. Got it?"

"Where are we going?" asked Rachel.

Leung looked at her for a second before answering. "That way," she inclined her head.

"Oh. Right. Got it," said Rachel.

"I'm going to go first," said Leung. "There may be shooting. Just keep going. Do not stop. Do not bunch up. Ready?" She turned and ran out onto the lawn. The rest jumped up as one and ran after her in a tight bunch.

They made it onto the roadway before the shooting started. It wasn't clear where it was coming from, but bullets whizzed by and puffs of pavement erupted around their feet. Leung dove into the drainage ditch on the far side of the highway. She located the source of the shooting and started firing back, giving cover to those behind her. Everyone tumbled into the ditch and squeezed flat in the damp bottom. Spot seemed to understand what was necessary and hunkered down next to Jamie. No one had been hit. The sergeant fired a few more shots, there was a distant scream, and then all was quiet.

Leung jumped up. "Now! Run! Go, go, go!" She pulled Adele up by the arm, pushed her out of the ditch and then grabbed Rachel. Adele sprinted for the treeline and then everyone was up and following. Jamie carried Maria, running awkwardly, and Leung brought up the rear. The younger of the two teenage girls stumbled and her companion pulled her to her feet and they ran together, hand in hand. There was no more shooting, and they all made it to the dark refuge of the forest.

PART II
CHAPTER 23

Leung stretched and looked around their campsite. What a mess, she thought. She stepped over to the firepit, careful not to kick the empty bourbon bottle or step on the blanket crumpled in the dirt. She uncovered the coals and blew them to brightness, added dry kindling, and soon had a crackling fire. She sat for a moment, soaking up the warmth. Mornings were still cool this high in the mountains, even in mid-summer.

There was some water left, and she put on a kettle. One of the kids would have to go for water today, she thought. I'm tired of schlepping it all the time. She ducked back into her tent to dig out a packet of instant coffee. She counted five packets remaining. They'd need to make another trip down to the town, soon. Going to town was like Christmas shopping in a bad neighborhood. It was exciting to get a bunch of stuff, and exciting simply to make it home.

Someone was stirring in one of the other tents. Maria spoke, her voice low, and Adele responded, her words indistinct. A few seconds later, the little girl emerged from the tent she shared with Jamie, Adele, and Spot. Adele followed. Maria sat on a tarp and pulled on her shoes. They had little Velcro straps and she tugged them snug before heading for the fire. Adele stepped into a pair of hiking boots and clumped along after Maria, laces dragging in the dirt. She pulled a heavy cardigan sweater closer around her and blinked at the early morning light.

"Do we have coffee?" she asked.

"We don't have coffee," said Leung, emphasizing the 'we'. "I have coffee."

Maria stared at the fire. Adele pushed her hair back from her face. She gathered it in a messy ponytail and winced as she secured it with a rubber band.

"Do we have water?" asked Adele, emphasizing the 'we'.

"Water is a great idea," said Leung. "Why don't you trot on down to the stream and fill up the fucking water jug?"

Adele stood for a moment, considering her response and then bent down and tied her boot laces. She picked up a plastic, five-gallon jug and held out her hand to Maria. "Come on, stinko. Let's go get some fucking water." Maria stood up and took Adele's hand, and the two of them started off down the slope.

Leung watched them go. She turned back to the fire and poured the boiling water into her coffee cup. The taste of it and the bright morning sun almost penetrated the cloud of irritation and outright anger that had been with her for days, now. The kids were total assholes, last night, she thought. All the older kids sat around the campfire, drinking bourbon. Emily, the older of the two girls Leung had rescued when they escaped Power City, had thrown up all over herself and her little sister, Eva. Rachel and Dwight had staggered off to Dwight's tent where they had sex — quick and noisy — while everyone had to listen. What are the idiots thinking, wondered Leung? They're acting like there's no tomorrow. She frowned down at the fire and blew on the steaming coffee.

* * *

The older kids started drinking in the early afternoon, everyone except Emily who had emerged from her tent only a few hours ago, shaking and pale. Leung looked at her. I risked my life so a bunch of spoiled, high school kids could get blotto in the woods, she thought. Emily looked up and met her gaze. Leung turned her head and spit into the fire.

Jamie was boiling oatmeal and cut up some beef jerky to put in it. Maria hung on his shoulder, and he gave her a slice of jerky which she chewed, mouth open, of course. Maria did not protest when Spot got a piece, too.

"That's not dog food," said Leung. "How much of that do we have left?"

Jamie looked over at Leung but said nothing. He unwrapped another piece of jerky and started cutting it up.

Caleb had the bottle, a big plastic liter of cheap vodka. He took a swig, made a face, and shuddered. "Ugh," he said. He held out the bottle to Leung who was sitting on a log next to him. Leung gave him a disgusted look and turned back to the fire.

"Come on, Leung," he said, and nudged her arm with the bottle. "It's medicinal. Good for what ails you."

Leung ignored him. Caleb got up and sat next to her on the log. He still had most of his linebacker bulk and Leung seemed much smaller. He crowded her. "Don't be that way, sarge," he said, and pushed the bottle in front of her face.

Leung slapped the bottle away. It flew out of Caleb's hand and landed in the fire which erupted in the splash of alcohol.

"Oh, shit!" said Dwight.

Caleb considered the bottle, melting in the flames. "Now what am I gonna do all evening, huh?" He turned his head to Leung. His lips were inches away from her ear. He leaned in. "Huh?" he repeated softly and licked her ear.

Leung stood up, took a step away and then turned to face Caleb. "Get up," she said.

Caleb looked at her and smiled. "Ooo," he said. "Is little Leung going to teach me a lesson?" He got to his feet and waited, head and shoulders taller than the soldier.

He doesn't move like he's drunk, she thought. And then her rage took her, and she lashed out, letting him block her first move but taking him down when he struck back and the big knife that she kept in her boot was out and on Caleb's neck and a drop of blood appeared where the knife's edge pressed into his pale skin. Caleb looked up at Leung's face, just inches above his. There was no expression in her face, just an absolute stillness, a readiness. He frowned and blinked, as if not quite sure how he had come to be flat on his back in the dirt. He tried to sit up, but Leung's eyes were very cold and the pressure of the knife on his neck increased.

Now the others were up and shouting.

"Leung," yelled Jamie. "Jesus Christ! Don't hurt him!" He moved toward her but stopped short, afraid to upset a delicate balance. "OK," he said. "He's an asshole. Everyone knows he's an asshole. And he's sorry. Tell her you're sorry, Caleb."

Caleb swallowed and licked his lips. "I'm sorry," he said. "I'm sorry."

Something changed in Leung's eyes. Some hint of doubt appeared as she looked down into Caleb's face. Did she see herself reflected in his eyes, a reflection of someone she barely recognized? She pushed herself up slowly, keeping the knife at Caleb's throat until she had her feet underneath her, and then stepped quickly to the side. She straightened up and looked at the faces around the fire, frozen, staring at her, mouths open. There was a low growl, and she looked down at Spot, his lips curled back showing his teeth.

She spun around and ran, following a game trail into the woods, her breathing ragged in her own ears. "Assholes! They're a bunch of little, fucking assholes!" she thought. She couldn't see right in the dim light under the trees. Her eyes were watering, and she tripped and fell hard. And fury, loss and sorrow overwhelmed her, and she stabbed the ground with her knife in a frenzy, over and over, sobbing, until exhaustion stilled her. She slept.

* * *

Jamie woke, bleary, and shifted in the warmth under the down bag. Adele's breathing was deep and regular, her head on her pillow next to Jamie's, invisible in the dark but close. Maria was curled between them, her head under the covers. Spot stood near the tent flap. His body was tensed, his head low and hackles raised. His growl had brought Jamie up out of sleep. Jamie turned his head and listened.

Spot growled again, and Adele's breathing changed. "What is it?" she said.

"Spot," said Jamie. He whispered. "But I don't hear anything." He sat up and held very still, breathing through his open mouth. There was the sound of wind in the trees. There was the crack of a log on the fire. "I'll go check," he said.

He picked up the rifle and crawled to the door. He had to shoulder by Spot who gave way reluctantly. He unzipped the door and pulled the flap in so he could see out. Someone sat at the fire, a familiar figure but somehow different. Leung stared at the flames, hunched and still.

"It's Leung," said Jamie. "She's back." The warmth of the down bags called, but he sat and watched the soldier for a few seconds. "I'll go see how she is," he said finally, and crawled out of the tent taking the rifle. He turned and zipped up the flap before Spot could slip out, too.

He walked up to the firepit, scuffing a bit so Leung knew he was coming, and holding the rifle casually in one hand. She did not look up when he approached. "Hey," he said. "I thought you were a grizzly come to eat us." He sat on a log and let the rifle lean against his shoulder. He clasped his hands around his knees.

The firelight cast shifting light and dark across her face, and seemed to paint it with expressions of anger, horror and grief. Jamie stared. Leung's body twitched, and the light glinted off the blade of her knife. She gripped it in her right hand.

"Leung? Are you OK?" he said. He shifted on the log, turning his body toward her as if waiting for her reply. His right hand dropped to the rifle and he drew his feet in beneath him.

Leung looked at Jamie. "I'm turning." She shook her head. Her eyes were damp. "I'm turning. I've got to go."

Jamie's eyes were stinging, and he blinked. "No." He shook his head. "No. You're... you're just mad, angry. Caleb was an asshole. He was way out of line. You were right to get mad."

"I can feel it, Jamie. Everything pisses me off. I'm going to explode. I've got to go."

"Go? Where? When?"

"Now. I'm going to walk until I drop. My only hope is that I drop before I lose it completely, because if I have the energy to make it back, I'll come back. And I'll kill everyone." She pressed the fist holding the knife against her forehead and closed her eyes. "I shouldn't have come back. I just wanted to say goodbye." She seemed to see the knife in her hand for the first time. She wiped it against her pants and hesitated, then stood and heaved it far into the night. "Tell everyone I said goodbye. Best of luck, Jamie. Take care."

Jamie jumped up. "Wait a minute. What about us? We can't do this alone. You were going to teach us stuff. What about first aid?"

"Too late, Jamie. If I stay, people will die. I guarantee it."

"Wait until morning, Leung. Things always look better in the morning." Jamie stepped over to her. He reached out and touched her on the arm. "Please," he said.

Leung swung her arm and backhanded Jamie across his face. "What the fuck's the matter with you," she snarled. "Listen to me." She grabbed the neck of Jamie's sweatshirt and pulled his face to hers. "You're all fucking dead unless I go. Now."

For a second, they stood like that, face to face, and then something changed in Leung's expression. Her eyes softened. She kissed Jamie on the lips. "Go with God," she said. She spun around and ran off, disappearing beyond the ring of light cast by the fire. Jamie listened to her footsteps, and when he couldn't hear them anymore, he stood unmoving, staring out into the darkness where she had gone. And when it got too cold, he crawled back into the fragile warmth of the tent and Adele's arms.

CHAPTER 24

Things were quiet at breakfast the next morning. Caleb's cut was not deep, and Adele cleaned it and stuck a small Band-Aid on it.

"Maybe we should apply a tourniquet," said Jamie.

A hint of amusement touched Adele's face. Caleb showed no reaction. Jamie sat down with Maria and stared at the fire.

"Where's Laura?" asked Maria.

"Who's Laura?" said Jamie.

"Laura... the Sergeant."

"Her name is Laura? How do you know that?"

"She told me."

Jamie pondered this.

"Where is she?" Maria asked again.

"She got sick, honey," said Adele. "She had to go away." She started packing up the first aid kit.

"Why did she have to go away?"

"Well, sometimes when people are sick they have to stay away from other people, so they don't get sick, too."

Maria blinked. She looked at Adele and then away. "When will she come back?"

"She's not coming back," said Caleb. "She turned. If she comes back, she'll kill us unless we kill her first."

Adele stood up with the first aid kit in her hand. "Ease up, Caleb. She's only four."

"You want her to make it to five?" he said. "Like she hasn't seen it all, anyway? What?" said Caleb. "Mommy and daddy are going to give their little princess a happy childhood? Get real. We're not playing house out here."

Jamie hit him with a flying tackle and they rolled over in the dirt. Caleb came out on top and held him down with one hand while hitting him in the face with the other. Jamie flailed at Caleb but with no effect.

"Get off him!" yelled Adele. She grabbed Caleb's arm with both of her hands, but he simply pulled her off her feet and she fell hard on her knees.

Rachel pulled at the neck of Caleb's jacket. "Stop it!" she screamed.

It was Dwight who finally put an end to it. He wrapped his arms around Caleb from behind and lifted him up off Jamie. Caleb twisted out of his grasp and started back but then Dwight stood between Caleb and Jamie and Caleb seemed to think better of it. He wiped his nose with the back of his hand.

"Little, fucking, prick," he said. "You were lucky, today, asshole." He walked back to his tent.

Adele helped Jamie up. He stumbled and sat heavily on a log. His fingers came away smeared with blood and dirt when he touched his face with his hand. Adele knelt in front of him and took his hand in one of hers. She touched his face with her fingertips.

"Here," she said. "Let me get that."

She picked up the first aid kit and started cleaning his cuts and bruises. Jamie watched her face as she worked. She was just inches away and put the first aid kit on his lap.

Maria came up and leaned on his knee. "I'm sorry, Jamie," she said.

"Don't be silly, sweetie," he said. He spoke carefully, moving his lips as little as possible. "You didn't do anything wrong. It's not your fault." He winced when Adele dabbed at a cut on his lower lip.

"We're just blowing up all over the place," said Rachel. "It's like we've all turned, and we just don't know it, yet."

Adele paused, and looked up from Jamie's lips to meet his gaze. They looked at each other without speaking, and then she dropped her eyes and continued cleaning his face.

* * *

Adele ran her fingers across Jamie's chest and down his stomach. He wasn't wearing pajamas, and her fingers kept going, tracing a slow line on the flat, taut skin, sliding in and then out of the dip of his belly button, and on. Every other night, she had found him ready and eager, but not tonight. She held him and kissed him on the lips.

"Ow," he said.

"Oh, I'm sorry, I'm sorry," she said. "Did I hurt you?" Duh, she thought. That's why he said ow.

"Let's just let it go, OK? Maria will be coming to bed soon, anyway." Rachel was babysitting Stevie and Maria at the campfire, and the sound of little voices learning a song came on the night breeze. It was a bitter sweet love song, "What becomes of the brokenhearted...", a cover of an old song, a big hit just before everything went to hell.

"Stupid song," said Jamie. He rolled over, away from Adele.

"I'm sorry," she said again. "Are you OK?" Jamie did not respond. "Is it me?" she asked.

At first, Jamie said nothing. Then "No. Of course not." His body was tense.

"Is it Caleb? The fight?"

"I couldn't do anything. It was like I was nothing. I was totally helpless. And he kept hitting me, and hitting me, and hitting me." Jamie's breathing was ragged. "I was helpless."

"Well, what did you expect? Caleb's a football player, for god's sake."

"He made me afraid. He's always made me afraid." Jamie's voice was coming from a place that Adele didn't know. "I wish Leung had cut his fucking head off."

Adele stared at nothing in the darkness of the tent. The singers were taking a break, and the only sounds were Jamie's breathing and the wind in the trees. She wracked her brain for the right thing to say, something that would make it all better.

"But you faced your fear, right? You jumped on him like...like a lion." Like a crazy man, came the thought.

"Next time, I'll just fucking shoot the motherfucker," he said.

Footsteps approached the tent. "Knock, knock," said Rachel. "Maria is sleeping over with me and Stevie, tonight. Enjoy!" Her voice was full of suggestion and a wink. It was pure Rachel, thought Adele, and she was shamed by a powerful desire to join them in the simplicity of singing stupid songs. She put a hand flat against Jamie's back and held it there, as if her love for Jamie could flow down her arm and through her palm and fill his man-boy body with goodness and light. She held it there until she fell into a restless sleep troubled by dreams of black bats that rose in a cloud from some dank cave and swarmed over her and Maria. She woke with a start and laid there until the early morning light of the mountain summer warmed the world and touched it again with color.

* * *

Jamie came stumbling out of the tent, maneuvering the long rifle awkwardly through the small doorway of the dome. He settled near the fire but a few steps away from Adele, Maria and the others. Spot watched him approach and when Jamie sat down he sniffed then shifted so Adele and Marie were between him and Jamie. Maria looked at Jamie, turning her head only slightly from the fire, and then turned back and poked at a burning log with a long stick.

"Oatmeal's hot," said Adele. "Maria found some blackberries." She tried a smile. Jamie glanced at her and away. He pushed himself up and hung the rifle by its sling on his shoulder. He picked up a plastic bowl and scooped steaming oatmeal directly from the pot. He retreated to his seat and started spooning up the oatmeal, but spit the first mouthful back into the bowl and sucked on the cool morning air.

"Did you burn yourself?" asked Adele. She poured a cup of water and brought it to him. He took it and sipped, sloshed the cool liquid in his mouth and spit it out on the ground. "That better?" she asked.

Jamie nodded but did not look at her.

"Berries?" She held out a small bowl with a few almost ripe-looking blackberries.

"Jesus, Deli. Can I just eat in peace?"

Adele stood for a second, bowl in hand, and then turned and sat down next to Maria. Maria leaned forward so she could see Jamie past Adele. She watched him blow on a spoonful of cereal, and then she sat back. She let the fire poking stick drop from her hands, and she pressed them together, palm to palm, between her knees.

Caleb looked from Adele and Maria to Jamie and back. He smiled at Adele. "I'll have some berries," he said.

Adele returned the smile and passed the bowl of semi-ripe berries. He dumped it into the crusty remains of his oatmeal and added a splash of hot coffee. "Mmmm! Best berries I've ever had." He was blinking rapidly and his mouth worked like he was trying to chew without touching the sour, acidic mouthful. Maria beamed.

Jamie glared at him from across the fire. "Who's playing house, now?"

"Hey, little daddy. No need to be that way. I'm just enjoying these great berries."

Jamie jumped up and unslung the rifle, but before he could get both hands on it, Caleb was standing with Leung's M-16 pointed at Jamie's face. Jamie froze. Caleb's eyes sighting down the barrel were very cold, and his finger was tense on the trigger.

"Put it down, Jamie," he said.

Jamie leaned the rifle against a log, holding it close to the muzzle with one hand, without taking his eyes off Caleb's gun.

"Step away." Caleb motioned with the M-16, and Jamie took two steps to the side, holding his hands out where Caleb could see them.

"Enough!" said Adele. She stood and put herself between the two young men.

"Yeah, that's it," said Rachel. She stood and faced Caleb, just a couple of feet away, directly in the line of fire.

Dwight walked over and picked up Jamie's rifle. Then he walked back to Caleb. "Why don't I hold the weapons for a little while." He put his hand on the barrel of the M-16 and Caleb let him push it down so it pointed at the ground and then let him take it from him.

"He's turning," said Caleb, loud enough so everyone could hear. "You're losing it, Jamie. You're turning." He looked at Dwight. "Keep him away from the guns." Caleb turned and stalked away. He grabbed the water bucket as he passed and headed down toward the stream.

Jamie started after him, but Adele stepped in his way and put a hand on his chest. "Let it go, Jamie," she said. "He isn't worth it."

"He's been a problem since the beginning," said Jamie. He looked past Adele at Caleb's back. "Someone's gotta straighten him out."

Adele blew out a breath and shook her head. "Some people are just that way. You can't change them. The only control you have is over yourself. That's it."

Jamie's face worked. He looked at Adele. "You're on his side." He looked around at the group. "You're all on his side."

His eye fell on Maria, sitting hunched over staring at the dirt in front of her shoes. She looked up at Jamie. Her face was tear-streaked, and strands of her dark hair stuck to her cheek.

"You're not nice, anymore," she said. "I don't like you."

Jamie breathed out hard, like he'd been hit, and for a second, he simply looked at her. Then he spun around and strode up the slope, away from the camp, away from Caleb, away from what he had seen in Maria's eyes.

CHAPTER 25

Adele put Maria to bed and then went back out. The fire had burned low, and she sat alone by the embers that glowed when touched by the fitful evening breeze. She pulled her coat closer. It was cool.

Everyone else had retreated to their tents. Rachel and Stevie's was dark as was Emily's and Eva's. A flashlight burned in Dwight and Caleb's tent casting silhouettes of two card players. After a while, the flashlight went out, and all was still. Adele sat and stared at the little fire, listening to its crackle, listening for his footsteps, listening for any hint of Jamie's return. Some time passed. She was chilled, and went to bed, but did not sleep.

She heard him pour water, drink, and then the spit and sizzle when he shook the last drops out on the dying embers. She went to meet him. He was standing close to the fire ring, one boot resting on a stone, his hands jammed in the pockets of his jeans.

"Hey," she said. She kept her voice low.

He didn't look up. His face was illuminated by the coals and the breeze chased a strand of his hair across his face. "Hey," he said.

She stepped up close and hooked an arm through his. His body stiffened. She waited a second to see if he would relax and accept her touch. He did not. So that's how it is, she thought. She let his arm go and moved a half-step away.

"You want something to eat?" she asked.

He looked at the food bag suspended high in a tree, a dark spot against the stars of the clear, mountain night. "Nah," he shook his head.

They stood there, silent for a few more seconds.

"I've got to go," said Jamie. Adele turned to him and put her hand on his arm.

"What do you mean?"

"Caleb's right. I'm turning. I can feel it. Everything makes me mad. Caleb makes me mad. The food makes me mad. The birds make me mad. Maria makes me mad." He turned to Adele. "You make me mad. I've got to go."

"Caleb makes everyone mad," she said. She stroked his arm. "I'm sorry about today. I know you thought I was taking Caleb's side, but I wasn't. Really. And Maria's just a little kid, you know? She didn't mean what she said."

"You said that we can't control other people. That we can only control ourselves. But I feel it, Deli. I can feel it. I can't control myself."

"We're all out of control, Jamie. We're all just like on the edge, all the time. We get up in the morning, and we don't know if we're gonna make it through the day." She pressed her body against his arm. "Let's go to bed. I'll rub your back. It'll look better in the morning." She kissed him on the cheek and tugged at his arm, but he didn't budge.

"It's not going to work. I have to go. Now," he said.

"OK... Look, I'll go with you. You'll see. A few days and it'll be good, again. Rachel can take care of Maria until we get back. It'll be like a vacation. We'll get away from everyone and just kick back. A vacation from the end of the world! Doesn't that sound good?" She tried to smile but it kept slipping off to the side. Her voice shook, and she swallowed. "We can leave first thing in the morning, OK?" She pulled at his arm with both hands, and Jamie let himself take a step toward their tent. He looked at her, his face barely visible now in the dark. His eyes glistened.

"Yeah," he said. "Sure. That sounds great. Let's do that." She hugged him and hid her face in his chest. "I love you," she said.

"And I love you, Deli," he said. And he put his arms around her and squeezed, hard, for a long time.

They went to bed, then, without speaking. There wasn't anything more to say and they did not want to wake Maria. Jamie folded his clothes and put them by the door where they would be easy to find in the dark.

* * *

He laid awake, and tried not to think of anything, because whenever he thought of something, his mind would run with it and spin it into a tale of grievance and anger. He wrapped Adele in his arms and snuggled against her back. It took a long time for her to fall asleep. He guessed she was responding to the waves of tension that swept over his body when he was ambushed by his emotions and they spiraled downward. He would come to himself with a start, recoiling from the ferocious feelings and images and willing himself to relax, to let it go.

Finally, her breathing became deep and regular. He touched the back of her head with his lips, barely stirring the cloud of dark hair, and slid out from underneath the down sleeping bags. He found his clothes and dressed outside. The summer morning was just a hint in the eastern sky.

He looked around the camp. No one was stirring. He picked up his walking stick but took no food or water. He went like a ghost, along the path he had chosen the day before, a path that led to a branching and then to another branch, all ways leading deeper into the mountains and leaving no clue as to which turn he had taken to any that might try to follow.

He walked as quickly as he could in the slow, dim dawn. His boot hit a root and he fell face-first onto the path. He climbed to his feet and kept going, brushing dirt from his face as he went. It hurt, and he tasted blood, but he did not pause. A cut was nothing, now. Only getting as far as he could from Adele and Maria was important. When he finally succumbed, he would go after anyone he could find, and he wanted to be so far away and so weak from hunger and thirst that it would be impossible for him to make it back to their camp.

He refused to think about Adele and Maria. He did not think of Adele waking and reaching for him but not finding him. He did not think of her emerging from their tent and looking around the campsite, doubt growing in her face. He did not think of the tears coming to her eyes, but his tears stung when they touched the raw skin of his cheek, and he could not see in the dim light whether it was blood or tears that now wet his collar.

And it never occurred to him to think that Adele, shaky from fatigue and grief, would eat a few bites of breakfast and then throw it up across the fire. And that far from setting out to pursue Jamie as she intended, she would clutch Rachel's arm and stagger back to her tent to lay in a tangle of sleeping bags, clinging to a bucket, as her stomach rebelled at the mere thought of food.

* * *

He walked all day without stopping to eat or rest. Once as he forded a mountain stream, he bent over and drank before he was conscious of the act. He could not stop himself and drank until satisfied. It's OK, he thought. He pushed on, up into the mountains, away from Adele and Maria.

He did not stop as it grew dark, until he stumbled and fell. He curled up against the cold and shivered there in the path until the morning came and it was light enough to go on. He was unsteady, now, on his feet and felt ill. Sometime in the midmorning, when the day had grown warm enough, he paused and sat on a rock.

He was shaky, and breathed through his mouth, panting. He tipped his head back to the sun, eyes closed.

This is so hard, he thought. That prick Caleb. It was clear now that he had maneuvered Jamie, provoking him in front of everyone. He looked back down the path, down the alpine valley he had been walking for the past hour. There was no way he could go back now. He was spent. He would never make it.

He looked up the path. It was a steady upward trek to a treeless ridge high above. Idiot, he thought. The whole point is that you can't make it back. He grimaced in disgust, revolted by his own hesitation.

Caleb's face came to him, and his anger gave him the energy to push himself up from the rock. He staggered but caught himself with the stick. He turned, taking small shuffling steps to point himself up the path. He looked down at his feet and back up to the way ahead. A flash of rage exploded in him, rage against Caleb, against Adele who had encouraged Caleb, against Maria who had failed to take his side against Caleb.

He lifted his walking stick high and flailed at the rock. The stick broke, and somehow his feet got tangled up and he lost his balance. He fell, or really just collapsed, folded up on the path. Nothing was within reach to destroy, nothing but himself. He clawed at his face.

He laid there panting. Black spots spun before his eyes. He blinked. The spots gathered and swarmed, and then there was a flock of black birds, wheeling and turning in the sky, coming up the valley. More and more appeared, so many that now they blocked the sun and turned the sky into a seething black cloud. Their cries were shrill, screeching.

The sky was full of cruel beaks and sharp talons, and Jamie sensed that these shrieking demons must not know about Adele or Maria or any of his friends. That if he thought of any of them, the black furies would see them and turn on them and tear them to pieces. He had to hide Adele and Maria and all of them. He had to conceal them utterly. He had to forget them, to eliminate every vestige of them from his own mind for their sake, to protect them.

And so he did. He emptied his mind, not just of Adele and Maria but of all his personal memories, all the things that now seemed so intertwined with Adele and Maria so that anything of his memory could lead the murderous flock to those he loved most. He renounced them, sealed them away in a box deep in the darkest recess of his mind, far from consciousness. And then he renounced himself, sent all his memories into distant exile, letting it all go, all that was Jamie.

The black flock was on him. The wings buffeted him, and their calls washed over him. He was swept away and could no longer feel the grit of the path on his face. He was falling through the swirling darkness and then he lost the sense of his body and its place in space, and there was nothing but the space, an infinite dark. All was still and black, motionless, timeless, shining. He rested for a second, for an eternity.

And then a song. A voice, distant, quiet, singing in some unknown language, a strange lilting tune. It stopped and then started again. It seemed to summon him, to draw him back into his body, back into a physical form, almost like he was condensing from nothing into something. He opened his eyes.

"Ah, you have come back to us." A dark, thin face loomed over him, framed by long black hair and a young man's silky beard. "Would you like some water?"

Jamie felt something touch his lips, and a drop of cold moisture trickled into his mouth. He tried to sit up, to take the canteen in his hands but fell back.

"Here. Let me help," said the man. He put a hand under Jamie's head. The canteen touched Jamie's lips again and he drank. He inhaled some water, and coughed, a painful spasm.

"Maybe just a bit at a time," said the man. "There is more where that came from." He smiled. "I think you will be OK, inshallah. For now, just rest. No? I will watch over you."

Jamie closed his eyes and let sleep take him. He sank into its sweet darkness.

CHAPTER 26

Ibrahim wrapped the fingers of both hands around the hot cup. He held it close to his face and let the warmth rising from the tea touch his skin. Tiny droplets condensed from the steam on his beard. He closed his eyes and inhaled through his nose. He smiled. His lips moved in a silent prayer of thanksgiving and then he sipped. The hot liquid burned all the way down. Ibrahim loved the mornings best.

He looked down at the young man sleeping on the floor of the cave. It had been a full day since Ibrahim had found him. At first, he thought the motionless figure sprawled across the mountain path was a corpse, but when he checked his thin wrist, a faint pulse tapped against his fingertips. It never occurred to Ibrahim to leave him, that the marks of fury on his face and hands were a warning that only a fool would ignore. It took an hour with several rests to carry him back to the cave.

Ibrahim touched a cup of water to the man's lips, wetting them and spilling a few drops on the downy red-blond beard. The man smacked his lips and licked at the moisture. His eyes opened. They wandered across the ceiling of the cave and then focused on Ibrahim's face.

"Water," said Ibrahim. He touched the cup again to the man's lips and this time the man drank. He raised his head and Ibrahim helped him with his free hand. The man finished the cup and let his head drop back onto the wadded-up coat that was his pillow.

The man moved his lips, but no sound came out, and he winced as if the effort was painful. He licked his lips and tried again. "More." It was just a whisper. Ibrahim poured another cup. He held it to the man's lips, and the man held Ibrahim's hand in both of his as he drank. He sighed when the cup was empty and closed his eyes.

"Next time we will try sweet tea, yes?" said Ibrahim. The man slept.

Ibrahim brewed another cup. This tea bag was on its last legs, and he stirred in only a single, heaping teaspoon of sugar. He mouthed the ancient words of thanks and tasted the sweetness.

He selected a branch from his small wood pile and broke off a piece. He put it on the fire and held out his hands for the warmth. The smoke from the fire rose to the ceiling and then some exhalation from the depths pushed it out the mouth of the cave. The temperature in the cave was constant, even in the cool nights. The cave could be livable in the winter, he thought, but then the image of the snow drifts around the mouth mounting until they sealed it shut and the stream outside freezing came to mind.

Ibrahim thought of another cave he had lived in when he was a boy, in the mountains of his homeland after his family had fled their village. The armed men, mujahideen, had come to their village in the night, and the next morning they lined up the village officials against a wall in the square and executed them. Someone told the men that Ibrahim's father taught at the school and was a Sufi heretic from the city, so they came for him, next. They dragged him out into the dusty street and shot him there in front of Ibrahim and his family.

The mujahideen were gone before noon. The next day, the government soldiers came, too late to save anyone but not too late to round up some villagers they thought were jihadist sympathizers. They put some of them against the pock-marked wall in the village square and shot them. Others they beat publicly and then loaded them into the backs of their trucks and drove off.

Everyone in the village fled to the mountains above the valley. They lived in caves and tents as the army and the mujahideen fought for control of the villages below. The fields were not tended, the meager crop was not harvested, and winter set in. They starved. They died in droves. One morning, Ibrahim could not rouse his mother from sleep and she was dead before sunset. The family that shared their cave took her clothes and cooking pot and pushed the little Sufi heretics, Ibrahim and his younger sister, out into the cold.

Ibrahim took another sip of tea. He would not stay in the cave. As soon as the young man was able, they would find another place. Perhaps they could find a cabin lower down in the valley but still far from the fires and gangs of the city. A warm, safe place where they could winter. "Inshallah," he breathed the prayer into the hot cup of tea. His breath mingled with the wisp of steam that rose from the cup and disappeared in the quiet air.

* * *

The young man woke again later that morning. Ibrahim had just come in from gathering wood and dumped the load on the floor of the cave.

"Water," the young man said, soft but clear.

Ibrahim turned toward him. His eyes were open and he looked directly at Ibrahim.

"May I have some water?"

"Of course, habibi," said Ibrahim. "Coming right up."

He poured a cup of cold water and knelt beside the young man. He reached out with both hands and took the cup from Ibrahim and drank. He was clumsy, and water spilled over the scratches on his face leaving traces in the dirt. He handed the cup back to Ibrahim.

"More?" asked Ibrahim.

The young man nodded. "Please," he said.

"Do you want to try some sweet tea?"

The man licked his lips. "Yeah. Sure." he said.

Ibrahim poured some hot water from the kettle and mixed in some cold. He considered using a fresh teabag - the man was a guest, after all - but decided the stronger brew might be too much for him. He did not skimp on the sugar.

Ibrahim did not let him take the cup but held it while he drank. "Go easy," Ibrahim said. "Your stomach might not be ready for this."

The man took a drink, and then another, and then he gulped down the sweet liquid.

"Slowly, habibi. It might be too much. You don't want to throw it up."

The man settled back. He drew a deep breath and let it out. "Where am I?"

"You are in a cave in the mountains. I found you on the path. You were unconscious."

He frowned. "There were birds," he said. He gripped Ibrahim's sleeve and lifted his head. "Black birds... Did they get us? Did they get..." His voice trailed off and the urgency went out of his voice. His eyes searched Ibrahim's face and then became unfocused.

"Did they get who?" asked Ibrahim. "Were there people with you?"

The young man looked around the cave. He seemed lost, more lost than simply waking in an unknown place would explain.

"Am I habibi?" he asked.

"Yeah, sure, man. You're habibi, you're my..." Ibrahim searched for the right translation. "...my friend."

"No, is habibi my name?" he asked.

"No. It's Arabic. It just means my friend. It isn't your name. Don't you know your name?"

The man stared up at Ibrahim, a look of fierce concentration on his face which turned to confusion and then dismay. He dropped Ibrahim's sleeve and collapsed back. He sighed, closed his eyes, and slept again.

* * *

Ibrahim looked at the face of the sleeping man. He was young, just barely a man, really. The scraggly beard and battered face had made him appear older. The fear and confusion of his first words though, the voice itself, was that of a youth.

Ibrahim wondered what the young man was doing on a path so high in the mountains. There had been signs all along that Ibrahim was not the only survivor taking refuge above the valley. But without food or drink? No backpack or sleeping bag? He wouldn't have lasted more than a couple of nights. It was suicidal.

Had that been his intent? Had he turned? Had the virus driven the young man to despair and he determined then to end it all? But that's not how it went with Rose, he thought. She had simply curled up on her bed one day and refused to eat or drink or even respond. He had cared for her and sang her the songs that he remembered from his childhood when the wali - the Sufi miracle worker - had called him back from despair and death's dark door. But she just sank lower and lower. Rose had waited for death, given herself to it, but not actively pursued self-destruction.

Ibrahim thought back to how he had found him, sprawled across the path, the shattered walking stick gripped in his hand. The young man had hit out at something with that stick. His final conscious moments had been filled with anger and violence, as if he had turned and descended into fury. Could that be? How was it that he was no longer furious? When he woke just now, he was confused, but certainly not a berserker. Had he turned and survived? Had he recovered?

Ibrahim clutched his chest, as if stabbed in the heart. What was that, he thought, and then it came to him. It was hope. His eyes stung. He could barely breath.

"Allahu Akbar," he whispered. "Allahu Akbar."

* * *

It took several days. Sick in the morning, fine in the afternoon. And the appetite... Adele was eating chips or Twinkies or clutching a stick of pork jerky nearly all the time.

"Are we out of sardines?" she asked.

"I thought you hated little fish," said Rachel.

"That was before the world ended. Jesus! Is pork jerky all we have?" Adele rummaged through the food pack.

"That's all that was left. Dwight said some other scavengers had already hit the store. Took all the other stuff. Pork was untouched."

Adele emerged from the food pack with a bag of bacon flavored chips. She tore it open and shoved her hand in and extracted a pile of crushed flakes. "Are they idiots?" she said speaking with her mouth full. "New rule: no packing soup cans on top of chips."

Rachel broke a stick against her knee and added the pieces to a pile of kindling. "I don't think we have to worry. There's nothing left down there. Dwight said the place was picked clean."

Adele stopped chewing and looked at Rachel. Rachel looked up from the pile of kindling. "At this rate, we've got maybe two weeks of food left," she said.

Adele swallowed. She looked at the little cluster of tents. "It was cold last night, too," she said. "This isn't going to work in the winter."

"No shit," said Rachel. "They get - like - ten feet of snow up here."

Adele tried to imagine ten feet of snow on the mountains, pretty but deadly. A doe and a fawn emerged from the trees a hundred yards uphill from the camp. They turned their heads toward Adele and Rachel and stared, poised to run, but then the doe continued on her way down the hill and the fawn followed. Their coats were sleek and glossy.

Adele watched them as they picked their way down into the valley. "I have Jamie's hunting rifle," she said.

"Too bad we don't have Jamie," said Rachel.

Adele winced and put a hand on her stomach.

"Sorry, Deli," said Rachel. "I wasn't thinking."

Adele shook her head, as if it were of no importance. She wiped a tear away, and bit off a piece of jerky. Rachel looked at her face and then down at the hand on her belly.

"You OK?" she asked.

"I'm fine," said Adele. "Don't worry about it."

"I mean, in general. You know... like, you're not... pregnant or anything, are you?"

Adele did not answer right away, then she turned to Rachel. "I don't know, Rache. I don't know. I'm scared." Her lips trembled.

Rachel knelt by Adele and put her arms around her.

"I just feel so all alone," Adele said. She started to cry.

"Don't worry, Deli. You're not alone."

"I need Jamie. I just need Jamie to come home."

Rachel stared at the mountain slopes without seeing them. "We're here. I'm here." She stroked Adele's hair. "Everything is going to be OK. It's all going to be OK."

CHAPTER 27

Adele poked her nose out the tent door and sniffed. The morning air was cool and pine-scented. She caught a whiff of breakfast and looked over at the campfire where Rachel, Stevie, Emily and Eva hustled around. The smell of oatmeal made Adele's mouth water. The weeks of morning sickness were behind her. The months of ravenous appetite were upon her.

Maria pushed by her. "Oatmeal, again?"

Adele stood up and pulled on her boots. "Don't worry," she said. "I'll eat yours." She sprinted for the fire.

Maria shrieked and ran after her. "No you won't!"

Adele leaned over and peered into the pot. "Mmmm," she said. "Looks like just enough for me." She ladled out a bowl. Maria stood, her fists on her hips, and a you're-in-big-trouble look on her face. Adele considered. "OK," she said, "you can have breakfast..." She held out the bowl to Maria, who snatched it and turned to find a place to sit. "...just this once," Adele finished. Maria sat and ate, ignoring Adele with all the dignity a four-year old with oatmeal on her face could muster.

Caleb emerged from his tent and stretched. He had lost weight as they all had, but he looked better for it. He had gone from beefy to lean, and it was an improvement. He looked over at the campfire and caught Adele looking at him. He gave her a toothy smile and Adele turned back to her breakfast.

He came over to the fire and picked up a bowl. He dipped the bowl directly into the pot and scooped up some oatmeal. He ate where he stood, watching Adele go at her breakfast. "Over the flu, then?" he asked.

"Yeah, I guess so," she said. "I feel fine, today."

"You look fine," said Caleb. She did look fine. In fact, she was glowing in the morning sun.

Rachel snorted. Maria came over and leaned on Adele.

Caleb stopped eating and studied Adele for a few seconds. His expression changed. "Holy shit. You're pregnant!"

Rachel watched Adele's face, waiting for her answer.

Adele considered her bowl. "Could be," she said. She refused to look at Caleb.

"Knocked up! That little shit," he said.

"Cut it out, Caleb. Don't be an asshole," said Rachel.

"What's he being an asshole about, now?" Dwight walked up.

"She's pregnant," said Caleb. "That little shit Jamie knocked her up and left her."

Dwight looked pained. "Wow, Deli. Are you OK?"

"Yeah, yeah. I'm fine."

"You look OK," said Dwight.

"She's eating like a horse," said Eva.

Adele stood and her bowl fell out of her lap. "Thank you, Eva," said Adele. She turned and marched off. Rachel and Maria followed.

"That little shit," said Caleb to her back. "I didn't know he had it in him." He laughed.

"What a prick," said Rachel.

"What's a prick?" said Maria.

"Don't worry, Deli. You've always got us. Everything's going to be all right."

"What's a prick?" asked Maria.

Rachel took Adele's hand and stopped her. Adele turned and looked at her friend. Rachel had a funny expression on her face.

"You know," said Rachel, "I don't get it, but ever since you told me, sometimes I just want to sing. I know it's dangerous. We don't know shit about this. And Jamie...and all. But sometimes I'm just..." she searched for words, "happy... for you. For all of us."

Adele looked in Rachel's eyes and saw the truth of what she was saying. She threw her arms around her. "Oh, thank you, Rache. I know it's crazy. It couldn't be a worse time and it couldn't be a worse place. But sometimes, I just feel the joy of it." Tears ran down her cheeks.

"What's a..."

Adele looked down at Maria. "I'll tell you later," she said. And Maria, who knew the final word on something when she heard it, just scowled.

* * *

Adele's emotions were all over the place. One moment everything was fine. The next, she was consumed with self-loathing. She stood up and walked to the dinner pot. It was her third helping.

"God, I can't believe it. I'm eating like a pig." Rachel glanced up, gave her a twitch of a smile, and then returned to eating stew. It made it better, right, if you voiced the criticism yourself? How stupid, how utterly stupid to say that, Adele thought. She sat back down and crouched over her bowl.

"You're eating for two," said Caleb. She was showing now, and he looked at her belly. Adele gave him a disgusted look, and his smile faded to a frown. "Just trying to be supportive," he said.

Adele started to say something but thought better of it. A sense of being utterly alone swept over her. She couldn't afford to piss off her friends. Not now. Not with a baby on the way. Jesus! How could this happen? An image came to her, of Jamie, of his neck and shoulders, smooth and bare. Oh, yeah, she thought. Like that, dumb-shit.

Jamie! She sent his name out, with all the power of her need and desire. She spoke to the baby forming in her womb. Help me call your father. Jamie, she called. Don't be dead, Jamie. I need you. We need you.

* * *

The next day was cool. Clouds piled up down toward the coast, threatening rain. The group gathered under a tarp next to the campfire. Dwight said he'd go look for some place they could hole-up for the winter. Caleb said he would stay and protect the women-folk, but then Adele held up her handgun and declared that they could take care of themselves. Caleb muttered something about a momma-bear and then said he would go with Dwight. Everyone agreed.

They packed enough food for a week. There was an old Forest Service road a couple of miles below them in the valley, and they would follow it, looking for cabins or other buildings that could give them winter shelter. They left after lunch. Emily gave Dwight a big hug and told him to be careful. Caleb carried Leung's M-16. They turned and waved when they reached the edge of the trees, and then stepped into the shadows. A heavy mist moved along the mountainside. It began to drizzle.

They stepped out onto the road without realizing what it was. Grass covered the bare dirt and at first, they thought it was just a clearing in the woods, but this clearing was long and thin, and it finally dawned on them that this was a dirt road that the forest was taking back. A game trail ran through the tall grass and scrub brush.

"Which way?" said Dwight.

Caleb blew out a breath and looked both up and down the trail. "Less snow the lower we go," he said.

"Yeah, but more people," said Dwight. "Let's go up first." They turned and followed the trail up the valley.

They kept an eye out for cabins along the way, and even more so for hints of a road or driveway heading off into the woods. These would be overgrown, easy to miss.

"That could be a driveway," said Dwight. He pointed to a gap in the trees about as wide as a car. It seemed to curve back up the slope to the right. He waded through some tall weeds and examined the ground. "Yeah, there are ruts." He peered up the slope. "Let's check it out."

Caleb made his way to Dwight and they moved through the gap, Dwight in the lead. Dwight pushed a branch aside and held it so it wouldn't slap Caleb in the face. Caleb reached out for the branch and snapped it off. "What?" he asked, when Dwight frowned.

"We should be quiet. Someone might hear."

"Like who?" demanded Caleb. "No one's been this way for fucking forever."

Dwight turned and continued on. They made their way around a sharp bend and stopped. Ahead, visible through the trees, was a structure, the straight lines and sharp angles a stark contrast to the tangle of the natural growth.

Caleb pushed past Dwight and tromped up to the cabin. Dwight watched him go but held back, waiting until Caleb waved him on. "It's been burned," he said.

The cabin was small, and only one wall still stood. Tall weeds had sprouted inside it. Dwight picked his way around the foundation and stopped. He stood, looking at something in the weeds.

"What is it?" asked Caleb.

"Look at this," said Dwight.

Caleb walked over to him. In the weeds outside what might have been the back door, lay a skeleton. Shreds of clothing still clung to the bones: blue jeans, bits of plaid flannel. Bright red suspenders had survived almost intact and suggested a substantial man.

"Huh," said Caleb. He squatted down by the skull and pointed to a neat, round hole in the back of the head. "Someone shot him."

Dwight squinted at the woods around the little cabin. The trees seemed threatening, the dark beneath them sinister.

"His hands were tied." Caleb pointed to plastic clothesline wound around the wrists. He shook his head. "Someone executed this guy." Now Caleb stood and took a step back from the skeleton. He rubbed his palms on his parka and looked around. "Let's get out of here," he said.

They walked back down the driveway to the road. They both moved carefully, making little noise. Caleb refrained from breaking branches and held the M-16 at the ready.

After a few minutes, Dwight looked over his shoulder at Caleb. "It must have happened a long time ago, like maybe in the first few weeks."

"Yeah," said Caleb. "Maybe crazies. Maybe scavengers looking for food. Who knows?"

Do crazies tie people up, wondered Dwight? Would scavengers bother to burn down the cabin? With a shock, he realized that the violence of the scene back in the woods could have been done by either. Crazies or normal people, they left the same destruction in their wake.

"Hey, do you want me to take the lead?" asked Caleb.

"Huh?" said Dwight.

"Well, you're just standing there, you know? We need to cover some ground."

"Oh. Yeah. Go ahead." Dwight stepped to the side and Caleb took up the lead. They walked on in silence. The drizzle turned to rain.

* * *

The hike up the road was a slog. Dwight and Caleb were in their rain gear, but their boots were not waterproof, and the blowing rain trickled down their necks and backs. Bushes scratched at their rain pants and tore small holes.

The road must have been well-traveled, at one time, with many driveways branching off. People had built cabins, vacation homes, and hunting shacks, but all were now looted and burned. Only once did they encounter any sign of other survivors. They came on a campsite next to a mostly burned house. A small firepit and a single camp stool sheltered under an awning next to an old-fashioned canvas tent. No one was around, but the smell of cigarette smoke lingered. They scanned the woods.

"No one home," said Caleb.

"Yeah. I bet they're watching."

"Maybe." Caleb stuck his head in the tent. "Hey, canned goods. Let's load up."

"Not ours. Let's leave it."

"Bullshit," said Caleb. "Nothing belongs to anyone anymore. We have the gun," he held up the M-16, "we have the food."

"Leave it, Caleb. We have enough."

"Enough pork jerky. I don't know, man. Another dinner of that shit and I might be ready for Dwight stew."

Dwight considered this. "Do a trade," he said. "They're probably sick of chicken noodle soup and would kill for some pork jerky."

Caleb disappeared into the tent. He rustled around a bit and then reemerged. "OK," he said. "I've done the deal. I'm sure they'll be ecstatic." He looked at a small bouquet of wildflowers sitting on the camp stool. "What's that?"

"Hostess gift," said Dwight.

"Shit," said Caleb.

Dwight turned and walked back down the drive. Caleb swung his pack up, glanced around at the trees, and then walked quickly after him.

A quarter mile on up the valley, the road was blocked. A big Doug fir had fallen across it, and they had to scramble up the slope of the ditch and pick their way around the exposed tangle of roots. Once they were by, the road seemed different. The weeds and bushes were thicker, taller. Dwight had the sense that they had entered a world more wild, one where the human touch had been gone longer than back down the valley. The air was sweeter, without the hint of burnt linoleum, lumber and siding that had been with them all morning. Dwight found breathing easier. A tension he hadn't been aware of left his hands, his back and shoulders.

That night, they made camp off the road, a bit away on the uphill side in a small clearing next to a stream. They had a couple of cans of soup for dinner - Campbell's Beef with Barley and a can of Progresso Lentil which they ate with reverence. The wind sighing in the trees lulled them to sleep.

They found several mostly intact cabins the next morning. They had all been looted. The doors were usually smashed in and the cupboards emptied, but only a few of the buildings were burned. Dwight imagined that the scavengers who made it by the fallen tree were smaller groups, on a mission, focused on essential supplies with no time or taste for wanton destruction. Less dangerous than the crazies? He wasn't so sure. They walked on.

The sun had dropped below the mountains and the valley was in shadow when the road crested a hill and ran along a small lake. The water was on their right, about a hundred feet from the road. The other shore was maybe a quarter mile away, a steep, forested slope with lots of exposed rock running all the way down to the water. This side was level, and the trees between the road and the water had regular gaps.

"Hey. Look at that," said Dwight. He pointed at one of the gaps. A picnic table and a rusted grill poked up above the tall weeds. "This was a campground."

Caleb looked up and down the lake shore. Most of the gaps in the trees by the road had a grill and a table. "Yeah, there's more," he said. "Like, maybe a state park?"

They walked on. At a branch in the road was a sign, barely legible, that read "Lakeside Resort Cabins and Camp - Office". "Let's check this out," said Dwight, and they turned right on the branch. Up ahead was a small, log building in a larger clearing. They stopped just before they stepped out into the clearing to survey the scene. The small log building straight ahead looked like the office. Off to the left was another log cabin. Dwight stepped farther out into the clearing and counted. There were five small log structures, strung out along the lake shore. None were burned. The doors all seemed intact. "Holy shit," he said. "This is it."

Caleb came and stood next to him. He held the M-16 ready and looked up and down the line of cabins. The grass in the clearing was tall. There were some trails through it, but they wandered past the cabins, indifferent to the presence of the structures. No one had beaten paths to and from the steps up to their doors.

The metal roofs were covered with pine needles and a few larger limbs. Stove pipes poked up above the debris. The pipe on one cabin had been knocked over by a fallen limb. Caleb moved out into the clearing toward the office. He stood on tiptoe to peer through the closest window, then walked around the corner and approached the door. Dwight followed.

The door was weathered but still on its hinges. Dull, red paint was peeling off and flakes lay on the doorstep in a pile of dirt, needles, and pine cones. Moss was spreading across the small porch, undisturbed. Caleb looked at the door. Dwight stepped by him and put his hand on the doorknob. He held his breath and turned it. He pressed on the knob and the door shifted slightly but would not open. "Locked," he said. He touched the faceplate of the deadbolt lock above the knob.

"Look out," said Caleb. He reared back and kicked the door. The frame splintered, and the door slammed open.

"Jesus, Caleb! Way to let everyone know we're here."

"Yeah? Like who? Look around, Dwight. We're it." Caleb stepped through the door. A high counter like a hotel front desk was on their left, and on their right was a small store, aisles, shelves and racks, all empty. Straight ahead was another door with a sturdy, deadbolt lock. Caleb walked up to it, turned the knob and pushed. It didn't budge. He stepped back and kicked. The door rattled in its frame but did not open. He kicked again, and again, and finally the frame gave a little with a loud crack. He kicked again, and the door swung open, revealing a room lined with floor to ceiling shelves. Every shelf was crowded with boxes. Caleb reached out and touched one box with the tips of his fingers. It was labeled "Mars Candy Company."

"Oh, yeah. Oh, yeah," said Caleb, nodding. "This is it. This is the fucking mother lode."

CHAPTER 28

Ibrahim stood at the mouth of the cave and looked out. Fall was upon them, and a storm was blowing in. One-by-one the mountain peaks disappeared into the dark, swirling clouds. A sheet of rain swept up the valley. The wind whipped a stand of trees on the mountainside below him and roared up the slope.

"Whoa!" yelled Ibrahim. "We're about to be hit, habibi."

He took a step back and then turned and ran deeper into the cave as the wind and rain blew in. He joined Jamie by the fire. Smoke which normally wafted toward the entrance was pushed back into the cave. The wind was cold, and the floor of the cave was quickly soaked several yards in. They scrambled for their winter coats and threw more wood on the fire.

Jamie watched the storm. Something was funny about the rain at the mouth of the cave. It was falling slowly and at an extreme angle. Jamie got up and walked to the entrance. Sleet stung his cheek.

"Oh, man." He turned back to Ibrahim. "It's snowing!"

Ibrahim came and stood next to him. "This is not good. I'm making tea."

Ibrahim went back to the fire and poured tea for both of them. He held out a cup for Jamie who sat next to him.

"You know, habibi, I don't think this cave is going to be viable for us when it gets cold." He sipped his tea. "We need to think about our options, no?"

Jamie looked around the cave. "Where can we go?" he asked. "I mean, we've been so safe here. Like maybe the winter isn't the worst thing that could happen to us."

"Yeah... I've been in caves in the mountains in the winter, habibi. It is better I think to take our chances down below."

"We don't know what's down there, who is down there." Jamie frowned and looked at the sleet lashing the mouth of the cave. It was almost there, a memory. He shook his head. Did he want to remember? It felt dangerous, somehow. Not for him, dangerous for others. Did I do something, he wondered?

"There is only one way to find out, yes? If you want, I will go scout out the situation. I will come back and tell you what I've found. Then we can decide."

"It would be safer if we went together."

"It is no matter, habibi. I have made many trips down into the valley alone. That is why we have so many delicious beef jerky." Ibrahim grinned.

"Hmmmm... Another good reason you should not be allowed to go alone. How long do you think it would take?"

"A couple of days, a week at most."

"Well..." Jamie shrugged, "OK. When do you leave?"

"I'll leave when it stops snowing."

Ibrahim moved around the cave. He emptied out his backpack and repacked it with just the things he would need.

"Don't forget the jerky," said Jamie. "Take it all."

"No, no, habibi. Keep it. I am sure I will find food on the way. I think there was some freeze-dried Chinese left at one place. General Tso's Chicken, Green Curry Shrimp..."

"Green curry isn't Chinese. It's Thai," said Jamie. How did he know that? It was unsettling. Things popped up like that, from nowhere, little isolated factoids. He picked up a bunch of packages of jerky and walked over to Ibrahim's pack. He shoved them in. "Take the damn jerky."

"OK." Ibrahim held up his hands in surrender. He finished packing in silence.

The snow let up, turned to rain and then stopped. Ibrahim shouldered his pack. They walked to the mouth of the cave together.

"Hey, sorry about the damn jerky comment," said Jamie. "I'm just a little off balance, I guess."

"Not a problem, habibi. You take care. May Allah protect you."

"Be careful. If you're not back in a week, I'll come looking for you."

"Thanks, but I will be back before that, for sure, inshallah."

Jamie knew that inshallah meant "God willing", that nothing was for sure for Ibrahim. He put out his hand. "Yeah, well, you know, thanks. For everything."

Ibrahim took Jamie's hand and pulled him into a hug. "It is my pleasure, habibi."

He turned and started down the slope toward the trees. He waved when he reached them, and then disappeared in the forest.

* * *

Ibrahim hiked all afternoon down the mountainside through dark, dripping fir trees. He came out of the forest and walked across an open area where the bedrock lay exposed, wet and glistening. His foot slipped, and he landed hard on his back but cushioned by his pack.

"Shit," he said. He rolled over and levered himself up, first to his knees and then to his feet. He turned slowly, placing his feet with care, and surveyed the flat expanse. A blackened area caught his eye, and he walked over to it. This close, it was obviously a fire ring. He squatted down and held his hand over it, and then lowered his hand closer to the ashes, and finally picked up a stick and stirred the ashes. There were no live coals, only fragments of glass, and some melted plastic. All was cold. It was an old fire.

He looked up and scanned the mountainside and the tree line for any sign of the camper. There was none, and satisfied that he was alone, he straightened up and looked around the firepit. The storm had scoured the open area, but the arrangement of logs around the campfire suggested a gathering spot for a small group, not just a single individual. Who were they, he wondered. A little scrap of plastic peeked out from beneath one of the logs, fluttering in the wind. Ibrahim bent over and picked it up. He smiled. It was weathered and torn, but still clearly the wrapper from a stick of pork jerky.

He walked around the campground. To one side was a small stand of trees and a sturdy limb bore the visible scars of a rope. Ibrahim imagined the food pack suspended there above the reach of bears. On the other side of the fire was an area where the bedrock was covered with a layer of soil and pine needles. It was large enough for several tents, perhaps five or six. He crossed over to that area and walked around it.

Off to one side, where someone might pitch a tent if they were seeking a bit of privacy, were three stones stacked on top of each other, each smaller than the one below, a little pyramid or crude Buddha figure. Under the top stone was a zip lock baggie with a smudged, mostly white piece of lined, notebook paper folded up in it. Ibrahim lifted the top stone and held the baggy up to his face. A single word was written on the paper in a girlish hand, "Jamie". The name was underlined.

Ibrahim let his pack slip to the ground and sat on it. He held the baggy in both hands and turned it over and back. "Jamie," he said, reading the name. The "i" was dotted with a heart. A sense of sadness swept over him, a sense of loss and hope and desperation that seemed to emanate from the paper in the baggy. It was a message left in the wilderness, by a young woman, for a young man, he guessed. How long had it been there?

He started to open the baggy and then stopped. Should he read this, he wondered. Was Jamie the young man back in the cave, habibi? Should he take the message back to him, unread? Should he read it and then leave it under the rock in case Jamie, whoever he was, returned? He took the paper out of the baggy and held it, then he unfolded it and read.

"Jamie, my love," it started. "Be alive, be alive, be alive! Come down off the mountain and hold this letter in your hands. It is my heart you hold, like I hold you in my heart. Where are you!? It has become so cold at night. Spot and Maria just don't cut it.

We're moving camp. We can't stay here. It is too exposed, and we will all freeze to death if we stay here. Caleb and Dwight have found some cabins down in the valley. With beds and doors and windows and wood burning stoves. It's called Lakeside. Come find us! Come find me!

Go straight down the slope until you come to an old BLM road. It is dirt, not paved. Go up the valley on the road. Be careful! Dwight and Caleb said there might be people we don't know on the road. At the end of the road are six log buildings by a lake. You can't miss it. Maria, Spot and I are in the second-to-the-last cabin from the office.

Oh, please find this, Jamie. Please be alive. Please, please. I love you, and I have a surprise for you. I know you haven't turned. I know it in my heart. You were just angry for a little while. Come to me! Find me!"

It was signed "Deli", with a line of "XO"s and hearts underneath.

Ibrahim looked off in the distance at nothing in particular for several seconds. Then he looked back down at the note and read it again. When he was done, he refolded it, put it back in the ziplock baggie, resealed it, and put it back under the top rock of the little cairn.

He checked the weather. The clouds appeared to be breaking up and sunbeams lit up parts of the valley down toward the river. He was almost sure that the young man up in the cave was the Jamie from the girl's note. The little group had found winter shelter and it seemed that Jamie would be welcomed back with opened arms, literally. Ibrahim was less certain about his own welcome. He was older, a foreigner, a Muslim, a Sufi. People had never been particularly generous or gracious to him. The sun touched the mountainside, blinding him for a second, warm on his face. He smiled. Only Allah had been gracious to him, always and in all things. That was all he needed. He would go back up the mountain and fetch the young man. Together they would find the cabins and a warm, secure winter. Inshallah, he breathed.

Ibrahim stood and wrestled the pack up onto his shoulders. He turned back the way he had come and started the long trudge up the mountain where winter had already touched the slopes with snow. The sooner we get off the mountain, the better, he thought. He had taken two steps when he heard the voice behind him.

"Excuse me," she said.

CHAPTER 29

It was half-way between a polite "excuse me" and a combative "excuse me", and the voice reminded Ibrahim of something, of someone. He turned slowly, holding his hands out just a bit from his body. She was standing about thirty feet away, a young woman in light gray ski bibs turned-down at the waist. A big dog stood next to her and her hand rested casually on something tucked into her belt. She looked directly at him.

"Hello," he said.

"Do you always read other people's mail?"

He was silent for a few seconds. "I'm sorry. I did not mean to intrude."

She frowned and cocked her head.

"Are you Deli?" he asked.

"Adele, yes."

"Adele...Prada?"

"Yes. Who are you?"

"I am Ibrahim Zarruq. From the CDC. I knew your mother, Rose Prada."

Something odd happened to her face. It seemed to come apart. She put her hand up to her mouth, revealing the butt of the pistol in her belt. She came forward until she was just a few steps away. The sun broke through the clouds and the tears on her cheeks glinted.

"Is my mother dead?" she asked.

"I'm sorry. Yes. She died shortly after you and I spoke on the radio. She never regained consciousness. I buried her on the CDC grounds."

Adele turned her face away and blinked. She wiped at her tears and took a deep breath. Then she turned back to Ibrahim. "Thank you," she said.

"It was an honor," he said. "It was an honor to know your mother and to tend to her."

Adele was silent.

"Would you like some tea?" he asked.

She looked at him and seemed to consider the offer. "Sure." She turned and walked away from him. "Let me get my pack."

* * *

The small fire burned hot, and the water boiled quickly. Ibrahim poured it over the slightly-used tea bag in Adele's cup and waited politely for her to finish with the bag. Adele stopped in mid-dunk and met his gaze.

"Oh, sorry," she said, and held the dripping bag out to him. He took it with a quick smile.

"It is not the best tea, unfortunately. And after four or five cups, it grows weak. Perhaps that's a good thing that the taste is weak."

Adele managed a smile.

"Do you like sweets?" she asked. "I have a chocolate bar, here."

"That sounds lovely," he said. He had to swallow the saliva that rushed into his mouth and almost slurred his words.

Adele dug through her pack and produced not one but two Almond Mars bars. She held one out to Ibrahim who took it with shaking hands. He held it and bent his head slightly. He said a silent prayer of thanks, then unwrapped the bar and ate it slowly, biting off small chunks and chewing deliberately. Eight billion dead, but this Mars bar... He couldn't help it. He was overwhelmed by gratitude.

Adele watched him eat. "Yeah, we were like that for a couple of days after we found the storeroom." Ibrahim grinned and Adele smiled back.

"So," he said finally. "How do you come to be here?"

"I keep checking our old camp, here," she said. "I'm looking for someone."

"You are looking for your young man, Jamie?"

Adele's lips twisted into a sort-of smile, and she nodded. "He left us. He was afraid he was turning, afraid he would become violent and hurt us." She watched a squirrel scamper up a tree. Ibrahim waited. "It's been a couple of months," she said. "I keep checking."

"Your Jamie," said Ibrahim. "He is a young man, blond, about six feet? Skinny, long hair, wispy beard?" He struggled to think of anything else that would be more descriptive. We all have long hair and beards, these days, he thought. And who isn't getting skinny?

Adele studied Ibrahim's face. He could see the wheels turning. She's not sure she wants to know, he thought. "There is a young man living with me. He was almost dead when I found him, but he is almost fully recovered."

"What's his name?" she asked.

"He cannot remember his name. He cannot remember anything about himself."

"He can't remember anything? Like where he's from? His friends? His family?"

Ibrahim shook his head. "Nothing. He knows how to tend the fire, and all that. He can speak English. He is highly intelligent, I think. Just nothing about his personal life."

"Where is he now?" asked Adele.

"He stayed back at the cave. He said he wasn't ready to go out into the world. It's like he is afraid of something."

Adele pondered this. "Why did you leave?"

"We can't stay in the cave over the winter. I'm looking for winter shelter. For both of us."

Adele stared at her teacup and nodded to herself. "I can't speak for everybody," she looked up at Ibrahim, "but you would probably be welcome at the cabins. There's one that no one is staying in. And if, you know, you've been taking care of Jamie... You know, if it is Jamie, you could stay, for sure."

"That is very kind," said Ibrahim. They sat silently for a minute, sipping tea.

"The young man in the cave..." Ibrahim spoke softly. "He is traumatized some. I don't know how he would respond to your offer. I wonder if the danger we live with, now, all the time, hasn't perhaps damaged him." He glanced up at Adele. She was watching him, listening. "And if he did truly turn, and recovered, we do not know what that does to you. We don't know what comes back. Or for how long."

Adele looked back at her cup and then off to the side. She looked back up at Ibrahim and studied his face. She frowned. "You think he really turned?"

"I do. He must have been very weak when he finally succumbed, but still the signs of violence that I saw when I found him... Things were broken and scattered. He had clawed at himself. The scars on his face... They might never fade."

Adele turned her face away from Ibrahim. Neither spoke for several seconds.

"It's Jamie. I'm sure," she said. "I have to go to him."

Ibrahim simply nodded.

"How far is your cave?" she asked.

"Half a day coming down. A full day going up, if we get an early start and push it."

"If we start now? We have a couple hours of light, still."

"We could do that. There is a good campsite along the way for tonight. Do you have overnight gear?"

Adele smiled. "Toothbrush and everything," she said.

* * *

Jamie stepped to the mouth of the cave and looked out. He held the cup of hot tea in both hands up close to his lips and took careful sips. The rising steam warmed his face but then a gust of chill wind cooled his moist skin. Ibrahim had been gone for several hours. Jamie hadn't expected the cave to seem so empty.

Off in the distance, up the valley, a flock of black birds rose above the snowy slopes of the mountain and wheeled in the air. More and more birds joined the cloud until the sky that way was filled with their dark motion. Jamie frowned as he watched and took a step back into the cave.

The flock seemed to form a shape, a face almost. A young man's face with a beard and long, wild hair. The mouth of the face was twisted into an evil smile and the thing in the sky turned as the birds wheeled through the air and it seemed to look at Jamie, directly at him.

Jamie dropped the cup. It shattered on the rocks, and he stumbled back, turned and ran into the cave. The fire was bright in the dim space and he took refuge behind it. He watched the opening, as if expecting something dark and evil to rush in. He grabbed an armful of wood from the pile and threw it onto the fire.

It seemed like hours that he paced back and forth behind the wall of flames before he finally sat down close to its light and warmth. The sense of alarm left him and he heated some things for a simple dinner. He shook his head as he wiped the frying pan clean. He had to laugh at himself, at how fragile he must still be to imagine a face – his own face – appearing in the sky. A gust of cold air blew in from the night and he threw another log onto the fire, heedless of how quickly the precious supply of fuel would shrink.

CHAPTER 30

At first, he thought it was the morning fire, crackling and snapping in the cold of the cave. But then it came again, louder, closer, clear in the frosty mountain air outside. He turned his head toward the mouth of the cave, now almost closed by a snow drift, and listened. Do wolves bark, he wondered.

Then it came bounding into the cave along the narrow opening Jamie had trampled through the drift, and it was definitely a dog, a golden retriever, barking and jumping with all the joy packed into that breed, and Jamie tumbled backwards laughing as the dog licked his face and the hands he put up to protect himself.

"Easy there, easy," he said. The dog backed off a step. "Sit!" he commanded, and the dog obeyed.

"Hello!" called a high voice and the sunlight at the mouth of the cave flickered as someone came in. The figure was bundled up in a hooded parka and wore shiny, well insulated ski pants. For all the concealment, it was obvious from the way she moved and held herself that this was a woman. She unzipped her parka and threw the hood back. She shook her hair out and it formed a thick cloud around her head. She was just a silhouette, with the sunlight behind her, and she paused to let her eyes adjust to the dim interior.

"Hello," replied Jamie. He got to his feet. "My god, another human being! What are you doing here? I am so glad to see you!" He walked up to the woman with his arms up and hands open, half in greeting and half in amazement. She was a young woman, he saw. The thick dark hair framed a pale, olive face. Her eyes were dark with long lashes that glittered with melted snowflakes. And she was smiling, grinning so bright her face seemed lit from within.

"Oh, Jamie," she said. She threw her arms around him and pressed herself hard against him. He touched her shoulder, tentatively, with one hand. She looked up at him, studied his face, and the smile faded. "Jamie?" she said. "You don't recognize me?" She traced the line of a scar on his cheek with her fingertips.

Jamie frowned, and shook his head slightly. "I'm sorry. Did I know you?"

The words seemed to take the woman's breath away. She stood frozen for a moment, and then moved back from him, her face working. She took her hands off him and held them awkwardly, as if unsure what to do with them, and then lowered them slowly. She stared at his face.

The light at the mouth of the cave flickered again, and Ibrahim came in, stamping his feet. "Hey, habibi," he called. He walked up to Jamie and gave him a bear hug, lifting him off his feet.

"Hey, Ibrahim," said Jamie, when Ibrahim set him down and he could breathe again. "Man, am I glad you made it. That snow... I thought I'd never see you again."

"That snow is getting deep, habibi. We almost didn't make it. Hey, you have hot tea?"

"Yeah, yeah. Come on. Sit down." Jamie stepped to the fire. He added a big log to it and started fussing with tea bags and cups.

Ibrahim looked at Adele and raised his eyebrows in a question. Adele nodded. Ibrahim turned to Jamie and took the steaming cup of tea. Adele took hers with both hands and blew on it, avoiding Jamie's eyes.

"So, look, habibi," said Ibrahim, once they were seated around the fire, Spot at Jamie's feet. "Adele recognizes you. From before." Jamie looked at Adele who gave him a brief smile but did not speak.

"Your name is Jamie Montane, and you used to live in Darnell, a town down on the river." Jamie looked from Ibrahim to Adele and then back to Ibrahim. "Adele knew you in high school."

"Do you remember anything?" asked Adele. The firelight glinted off drops of melted snow on her eyelashes.

"I've been trying," said Jamie. He shook his head. "I...I remember English. I mean, I can talk. I can dress myself," he held out his arms to prove it. "But the personal stuff, you know, like my name or my age or my parents, or my friends," he looked up at Adele. A tear trickled down her cheek. This was all wrong, he thought. "I can't remember anything."

"You were camping with a group of friends down the mountain," said Ibrahim.

"Maria, Rachel, Stevie, Caleb, Dwight?" Adele listed the names. "Deli?" She searched his face.

Jamie sat still for a second, staring at the fire without seeing. Then he looked back at Adele and shook his head. "Nothing," he said. "I just can't remember."

"What happened to you?" she asked.

"I don't know. The first thing I remember is waking up in this cave with Ibrahim singing."

"Adele says you exiled yourself," said Ibrahim.

"You thought you were turning. You were afraid you were going to turn on me, on us. You were afraid you would hurt us. So, you ran off. In the middle of the night." Adele paused. "I... We... looked for you for days but we couldn't find you. Even Spot couldn't find you."

"Spot?" said Jamie. The dog lifted his head and looked at him. "He doesn't have any spots." Jamie frowned, as if trying to think of something.

"Yeah," said Adele. "You said his name was a joke. He was basically your dog."

Jamie and the dog looked at each other for a second, and then Jamie reached down and scratched him behind the ears. "Good dog," he said. Spot closed his eyes and grinned. Jamie scratched the top of his head and down his back. It seemed like just the right thing.

He looked at Adele, at the tears, her posture, how she clasped her hands together. "We were close," he said to her, a statement, not a question. She met his gaze and nodded.

"I'm sorry. I'm trying to remember."

Adele stood up and walked out of the cave. The light flickered as she passed through the narrow opening.

"You see much, habibi," said Ibrahim. He opened his mouth to say something more, but hesitated.

"So much pain," said Jamie. "Maybe it would have been better if you had just left me on the path."

* * *

Jamie was packed and ready to go. It had taken less than an hour to do the job. Food, tea bags, one of the down sleeping bags and a thick sleeping pad was all they took. Jamie had almost no extra clothing, and they left behind most of the equipment Ibrahim had packed up to the cave over the summer months. The kitchens down at the cabins were well-equipped.

They ate a quick lunch. Adele plowed through beef jerky and oatmeal like there was no tomorrow. The beef jerky was such a relief after all the pork jerky she had been eating. She shared that with Jamie who welcomed the pork flavor. It was a change of diet for him. Jamie and Ibrahim insisted on tidying up after the meal. "We might want to come up here next summer," said Ibrahim.

They shouldered their packs and started for the mouth of the cave. Jamie paused there and turned to look back. The cave and the mountainside were all he knew of the world. This had been his only shelter and the bare rock walls seemed suddenly cozy and safe. Outside, the wind howled. "Did you hear that," he asked.

"Yeah, I think the weather might be changing," said Ibrahim.

"It sounded like wings, like a flock of birds," said Jamie.

"It's clouding up," said Adele. "We need to get going."

"OK. Let's roll," said Jamie, and they walked out into the gathering storm.

* * *

Spot led the way, running ahead and then back, breaking a trail through drifts that had formed in the few hours since Adele and Ibrahim had come up the mountain. Ibrahim and Jamie trudged along behind the dog. Adele brought up the rear, welcoming the privacy of being last.

She watched Jamie, how he held himself, how he walked. She listened to his voice when he spoke a word of warning about the path or complained about the wind. It was definitely Jamie, and she could almost pretend that all was well again, that she could speak of a time before and they would laugh at the shared memory. But he would turn, perhaps holding a branch so it wouldn't slap her in the face or reaching out for her hand to help her over a rough patch, and their eyes would meet. Adele would look in vain for the flash of recognition or heat or amusement that had always been there. Instead, Jamie's glance was guarded, as if he was aware of the pain that his failure to remember brought her and he felt it as a personal failure, a shameful weakness.

The storm came up the valley, a wall of dark clouds moving fast. They entered the trees just before it hit and welcomed the shelter. They had maybe an hour of light left, and it was already dim under the firs.

Jamie and Ibrahim stopped and were talking when Adele came up. Ibrahim turned to her. "There are some rocks a little way ahead that will shelter us from the wind. It is a good place to camp for tonight, I think."

"Yeah, I remember. Sounds good," said Adele. A dark strand of hair escaped her hood and fluttered around her face in the wind. She pulled the mitten off one hand and tucked the strand back into place. Jamie watched. Adele pulled her mitten on and pushed ahead. Jamie and Ibrahim fell in behind, and Spot shouldered by her legs, anxious to be out ahead of everyone.

They pitched a single tent in the lee of the rocks and crawled inside to eat a cold meal of jerky and hard, frozen candy bars. They still had a working flashlight, but after the meal Adele turned it off to preserve the batteries. It was pitch black in the tent, and they got in their sleeping bags for warmth. This was a complex maneuver in the little tent with three people and a dog, three back packs, boots and the puffy down parkas. Adele smacked someone in the face. "Oh, sorry!" she said.

"A mere flesh wound," said Jamie.

Adele smiled in the dark. She lay next to him, her back turned, trying not to invade his space. Ibrahim and then Spot started snoring. She sensed Jamie's presence. It was like the ground sloped toward his body and she curled up away from him so she wouldn't slide down that slope and crowd him. Was it just her, or was he, too, awake? She could hear his breathing, and it seemed he was close, turned toward her. Finally, his breathing became deep and regular.

She put her hands on her stomach. Had it moved? When did that normally happen? Where was YouTube when you needed it? Did it feel the closeness of its father? Or was this just indigestion? Sleep was a long time coming.

* * *

He came awake as soon as she moved. They had shifted in the night and somehow Adele was snuggled up against him and his arm was as much around her as his sleeping bag would allow. He drew it back and rolled away from her as far as he could in the cramped space. He started to whisper an apology, but an overwhelming sense of fear rose up in him and he struggled to form the words.

"Sorry," he managed finally, a whisper.

"I'll be right back," she said. "Gotta pee." She fumbled around and pulled on her boots and a coat. Jamie heard the tent door unzip and a flood of cold air hit his face until Adele zipped it up again.

He lay there in the dark, wrapped in his own arms, while the fear slowly diminished. What was this, he wondered. What am I afraid of? But he knew exactly what he was afraid of. He was afraid of himself and what he was capable of, afraid that he was a danger to others and Adele most of all.

Adele returned and crawled into her sleeping bag. She seemed to sense his reserve and settled as far from him as the small space would allow. The wind had come up in the night and the fabric of the tent fluttered. Jamie stared upwards into the dark which seemed to extend beyond the tent ceiling, a limitless expanse where one could fall forever. He lay awake for what seemed hours, listening to the wind and the beat of it against the tent, so like the sound of a million wings flapping in the endless black of the night. All he wanted was to reach out and touch Adele, but something whispered to him that to allow himself to touch her would put her in the gravest danger. So he laid there, fingers digging into the flesh of his own arms until shortly before dawn when, exhausted, he fell asleep.

CHAPTER 31

"Almost there," said Adele. "They're at the top of the hill." It was after dinner, and the light was fading as they approached the cabins.

Spot was in the lead, running ahead and then turning and waiting for them to catch up or sprinting back to urge them on. Adele was next. Ibrahim and then Jamie brought up the rear.

Jamie paused and shifted the weight of the pack on his shoulders. The journey had taken more out of him than he expected. They had pushed to make the cabins in three days, and this last uphill leg seemed especially hard. Jamie leaned on his walking stick and watched as the others pulled away from him. He was afraid. Adele had explained to Jamie and Ibrahim who all was living in the cabins and had told Jamie a little about how he knew them. Maria, Caleb, Dwight, Rachel, Stevie, Emily and Eva. Each name landed with a little shot of anxiety. Each brief history Adele offered felt like an indictment to Jamie, a description of how he would disappoint and fall short.

Spot ran back, past Adele and Ibrahim all the way to Jamie. The dog jumped up on him and put his paws on his chest and tried to lick his face. Jamie smiled despite himself and scruffled Spot's head. "Good dog," he said. It was easy with Spot. The love had been immediate and mutual. No history seemed to be required. Adele and Ibrahim had turned when Spot ran by and stood looking down at them.

"All good, habibi?" called Ibrahim.

"Yeah, I'm good," said Jamie, and started after them. They waited until he caught up, and then they pushed on up to the top of the hill. Spot ran ahead, barking now.

"See the picnic tables?" asked Adele, pointing. "We were, like, what the hell are picnic tables doing in the middle of the wilderness?" She seemed to be chattering, as if the silence had become awkward. "And then Caleb and Dwight showed us the resort." At the end of the road was a small cabin, and several people came into view. Spot rushed to them and then back to Adele, Jamie and Ibrahim, leaping into the air and barking.

A small figure broke from the group by the cabin and came running toward them, dark hair flying behind her. "Jamie," she yelled.

This is going to be very, very hard, thought Jamie.

It was as bad as he had feared, perhaps worse. Adele handled the introductions, explaining to the group that Jamie had no memory of the time before he woke in Ibrahim's cave. No one seemed to get it except perhaps Caleb. Dwight, Rachel and the rest gave Jamie big hugs, but Caleb reached out and shook Jamie's hand like they were being introduced for the first time. Jamie felt a flash of gratitude at Caleb's sensitivity, but despite Caleb's smile, something in his expression – in the eyes – made Jamie think that Caleb's reserve reflected what had gone before just like the hugs from everyone else.

Maria had clutched Jamie's leg and wailed. "You don't remember me," she accused.

Without thinking, Jamie picked her up and kissed her on the cheek. "Hey, sweetie," he said. "There's no reason to cry. It's all OK." He stroked her hair, but she wriggled out of his grasp and ran and threw herself into Adele's arms. She rested her head on Adele's shoulder and refused to look at him for the rest of the evening.

Ibrahim got a warm welcome. He teared up a bit as the group gathered around him and for a second, he seemed to gasp for air as if drowning in a deep ocean though there were only eight of them. Jamie wondered how long it had been since Ibrahim had been around this many people.

They all trooped over to Rachel and Stevie's cabin, and she heated up some cans of beans on the old wood burning stove. Everyone crowded around the table while the three travelers ate. All the bodies made the room warm, and soon the couch in the sitting area was piled high with discarded coats and scarves.

"Tell us everything," Emily said to Jamie, who looked up at her and then quickly back to his plate.

Dwight watched Jamie. "Yeah. Ibrahim. You especially," he said. "We know how things went down in the valley, you know? But we don't know anything about the rest of the world."

"Ibrahim worked with my mom at the CDC," said Adele. "He took care of her...when she turned."

"Ah," said Dwight. Everyone was silent for a second.

The warmth, the food, all the people were too much for Jamie. Fatigue swept over him and he swayed in the chair. Ibrahim put out a hand to steady him.

"Whoa, habibi. Maybe it is time to rest, yes? It has been a long day."

"Oh, yeah, of course," said Rachel and everyone jumped up, talking at once, apologetic and solicitous.

"I figured Jamie and Ibrahim could take the empty cabin," said Adele.

"Yeah, yeah," said Dwight. "Let's get you moved in." He hoisted Jamie's backpack on one shoulder and Stevie and Eva both picked up Ibrahim's pack, each grabbing a strap and lugging it between them. The group walked across to the cabin, their passage marking the virgin snow around the dark building.

* * *

It was a bed, a big double bed that crowded the small room. After sleeping on the ground in a big cave for all his known life, Jamie found it hard to breath in that room. He stared, then he turned around and stepped across the narrow hall into the other bedroom. It had two small twin beds with thin mattresses on bare metal springs. Ibrahim had thrown his pack on one and sat on the other.

"Hey," said Jamie. "Why don't you take the big bed."

"No, no, habibi. I am fine here."

"Please," said Jamie. Ibrahim looked at him.

"Yeah, sure, I'll take the luxury room," he said. Jamie stepped aside, and Ibrahim carried his stuff across the hall. He dropped his pack on the floor, turned around, and then fell back onto the bed with his arms stretched wide. The bed springs screeched.

"Ahh!" he said, a long, drawn out sigh.

Jamie stood at the door and waited a second. Ibrahim did not move, and Jamie frowned. Then Ibrahim started snoring. A smile flitted across Jamie's face. He returned to his bedroom and sat at the foot of a bunk. He flopped back, and a cloud of dust rose. It swirled around above him in the light of the kerosene lamp like a distant flock of birds. Jamie closed his eyes and slept. He dreamed of clouds of black birds, beaks and talons tearing.

* * *

"Why doesn't Jamie remember us?" asked Maria.

Adele pulled the covers up to Maria's chin and tucked them in. It got cold in the cabins at night unless someone got up in the dark and fed another log to the stove.

"He's been sick," said Adele. "He can't remember anything. He can't remember any of us. He can't even remember his mom and dad."

Maria looked up at Adele. Does she remember her mom and dad, Adele wondered. And would it be a bad thing if she couldn't?

"Will he get better?" Maria asked.

"We don't know. Sometimes memories come back." Adele looked out the bedroom window into the winter-dark night. A window in Jamie's cabin was dimly lit by the low glow of a lamp.

"He just doesn't want to remember." Maria turned to face the wall and pulled the covers over her head.

Adele laid her cheek down close to Maria's. "Sure he does, pumpkin," she said, but now she wondered. There was a wariness in Jamie, like he was guarding against some danger. But what danger could the group of friends pose? He doesn't trust us? He doesn't trust me, she thought. She sat up.

"Where's Spot?" she asked.

Maria did not answer. Adele got up and walked through the cabin. Spot was not curled up by the stove or on the couch. She opened the front door and checked, but there was no Spot waiting there. She threw on her down jacket, flipped up the hood and went out to stand on the little porch. There was one obvious place to look. She started off toward the cabin with the dimly lit window.

Spot sat up and whined as she approached Jamie's front door. "What are you doing out here in the cold, doofus?" she asked. She patted him on the head. She looked back toward her cabin but then turned and tapped on Jamie's door. There was no answer, so she tried the doorknob. It turned, and the door swung open. Spot pushed by her and she followed him in.

Spot padded through the main room down the short hallway. He paused at the doors to the bedrooms and looked first one way and then the other. He disappeared through one of the doors, and bedsprings creaked.

Adele walked to the doorway and stood looking in. Jamie was curled on his side on the bare mattress. His boots were still on. Spot had wedged himself between the wall and the sleeping figure and looked at Adele as if to say "Yeah, I'm on the bed. So what?" Jamie shifted in his sleep and threw an arm over the dog.

It was all she could do not to climb into the bed with them. She looked over her shoulder at the room with the double bed where Ibrahim snored. Jamie had made a choice, she knew. Maybe Maria was right. Maybe he did not want to remember.

She unstrapped the sleeping bag from Jamie's pack and pulled it out of the stuff sack. She unzipped it and spread it out over the sleeping man/boy and his dog. She bent over and put her face close to his. She breathed in and could smell him, almost taste him. She touched her nose to his cheek and put her lips close to his ear. "Remember me," she mouthed, silently she thought, but he stirred in his sleep and murmured something. When he was still, Adele straightened up. She looked at the lantern, debating whether to blow it out but decided Jamie might need some light, something that let him see where he was and that he was safe if he woke in the night.

She returned to Maria and her own cabin. Adele was exhausted but laid there staring for what seemed hours into a dense dark that hovered above her bed just below the ceiling. Finally, she slept.

CHAPTER 32

He heard the hard crack of the first gunshot in his dream. His eyes were open when he heard the echo and he was on his feet at the window when he heard the second shot. A small group of people stood at the edge of the cabins looking off into the woods. One held a long gun, an M-16 it looked like, and aimed it at something out of view.

The shooter pulled the trigger again, and this time let off a long burst of automatic fire. Spent shells spewed from the rifle and glinted in the sunshine as they fell into the snow. Small figures, Maria and Stevie, Jamie guessed, clapped their mittens to their ears and jumped up and down. The gunman turned, and Jamie recognized Caleb. Caleb grinned at the others and pumped the rifle above his head, triumphant.

Jamie grabbed his coat on his way through the main room and jerked the front door open. Something made him close it quietly behind him, and he paused before he rounded the corner of the cabin. He stuck his head out and looked at the group. They seemed at ease, chatting and smiling. Jamie searched the woods where Caleb had aimed. There was nothing but the tangle of brown, winter brush beneath dark fir trees.

Caleb waved. "Hey! Don't worry! I won't shoot you." He laughed, and Jamie stepped out from behind the cabin. He walked over to the group, the snow making squeaking sounds at each step as he approached. Caleb gave him a big grin, and Adele and the others gave him very welcoming smiles. It looked like they had to work at it. Maria stood back, her expression unreadable.

"Hey," he said.

He got a chorus of hey and good morning, back.

"What are you shooting at?" Jamie asked.

"Target practice," said Caleb. "Dwight and I are going hunting."

"Oh, wow," said Jamie. "What for?"

Caleb and Rachel spoke simultaneously. "Deer," he said. "Anything he can get," she said. She grinned, and Caleb's smile slipped a bit.

"We're running a little low on food," said Adele. "There was a storeroom with some stuff in it, but we kind of plowed through it."

"Mars bars," yelled Stevie. He did a little dance in the snow.

Ibrahim walked up. "We have some food," he said. A sunbeam seemed to brighten everyone's faces.

"Some cans of chili, beef jerky," said Jamie. The light seemed to dim.

"At least it's not pork jerky," said Dwight.

"Venison steaks, tonight!" said Caleb.

"You serve steaks tonight and I'll put you back on my nice list," said Rachel. She batted her eyelashes.

Ibrahim looked embarrassed.

"Don't worry," said Rachel. "My virtue is safe."

Dwight snorted.

And Rachel couldn't help herself. She hooked an arm through Ibrahim's, cocked her head just so, and looked up at him out of the corner of her eye. "So, how much of that chili did you say you had?" she asked.

Ibrahim stammered, and everyone laughed, even Ibrahim.

* * *

The bread was a revelation. Rachel had baked it fresh that morning and the slice that she cut for Ibrahim was still warm when he picked it up. He looked down now at his plate and the few crumbs scattered on it. Some were blackened: wood stoves were tricky. Ibrahim resisted the urge to lick the plate. Instead, he pressed his finger onto each crumb and brought it to the tip of his tongue.

Rachel watched and smiled. Adele, Stevie and Maria were clearing away the lunch dishes. Jamie had gone back to his cabin to rest.

"That was wonderful," said Ibrahim. "I didn't think I would ever taste bread, again. God is good."

The smile faded from Rachel's face. She sat back and waved a hand dismissively. "Right," she said. "Not including the eight billion people thing."

Ibrahim looked up at her. "What thing is that, Rachel?" he asked.

"You know... The both-my-parents-dead thing. The all-our-families-dead thing. The eight-billion-people-dead-thing." Rachel gave Ibrahim a big, phony smile.

Adele turned from the sink. She crossed her arms and leaned back against it, watching her friend.

Ibrahim was silent. For some reason, a Zen story, a Zen koan he had heard once came to mind.

The Zen master asks the student an impossible question. He places a cup of tea in front of the student. "Does the tea have buddha-nature or not?" he demands.

The student knows that everything has buddha-nature. So why is the master asking?

"Yes," he answers. "The cup of tea has buddha-nature."

"Wrong answer," says the master. "Does the cup of tea have buddha-nature or not?"

The student is confused. "No," he tries. "The cup of tea does not have buddha-nature."

"Wrong!" replies the Zen master. "Does the cup of tea have buddha-nature?"

Now the student sits, staring at the cup. After a few seconds, he reaches out his hand, picks up the cup, and sips the tea. Then he puts the cup down again.

The Zen master grins. "Right answer!"

Is Allah merciful, wondered Ibrahim? He looked at Rachel's hand and then into her eyes. He reached out his hand and placed it gently over hers.

Rachel searched Ibrahim's face. A single tear rolled down her cheek. She stood, picked up her dishes and walked them over to the sink and then turned and walked out the door.

"What's the matter with Rachel?" asked Maria.

"Nothing," said Adele. "She's OK. It's OK."

And Maria seemed satisfied.

* * *

The hunters returned after dark, empty-handed. Caleb and Dwight stopped by their own cabin to change out of wet clothing and then joined the group in Ibrahim and Jamie's cabin. The newcomers were hosting a dinner of chili and beef jerky. Not fresh meat, but a welcome change from lentil bean soup and pork jerky.

"Yay, the hunters!" cried Rachel and everyone raised their glasses.

"We almost had a deer," said Caleb. "We hit it, but it got away."

"Did it leave a trail?" asked Jamie. "Could we find it tomorrow?"

"Yeah... I'm not sure," said Caleb. Dwight was busy dishing up his plate at the stove and said nothing.

"Not sure about what?" asked Rachel.

"Well, it was getting dark..." said Caleb.

"Oh, yeah. Not smart to go wandering around at night in the mountains in winter," said Emily.

"No shit," said Caleb. He smiled at her, and she smiled back.

"We found the start of the trail. There was blood, you know, so we know Caleb hit it at least once," said Dwight.

"What do you mean, at least once?" asked Jamie.

For a second no one answered. Then Caleb picked up a glass of vodka and sipped. "I'm pretty sure I hit it more than once."

"How many shots did you get off?" asked Jamie.

Caleb looked annoyed. "I emptied the clip. It was on full-auto."

"You machine-gunned Bambi and we don't even get a steak?" asked Rachel.

"We'll have steak tomorrow. Bambi won't last the night."

A wolf howled in the distance, and Jamie frowned. "I'm not so sure the steaks will last the night."

"You want to go get it? I'll point you in the right direction," said Caleb.

Jamie looked at Caleb and thought of the hunting rifle. Adele had brought it to him that afternoon. "It's yours," she said, and he took it from her and without thinking had worked the bolt to make sure it was unloaded. How had he known to do that, he wondered? The rifle had been heavy and felt right, familiar in his hands.

"I'll pass," said Jamie. Something stirred in his chest, a rustling of wings. Caleb looked away.

* * *

Jamie stood at the kitchen window and watched Dwight and Caleb set out to find the deer. It was a still morning, and the sunlight glistened on the snow. They tromped off through the drifts, following their own tracks from the day before.

Lunch time came, and they were still not back. Jamie sat on his front porch whittling a ramrod for the rifle from a piece of hardwood he had cut in the forest. He stopped and listened. The sound of the M-16 came, faint but clear in the cold air, a short burst of automatic fire, then a longer burst. Jamie waited for more, but there was only the sound of snowmelt dripping off the cabin's roof.

Adele and Maria walked up. "Well, at least we know they're still out there trying," said Adele.

Jamie look at her. Was this implied criticism, he thought? Should I be out there? He studied her face.

"Not that anyone else should be out there," she said. "I didn't mean you... I mean, like, everyone understands you're still not, you know, a hundred percent."

He smiled to let her off the hook. "Don't worry about it. I'm feeling OK."

Maria sat next to him, dangling her legs off the porch. "What's that?" she asked.

"I'm making a ramrod. You use it to push a cloth through the barrel of the rifle to clean it."

"Does it get dirty?"

"It does if you shoot it."

"Are you going to shoot it?"

Jamie looked up at Adele. "Yeah, I'm going to shoot it. I'm going to help with the hunting."

"You don't need to push yourself," said Adele. "How long will a deer last us, anyway?"

Jamie considered. "How many are we?" He counted on his fingers and then looked back to Adele. "Ten?" She had a funny expression on her face. Jamie couldn't quite figure it. He shrugged. "Hell, if I know. We'll see. I hope."

"Rachel says Deli is eating for two," said Maria.

Jamie looked at Maria, and for several seconds, no one spoke. Then he looked at Adele. His eyes dropped to her stomach and then he looked back at her face. She was watching him.

"We should talk," she said.

CHAPTER 33

Maria protested, but finally went off to hang out with Stevie and Rachel. Adele sat on the porch steps. She watched Jamie whittle at his stick.

"So, um..." she began. "Like Maria said, I'm pregnant." She waited for Jamie to say something, but he was silent. She swallowed. "You're the father."

Jamie stopped whittling. He stared at the ground in front of him.

"I know you don't remember any of this. About us..." She watched his face, searching for any sign of recognition or memory. "And it's not like you knew about this, you know, when you left." His face seemed hard, now. He frowned at the pile of wood shavings at his feet. He turned his head and looked at her. He seemed stricken, his lips slightly parted, the cloud of his breathing coming in short bursts. "I'm somewhere in my first trimester. Due in the summer... sometime." What else could she say? "I'm fine," she said. "We're...healthy... I think."

Jamie stood up, knife in one hand, stick in the other.

"You're not... I don't expect anything from you," she said. "I just had to tell you. You had a right to know. Everyone else knows. It was going to come out one way or the other."

"Does everyone know I'm the father?"

"Yeah." She nodded.

"And... And like there's no doubt about that?"

Adele eyebrows went up. "None." She enunciated carefully.

Jamie looked away, out across the open area around the cabins to the woods and the mountains beyond.

"I have to think," he said. He turned and walked into his cabin. The door slammed behind him.

Adele felt the chill of a tear on her cheek. She wiped it way with the sleeve of her parka and got up. She walked back to her cabin. It was cold inside and she threw a log onto the coals in the stove. She put the kettle on and made herself a cup of instant coffee when the water boiled. She sat at the kitchen table where she could see Jamie's cabin out the window. She had lost him. She lost him when he first ran away. And then she lost him all over again when she saw him in the cave but he did not remember her. And now again. She was alone, over and over and now finally. A darkness came into her mind. Her coffee grew cold.

She watched Jamie when he emerged from his cabin, rifle in hand, and set off into the woods. He did not follow the tracks left by Dwight and Caleb. He went another way.

* * *

Jamie pushed on up the slope. He was breathing hard and soon unzipped his down jacket. The rifle was heavy, an older model with a wooden stock. He shifted it from one hand to the other and finally slung it over his shoulder. He reached a level spot and leaned on a stump to catch his breath. The snow around him was unbroken by tracks.

Jamie held his breath and listened. There was no sound but the creaking of trees and the whisper of the afternoon breeze. Off in the distance, a lone bird soared in the clear air, big and black. It called. A raven, thought Jamie. He watched it, trying to think only of the expanse of air over the mountains and the movement of deer through the woods above the valley.

He walked along the mountain until he crossed a stream. Then he turned and walked down along the stream, moving slowly, placing his feet carefully. He unslung the rifle, checked that it was loaded, and held it in both hands.

He stopped. Ahead a ways, the snow was disturbed, a path crossing the stream. The saplings there along the bank had bare spots gnawed in their bark. Jamie stepped over to an outcropping of rock and settled behind it where he could see up and down the path through the trees. The wind was blowing in his face. It was right.

The sun was lower in the sky and the shadow of the mountain across the valley crept closer. The air was colder, and Jamie zipped his jacket and adjusted his scarf. Something caught his eye, a flicker of dark through the trees down the path. Jamie aimed the rifle at the spot where the path crossed the stream and waited.

A doe appeared and paused at the edge of the trees. She tested the air and looked both up and down stream. Jamie was absolutely still and held his breath.

The doe stepped into the open and a yearling followed. They walked to the edge of the stream and stepped into it. The yearling drank, but the doe took one last glance around before it lowered its head to drink. Jamie took a breath and held it. He aimed for the doe's brain - the quickest and least painful death, but then lowered his aim to the doe's chest - less likely to miss. He clicked the safety off like Bonney had taught him - the last thing you do before pulling the trigger. The doe and the yearling both looked up, directly at Jamie, and leaped away.

Jamie crouched, unmoving, behind the rocks. Who is Bonney, he thought. He let his breath out. The image of a tall thin man with longish hair and beard touched with gray came to mind. Jamie pushed at the edges of the image, tried to add to it. What was the man wearing? Where was he? What was around him? Who was he? But the image faded like a dream, and Jamie was left knowing a memory had come back but only that knowledge remained. He rubbed his eyes as if waking up from sleep.

His stomach growled, and Jamie walked to the stream and drank. He looked around, considering, and then returned to the rocks. He would wait another hour, but no longer. He did not want to be caught out in the winter night. He positioned the rifle, resting the barrel on a rock. He left the safety off.

The light shifted and dimmed. The sun dropped below the mountains across the valley and the little stream was in shadow. Jamie put his finger on the safety but then froze. Again, something moved in the trees, approaching the stream. This time, a lone buck stepped out into the open and sniffed the breeze. Jamie had a clear shot and took it. The recoil of the big gun was only partially cushioned by his down jacket, and the report banged back and forth across the valley. The buck leaped up and fell back into the snow. Its legs kicked and then were still.

Jamie jumped up and rushed down the slope to the buck. The snow was stained red. The buck was dead. Jamie threw his head back and yelled up into the sky. He held the rifle above his head and danced in the snow. The hunt was successful. A sense of power swept over him, followed immediately by fear. There was a darkness in his exaltation. This power was dangerous, not to be trusted.

Jamie knelt by the buck's head. He pulled off his glove and placed his hand on the animal's neck. He mouthed words of thanks, words that felt familiar for a brief second, but the feeling faded. Jamie looked up at the late afternoon sky. No time for memory. No time for celebration. He pulled a knife from the sheath on his belt. He had to get to work.

* * *

The buck was young and scrawny after the long winter. Field dressing it reduced its weight even more, but Jamie staggered when he got it on his shoulders. He hadn't thought this through. Getting the deer back to the cabins was going to be a tough job for a single hunter. And messy. He followed the game trail from the stream along the mountain slope. It descended gradually to the valley floor.

The road up the valley ended at the cabins, but a clear path continued beyond. It was dusk when Jamie reached that path. He leaned his weight against a tree but kept the deer on his shoulders. He was afraid to drop the deer to the ground because he didn't know if he would have the strength to hoist it up again. He rested.

It was dark by the time he approached the cabins and emerged from the treeline into the open area. He could hear Spot in one of the cabins, barking his head off. Kerosene lamps lit several windows with a weak, golden glow. Jamie almost wept. The sense of returning to civilization, to humanity, to his people was overwhelming. He staggered as he walked to his cabin, only partly from exhaustion.

He dumped the carcass in a snow drift below the kitchen window and went in.

"Whoa, habibi!" said Ibrahim. "Are you all right?"

Jamie's jacket was soaked with blood from carrying the deer. His face was haggard from fatigue and hunger. He shrugged off the rifle and let the jacket slip off his shoulders onto the floor. He collapsed into a chair at the kitchen table.

"I'm fine." He held up a hand to stop Ibrahim who was examining him. "I bagged a deer. It's outside."

The door opened and Adele, Maria, Rachel, Stevie and Spot rushed in. Spot jumped up on Jamie and then whirled around and attacked his bloody jacket, licking and biting. Adele put her hand on Jamie's cheek and turned his face, looking for the source of the blood smearing his hair and beard. Jamie pushed her hand away, gently. A flash of memory came at the touch, a bridge at night, a kiss.

"I got a deer. It's outside," said Jamie.

The small kitchen erupted in cheers and the little kids jumped up and down, clapping.

"I need something to eat. And then I'm gonna crash."

"We've got some chili. How about that?" asked Ibrahim.

"Please," said Jamie. Ibrahim maneuvered around the crowded table to the cabinets and got a can of chili going on the stove. Caleb and the rest of the group came in, stomping snow off their boots. There was more celebration as Maria and Stevie announced the deer. Caleb's cheers, however, were muted and short.

"We can't leave the carcass outside overnight," said Jamie.

"Yeah," said Dwight. "There was nothing left when we found the deer we shot yesterday."

"Rachel and I will take care of it," said Adele. "We'll hang it in a tree."

"I'll help," said Dwight.

Adele nodded.

"I'll help, too," said Stevie.

Dwight looked at Stevie for a second. "You know, there really was just nothing left of that deer. It looked like something big got at it, like a mountain lion or a pack of wolves, or something." The group looked at him. "I think we should make sure the kids have an adult watching them whenever they're outside, like even just outside the door or on the porch, you know?"

"Makes sense to me," said Rachel. She looked at her little brother.

Adele spoke to Maria. "You understand what that means?" Maria looked puzzled. "It means you tell me whenever you're going outside. And there has to be a grownup outside, too. Always."

"OK," said Maria. She looked less than enthusiastic, and none of the teenagers blinked an eye at being called a grownup.

CHAPTER 34

Jamie shook out the sleeping bag and arranged it on his bed. Morning light streamed through the window and the dust swirling in the air glowed. He looked outside. Adele stood under the buck's carcass with her head tilted back, squinting. She had a big kitchen knife in her hand.

Jamie grabbed a stick of jerky on his way out the door. He walked up to Adele, who turned to him and smiled. Her face seemed as bright as the sun, and Jamie felt something move in his chest. He put his fist to his lips and cleared his throat.

"Good night?" she asked. "You look way better."

"Yeah, I was like the walking dead, or something." He smiled back. They stood for a moment. Then Jamie looked at his feet. The snow showed tracks.

"Looks like something tried to get at the buck," he said. He looked up at the carcass hanging above them. It was untouched. "Spot barked a lot last night. Guess that's why." He looked down and around. The sun was melting the snow and the tracks were vague. There were a lot of them.

"A pack of wolves, maybe," said Adele.

Jamie frowned. He scanned the treeline. Its shadows were darker in the bright sunshine. The civilized world of the cabins felt tenuous, fragile. So what else is new, he thought.

"So, how do we do this?" asked Adele. She looked behind Jamie. He turned. Ibrahim approached. He carried an ax in one hand and a saw in the other.

"I helped my mother butcher a goat, once," he said. The memory brought a touch of sadness to his face, but then he smiled. "First we skin it. Then we cut it up until it looks like meat."

Jamie's mouth watered. He swallowed.

They worked the rest of the morning. Rachel, Stevie and Maria brought them lunch and then hung around. The little kids poked at bloody pieces with sticks and made a general nuisance of themselves, until Rachel had them gather wood and build a fire. Ibrahim cut some strips of meat and showed them how to roast them over the open flames.

The smell of cooking meat brought the others. Dwight and Caleb produced a bottle of vodka and passed it around. When it came to Ibrahim, he just grinned and passed it to Jamie who took a swig. He looked at Adele. She brushed some dark, unruly hair off her forehead with the back of her hand, leaving a smear of sweat and blood behind. She smiled and shook her head.

Her cheeks were rosy from their work and she stood tall with her shoulders thrown back. They had shucked their coats and jackets and Adele was down to a long sleeve T that seemed way too small for her. A memory came to him, a school fair and his hand on her back. He wanted to put his hand there, again, and when he looked at Adele's face, it came to him that she knew what he was thinking and she would let him, if he wanted. But in that very moment, it also came to Jamie that something dark was still in him, that he had turned and come back, but he feared not all the way. He was a danger to her, and to the child, and he had to look away, and did not see the disappointment in her face when he did.

Rachel took the first piece that came off the fire. When she turned around, Maria and Stevie were standing right there. "One bite, each," she said. "There's plenty more coming." She held the stick while the kids took the first bites.

She walked it over to Jamie. "Yay, the mighty hunter!" she said. His hands were a mess, so she held it up to his mouth and he took a bite. Then she walked over to Ibrahim and Adele, each of whom took one bite. She ate the last fragment herself.

"What am I, chopped liver?" asked Caleb.

"I wish," said Rachel. She skewered another slice and put the stick back on the fire. She delivered the next piece to the others and each took just a bit, like a sacrament.

Spot gnawed on the buck's head and they left him to it. The sun dropped below the mountains and the open area was all in shadow when they finished the butchering. They wrapped the meat in old newspapers and packed it in an army footlocker. Ibrahim and Jamie carried the footlocker to the office building which was never heated. Adele walked with them and handled doors. They set the footlocker down on a shelf in the back storeroom.

"What do we do when it gets warm?" asked Jamie.

"Ice from the mountains?" suggested Adele.

"We'll see," said Ibrahim. "Let's go eat steak. Allahu Akbar!"

And they trooped out into the evening through the snow that was freezing hard again. Across the way was the fire, bigger now with bigger cuts of venison roasting and they could smell the meat and hear the voices of their friends.

They ate their fill, and everyone laughed when Maria chased Stevie around trying to touch him with a piece of pork jerky.

"Time for bed," said Adele. The kids whined but went with Adele and Rachel.

"Good night," they called over their shoulders.

Ibrahim and Jamie were the next to leave. Jamie went directly to bed, but lay awake, thoughts of meat and flesh, desire and fear circling in his mind.

* * *

Jamie welcomed the moonlight. It reflected off the snow and came in through the small window in his bedroom. The rafters above his bed were lit in the glow, and he could see his breath in the cold air of the room. He pulled the down bag closer around his ears.

It had been a feast. A feast that he had brought about, and he knew that everyone - except perhaps Caleb - was glad to have him there, glad to have him back.

But I'm not back, am I, he thought.

Bits and pieces of memory had come to him that day. Isolated fragments that were like pieces of a puzzle. He didn't know how to put the pieces together, though. He had no picture of what the pieces should look like when they were all assembled again. But there was one thing about the picture that he knew, and that was the anxiety that never left him, the sense that when that picture was finally assembled, it would reveal a darkness in him, a real threat he posed to those around him.

Deli was pregnant with no one to help her, no doctors or nurses, not even her mother. He had done this to her. It was his fault. His desire for her was no memory of the past but a clear and present danger, a destructive force with him now, part of the darkness. What future could she have with him?

And Caleb... Once that evening Jamie had been cutting a piece of venison and glanced up. Adele was sitting on a chair by the fire and Caleb was standing in front of her. He said something, and Adele laughed. Caleb held out the bottle of vodka to her, but she waved it away. Caleb had pushed the bottle past her hand towards her face, and she had taken the bottle from him but put it down in the snow rather than drink. Caleb's smile didn't change, but he said something to Adele and her smile had faltered as she looked up at him. Caleb leaned over to retrieve the bottle and put his hand on her knee as if to steady himself. Jamie had gripped the handle of his knife with such force that his fingers ached. He had to look away from Caleb, and it took an effort of will to relax his hand. He put the knife back in its sheath on his belt and did not take it out again that night.

He had to keep his distance, build a wall around himself for the sake of everyone else. He had done enough damage. There must be no more.

He rolled onto his side and pulled the sleeping bag over his head. He took shelter under the covers, as if the dark there could give him shelter from the darkness in his mind. He squeezed his eyes shut. He breathed through parted lips and listened. There was a sound like breathing or the beating of wings. He held his breath, but the sound continued, and he felt the presence of a dark thing, just on the other side of the sleeping bag, waiting and watching.

CHAPTER 35

Things were getting basic. She wasn't worried anymore about school art fairs and whether the black jeans would go with the red top. This morning it was an issue of keeping warm, staying safe, and meat. Adele thought of the footlocker full of venison and smiled. Sunlight flooded the little kitchen. Maria looked up at her from her breakfast bowl. The little girl smiled, too, and then got back to business with her spoon.

Adele looked out the window. Jamie and Ibrahim were building some sort of framework over the firepit. They had been talking about how to preserve food the night before, and Adele guessed the framework was for drying or smoking meat. Jamie took his hand off it and the framework slumped to one side. The baby kicked. Adele put her hand on her stomach. She frowned.

"What're Jamie and Ibrahim doing?" asked Maria.

"Are you done? Let's go see."

Maria pushed her bowl away and stood up. Adele pulled on parka, scarf and hat. Maria protested at the delay but let Adele bundle her up before they went out the door. Spot saw them coming and bounded over to greet them. Some breakfast was left on Maria's face, and Spot got it with a quick lick before Maria could push him away.

Ibrahim turned to greet them. "What's with the sour face, little one?"

"Spot licked me," she said.

"Oh, Spot. What a bad doggie!" he said.

Spot grinned and wagged his tail. Maria pouted.

"Hey," said Adele. She looked at Jamie who was giving the framework all his attention.

"Hey," he said. He didn't glance up.

"Watcha doin'?" asked Maria.

Jamie didn't answer.

"We are building a framework for drying meat," said Ibrahim. "We can do this when it gets warm. Then we'll have venison jerky."

Maria made a face. "Jerky?! Ew!"

Ibrahim and Adele laughed. Jamie just smiled and tightened a knot.

Adele stepped over to the framework. "Looks a bit rickety," she said.

Jamie didn't respond. Adele put out her hand and gave it a shove. The framework collapsed.

"Oh, shit! Sorry!" said Adele. Now Maria laughed. Jamie stood, arms at his sides, staring at the pile of sticks and string on the ground.

"Not to worry," said Ibrahim. He bent over and pulled on one of the larger sticks. The structure came up, a tangled mess.

Caleb and Dwight walked up. "Let me guess... Modern art?" said Caleb.

Adele put her hand to her mouth and stifled a laugh. Ibrahim smiled. Jamie's expression hardened. He looked up at Caleb and Dwight and then at Adele. She met his gaze. He was still for a second, then turned and walked off without a word.

"Hey, man!" called Caleb. "Don't be like that. Just kidding!"

Jamie kept going. He went into his cabin and closed the door.

Something about it felt final, to Adele. Whatever it was that had come back, it wasn't the Jamie she remembered, the Jamie she had loved. This Jamie was remote, unavailable. It was like he refused to listen to himself, to his own feelings. Several times, she had sensed a response in him to her, a response he seemed to kill as soon as it arose. Now there was just a blankness, no warmth, no help.

She turned to Caleb and put a hand on his arm. He smiled at her and she mustered a smile in return.

"You guys have fun last night?" she asked.

"Oh, yeah. You left way too early."

"Well... Had to put Maria to bed, you know."

"Sneak out when she's asleep. It's OK. She's right there." Caleb nodded toward Adele's cabin. "You can keep an eye on her from here."

Adele looked at her cabin. It seemed close in the bright, morning light. At night in the dark, it would seem a million miles away. She smiled at Caleb and then waved to Rachel and Stevie who were making their way toward the group.

"What's that?" asked Rachel.

"It is modern art," said Ibrahim.

"Awesome," she said. "We could really use some of that."

* * *

They were all out there, laughing, talking. Jamie shifted to one side and peeked out the window. Caleb stood close to Adele. She still had her hand on his arm. She smiled up at him and laughed at something he said. Jamie turned his face away and squeezed his eyes shut.

This was good, right? He needed to put distance between himself and Adele, for her sake. She had to see how unreliable he was, with the fragments of memory that came and then faded like a dream so you could remember you had them but that was it. And the anger... It rose in him like a storm tide. Caleb provoked it, of course. But it had appeared other times. When he shot the deer, that exultation at the kill, wasn't that a form of anger? And his feelings for Adele... They were darker, yet. She had pushed the framework over with one hand, contemptuous. The image of Adele, her dark hair wild, the skin of her neck and shoulders pale, came unbidden to his mind and something in him stirred, powerful, hungry and careless.

Jamie walked to the stove and put the tea kettle on. He stared at it without seeing it.

He went back to the window. Rachel was helping Ibrahim with the framework, now, along with Stevie. Adele and Caleb were horsing around. She hit him with a snowball and shrieked when he rushed her and twisted her arm around behind her back. She struggled but he wouldn't let her go, and Maria jumped up and grabbed his arm with both her hands and appeared to be biting. He swatted her away and she fell back into the snow. He laughed, helped her up and started brushing her off. She pulled away from him and ran to Adele who knelt down and put her arms around her. Adele put her face close to Maria's and said something. Maria said something back and pointed at Caleb.

The kettle whistled. Jamie turned from the window and poured a cup of tea. He leaned against the kitchen table and sipped. His eye fell on the rifle by the door and he stared at it, absently, not really thinking of anything at all.

* * *

The others had trooped off to lunch and Ibrahim worked alone at the framework. He looked up as Jamie approached. "Hey, habibi. I think it's done." He stepped back and surveyed the structure.

Jamie held out a steaming cup of tea and Ibrahim took it. "Thanks." He sipped it.

"Yeah. Looks good," said Jamie. He put out a hand and tested it.

"Adele finally worked it out," said Ibrahim. "We should get her working on running water."

"Yeah, she could probably figure something out." He kicked at a small pile of firewood stacked next to the framework. "We're going to need lots and lots of wood."

Ibrahim looked around. They had already collected and burned most of the nearby tree fall. A big stack of wood would be a group effort.

"Have you had lunch?" Ibrahim asked.

"Not yet. I'll cook. What do you want, jerky or steak?"

Ibrahim grinned. "Yeah... I think steak."

They started for the cabin.

"Habibi, how are you doing?" Ibrahim glanced at Jamie, who looked straight ahead. "You are settling in OK?"

They walked several paces before Jamie replied. "I feel like it's not good for me here," he said.

"How so, Jamie? These are your friends. Adele is pregnant with your child. If not here, then where?"

"I don't think I'm good for Deli. I'm not... It's like, I feel like I'm a danger, you know? I'm afraid I could hurt her, hurt the child."

"Ah." Ibrahim frowned. "But why would you do that?"

Jamie shook his head. "I don't know what I was before. And I don't know what I am now, really. When I look at her, it's like I'm afraid for her. There's something inside me. I'm afraid of it."

Ibrahim waited, but Jamie did not continue.

"And what is this thing inside of you?" he asked.

"It's dark," said Jamie. "It's like... When I think of Caleb, I think he's a complete asshole. Like I could just kill him sometimes. I mean like, really. Really kill him. It's strong, Ibrahim."

"And when you think of Adele?"

Jamie shook his head. "I don't let myself think of her. It's too scary. I just turn away."

Ibrahim stopped. Jamie took a few steps and then turned back. Ibrahim looked at something in the snow, something that was tucked down against a fallen log a bit to the side of their path. It was the head of the buck, or what remained of it after Spot and who knows what else had gnawed at it. The skull was placed upright, and two bright pennies had been placed in its eye sockets, one in each one. They glinted in the sun, and Ibrahim had the feeling that they watched him.

Jamie came and stood next to Ibrahim. "What's this?" asked Ibrahim. He looked at Jamie. Jamie's mouth was open, and his eyes were fixed on the skull.

"It's Maria," said Jamie. "I showed her how to do this. Her mother was dead, and we put pennies on her eyes."

CHAPTER 36

The memories were a flood, now. It was all coming back. He sat at the kitchen table and wept. He wept for his mother and Bonney, and for their house up the hill from town. He wept for Maria and Maria's parents. Spot put his head on Jamie's knee and whined. Jamie put his hand on Spot's head and wept for Mr. Schultz, and Mrs. Yates. He wept for Adele, so alone, and for the child they would bring into a savage world. He remembered turning, the insane fury of it that rose up and swept him away, and he wept for himself, for who he had once been and what he feared he now was.

Ibrahim sat at the table with his cup of tea. He was silent.

Jamie rubbed his eyes with the heels of his hands. He drew a deep breath and let it out.

"I wish I had never come back," he said.

Ibrahim looked at him and waited.

"Why did you save me, Ibrahim? You knew I had turned. You knew what I was. Why didn't you just leave me? It would have been all over, then."

Ibrahim frowned. "I don't know why I did that, habibi. I just did it. I didn't know for sure how it would be for you. And it worked out. You came back."

"Did I? Is this back? I can remember now and I'm not like I was. I'm different. Why didn't you just leave me?"

"I've been thinking, Jamie. I was twenty-five when it all started. Everyone my age was turning. But I didn't."

Jamie waited.

"When I was a kid, in Pakistan, things were tough. I lost my father and then my mother. I almost starved. I almost froze in the mountains." Ibrahim looked out the window at some distant thing. "They took me to an orphanage in Peshawar, but they didn't think I would live. I wouldn't speak, wouldn't eat. They brought in doctors, but they couldn't do anything. I was just wasting away."

Ibrahim sipped his tea.

"There was an old woman. She did laundry at the orphanage. She knew my family was Sufi, so she brought in a Sufi healer, a saint. She had to sneak him in." Ibrahim smiled. "Sufi healers..." He shook his head. "They were not respected. They were just uneducated, country bumpkins. Or con-men. At any rate, he sang for me, like I did for you. And it worked. He healed me. And that's the thing, habibi. I think I had turned. And he brought me back."

He looked at Jamie. "And when I saw you there, on the path, I couldn't just leave you. You looked so young. And I was so tired of everyone dying. And so I tried it. And it worked. You came back."

Jamie's face was sad. "But what came back, Ibrahim? What am I?"

* * *

The septic system at Lakeside was a blessing and a curse. It meant they had indoor plumbing and indoor bathrooms - a big deal in winter, thought Jamie. The curse part was how much water it required, and the water pumps at the little resort depended on the generator and the generator depended on gasoline and there wasn't any gasoline so there wasn't any running water piped into the cabins. Jamie stood looking at the water buckets on the floor under the bathroom sink, both bone dry. He glanced out the little window at the night sky.

"Shit," he said.

He picked up the buckets and started for the door.

"Thanks, habibi," called Ibrahim as Jamie went by his bedroom.

"My pleasure," said Jamie.

He filled the buckets from a little stream just above where it entered the lake. His boots got wet, but he figured they would dry by morning and he hustled back to the cabin, a full, sloshing bucket in each hand.

He looked up as he passed Caleb and Dwight's cabin. Caleb's bedroom window was dimly lit, and a figure stood there looking out. She had wild hair and had wrapped a blanket or sleeping bag around her pale shoulders. Jamie slowed and stopped. For a second the figure in the window didn't move and Jamie wasn't sure if he was visible to her or not. Then she bent and blew out the lamp, and the bedroom was dark.

This is good, he thought. Adele needs to know she can't depend on me, right? But it didn't feel good, and the cold penetrated his wet boots as Jamie trudged on home.

* * *

Emily and Eva were hosting dinner and were juggling pots and pans at the stove. It had turned cold in the afternoon and the group was gathered inside where all the bodies would have warmed the place even without the cooking. They had been eating fresh meat for several days now, but the steaks were still a novelty. No one complained that it was venison, yet again.

Caleb and Dwight slouched on the couch. Caleb had his feet up on the battered coffee table next to a big jug of cheap red wine. He leaned forward and picked up the jug. Dwight held out his glass and Caleb filled it before refilling his own tumbler.

Adele made her way around Ibrahim and Rachel who were standing in the short hallway deep in conversation. Rachel took a step toward Ibrahim to make room for Adele as she passed, and then took only a half-step back. She gave Adele a quick smile.

Something crashed in one of the bedrooms and Adele stuck her head in. Maria, Stevie and Spot all looked up at her like deer in headlights. Nothing seemed broken, so Adele just gave them a warning look and went on to the bathroom at the end of the hall. She checked herself in the mirror and touched up her makeup. It only partially concealed the black eye. She was counting on the dim light from the kerosene lamps. She returned to the main room.

Jamie had come in while she was in the bathroom and was sitting in a corner far from the lamps. Adele assessed the geometry of light and shadow in the room and started for a chair in a corner on the other side of a small table from him. She had to pass Caleb on her way, and he reached up and pulled her down onto his lap.

"Hey, there, little momma," he said. "Come sit with papa." He put his arm around her neck and pulled her face toward him. He kissed her on the lips and gave her a big grin. Adele let him kiss her, but then pulled away and stood up. She stepped over his legs and went on to the chair in the dark corner. She sat so the eye with the bruise was turned to the wall, away from Jamie.

"Hey," she said.

Jamie turned and looked at her. He cocked his head. "So... You and Caleb are like, hooking up now, or something?" He kept his voice low so only she could hear.

She turned to him. "What's it to you?" The light from the lamps in the kitchen fell on the battered side of her face.

Jamie looked at her eye and then leaned forward to get a better look. He frowned. He turned to look at Caleb sitting on the couch and then back to Adele.

"Did he do that?" he asked.

Adele put her hand up to her cheek. "No," she said. "I walked into a door." She regretted it immediately. The door thing was such a cliché that it was just like saying "he hit me." Even if it had been true, she should have said anything else.

For a second Jamie just looked at her. Nothing obvious changed in his body, but she sensed a gathering in, a hard, dark focus taking shape in him. "Jamie," she said and reached out a hand, but too late.

Jamie stood and walked over to Caleb. He pulled his hunting knife from its sheath on his belt and grabbed Caleb's hair. He put his knee in Caleb's stomach, pulled Caleb's head back and laid the edge of the knife against Caleb's throat.

"Hey!" said Caleb but then he fell silent when Jamie pushed the edge harder against his throat. Jamie put his face close to Caleb's.

Adele held her breath. Everyone in the room seemed frozen, staring, their mouths open. She saw Caleb move his hand, as if to grab Jamie's wrist.

"Don't move," said Jamie, and Caleb stopped. "Here's how it's gonna be. Tomorrow morning I'm going to come looking for you. And if I find you, I will shoot you dead. Do you understand?"

Caleb was shaking. "You're not the only one with a gun."

Jamie seemed to consider this. "Yeah, but I'm the only one with bullets left, aren't I?"

Caleb just looked at him.

Adele sucked in her breath. "Jamie!"

"Easy, man," said Dwight. He stood up slowly and took a step away, holding his hands out as if to show he was not armed.

"Enough!" said Ibrahim. "Let him up, Jamie."

Jamie stood up, turned and walked out of the cabin.

Caleb put his hand to his neck and looked at his fingers. They were smeared red. "Jesus fucking Christ! He's turned again," he said.

Emily rushed over with the kitchen first aid kit. "Let me see," she said. She pushed Caleb's hand out of the way. "It's not bad. Don't worry."

Maria and Stevie stood in the hallway entrance and stared at Caleb. Ibrahim knelt by the couch and patted Caleb's arm. Rachel stood behind the two kids, holding them. Adele looked at her. Rachel alone looked at Adele, where she sat silently in her chair, one hand resting on her stomach and the other on the little table, still stretched out to Jamie's chair. She understands, thought Adele. She's the only one.

Adele stood and walked out the door, without her coat. She went to her cabin. She curled up on her bed and pulled the down bag over her. She closed her eyes and lay still in the cold and dark.

* * *

Jamie stood motionless in the still dark shadows of the treeline. The first light of morning touched the tops of the hills to the west of the valley, but the cabins below were barely visible. He shifted the rifle from one shoulder to the other.

The lamps in Caleb and Dwight's windows had burned all night. Figures came and went. Jamie could make out Ibrahim, Rachel, and Emily as they stepped through the front door. Now the door opened, and three figures emerged, Dwight, Caleb and Emily. Caleb and Emily had packs. Caleb carried Leung's M-16.

Dwight hugged each in turn, and then Caleb and Emily stepped off the little porch. Emily waved, and the pair walked to her cabin. The door opened and a smaller figure, Eva, came out to join them. The three turned and started on the road down the valley, back toward the Darnell River.

Jamie squeezed his eyes shut and then opened them again. He had meant for Caleb to go, but he was filled with sadness to see Emily and Eva go, too. Had his outburst so frightened them that leaving with Caleb seemed the safest course? What if it had been Deli and Maria leaving with Caleb? What had he done, he wondered. Would everyone leave, slipping away a few at a time until Jamie was left alone? He had felt so powerful, but what had come of it?

Jamie sat on a log and watched the cabins in the slow morning light. Ibrahim lit a lamp and a few minutes later he came out with an empty bucket. Spot slipped by him before he could close the door. The dog stood on the porch and looked around. Ibrahim let him stay outside.

The dog jumped down off the porch and ran across the open area, making a beeline for Jamie. He jumped up on Jamie when he reached him and licked his face. Jamie pressed his face into the fur of the dog's neck and hugged him. Ibrahim had stopped walking. He turned toward where Spot had disappeared into the trees.

Jamie stood up and walked out to meet Ibrahim.

"So... Habibi, you have chased Caleb away. Emily and Eva went with him."

"I saw." Jamie nodded. He did not look at Ibrahim, but studied something off in the direction that Caleb, Emily and Eva had taken. Then he turned to Ibrahim. "Caleb hit Deli. She had a black eye."

Now Ibrahim looked off into the distance. He shook his head. "Poor Adele. She must feel so all alone." He looked at Jamie. "When you came back, it was not what she had hoped."

Jamie covered his eyes with his hand. "I couldn't let him hit her."

"Adele needs your help, habibi, but not that help."

Jamie looked at Ibrahim. Was I even trying to help Adele, he wondered? Or was I just indulging my own sense of grievance? "I don't know what to do," he said.

Ibrahim considered. "Do you love Adele?" he asked.

"Yes. I do. Both the old me and the new me."

"Then what's the mystery, Jamie? Let her know, before it is too late."

PART III
CHAPTER 37

Jamie straightened up and pulled off his work gloves. He stretched, clasping his hands together high over his head and arching his back. Adele ignored this display and stacked a piece of firewood on the pile placing it just so. Jamie pulled his sweaty t-shirt away from his chest. He glanced at Adele, but she turned away to the next piece of wood. They could work together. They all had to work together. But with Jamie, that seemed to be all that Adele could stand.

Spot lolled in the sun a few steps from the woodpile. He looked up and growled, low in his throat. Adele looked past Jamie at something in the distance. She frowned and shaded her eyes with her hand. "Who the hell is that?" she said.

Jamie turned. In the distance was a figure coming down the road to the cabins. Something was wrong with the walker. He or she staggered, and the human shape seemed deformed. Then it became clear: the person was carrying someone piggy-back and struggled under the load.

Adele took a step toward them, but Jamie put his hand on her arm, and she stopped. They remained unmoving for a few seconds, watching the pair approach. Dwight came out of his cabin and stood on the front porch where he could see the newcomers. He glanced at Jamie and Adele and turned back to the strangers.

The walker stumbled and dropped to her knees. The figure on her back slid to the ground and lay there. Adele and Dwight started running toward them. Jamie hesitated, then picked up the axe and followed more cautiously. Spot walked at Jamie's side.

Dwight got there first. He knelt by the young woman and put his hand on her shoulder. She turned her face up to him and they spoke. Adele was a few steps behind Dwight and when she arrived, Dwight moved to the man that the woman had been carrying. He lay on the ground, limp and unmoving.

Dwight looked up when Jamie and Spot got there. “Help me with this guy,” he said.

“What are we doing?” asked Jamie. Spot sniffed at the still figure and growled.

“Let’s put him in Caleb’s bed,” said Dwight. He got the man’s arms and Jamie got his legs under the knees. The man was very thin, and Jamie had no trouble hoisting him up.

“Is he still alive?” asked Jamie. Dwight did not answer.

Ibrahim ran up. The man’s head hung down and Ibrahim lifted it clear of the steps while Dwight and Jamie climbed onto the porch. Ibrahim pushed the front door open for them. They made their way to Caleb’s bedroom and lowered him gently onto the bed.

The man lay completely still. He was just skin and bones, and Jamie thought of pictures of the starved survivors of Auschwitz. His hair was long and tangled with bits of leaves in it. He had a full beard, but Jamie guessed his age as mid-twenties. The man’s chest rose and fell. He lived.

There were footsteps on the porch and Jamie turned toward the door. Adele and the young woman came in. Adele had her arm around the woman’s waist and helped her walk to the bed. She sat down next to the thin man and put her face close to his. Her hand rested on his chest. He took another breath and she smiled. She looked up at them. “He’s still alive. You can bring him back!”

“He’s pretty far gone,” said Adele. “We can try. Can he eat? Does he wake up?”

“His name is Peter,” said the woman. “He’ll wake up. You can sing to him, right? You can bring him back. Then he’ll eat.”

A low growl from Spot broke the silence.

“He’s turned?” asked Jamie.

“Emily and Eva said you could sing him back.” The woman turned to Ibrahim. “You’re Ibrahim, right? Sing to him.” Peter took another breath and the woman’s hand rose and fell on his chest. “Please!” she said. “He’s almost gone.”

Ibrahim frowned. “We...” He shook his head. “We don’t know. We don’t know what made a difference.” He looked over to Jamie. “It was just Jamie. Just one time.”

“Please,” she said. Her voice was low and tremulous, but clear in the quiet room.

Ibrahim pulled a chair over to the bed and sat. He reached out and pushed Peter’s hair away from his face and then put one hand on the skin of Peter’s neck close to his shoulder. He cleared his throat, licked his lips, and began to sing, the same odd tune and foreign words that Jamie remembered had filled the dark expanse of his mind back in the cave. Someone was singing with Ibrahim, and Jamie recognized his own voice.

Peter's chest rose and fell. Ibrahim started another song, one that Jamie did not know. He caught the refrain, though, and he hummed along. He took Peter's hand in both of his, and Peter's chest rose and fell again, and then again.

The woman was rocking back and forth in time with the song. Her eyes were fixed on Peter's face. A tear made its way down from the corner of her eye, trembled on her chin, and then fell. It made a wet stain on Peter's shirt, next to where her hand rested on his chest. It rose and fell now, slowly but continuously.

Peter's eyelids flickered, and his chapped lips parted. Then he opened his eyes and looked up into the face of the young woman who bent over him. His lips moved, but he made no sound.

"Water," said Jamie. "He needs water."

Adele dashed to the kitchen and came back with a glass of water and a rag. She dipped the rag in the water and swabbed Peter's lips. He licked his lips. "More," he said, his voice just a rasp.

The woman took the glass and rag from Adele. She soaked a corner of the rag and then touched it to Peter's lips. He sucked it dry, and she put the glass to his lips and tipped just a bit. Peter drank.

* * *

Her name was Ramona, and she stayed by Peter's side for the next week. She slept on the floor by his bed and fed him whenever he woke. She cleaned him up when he threw up the first bowl of venison broth and wept for joy when he kept down the second.

Peter gained strength. At the end of the first week, she helped him down the short hall to the bathroom, and back again. He was still too weak to move around much, but at times he was restless. She started reading him one of the trashy novels someone had left in the cabin. He would lie still, listening, and then his eyes would close, and he would sleep some more.

They all looked-in on the newcomers several times a day for the first couple of days. New faces were still exciting then, and Maria and Stevie would make pests of themselves, standing at the bedroom door staring until Dwight chased them away.

Ramona was always sweet with the kids. One day, she tried some Spanish with Maria, but Maria could remember only a few words. She seemed unsettled when Ramona spoke Spanish to her, as if the language recalled painful memories. Ramona stuck to English after that.

Peter seemed a gentle soul, but no one was surprised to learn that he had been violent when he turned. They had all seen too much and knew what the virus could do to even the sweetest of them.

* * *

Another group showed up at Lakeside several days after Ramona and Peter arrived. This time, Jamie left the axe behind when he went to meet them: two young men carrying a woman on a stretcher. Her name was Rita and she had bleached blonde hair that spilled out from under the blankets that covered her. She was curled up in a tight ball.

"It's like she's a black hole, or something," said Stan, one of her stretcher bearers. "She went so far in and then - boom - just fucking disappeared. You can help her, right?"

Stan asked Ibrahim to sing for her, which he did, and Stan gave Ibrahim some canned goods. Then Stan and his friends pitched a tent on the other side of the road and waited.

That afternoon, Jamie and Ibrahim went to check on Rita. They found Stan sitting on a stool outside the tent. "How's she doing?" asked Ibrahim.

"She's moving around, some," said Stan. "It's like she's sleeping now, you know, like it's natural. Not like before."

"OK... That's good," said Ibrahim. He glanced at Jamie.

"Did Emily and Eva send you to us?" asked Jamie.

"No," said Stan. "Caleb did. He says everyone who's sick should come here and get cured."

"Really?" said Jamie. "How many people did Caleb tell?"

"Well, everyone. He made an announcement at a Darnell town meeting."

"There's still a Darnell?"

"Well, sort of. There's like maybe a hundred people there now."

Jamie was silent for a second. "Do you know a Nat Bonney or Ellen Montane?" he asked.

"Nope." Stan shook his head. "They friends of yours?"

"They're my mom and dad."

"Oh...Sorry, man," said Stan. "There just aren't any old people left, you know."

Jamie looked away and blinked. "So, how do people live now? In Darnell?"

"Mostly scavenging... Not all the houses are burned. There's still canned goods and stuff. Caleb set up a system. Everyone brings their stuff to the grocery store and then they get rations from there."

"How's that working?"

"It's working..." Stan shrugged. "Caleb's crew encourages participation."

"Caleb has a crew?"

"Yeah. There's like ten guys. They do what he says, so everyone does what he says."

"Sounds like Caleb."

"What's going on down in the city?" asked Ibrahim.

Stan shook his head. "Totally screwed-up. Gangs and stuff. But there's some business, you know, back and forth. Some of Caleb's guys found a big marijuana grow operation back in the hills. Took some plants down to the city. Came back with a load of useful shit." He pulled out a joint and lit it. He took a drag and then held it out. "Want some?"

"No, thanks," said Jamie.

Ibrahim shook his head. "How about the rest of the world? Anyone out there? Any news?"

"Pretty much like us, you know. Just scattered, small groups."

"Does the government exist?"

Stan grimaced. "Some guys in uniform came down from upriver – from Power City. Said they were the army and they were here to help us. Sorry looking bunch. Caleb chased them off. That's when Caleb promoted himself to mayor. Seemed like a good idea at the time." He took another puff on the joint.

"You from Darnell? Originally?" asked Jamie.

"Naw. I grew up in the city. When everything blew up, Rita and me and a couple of buddies split. We made it as far as Darnell before winter hit."

"Where were you going?"

"Anywhere. Nowhere." Stan smiled.

Dwight walked up. Stan offered him the joint and Dwight took a toke. "How's Rita doing?" he asked, blowing out smoke with each word.

"Better," came a woman's voice from inside the tent, and Stan turned and ducked through the door.

Ibrahim and Jamie followed. Stan was kneeling by the stretcher, his head resting on Rita's chest. Her hand was on his shoulder, which shook with his sobs. Ibrahim touched Jamie's arm and they stepped out and rejoined Dwight.

"That's three for three," said Jamie. He smiled.

"Yeah. So, three people have recovered. That's huge. But we really don't know anything about what cured them. You know, Jamie, when you flip a coin you can have runs of all heads or all tails. It looks like a streak, but it's just random."

Stan emerged from the tent. His eyes were red rimmed. "She asked for something to drink. It's been days since she's had anything to drink." He hugged Ibrahim. "I owe you, man. We owe you."

"I am glad to help, Stan. Allahu Akbar."

Stan looked startled for a moment, but then went on. "Say... You guys look like you have an OK setup here. Mind if we stay a while? I'm in no rush to get back to Darnell, you know?"

Ibrahim looked at Jamie and Dwight. "What do you think, Dwight?"

Dwight took another drag on the joint and tried to look thoughtful.

"There's more where that came from," said Stan. He grinned.

"Yeah. Why not?" said Dwight. He looked around. "We've got room."

Stan considered the open area along the lake. "Thanks, man. You know, you should probably be ready for more people." He pushed back into the tent.

"Is it dinner time yet?" asked Dwight.

Jamie and Ibrahim exchanged a glance. "It is any time you want," said Ibrahim.

"Time for pork jerky," said Dwight and started for his cabin. Ibrahim and Jamie watched him go.

"This thing that Caleb is doing... Sending us everyone who's turned." Jamie shook his head.

"You think he means us harm?"

"Being around people when they turn... Been there. Done that."

* * *

The next morning, Jamie stepped out onto the front porch with a steaming cup of tea. He stopped with his hand resting on the door knob, the front door still open.

"Uh, Ibrahim," he said without turning. "You better come see this."

"What is that, habibi?" asked Ibrahim. He came and stood behind Jamie in the doorway.

In front of the cabin were fifteen or twenty people, sitting in small groups each gathered around a person on a stretcher or just lying on the ground. They all looked up when Jamie stepped out, and several stood when Ibrahim came to stand behind him.

"We're ready," said one young woman.

"We were here first," said a man with the group closest to the porch. He turned and glared at the young woman who did not look away but reached for something in her coat pocket.

"Wait a minute," said Ibrahim, his hand raised. He pushed past Jamie and stood on the edge of the porch. "All these people have turned?" he asked.

"Yeah," said the man closest to the porch. "Caleb said you could cure them. He said you could sing for them."

"Ah," said Ibrahim, softly. He nodded, his eyebrows raised.

Jamie scanned the crowd. Many were armed with rifles and shotguns slung over shoulders or handguns tucked into belts. Jamie guessed that the young woman had been reaching for a weapon in her pocket and that those who were not obviously armed had guns or knives tucked away somewhere.

"Yeah... OK..." said Ibrahim. "I will sing for everyone. Who's first?"

The crowd got up and pushed toward the porch. People started shoving and words were exchanged.

Ibrahim raised his voice. "I will get to everyone," he said. "There is no need to fight. Anyone who fights, I will not sing for him."

Jamie looked at Ibrahim and wondered if he could carry out that threat. He couldn't remember a time when Ibrahim was anything but giving. And most of these people were armed. He thought of the rifle back in the cabin, but before he could step back through the door, Adele and Rachel came up.

"Listen up," said Adele in a loud voice. She stood to one side, visibly armed and pregnant, and the crowd quieted. "Make a line from here out." She motioned with both arms and the newcomers fell into line.

Ibrahim came down from the porch and knelt by the first stretcher. "Was he violent?" he asked.

"No," said the young man who had been carrying the stretcher, but he had hesitated before answering and Ibrahim looked at him. "He's comatose," said the young man. "He can't hurt anyone."

Ibrahim looked at the man on the stretcher. He was still, eyes closed, his face slack. Ibrahim put his hand on the man's forehead and started singing. He rocked back and forth in time with the song, and Jamie found himself singing under his breath along with Ibrahim.

Ibrahim finished the song and stood to move on to the next group. "What happens now?" asked the young man.

"Everyone who has recovered, came out of it within a day or so. If he is going to recover, you should know soon," said Ibrahim.

"What if he doesn't?" asked the man.

"I am sorry," said Ibrahim. "The song is all I've got. There is nothing else I can do."

The man looked down at the still figure on the stretcher. Then he nodded. "Let's go," he said and the others in his group picked up the stretcher and moved off. Ibrahim approached the second group.

Jamie watched from the porch as the first group walked away from the cabins. They crossed the road and put the stretcher down next to Stan and Rita's campsite, and then started putting up tents.

The young woman who had reached into her pocket stepped toward the porch. "Why do we have to wait?" she asked. "Why aren't you singing?"

"Me?" said Jamie. "I can't sing."

"That's not what Caleb said. He said Jamie could cure people, too. You're Jamie, right?"

"I can't do it," said Jamie. "Caleb's just trying to cause trouble. I'm sorry."

The woman pulled her hand out of her pocket and held up a revolver. "Sorry doesn't cut it," she said.

"It's going to have to," said Adele. All eyes turned to her. She held her own revolver pointed at the woman.

For a second no one moved. Then Jamie put down his tea, stepped off the porch and walked over to the still figure of the young man the woman had been tending. He knelt down and placed his hand on the man's cheek and started to sing. His mouth was dry and his voice caught. He licked his lips and began the song again from the beginning.

The woman came over. She knelt down next to Jamie and placed one hand on the man's chest. She still held the revolver in her other hand, resting it on her knees. It was pointed at Jamie.

Jamie started rocking in time with the song, and the woman rocked with him. Out of the corner of his eye, he caught a glimpse of Adele who had come over and stood behind the woman kneeling next to Jamie. Adele held her pistol out a little from her body, the muzzle pointed at the back of the woman's head.

This is it, he thought. A feeling of love for Adele welled up in his heart, and gratitude. His eyes brimmed and a tear trickled down his cheek. His voice became strong and though he did not know the meaning of the words of the song, in that moment it became a love song and a song of thanks.

The man on the stretcher opened his eyes. They wandered across Jamie's face and then came to rest on the face of the young woman. His mouth twitched, almost a smile. He spoke, his voice barely a whisper. "Baby," he said, and the woman clutched his shirt with both hands and buried her face in his chest.

* * *

A few more groups arrived later that morning, and then a few more the next day and then it was a steady stream of people bringing their friends and loved ones who had turned. The tents across the road spread around the cabins and grew into a tent city. When carts pulled by horses arrived, Dwight walked down the road and returned to report that the fallen tree blocking the way up the valley had been cut up and dragged aside.

Ibrahim and Jamie were overwhelmed and grew hoarse. First Adele but then also Rachel and Dwight were pressed into singing. And it seemed to work, at least often enough to keep the peace.

Not everyone recovered. Some were so far gone that they never woke from a coma of starvation and dehydration. Perhaps they simply couldn't hear the singing. But there were others who were definitely conscious, fighting against their restraints or cursing at everyone they saw, and some of them also did not come back.

Ibrahim had the singers keep track of how many people they treated. He asked people to report back and tell them if the one who had turned did indeed recover or not. The statistics showed that more than half recovered, and it was probably more than that since not everyone bothered to report back.

* * *

"Stevie and Maria," called Rachel. "Breakfast!" The kids shoved their way through the bedroom door down the hall and into the kitchen. Maria got to the table first and stopped short, staring at her plate. A fully wrapped, pristine Hostess Ho Ho sat there. Stevie's plate had one, too.

"Sit," said Rachel and the kids scrambled into their chairs. Adele turned to watch and leaned back against the counter. She smiled.

"What is it?" asked Maria.

"It's a Ho Ho," said Stevie. He attacked the package, threw the torn plastic on the floor, and took a huge bite. Spot crawled out from under the table and went after the wrapper.

Maria watched Stevie and then grabbed her own Ho Ho. She was fast and efficient but messy. Maria's face was smeared with frosting and crumbs, and Spot – who judged Maria the best bet – sat next to her chair watching her every move.

When Maria was finished, her hands were sticky and she held them up. Spot whined and she looked down at him, considering, and then held out a hand for him to lick.

"Maria," said Adele. "Don't let Spot lick you. Go wash your hands and face."

Maria ignored Adele. Spot went at her hand and fingers as if he knew he had only a short window of opportunity.

"Maria," said Adele.

Maria offered Spot her other hand.

"Hey," said Adele. "Don't ignore me when I'm talking to you."

Maria looked over at Adele and then turned and offered her face to Spot who rushed to lick her cheeks. Adele pushed off from the counter and started around the table. Maria jumped up and made a break for the door, but Adele grabbed her by the arm before she reached it.

"No!" said Maria. She hit at Adele's hand and made to bite it. Adele jerked her hand away and stood with her back against the door. They faced each other.

"Let me out," demanded Maria.

"Go wash your hands and face," said Adele.

"You can't tell me what to do."

"Oh yes I can."

"You're not my mother!"

A change came into Adele's face. The anger drained from her expression and she cocked her head to one side. She looked at Maria, almost as if the little girl was something Adele had never seen before, as if she were seeing her for the first time. Maria waited.

"You know," said Adele, finally. "Maybe I am." And she stepped away from the door to the table and started to stack dishes.

Maria watched her for a few seconds, anger, puzzlement and something else – perhaps wonder – touched her face. Then she turned and walked down the short hallway to the bathroom. Water splashed in the sink.

Adele carried the dishes over to the kitchen counter. Rachel looked at her as she squeezed past and then glanced at her little brother.

"You are definitely not my mother," he said.

Rachel made a face. "That's a fucking relief," she said and turned to help Adele.

Stevie studied the top of the kitchen table. He spotted a Ho Ho crumb and mopped it up with his forefinger. Then he stood and walked down the hall back to the bathroom, where water splashed again.

CHAPTER 38

"You ready?" asked Rachel.

Adele looked out her kitchen window at the crowd of tents, people, carts and vendors that filled the open area around the cabins. She couldn't see out to the road anymore, but she didn't need to.

"They just keep coming," she said. She drank the last of her tea, black for the caffeine kick and with fresh cream to soothe her throat. "Let's go," she said. She got up and dumped her lunch dishes into the sink where they joined her breakfast dishes. The remains of eggs and bacon had hardened. Rachel added her plate and Adele filled the sink with hot water from the kettle on the stove. "Let 'em soak," she said. She went to the door, steeled herself, and stepped out.

The open area around the cabins seethed with motion. It was half county fair and half Woodstock. Streams of people made their way through the tangle of tents and booths that filled the space. Most were in small groups, and many of these carried someone on a stretcher that they hoped the singers could save.

"Look out," said Adele. A bound figure on a stretcher struggled wildly and those carrying the stretcher dropped it when an arm came free from the ropes, flailing at anyone in reach. Two of the stretcher-bearers wrestled with the arm and a third man lashed it down, immobile again.

One of the men looked up at Adele and Rachel on the porch. He nudged the man next to him and said something, and then he got to his feet and approached the porch. He took off his hat.

"Pardon me," he said. "You're singers, aren't you?" He looked from one to the other and back. "You're Adele and Rachel, yes?"

Neither Adele nor Rachel spoke.

"My brother," he motioned to the man tied to the stretcher, "could you sing to him? He's been like this for days. I don't know how long he's got."

"Have you checked-in?" asked Rachel. "He still looks strong. The wait isn't long. He'll make it, just fine."

The man considered this. He put his hat back on and his hand came to rest on the hilt of a large knife tucked in his belt. "People can die, waiting," he said. His face was hard.

Adele stopped breathing.

"What?" said Rachel. "You think you're the only one around here who's got someone who needs singing?" She had raised her voice, and people stopped and turned toward the porch. "What about all the people who came yesterday? Huh? You going to butt up in front of them?"

The man took a step back and looked nervously left and right.

A big guy with a rifle slung over his shoulder spoke up. "Everybody checks in and waits their turn, asshole. Even a pussy with a big knife."

The man took his hand off the knife and held up his hands, empty. "Yeah, yeah, sorry... I didn't know. I didn't know how it works. We'll go check-in." He rejoined his friends around the stretcher, and they picked it up and made their way through the crowd which parted to give the still struggling cargo wide berth.

Adele exhaled. She glanced over at Rachel. Rachel's hand rested on the butt of a small handgun in her belt.

"You're my BFF," said Adele. "Promise me we'll hang out forever."

"Don't worry, momma-girl," said Rachel. "Besties, forever." She watched as the crowd that had gathered broke up and the flow of people resumed. "Let's go rescue the boys. They get hoarse, quick."

They went down the steps and started for the hospital tent. The crowd parted for them, too.

* * *

Adele and Rachel made their way through the crush of people, stepping aside for a small herd of goats driven along by two shouting kids with long sticks. They balanced on a two-by-four laid across one of the bigger mud puddles churned up by all the traffic after the late spring rains. The grassy area between the cabins had become a sea of sucking mud.

At first, they had set up the hospital tent near where the road entered the cabins, but too many newcomers went directly to the tent and demanded immediate attention. By this time, Adele and Rachel had instituted the check-in procedure, and those waiting their turn resented the people who were butting-in. Fights broke out. The cemetery on the hill overlooking the cabins was started to hold the bodies of three men killed during one particularly vicious melee.

After that, they moved the hospital tent as far from the road as they could. Something about walking through the suffering but orderly crowd on the way to the tent to check-in inspired patience in the newcomers. Or perhaps it was the large number of guns, knives, machetes, and pointy garden implements carried by those already waiting that discouraged line-jumping. At any rate, even after hundreds of people gathered at Lakeside (one afternoon, Dwight walked around the area and tried to count - he quit after 500), there were few disturbances.

Not everyone who made the trip to Lakeside came for the healing. Hundreds of desperate people in one spot was a business opportunity, and food booths, tables of used but almost wearable clothes, and equipment vendors selling backpacks, weapons and ammunition lined the pathways through the tents.

Most amazing to Adele were all the quacks selling cures for the virus. People who claimed to be cured themselves set up little kiosks where they laid on hands, closed their eyes and murmured special words. More than one tent had a table out front full of small bottles with water from the lake. "Holy Water" or something like that read the hand-lettered signs.

One early morning when she was still fetching her own water, she came upon a line of people at the lake shore. A woman in saffron robes stood waist-deep and washed each person while singing some sort of blessing. Her voice came high and clear across the lake to Adele. The woman had a lovely singing voice, and though Adele knew better, she felt the power of it. She looked at the people in line, some alone, some helping a friend or family member, and the contempt she had begun to feel for all of them left her, and never came back.

Adele's foot slipped off the two-by-four and her boot sank into the mud. She bunched up her toes and pulled but her foot slipped out and the boot stayed buried up to the ankle. "Shit," she said.

Rachel turned and held out her hand. Adele grabbed it and bent over to pull the boot free but lost her balance and had to put her bootless foot down in the mud to keep from falling. "Fuck," she said. She waded to the edge of the puddle and leaned on a table to pull the muddy sock off.

"Hey!" said a sharp-eyed woman behind the table. Adele turned to her and the woman's expression softened. "Oh, sorry," she said. "I didn't recognize you."

Rachel walked up. "Hang on," she said. "I've got some socks at my cabin."

But before she could turn back to her cabin, the woman behind the table held out a pair socks to Adele, brand new still in their packaging. "Here," she said.

"I don't have anything..." Adele started, but the woman held up her hand and stopped her.

"Take 'em." She smiled. "Your money's no good here."

Adele smiled back, both in gratitude and amusement. No one's money was any good anywhere, these days. Everyone bartered. "Thanks," she said, and took the socks.

Main Street was the widest, muddiest pathway through the camp. It wound between tents and tables from the entrance road to the hospital pavilion at the far end. It was usually jammed its entire length during daylight hours and often into the night. Within a few weeks of its existence, it had developed neighborhoods and business districts. Vendors of various sorts clustered around the hospital. The residential tents were pitched in rings farther out.

Rachel and Adele made their way through the press, passing general merchandisers, then arms dealers, then bars (hard cider and grape juice at the cheaper spots, some real, dark, home-brew beer or moonshine at the classier joints), and finally through the densest section where they offered the wildcat cures: holy water, laying on of hands, and singing - everything from hymns to hip-hop.

Somehow, it was never difficult for Adele and Rachel to walk through the crowd. Something moved with them and a little ahead of them, some subliminal message or vibration sensed by the people in their path so everyone turned and stepped to the side, letting the two singers pass easily.

Closer to the hospital tent, the flow of people split going on either side of the line of those waiting for admission and the cure. "Wow. Long line, this afternoon," said Adele.

"Longer every day," said Rachel.

They ducked through the opening to the pavilion and nodded to Ramona and Peter behind the check-in table. Adele hurried to Ibrahim's side of the tent to relieve him, jostling Rachel in the process. Rachel snorted in exasperation but went over to Jamie's side. He sang, his voice low and his lips close to the ear of a man curled up on a stretcher. Jamie's hand rested on the man's head, his eyes, though, followed Adele as she joined Ibrahim.

Rachel put her hand on the shoulder of the man on the stretcher and joined in with Jamie, picking up the tune and words they had all learned from Ibrahim. This was how they always did the hand-off, when one singer relieved another, as if the song had to be unbroken for it to have power. And it seemed to soothe the families that carried their loved ones in and out of the pavilion, like the song was a living thing passed from one singer to the next and from the singers to the sick. The group had never discussed this. It was just a custom that one day seemed right and obvious to them all.

Jamie and Rachel finished the song. The family rushed to pick up the stretcher to make room for the next group. Rachel smiled and nodded as they thanked her. Jamie sipped from a glass of water, barely acknowledging the thanks, fatigue clear in his face. "See you in an hour," he said. He stood for a second, watching Adele across the way, and then turned and went out the back entrance.

Rachel moved to the next stretcher where a teenage boy, strapped down and gagged, glared at her. She was used to this and barely noticed anymore other than to ascertain that he was secure.

Two young men and a girl stood beside the stretcher. "What's his name?" Rachel asked. She didn't need to know, but Jamie had started asking this question and they had all adopted it as part of the ritual.

"He's Jonah," said the girl.

Rachel smiled at her and placed her hand on Jonah's arm. "He's young."

"Yeah," said one of the young men, nodding. "We're seeing a lot of that. It used to be that it was only the old, like mid-twenties and up. But none of them are left, you know? Now it's coming for the rest of us."

Rachel considered the boy's face. He looked back at her and growled through his gag. It was partially chewed through, and Rachel decided it was time to sing. She didn't ask the question that had come to her: how young were they turning, now?

CHAPTER 39

"Dinner's here," said Jamie. He draped the hand towel over the edge of the kitchen sink and turned to the singers gathered in his cabin. There was a quick knock-knock at the door and Ibrahim opened it. A young man and woman stepped in carrying big serving dishes that steamed.

"Hi, Tamara. Hey, Larry" said Ibrahim.

They set the dishes on the table where plates, knives and forks were already laid.

Tamara lifted the lid off the biggest dish. "Roast lamb," she said. She pointed to the other dishes. "Potatoes, spring greens."

"Oh, that smells so good," said Adele. She plopped down at the table close to the lamb. Maria and Stevie battled briefly for the chair next to her. Maria won.

"It is so awesome that you guys are doing this," said Jamie, and there was a chorus of appreciation from the others.

"We're just trying to keep you guys going," said Tamara.

"What's with the matching scarves?" asked Rachel. She held out her plate and Adele gave her a big helping. "I mean, saffron looks good on you, of course" she said to Tamara.

"It's the Helpers. We're getting organized. The saffron scarf's our insignia."

Jamie and Ibrahim held out their plates to Adele and she took Ibrahim's.

"The Helpers?" asked Dwight. Adele ignored Jamie's plate so Dwight took it and dished it up.

"Yeah," said Larry. "People were just doing things. You know, the burial team, the guys who were helping with stretchers, meals for the practitioners... Ramona said we should get organized and do what most needs doing."

Ibrahim put down his fork and looked from Tamara to Larry. "We could not do what we are doing without your help." He put his hands together and gave each a slight bow. "Thank you. Thank you."

"Who are the practitioners?" asked Dwight.

"Well, you all, of course," said Tamara. "Kelalah-sha, Saint Tommy, and a couple of others."

"Kelalah-sha?" Dwight raised his eyebrows.

"Yeah, you know, saffron," Larry waved his hand up and down his body. "She does the baptism-washing thing in the lake."

"Oh, yeah," said Dwight.

"Is it OK if we clean up when we bring breakfast?" asked Tamara. "We're putting up another hospital tent and it's probably going to take all of us the rest of the night."

"No problem, at all," said Ibrahim.

"Why do we need another hospital tent?" asked Dwight. "We can hardly sing to all the people as it is."

Tamara held up her hand and smiled. "It's not for you guys. It's something different. You get this many people," she gestured to the encampment outside the cabin, "and someone breaks an arm, has an upset stomach, you know, whatever."

"A lot of diarrhea and fever," said Larry. He frowned.

"Got it," said Dwight, and got busy with his lamb.

* * *

After dinner, they moved to the small living room and collapsed on the couch, into chairs, and on the floor. The only sound was the clatter of Maria's dinner plate as Spot chased it across the kitchen floor with his tongue. Adele gave Maria a look. "Whose plate is that?" she asked.

"I don't know," said Maria. She climbed up on Jamie's lap.

"Oof," he said.

Adele looked away.

"What should we do about all the phonies?" asked Dwight. "Saint Tommy? Lady La-la what's her name?" He snorted.

"How do we know they're phonies?" asked Jamie. "How do we know their stuff doesn't work?"

"Oh, come on," said Dwight.

Ibrahim looked over at him. "How do we know that our stuff does work?"

"What do you mean?" said Dwight. "Of course we know. Everyone knows. You brought Jamie back. Peter... Every day I see people walking around like normal who were curled up in a ball or foaming at the mouth the day before."

Ibrahim shook his head. "We don't know. All we know is that the virus used to kill everyone and now it doesn't. We don't know if it's the song that brings people back, or the touch or just our breathing on people. Maybe people are getting better on their own."

"Yeah, so, not everybody comes back right away. I get that. Sometimes it takes a day or a few days. And maybe it doesn't always work. But we sing, and people get better, right?"

"Viruses mutate all the time." Ibrahim shrugged. "Lots of them become less lethal."

Jamie watched Ibrahim. The Pakistani pushed his hair back from his face and blew out a breath. "I'm a statistician. I know the difference between correlation and causation, and truly, truly, we do not know what's really going on."

"Well, let's not mention that to the Helpers, OK?" said Rachel. "I'm getting used to catered meals."

No one spoke for a few minutes.

"I used to feel like we were in control of things," said Jamie. He studied his hands, laying in his lap. "You know, we were the healers and Lakeside was our place. We had respect." He paused. Adele looked at him, waiting. "But now I feel like we're just along for the ride. Like there's five of us and five hundred of them. And we really don't know shit. About anything." Jamie looked up and met Adele's gaze. "Sometimes I wish things were the way they used to be. I wish things were like they used to be."

Adele got up and walked quickly to the bathroom. She stayed there a long time.

* * *

Jamie walked into the hospital pavilion, past the usual line of families and stretchers. Peter sat alone behind the check-in table.

"Where's Ramona?" asked Jamie.

"She's over at the new hospital tent. The Helpers put out the word that they needed anyone with medical training, stat." Peter turned to the next group and motioned them forward.

"Ramona has medical training?"

"Yeah. She's an R.N."

"Oh, wow," said Jamie. He thought of his mother. "Why stat?"

"Lots of sick people. Lots of diarrhea, fever." Peter frowned. "You know what cholera is?"

"Oh, yeah. My mother was an R.N."

"Ramona says they think that's what it is."

Jamie thought of a thousand people crammed in around Lakeside, with no bathrooms except the forest and the lake. The place was beginning to smell. And how many people were drinking out of the lake, he wondered.

He looked over at Adele who was singing to a red-haired woman, all curled up. Adele looked exhausted. Jamie searched for Ibrahim who usually relieved Adele, but he was not back from lunch, yet. "I'm relieving Adele," he said.

Peter looked at him and frowned. "Good luck with that."

Jamie walked over to Adele's station and put his hand on the red-haired woman's head, next to Adele's hand. Adele looked up and faltered, but Jamie's voice carried the song without a break. Adele looked back down at the woman and they finished the song together. Adele's voice was barely a whisper, and at times Jamie thought she was just mouthing the words. They finished, and Adele turned to go.

"You look like shit," he said. "Maybe you should go see Ramona."

Adele turned toward him. Her face was thin, pinched, and her skin had a bluish tint, her lips chapped and cracked. She tried to speak, but then staggered and fell toward Jamie. He caught her and lowered her gently to the ground. He put his hand on her forehead. It was cold. She gasped for breath.

He gathered her up, shocked by how light a pregnant woman could be. Rachel ran up. "I'm taking her to the new tent," he said. He started for the door. "Can you do another shift?" he called back to Rachel.

"Got it! Go!" she called back.

When he got close to the new tent, he saw the line of people waiting. The line snaked out the tent's front door and wound around, and then down the lane. Jamie blew by the line, ignoring protests, and pushed through the door. The tent was big with four rows of makeshift beds along two aisles. Jamie saw Ramona, halfway down one aisle, and made for her. Several men with saffron scarves stepped in his way but then let him pass, whether because they recognized him as a singer or because they recognized his determination, it didn't matter.

Ramona looked up. She saw Adele. "Oh, shit," she said. She rushed to an empty bed. "Here," she said, and Jamie laid Adele down.

Jamie put his hand on her cheek. "Deli... Deli," he called her name softly. Her eyelids fluttered, and her gaze wandered before coming to rest on his face. She looked at him for a few seconds and then closed her eyes.

CHAPTER 41

Jamie stayed by her all that night. She woke up occasionally, and Jamie would put a straw to her lips. She sipped the water, but often could not keep it down. He cleaned up after her.

Ramona stopped by at the end of her shift to check on Adele. "Ibrahim says he can spell you."

Jamie looked around. "Where is he?"

"He's outside," she said. "We're sort of quarantined. Limit the spread of the disease."

"Tell him no thanks. No reason to expose more people. I'm fine."

Ramona looked skeptical. "You sure?"

Jamie looked at her and smiled. He shook his head. "I'm not leaving."

"OK," she said. She bent over, put her arms around him, and touched her cheek to the top of his head. Then she straightened up and walked away.

* * *

Sometime in the early morning hours, there by her side, he fell asleep and dreamed. She stood, her back to him, tangled hair a dark cloud above slim shoulders. A child, a little girl with the same hair, stood next to her and held her hand. The woman and the little girl started off, walking into the great beyond of a limitless plain, and he tried to call out to them, to call them back, but fear welled up in Jamie, choking off his voice. He struggled, strained to speak past the cold grip of it around his throat, but no words passed his lips. They walked into a gathering mist, now concealed and now glimpsed in the dimness. Jamie opened his mouth. "Wait," he called, but no sound emerged. "Wait," he tried again with all his desperate need, and this time there was the faintest whisper. The little girl stopped. She turned and looked back at him. "Come back," he called. And the girl pulled at her mother's hand so Adele turned, as well.

* * *

Jamie opened his eyes. Adele was looking at him. Perhaps she had made some sound that woke him. Her face was sunken, the skin stretched tight over the bones. Her hair, usually so untamed, lay flat against her skull. Jamie put the straw to her lips, but she seemed unaware of it. He put the cup down and laid his palm on her cheek. Her skin was cold.

She moved her lips, and Jamie waited. It was barely a breath, and he was really just reading her lips.

"I'm sorry," she said.

"Deli." A tear ran down his cheek and he wiped the salt taste of it off his lips. "It's OK. It's all going to be OK." He smiled. Another tear dropped onto her face, on the corner of her mouth. She licked at it, smiled, and closed her eyes.

She woke several more times during the night. Each time, Jamie put the straw to her lips and urged her to drink. She seemed to study his face as if looking for something, and then slowly wrapped her lips around the straw and sipped.

Again Jamie slept, but a commotion at the next bed woke him. Two Helpers picked up the bed like a stretcher and carried it off with the patient, a young woman in saffron robes. Her arm dangled loose, the hand dragging on the ground. The stretcher bearers made no effort to prevent it.

"Her arm..." said Jamie as they passed him.

The Helper just shrugged and they went on.

When it grew light, someone came around and blew out the lanterns. Jamie held up the water bottle and a Helper refilled it with apple juice. "Let's see if she can keep that down," she said.

Ramona arrived with a sandwich, and Jamie took a bite while she examined Adele.

"Is she taking the juice?" she asked.

Jamie nodded.

"Keeping it down?"

"Yeah."

Ramona bent over and studied Adele's face, touched her forehead.

"She looks better," said Jamie.

"Yeah, she does." Ramona nodded. She put her hand on Adele's stomach and waited. She moved her hand to another spot and waited again. Then she smiled. "Still kicking," she said.

* * *

Jamie felt a hand on his shoulder and looked up at Rachel. He smiled. "She's better," he said.

Rachel nodded. "Ramona filled me in." She studied his face. "You should get some sleep. I'll watch."

Jamie looked down at Adele. Her eyes were closed and she breathed easily. "Yeah, OK. I'll be back after lunch." He stood up and turned to go. Rachel gave him a hug and sat down in the chair by Adele's stretcher.

The morning was bright and warm. Jamie blinked when he stepped out of the hospital tent and stood to the side to let the constant stream of people - Helpers, patients, family - pass by. The check-in line seemed shorter than the day before. He thought of Ibrahim and Dwight. With Adele, Rachel and Jamie out of the rotation, the two remaining singers would be feeling the strain. He set off toward the pavilion.

The lanes weren't as jam-packed as usual. There were still crowds around the various vendor booths, especially the bars and herbal remedy shops, but Jamie wasn't chanting "excuse me" continuously as he threaded his way through the crowd, and it wasn't until he got close to the singing tent that he came upon the end of their check-in line. It too was shorter than the day before. He stepped up to the table at the entrance.

"Hey, Peter."

"Hey, Jamie. Ramona gave me the news about Adele and the baby. That's really great."

Jamie nodded. "Yeah. It was scary."

"You look beat. You should go sack out. We've got it covered, here."

Jamie looked around the tent. All the beds were occupied. He spotted Ibrahim and then Dwight, both singing. Then he noticed several others, also singing, people he did not recognize. He frowned "Who are they?"

Peter did not ask who he meant. "They're new singers. Ibrahim recruited them."

"Can they do it? Does it work when they sing?"

Peter shrugged. "Looks like it. Ibrahim says they are all people he brought back." He glanced at a piece of paper. "We've been keeping track of their results. They're doing about as good as he and Dwight are."

Jamie stood for a moment, taking in the scene. He had been exhausted but elated by Adele's recovery. Now he felt deflated, unnecessary. Maria came through the tent door and leaned against his leg. She looked up at him.

"Is Deli OK?" she asked.

Jamie smiled down at her and put his hand on her head. "Yeah. She's real good, drinking juice and everything."

Maria buried her face in the leg of Jamie's blue jeans. She wrapped her arms around his leg and squeezed. Jamie bent down and lifted her up, kissed her on the forehead and held her tight. At least I'm necessary to Maria, he thought. And to Adele, even if she doesn't know it yet.

* * *

Jamie reached for his phone and silenced the alarm. Four hours of sleep hadn't refreshed him, but he figured now he could stay awake for the rest of the day.

He disconnected the phone from the solar charger and looked at it. The phone and charger were gifts from a young woman he had brought back. The screen was cracked, and the battery held a charge for only an hour, and it was useless for calls or texting, of course. It was good for the clock and for a couple of games, but that was about it. That and the trade value. Cell phones had become money, like cigarettes in prison, whether they worked or not. He turned it off, slipped it in his pocket, and went into the kitchen for lunch. He wolfed down a peanut butter and jam sandwich and headed out to check on Adele.

Main Street was bustling but not overly crowded. Jamie stepped around a group of new arrivals putting up a tent. They were using half of the space available, and Jamie could see several more empty campsites along the lane. Just yesterday, it seemed, new arrivals were pushing into the woods on the hillsides around the cabins to find space. But not today. For the last several weeks, people had been coming and going, but Jamie sensed that more people were going than coming, now. Lakeside was emptying out.

"Hey, habibi," called Ibrahim. Jamie turned, and Ibrahim waved. Jamie waited.

"Are you going to visit Adele?" asked Ibrahim. "Mind if I come, too?"

"Sure. Come on," said Jamie, and they walked together toward the new hospital tent.

"Sorry I couldn't do a shift this morning," said Jamie. "I just had to sleep."

"No problem, Jamie. It was slow. I don't think as many people are coming, now."

They approached the end of the check-in line at the hospital tent.

"This line is longer today" said Jamie. "Maybe cholera is scaring people off?"

"I think it is more than that," said Ibrahim. "Peter said that the road up from the valley is lined with people offering cures for the virus. He said that many people don't bother to come all the way up to Lakeside."

"That's a relief," said Jamie. A crowd around a beer tent spilled out into the lane and pressed Jamie and Ibrahim close to the line of sick people waiting to check-in. Jamie made sure he did not touch any of them. He frowned at the beer drinkers. "Bunch of drunks," he muttered.

"Cholera is in the water," said Ibrahim. "It is safer to drink beer."

"I don't see you drinking beer."

Ibrahim smiled. "It is forbidden for me. I'm boiling drinking water."

"Why can't they boil water?"

"Fuel is scarce, Jamie." Ibrahim looked out over the tent city to the surrounding hillsides.

Jamie followed his gaze. The lower slopes looked trampled down and picked clean. Here and there a fresh tree stump showed where desperate campers had resorted to harvesting wet wood.

"I can boil water because the Helpers make sure we have enough good firewood. We are getting special treatment, Jamie."

"For good reason."

Ibrahim stopped and turned to Jamie. "It used to be, habibi, but I am not so sure anymore. I think people we bring back maybe can bring back other people. Or maybe the virus just isn't as lethal as it used to be. A couple of weeks ago, we were special, and Lakeside was a special place. But maybe not anymore."

Jamie looked at Ibrahim. "You're special," he said. "Deli is special."

Ibrahim smiled. "Amen to that, habibi" he said.

CHAPTER 42

Jamie walked through the hospital tent, down an aisle lined with the sick on either side. Ramona said that nearly every patient was suffering from cholera. The stench was penetrating. Ibrahim put a blue bandanna to his nose and murmured something - a prayer, Jamie guessed.

Adele's eyes were closed when they reached her. Rachel got up from the bedside chair and led them a few steps away. "She's sleeping. She's doing good. She took some broth for lunch."

Jamie blinked away something in his eye. "I'll take over, Rache," he said.

"OK. I'll swing by around dinner time. Here's the broth." Rachel pointed to a cup with a straw on the bedside table. "Ramona says give her as much as she wants, and then some."

"Yeah. Got it." Jamie nodded.

"She asked for you."

"Come get me. Next time just come get me."

"I told her you'd be here when she wakes up."

Jamie just nodded. Something was in his eye again and he wiped at it with the heel of his hand.

"Have you had lunch?" asked Ibrahim. "We have bread and stuff at our cabin. I can make you a sandwich."

"A man who cooks," said Rachel. She hooked her arm in Ibrahim's and batted her eyelashes. "Oh-la-la!"

Ibrahim looked impossibly pleased with himself. He smiled down at her, and they walked down the aisle together to the tent door.

Jamie watched them go, a puzzled expression on his face. When they were out of sight, he turned back to Adele. Her eyes were open, and she was watching him. She smiled and her hand on the blanket twitched. Jamie sat on the chair and took her hand in his. Neither spoke.

"Water," said Adele, after a minute. Just a whisper.

"Here's broth," said Jamie. He held the cup and lifted her head so she could wrap her lips around the straw. She sucked until the cup was dry, and Jamie lowered her head back to the pillow. He looked around and caught a Helper's eye and held up the empty cup. The Helper nodded.

Adele licked her lips. "Jamie..." she said. Her voice was weak.

Jamie put his finger to her mouth. "Shh," he said. He took her hand in his. "I'm sorry, Deli. I'm sorry I chased Caleb off. I know you needed someone, and I wasn't there for you. I was too tied up in my own thing. I... I remembered. It all came back. Everything, you and me. But I was afraid. I didn't know who I was, what I was. I was afraid for you. For the baby." He shook his head. "I'm sorry, Deli."

She smiled, and a tear trailed down from the corner of her eye. "I love you," her lips formed the word, soundlessly. She closed her eyes.

Jamie sat with her for the rest of the day, his hand in hers. When she woke, he held the cup of broth for her, and she drank it down. When Rachel came at dinner time, Adele was sitting up and taking her first bites of solid food.

* * *

They carried Adele on a stretcher back to her cabin. She protested at first that she could walk it, but Jamie had glanced at Ramona who had pursed her lips and shook her head ever so slightly. They let Adele take the few steps from her bed to the stretcher, though, and after that she seemed content to ride the rest of the way to the cabin.

Ibrahim took the front of the stretcher and Jamie the back. Rachel walked on one side with her hand resting on Adele's arm. Stevie, Maria and Spot were all over the place, at one point trying to duck under the moving stretcher during a game of tag. Rachel put an end to that.

It was an easy trip. The last few days had been dry and sunny so the road surface was not mud. And traffic on Main Street was light.

"Where is everyone?" asked Adele.

Jamie looked up and down the lane. Today, just about every other spot along their path was empty. In place of the tents and makeshift lean-tos crowding the street when Adele had gone into the hospital, there were now many bare patches of dirt usually strewn with discarded clothing and trash.

"They're leaving," said Jamie. "Everyone's a healer now. So, they're like, why hike all the way up to Lakeside and get cholera?"

They passed a young couple carrying a man on a stretcher toward the hospital. The stretcher bearers had saffron scarves around their necks.

"Thank God the Helpers are still here," said Adele.

"Yeah," said Jamie. "They're actually staying. At least some of them."

"Like, permanently?" asked Adele.

"Yeah. They're starting a community. Farther up the valley. Like a retreat center. A spiritual thing."

"Like a cult?"

"I don't think so. Peter and Ramona helped start it."

Adele seemed reassured.

They approached Adele's cabin and Rachel went ahead to open doors and clear the way. They stopped in the main room and Rachel helped Adele off the stretcher while Jamie and Ibrahim held it steady. Rachel started Adele toward her bedroom, but Adele hesitated.

"Can I sit up for a bit?" she asked.

"Yeah, sure," said Rachel, and she and Jamie helped Adele get comfortable on the broken-down couch in the sitting area. They bustled around, setting a glass of water in reach and tucking a down bag around her. Then everyone cleared out except for Jamie, who had the first shift. Adele watched them go.

Jamie stood in the middle of the room. "Do you need anything? A book? Tea?"

"Tea," said Adele. "I'd love some tea. There's some chamomile in the cabinet to the right of the sink."

Jamie made the tea and gave the cup to Adele. She sipped.

"Could you rub my feet?" she asked.

"Sure." Jamie sat at the far end of the couch and put Adele's feet on his lap. He pulled off a sock and got to work.

Adele put the cup down on the coffee table, laid her head back, and closed her eyes. "Mmmm..." she said.

After a few minutes, Jamie switched to the other foot, and after a while, he stopped and let his warm hands just rest on her feet.

Adele appeared to sleep, but then opened her eyes and looked at Jamie. "We need to work on a nursery," she said. "And you should move in."

"Yeah... OK," he said.

CHAPTER 43

Lakeside emptied out over the next several days, leaving nothing but a field of dirt, rubbish, and a few, isolated tents still standing. Ibrahim surveyed the scene from his front porch. His morning cup of coffee warmed his hands. A breeze came up the valley and the fabric of the tents flapped loosely. Ibrahim frowned. Something about the tents worried him.

Peter came walking down the road from up the valley. He waved, and Ibrahim raised a hand in response.

"Hey, Peter," said Ibrahim. "Coffee?"

"Thanks." Peter shook his head. "I'm good." He stepped up on the porch and stood next to Ibrahim, looking out at the debris. "What a mess."

They were silent for a few seconds.

"Have you checked the tents?" asked Peter.

"Not yet. I'll do it right after breakfast."

"I'll do it," said Peter. "The sooner the better, probably." But he didn't move.

"Yeah... I'll come, too." Ibrahim put his coffee down on the edge of the porch and they started off together.

The first tent was tattered and slumped. Ibrahim used a stick to lift up the door and peered inside. A small pile of discarded clothes lay against one side. A single hiking boot with no mate sat in the middle of the floor.

"Let's knock it down so they know we've checked it," said Peter. He pulled up stakes and the tent collapsed, flat except for the little lump of clothes and the boot.

The second tent was completely empty. The third had a few empty bottles and a dirty blanket. The fourth had a dead man. They could tell by the smell that he had been dead for several days.

Peter pulled the saffron cloth from around his neck and tied it to a tent pole and zipped the tent door closed. "I'll tell Tommy," he said.

"Who's Tommy?" asked Ibrahim.

"Saint Tommy. He's in charge of the body squad. They'll do the burial. They've done a lot."

They went on to check the other tents, but the smell of the body stayed with Ibrahim. Most of the tents were empty or littered with trash. They found one other body: a child wrapped in a blanket with the head of a flannel teddy bear poking out snugged into the child's cheek as if giving him a kiss.

"Are you doing any ceremony when you bury them?" asked Ibrahim.

"Yeah, but we just kind of made it up. Would you perform a ceremony? Sing, maybe?" said Peter.

"Come get me when it's time," said Ibrahim. He started back to his cabin, but then walked by it and on to Rachel and Stevie's. His cabin was empty and quiet now that Jamie had moved in with Adele. As he approached, he could see Rachel moving around in the kitchen. He knocked, and she opened the door. She smiled.

"Just in time," she said. "Pancakes," she ticked off on her fingers, "real maple syrup, and butter."

The cooking smells rolled over him. Stevie waved a fork full of pancake, dripping syrup and melted butter on the table and across his shirt.

Ibrahim stepped through the doorway. Rachel didn't move. He put his arms around her and pulled her close. "I'm in," he said.

* * *

The cleanup took days, and they couldn't have done it without the Helpers. About twenty people had decided to stay with Ramona and Peter in their new community, and each morning a crew came down from their camp to lend a hand.

Dwight had started going through stuff, trying to find anything worth salvaging, but the stink and filth of it was too much, so they just piled everything up and set it on fire. The smoke was foul. They stayed upwind and added wood to burn it all completely. The bonfire lasted all day and into the night.

When the next day dawned, the open area was cleared of all the debris except for a small dresser that swarmed with bees.

Jamie stood a ways off, frowning at the hive. "Maybe later," he said.

"No shit," said Dwight. He swatted at a bee and they moved off to join Peter and the crew taking down the hospital tents.

Peter sent one of the Helpers to fetch Ramona and the rest of their group. They rolled each tent up and heaved it onto their shoulders, and Stevie told Maria they looked like a giant centipede. They made two trips up the valley to the Helpers' campsite and then spent the rest of the day setting up the tents. The first was housing for the Helpers, kitchen, dining room and sleeping quarters, all in one. The second continued to function as a hospital, as news spread down the valley that the cholera epidemic had passed, and a steady stream of the sick and injured kept Ramona and her medical crew busy.

For the next couple of months, the sound of chopping and sawing came down to Lakeside when the breezes blew in the right direction. Ibrahim started going up to the campsite to help them build log cabins and, after a while, he joined the Helpers for morning meditation and chanting. The Helpers made a bell out of a big gas cylinder, and the deep sound of it rang through the hills. The rest of the Lakeside group pitched in with the construction effort and had a standing invitation to meals.

* * *

Early summer was still cool in the mountains, but the sweat dripped off Adele's face. She reached out and grabbed Jamie's arm to steady herself as they walked across a section of road washed out by a recent rain.

"You all right?" he asked. He looked alarmed. He always looked alarmed, these days. Adele was huge. Adele was ready for this to be over.

"Yeah," she said. He waited for her to expand on that, but she just pushed on ahead.

She looked up when the cabins came into view. "Who's that?" she asked. A horse was grazing in the open area and an old-fashioned wagon with wooden wheels stood nearby.

A door slammed open. Maria jumped down from their porch and ran toward them. She grabbed Adele's hand when she reached them. "Eva and Emily are back," she said. She pulled Adele toward the cabin, but Adele stopped.

"Is Caleb here, too?" she asked.

"No. Just Emily and Eva."

Adele glanced at Jamie who was watching her. "That's a relief," she said, and the perpetually worried look on Jamie's face softened for a second.

Emily stepped out onto the porch and came to meet them. She had a big smile on her face. "Look at you," she exclaimed.

Adele couldn't help but smile back. "Welcome home!" she said.

Eva ran up and Adele put one arm around her and one around Emily. Maria skipped on ahead, and Rachel, Ibrahim and Stevie came across the open area and met them on the porch.

"I'll make tea," said Adele when they walked in. She started for the stove, but Emily protested.

"You sit," she said. "I'll make tea."

Adele lowered herself into a chair at the table, and her water broke. "Oh, shit," she said. She looked up at Jamie, a stricken expression on her face. "Jamie..." He rushed over and knelt by her chair.

"What?"

"My water broke."

"What? Now?"

"Yes, now."

"OK. OK." Jamie jumped up and rubbed his hands on his jeans. "Here's what we'll do. We'll go get Ramona. I'll go get Ramona." He started for the door.

"Jamie..." Adele reached out and snagged his sleeve. He stopped and turned toward her. "Eva will go get Ramona. Eva?" The girl stood up.

"Yes?"

"Ramona is a nurse. She's at the Helpers' center. That's straight up the road. A bunch of tents. Tell her my water broke and we need her right away. Got it?

Eva nodded.

"Maria, go with Eva. Show her where the Helpers are. OK?" Both girls nodded. "Go!" said Adele, and the two went out the door like a shot.

Adele stood. "I'm going to go lay down." She managed to make it to her room, despite a crush of babbling friends bouncing off the walls and each other as they helped her down the hall and through the bedroom doorway. The room seemed very crowded.

"Everyone..." They all stopped and looked at Adele. "Out! Jamie, you stay." The room cleared out and Jamie sat on the edge of the bed. "You ready for this?" Adele asked. Jamie looked like a deer in headlights. "Hello?" said Adele.

"Yeah, yeah. Sure," he said. "Are you OK?"

"You're sitting on my hand."

"Oh!" Jamie jumped up and Adele rubbed her hand.

"I'm fine, Jamie. Everything's going to be OK."

"Yeah, yeah. Everything's going to be OK."

"Sit," said Adele.

Jamie sat in the chair by the bed. "Any contractions?"

"No. Take it easy. I'm ready for this. I am so ready."

Jamie looked around the room, filled with the double bed and a dresser that would double as a changing table. "Five minutes ago, I felt ready," he said. "Now I can't even remember my name, let alone what we're supposed to do."

"You're as ready as you're going to be," said Adele.

Jamie did not look reassured.

* * *

Lydia was born June 9th at 8:34 AM, according to Ramona's watch. Adele was in labor for over twelve hours and Jamie never left her side. He let her squeeze his hand hard when she pushed and apologized from the bottom of his heart when she cursed him for what he had done to her.

Ramona wrapped Lydia in a baby blanket and laid her on Adele's chest. "She's not crying," said Jamie. "Is she breathing?"

"Oh, yes," said Ramona. She smiled. "Not all newborns cry. She's in good shape. Everyone's in great shape."

Jamie leaned forward and peered into the little, scrunched up face. He touched a tiny hand with his finger and she gripped it in her tiny fist.

"Whoa," said Jamie. "She's so strong."

Adele beamed.

Lydia opened her eyes and looked at Jamie. She looked directly into his eyes and held his gaze for a second. Then she smiled up at him, yawned, closed her eyes, and slept. What's the big deal, she seemed to say.

"Gas," said Ramona. "Or just reflex. She won't really smile for a couple of months."

Jamie didn't protest, but he knew better. She had looked at him and knew him and smiled. He grinned back, a silly grin that seemed bigger than his face could hold. And he had a sense that they were not in a small room crowded with Adele, Ramona, Rachel and Emily, but a room with only one person in it, this small wrinkled being. And he felt the walls of the little bedroom drop away so there was a vast, shining expanse now, of possibility, something utterly mysterious and unknowable. He was astonished.

"Steady, there, daddy," said Adele. Jamie looked at her and realized his mouth was hanging open. He closed it. He bent over and kissed Adele on her sweaty forehead.

Anything, he thought. I'll do anything necessary to keep you and Lydia safe. You will be safe, forever. I promise. "I love you, Deli," he said. And then she, too, smiled, closed her eyes and slept.

* * *

Jamie poked at the fire pit and checked the venison on the racks, then moved back when the thick smoke stung his eyes. He almost stepped on Spot, who had been closely supervising the operation all day. They both looked up as Adele, Maria and Emily came over. Adele walked carefully, still sore a week after giving birth. She put Lydia down in the little hammock she had rigged and coochie-cooed her. Lydia giggled.

"How's it going?" asked Emily.

"Looks good," said Jamie. "Should have a load by tomorrow."

"Excellent," said Emily. She turned to Adele. "Got your shopping list done?"

"Oh, yeah. How much do you think we can we get with a load of jerky?"

Emily shrugged. "We'll see. People are getting hungry. The civilized world isn't doing so well without refrigerators." She put civilized in air quotes. She considered the racks of venison. "I think they could be hot-to-trot for meat that lasts."

Maria wrinkled her nose.

"Show me your list," said Emily. "Tell me what's most important."

"It's in the cabin," said Adele. She looked at Jamie. "You got Lydia?"

"No problem," said Jamie.

Adele and Emily started for the cabin. Maria checked on Lydia and then ran to catch up. She went in with them but came back out almost immediately and settled on the little porch with a book in her lap.

There was a shout and Jamie turned to look. Dwight was running from the bee-hive dresser waving his hands around his head. He didn't run far and soon slowed to a walk. He swatted at something and jogged a few more steps, then turned toward Jamie and the smoking pit.

"What was that all about?" asked Jamie.

"Honey," said Dwight. "Emily said she thought people would trade for honey."

"Ah," said Jamie. "Do you know anything about harvesting honey?"

"Guess not." Something in the air caught Dwight's attention and he frowned.

"Smoke's supposed to stun bees," said Jamie. "Maybe try that?"

"Huh," said Dwight. He squatted by the fire and selected a particularly smoky piece of wood. He stood and looked back at the hive. The angry buzz came to them across the field. "Maybe I'll wait until things quiet down."

Lydia started fussing and Jamie stepped over to her. She took a deep breath and wailed.

"OK... Time to harvest honey," said Dwight. "Good luck." He made for the bee hive.

"Hey, little stinko," said Jamie. "Everything's good. Daddy's here." He laid his hand on her chest and gave a little push so the hammock began to swing back and forth.

"Rock-a-bye baby, in the tree top," sang Jamie. "When the wind blows, the cradle will rock." It seemed to be working. "When the bough breaks, the cradle will fall. And down will come baby, cradle and all."

Jamie looked down into her face and smiled. She had dark hair, like her mother, but her eyes were Jamie's. She slept.

He heard another shout, and watched Dwight sprint away from the hive, flailing at the air with the smoking stick. He was coming toward Jamie and Lydia, but Jamie waved him away and Dwight got the message. He made for the lake and dove in. He stayed under for several seconds, and then surfaced. He waved to Jamie who waved back.

Jamie heard an angry buzz and put his hand over Lydia's face without touching her. He looked up and searched for the bee but didn't see one. He didn't hear it again, and relaxed. Lydia was looking up at him, smiling.

Jamie started to smile back but stopped. An ugly, wasp-like thing was on her forehead. It moved, testing her pale skin with its feet and antenna, and its abdomen with the wicked stinger flexed. Jamie froze. Hold still, baby girl. Don't move, he thought. The bee buzzed off, and Lydia waved her little fists and kicked her little feet. Jamie smiled down at her, but it took his breath away, and he saw how it really was, how helpless he really was, finally, to protect this little girl. He could summon that dark power all he wanted and it wouldn't make a difference. And the world seemed a vicious place. If the bees didn't get her then the wolves would get her. And if they didn't, then a virus or the people down the valley somewhere would get her. He would give his life to protect her, but the terrible knowledge was like a knife in the heart: it wouldn't be enough. It would never be enough. He would never be enough.

CHAPTER 44

The first of the orphans showed up unannounced and all alone, cast out and ragged. Ibrahim sensed her presence out in the late-summer trees beyond the clearing. He straightened up from the stone he had been setting in the fireplace at the north end of what would be the meeting hall and scanned the tree line.

"Ready for a break?" asked Jamie. He pulled his gloves off and took a swig from his water bottle. He looked at Ibrahim and followed his gaze to the trees. "What is it?" he asked.

Leaves fluttered on scrub brush and higher up the slope branches of Douglas fir trees swayed in the morning breeze. "Huh..." said Ibrahim. "Thought I saw something."

They stood for a minute, alert, searching.

"Like an animal?" asked Jamie.

"Not like an animal." Ibrahim frowned. "I think we are being watched, habibi."

Jamie looked over at his jacket, draped on a tree stump and the rifle leaning against it, and then looked around the work site. Most of the Helpers were at the far end of the clearing by the road, tamping the earth of a terrace. He walked over and picked up the rifle.

Ibrahim listened. The wind sighed through the needles of the fir trees and rustled through the leaves of the brush. The thump, thump, thump of the work crew packing the dirt by the road was dull and distant. The hillside above him was bright in the morning sun, alive, but not threatening.

Ibrahim walked over to Jamie. "I don't think we will need that, Jamie," he said and laid his hand on the barrel of the gun.

Jamie leaned the rifle back against the stump and followed Ibrahim to a log that lay a few steps closer to the slope. Ibrahim rummaged through his pack and laid out his lunch on the log. He looked up the slope, smiled, and then motioned toward the food like a maître d' guiding a diner to her table. Then he went back to the fireplace. "Help me out with this one," he said, and he and Jamie wrestled with a big rock.

When they got the rock positioned right, Ibrahim looked back at the log. The lunch was gone. He smiled.

They worked for another couple of hours and then took a lunch break. Jamie held out half of his sandwich to Ibrahim. "Yeah, thanks, habibi," he said and took it. Ibrahim murmured a prayer and then ate without speaking.

When he was done, he opened a thermos and held it out to Jamie. "Sweet tea?" he offered. Jamie poured some into a cup and handed the thermos back. Ibrahim filled his own cup and sipped the steaming liquid.

"I feel it, too," said Jamie.

Ibrahim looked up at the slope and nodded. "Do you have any more brownies?" he asked.

Jamie sighed. "Yeah." He handed a bag to Ibrahim who took it and walked back to the log. Ibrahim laid out the brownies, but not without a twinge of regret. These were home-baked by Adele. Then he rejoined Jamie and they got back to work on the fireplace and chimney. This time, he kept an eye on the food.

She stepped out from behind the trunk of a huge, old-growth fir about a hundred feet from them. She was young, not a child but not much more. She was dark and her hair was a black cloud around her face, full of twigs and leaves. Her clothes were dirty and torn and did not conceal how thin she was. Ibrahim hoped she had a sleeping bag or blanket tucked away somewhere because the nights in the mountains were chill even in summer.

She made her way down the slope, silent and sure-footed with thoughtless grace, and stood for a few seconds watching Ibrahim and Jamie before she moved out into the clearing toward the log. She stood at the log for a second as if unable to believe her eyes, and then grabbed the brownies, gave them the finger, turned and sprinted back up into the trees.

Ibrahim grinned at Jamie. "I am filled with admiration for this wild thing."

"Yeah," said Jamie. He smiled. "Let's not piss her off."

Adele and Rachel came up. "Piss who off?" asked Adele. She checked Lydia who was awake but content in her sling.

"There's a girl hiding in the woods. Ibrahim put some brownies on the log for her and she took them and then gave us the finger."

"I thought people liked my brownies," said Adele. She scanned the hillside. "Where is she?"

"Somewhere up there. Around the big fir."

Adele took a couple of steps toward the log and stood looking out at the woods.

"How's the peanut?" asked Jamie.

"She's a happy little girl, today." Adele walked to the log and sat facing the slope.

"Why don't you boys go help with the terrace for a while?" said Rachel. "We're taking a break." She sat next to Adele and Lydia.

Ibrahim and Jamie looked at each other. Ibrahim shrugged and they started for the far end of the clearing.

"I'm leaving the rifle," said Jamie over his shoulder.

"No, no," called Adele. "Take it."

Jamie turned back to pick up the rifle, and Ibrahim waited.

"I hope they know what they're doing," said Jamie.

The crew working on the terrace seemed glad to have Ibrahim and Jamie join them. They were filling in the area behind a low retaining wall to create a raised, level surface for the log structures that would get them through winter. A guy named Wynston knew about retaining walls and drainage from before when he worked for a landscaper and was leading the effort. He had Ibrahim and Jamie relieve a couple of tampers who looked exhausted. They soon knew why.

Ibrahim and Jamie kept an eye on Rachel, Adele and Lydia, who remained sitting on the log for most of the afternoon. Nothing happened until the sun dipped below the hill and the slope was in shadow. The air became cool.

Ibrahim glanced up and saw that a fourth figure had joined the two young women and the baby. The thin, dark girl stood four or five steps away from them. There was some back and forth - the log was too far off to make out the words - and then Adele held something out in her hand. Ibrahim nudged Jamie who stopped tamping and watched.

"Shit," said Jamie. "There go the rest of the brownies."

The girl hesitated and then came up to Adele and took the offering. Whatever it was, she devoured it quickly. Rachel held up a jean jacket that had been draped over the log and the girl took it and pulled it on. Rachel motioned for her to approach, and the girl let Rachel roll up the sleeves for her.

"Shit," said Ibrahim. "There goes my jacket."

* * *

Jamie leaned on the tamper and watched Adele and Lydia, Rachel and the feral, dark-haired girl approach. Ibrahim and the others in the work crew also stopped and waited. The girl seemed uncertain and dropped a few steps back as if intimidated by all the strangers. Adele and Rachel turned to her. Adele said something and held out her hand. The girl refused it but came on and walked the rest of the way with them. Jamie gave them all a big, encouraging smile.

"Hey, everybody," said Adele. "This is Miriam. She's been hanging out in the woods for a couple of weeks, but she's gonna stay with us for a few days."

Everyone nodded and said hi or welcome or glad to meet you. Ibrahim stepped forward and held out his hand. Miriam looked at it and then up at his face.

"I saw you," she said.

Ibrahim nodded. "Yeah. I was by the log this morning."

"No. It was a dream. I saw you in a dream."

"Ah," he said, and nodded. "You have dreams?"

"I'm like you." She glanced over at Jamie. "And him," she said.

Ibrahim turned to Jamie. "You have dreams, habibi?"

"Yeah. Sure. Everyone has dreams."

Miriam shook her head. "Not like everyone."

Adele looked from Miriam to Jamie, but Jamie would not meet her eyes.

"Well... OK. We're heading down to the cabins," said Adele. "Miriam can share Maria's room for a few days."

"Yeah. Good," said Jamie, but he wasn't really sure it was good. "I'll be down in a few." He watched Adele, Rachel and Miriam head down the road and tried not to think about how the late afternoon breeze in the trees made a sound like air flowing over black wings.

"We're doing good," said Wynston. "Let's break for the day." The work crew shouldered their tools and started for the main tent. Jamie lagged behind and Ibrahim waited for him to catch up.

"You did not tell me you were having dreams, habibi. Are these dreams not like before?"

"Hey, like I'm supposed to tell you everything?" asked Jamie.

"No, no, Jamie. I do not mean to pry, but there are some things about the virus that I haven't told anyone. Some things that we learned at the CDC."

Jamie stopped and turned to Ibrahim. "Like what?"

"They did some MRIs on people who had succumbed to the virus. There were abnormal patterns of activity in their brains."

"No shit?" said Jamie.

Ibrahim blinked, but went on. "It was like parts of the brain that normally communicate only a little were communicating a lot. I don't remember the details. My Ph.D. is in math and statistics, not neurology." Ibrahim seemed apologetic. "But areas that handled subliminal perceptions seemed to be flooding the parts of the brain responsible for constructing what we see and hear consciously."

"OK. So, what?"

"So, it looks like the virus has mutated, right? It is less lethal now. But it still makes a difference. I think some of us see things differently, now. It's like the unconscious is much closer to the surface for some of us. We have become more sensitive to physical stimuli and we make sense of these inputs in a new way." Ibrahim paused.

"What's that mean, Ibrahim?"

"We have dreams. We hear things. Maybe we see visions, even." He watched Jamie's face.

Jamie looked at Ibrahim for a second, and then he turned and stared down the road toward the cabins. He remembered a flock of crows covering the sky, and how his own face looked out of that black cloud and had smiled at him, a smile full of malice.

"You know what I'm talking about, don't you?" asked Ibrahim.

A sense of desolation swept over Jamie. He shrugged.

"I think Miriam is like that, too," said Ibrahim. He and Jamie looked down the road to the cabins. Adele, Rachel and the girl were walking around a bend and then were out of sight. "It is a powerful gift and she is young and vulnerable. She will need much care and attention to survive."

"This is no gift," said Jamie. "This is a fucking curse." And he picked up his tamper and walked on toward the tent, through a golden, late summer afternoon that he could not see.

CHAPTER 45

It took Jamie and Adele several days to learn Miriam's story. Maria was the key. Miriam seemed to respond immediately to the little girl but was watchful with everyone else. This went on until the second night after dinner when Maria and Jamie were sassing back and forth. At one point, with mock severity, Jamie had pointed at Maria and commanded "Sic-em, Spot." Miriam looked on with horror as Spot leapt up onto the couch and started licking Maria's face. Maria shrieked and tried to push the big dog away but with no success. Miriam looked from Jamie and Adele to Maria, all three laughing their heads off, and something seemed to click for her, and she had burst out laughing too. It wasn't all smooth with Miriam after that, but it was different.

She was thirteen. She was from one of the few black families in Darnell and her big brother, Trayvon, was on the edge of Caleb's group in high school. Jamie remembered Trayvon. He was a quiet, kind of nerdy guy who played basketball. He played so-so, and Jamie had the impression that Trayvon joined the team reluctantly, hoping to find a place for himself and some acceptance in the mostly white community.

One night, when the town was burning, a mob had attacked their house. Trayvon held them off for a few desperate minutes, and Miriam made it out the back door and into the woods. She survived. Trayvon did not, and she was left alone in the world.

The first months in the valley were chaotic, and nearly everyone, Miriam included, welcomed Caleb when he came down from Lakeside and took power. He was a hero. He set rules and his guys had the weapons and the will to enforce them. And one of those rules was that anyone who showed signs of turning was expelled from the town. Inevitably, some of those who were expelled returned, berserk and deadly. Caleb changed the rule, then: If you showed signs of turning, you were tied up. If your friends or family wanted to take you away (like to Lakeside), you could go. If no one stepped up for you, you were killed.

The virus mutated. Many people recovered, more or less, but those who recovered less were often still killed. It was a judgment call, who was too far gone or was on the way to too far, because by the time they were too far it was too late, and some innocent bystander was dead at the hands of a berserker.

Caleb was the one who made the judgment call, and at first Miriam thought he was right on. Miriam could look at someone who was turning and pick up the cues before anyone else, sometimes even before the person turning was aware of it. Caleb was like that too, and it made her feel safe.

But then one day a pretty young woman accused Caleb of rape and Caleb denied it. He said she was turning and since she was without family or friends, ordered that she be killed before it was too late. Miriam looked at Caleb and at the young woman and it seemed obvious that Caleb was lying and that she was telling the truth. But no one else saw it or was willing to speak out.

Then, Caleb made a big show of being magnanimous and made an exception with the young woman. He had her exiled from the town rather than executed, and she went alone up the valley. Later that morning, three of Caleb's guys went up the valley hunting and Miriam heard a single gunshot off in the hills. The hunters came home empty handed but seemed somehow satisfied with the hunt. That night Miriam dreamed, and the next day she left Darnell.

* * *

Jamie leaned on the long handle of the tamper and wiped the sweat off his face. He looked up the hillside where Miriam dumped a final shovel of dirt into a wheelbarrow. Ibrahim started the load down the slope, not so much pushing the wheelbarrow as trying to slow its descent.

"I think that should do it," said Jamie. He stepped back as Ibrahim went by him and dumped the dirt at the edge of the retaining wall.

Ibrahim stretched. Wynston walked up and pulled off his work gloves. He looked up and down the line of stones that was all that was visible of the wall now that the dirt had been piled up and packed in behind it. "Awesome," he said.

"Yeah. I think this'll be it," said Jamie. He looked over the hard-packed and level surface of the terrace. "It's weird," he said.

"How so?" asked Wynston.

"It's like everything falls apart, and here we are rebuilding already."

Wynston shrugged. "We need a solid structure to make it through the winter and we need a level lot to build it. That's all I know."

Ibrahim grinned. "We are building something different here, habibi. Our community will not be like before."

Jamie squinted at the main hall just taking shape at the far end of the terrace. The first few rows of logs had been laid, and at each end of the large rectangle a stone fireplace and chimney rose high and bare. New and different? He wasn't so sure.

"You guys OK with doing logs, next?" asked Wynston. "We need to push this thing along."

Jamie welcomed the cool breeze on his face, but he knew what that breeze meant, too. Fall was approaching and behind that winter. "Yeah. Sure," he said. He looked at Ibrahim. Ibrahim stood, his face turned up the slope, watching Miriam. "That work for you, Ibrahim?" prompted Jamie.

Ibrahim turned to them. "Absolutely. I am happy to work wherever the need is." He smiled.

"OK. Peter is lead on logs," said Wynston. "I'll tell him you'll be over in a bit." He looked at his watch. "After lunch?"

"Perfect," said Ibrahim. Wynston turned and walked back to the crew working on the hall.

For a few seconds neither Jamie nor Ibrahim spoke. Ibrahim looked back up the slope to Miriam and Jamie followed his gaze. She was standing quietly, leaning on the long handle of the shovel. She looked back at them.

"How is she doing, habibi?"

"OK, I think. Maria complains about being woken up at night. I guess Miriam dreams a lot. Talks in her sleep, thrashes around, that kind of stuff." Jamie shrugged. "She's quiet around me and Adele. Kind of cautious. But she seems like a good kid. No trouble, at all."

"She is aloof, no?"

Jamie nodded. "Yeah. I get the feeling the family vibe of our cabin might be too much for her, you know. Like too close too soon."

Miriam put the shovel over her shoulder and started down the slope toward them. "What's this shit?" she said when she was close enough. "Wynston give you guys the day off?"

Ibrahim grinned. "No, no, Miriam. We were just hoping you would come down and show us the right way to do the tamping."

Miriam rolled her eyes. She turned to Jamie. "Hey, I'm thinking I could stay up here tonight. Like in the tent."

"Fine by me," said Jamie. "Check with Ramona."

"OK."

"Getting tired of sleeping with Spot?" asked Jamie.

Miriam smiled. "No," she said. "Where'd Wynston go?"

"Somewhere over there by the hall." Jamie pointed with his chin.

Miriam turned and started for the log structure.

Jamie waited until she was out of earshot. "Pretty independent. Grown up," he said.

"She had to grow up fast, habibi. I think we all did, yes?"

They watched her go, tall for her age and wiry. Something in how she held herself told Jamie that she was aware that they were watching. "Maybe she won't stay," he said. "Maybe she prefers the woods." Ibrahim turned to him, waiting. Jamie met his eye and then looked back toward Miriam. "It's not like we're her parents or anything," he said.

Ibrahim seemed to consider this, then made a face and picked up a shovel and started spreading the dirt. Jamie gripped the tamper with both hands and started hammering it down, hard and flat.

* * *

The next day, Ibrahim and Jamie were on the crew trimming and shaping logs. It was a warm morning, and Jamie was glad to see Miriam coming across the terrace lugging two water jugs. Halfway across, she put them down and shrugged her shoulders. Jamie made one more cut on the saddle notch in his log and then put down the draw knife and walked to meet her.

He reached for one of the jugs. "Need a hand with that?" he asked.

"Nope," she said. "It's harder with one. I'm balanced with two."

She picked up the jugs and they walked together. "How's sleeping in the tent?" he tried.

"OK."

"Is it funny being around a bunch of people, again?"

"It's OK," she said. "It's easier to be alone, you know, in a crowd. Not like..." She stopped speaking and glanced at Jamie.

"Not like being in a little, strange family, huh?" Jamie completed her thought. He gave her an encouraging smile.

"I'm not so hot on families, right now," she said. They walked a few steps in silence. "I mean, you guys are great, Maria, Spot, and all..." She trailed off.

"That's OK, Miriam," said Jamie. "I think we're all kind of bent out of shape." He watched a bird soaring above them, black against the bright sky. "I think we're still trying to figure out how to be together again. It's not like before." He paused. "We're not like before."

They made it a bit farther and then Miriam put down the jugs again. She rubbed her shoulders.

"You need a shoulder yoke," said Jamie.

"How do you do it?" she asked.

"It's like a stick and you..."

"No. I mean the dreams and stuff. How can you be around people?"

Jamie frowned. "Is it hard for you?"

"I feel like I'm in a big parking lot and all the car alarms are going off all the time." She looked at Jamie and then away. "There's so much pain. Everyone's in pain and it's in my dreams every night and I can't get away from it." Her eyes glistened.

"That sounds awful. It's not like that for me." Jamie shook his head. "I see...things... sometimes," he said. "Sometimes I dream." He remembered calling to Adele and a little girl. "But it's not all pain."

"I see pain," said Miriam. "I see it everywhere, all the time. Like for you, I see how you're afraid of yourself. You don't know what you are. And like Ibrahim and Rachel... He's afraid to love her."

"Why would he be afraid to love her? Because she's not a Sufi?"

Miriam shook her head. "No," she said. "You know."

And Jamie did know. Loving was hard enough, before. But now, every heart was sure to be broken, and soon it seemed. He sighed.

He remembered something Bonney used to say. He lifted his hands, empty and helpless. "Chop wood. Carry water," he said. "It's won't always be like that. It gets better. You'll see." He smiled. It was all he had.

She stooped and picked up the water jugs, turned and walked away.

* * *

Jamie watched Adele in the dim light of the oil lamp. She sat across the small room on the couch, her feet up on the battered coffee table. She was knitting a tiny sweater with red yarn and she looked very tired. Lydia was snug in her sling on Adele's chest.

The lamp cast a golden glow and Adele's face was not so much lit as suffused by light. The kitchen behind her was dark and her eyes were dark in a face that seemed to give back the sunshine of the late summer days. Jamie thought she looked like the Madonna in a painting by one of the old masters.

"How's Miriam doing?" she asked.

"She likes it better up there," said Jamie. "Fewer nightmares."

"Did we drive her off?"

Jamie looked past Adele and searched the darkness of the kitchen. "She said it's easier to be alone in the crowd. Like it was too intense with just us. Not bad... Just too close or something." He sat silent for a minute. "The Helpers are really sweet people, you know, but... I don't see how she's going to make it there, either."

Adele put her knitting down and shifted on the couch. "Oof..." she said.

Jamie sat up straight. "You OK?"

Adele waved him away. "Yeah, yeah. I'm fine. Just achy." Jamie slumped back in his chair. Then, as if she regretted her brusque dismissal, "Maybe a backrub later?"

"Yeah, for sure," he said. And it was for sure. He would do anything to help her and Lydia through this time. And all the times that would come after, too. But that future seemed a vast abyss that they would plunge into and fall through forever with nothing to hold onto and nowhere to stand. The darkness of the kitchen filled him with fear, as if the howling abyss had opened up on the other side of the couch and they were already sliding in. He sensed that the little help he could offer was nothing compared to the failures and shortcomings that were inevitable. Chop wood, carry water, he thought. He could give a backrub. That's what he would do.

"You good?" asked Adele. She was looking at him, one hand resting on Lydia and the other holding the knitting.

"Yeah," he said. "I'm good." But he thought he could see the doubt in her eyes.

CHAPTER 46

Ibrahim watched her go. Miriam walked toward the outhouses but kept going when she reached them. She retrieved a small backpack from behind a tree stump and then made her way up the slope to the treeline. She looked back then, and their eyes met. Ibrahim put his palms together and bowed. She hesitated, then bowed back, turned, and disappeared into the forest. Ibrahim murmured a blessing.

The work crews were getting their morning assignments from Wynston when Ibrahim came up. He and Jamie were on logs again, this time with the crew that hoisted a trimmed and shaped log up to its permanent place on the wall of the meeting house. A system of pulleys and winches made it possible, since even the smallest logs were too heavy to lift by hand.

Wynston looked around at the gathered workers, about 20 men and women. "Any questions?" he asked.

"I would like to say something," said Ibrahim. He stepped forward and stood next to Wynston, facing the group. Wynston took a step to the side, giving Ibrahim the floor.

"Miriam has decided to go back to the forest." Ibrahim scanned the faces of the Helpers. Some seemed sad, others shocked, some just puzzled.

"Why is she leaving?" asked Ramona.

"Yeah... Like, how is she going to make it through the winter?" asked a man.

Ibrahim paused to collect his thoughts, and the group waited. "Miriam is a very sensitive girl. That is why she so much held herself apart. It is nothing that we have done. It is nothing we could have not done." He paused.

"I don't get it," said a voice from the back of the group.

Ibrahim nodded. "Miriam... We think the virus has mutated, yes? And it seems that some people who recover are different afterward. The dreams... Many of us are having very vivid dreams." Several Helpers nodded and frowned. "Well it seems some of us have waking dreams, visions even. Miriam was kind of like that. She could see or sense people's pain." Ibrahim made a helpless gesture. "Being around us all was just too much."

"How is she going to make it out there?" asked Ramona. "How is she going to make it through the winter? How could you let her go?"

"How could I stop her?" asked Ibrahim. "I talked with her. I tried to convince her to stay. I even offered that we would build her a little place off to the side." Ibrahim sighed. "She said none of it would work."

Multiple conversations broke out in the crowd. Then Ramona spoke up. "We can leave food out for her. She doesn't have to join us for meals or sleep with us, or anything. She can come down, pick up stuff and then go back to the woods."

Ibrahim looked slightly surprised. "Yeah, that's a great idea. Let's do that."

They started the next day, leaving a day's worth of food out at the foot of the slope in a bag. The first day, the food went untouched. The second day, the bag was torn to shreds and the area covered with small animal tracks. The third day, they put out a new bag. It disappeared and was replaced by a small, human figurine made out of sticks and leaves tied together. The head was a dark-skinned walnut with a halo of black hair made from god-knows what. A smiley face had been painted on the walnut with what looked to be sparkly nail polish.

The system worked well for several years, and over time the figurines became more artful and were left more frequently. Visitors to the center started buying them and would put them in little shrines outside above their doors to ward off evil spirits. It got to the point that Miriam was paying for her keep, in full, and the Helpers never regretted supporting her and the other hermits who took refuge back in the hills.

* * *

Jamie held Lydia and walked around the cabin. He hummed to her and bounced her just a little as he walked. She was having none of it, though. She fussed and cried.

He stuck his head in the bedroom. "I'm taking her to Ramona."

Adele heaved a sigh and sat up. "OK. Hang on and I'll come with."

"Why don't you stay here? Rest up a bit. I've got this."

Adele looked at him. There were dark circles under her eyes.

"That way you'll have more energy when she keeps us awake for the next week," he added.

Adele gave him a disgusted look and then fell back onto the bed. She waved a hand. "Go," she said.

Jamie grabbed their baby-go bag and stepped out onto the front porch. Maria looked up from a book on her lap. "What's this word?" she asked.

"Let me see," said Jamie and Maria held the book for him and pointed. "You can sound that one out. What's the sound of the first letter?" Lydia wailed. "Microscope," he said. "The word is microscope." He put his hand on Lydia's forehead. It was hot.

"Hey, I'm going to visit Ramona. You want to come?"

"Sure." She put the book down on the porch and skipped along with Jamie.

"What's a microscope?" she asked.

"You use it to look at things that are too small to see."

"There are things too small to see?"

"Oh, yeah," he said. "We need to send you to school. You'd learn about all that."

Maria was silent for several minutes and she fell behind Jamie as they walked. Finally, she stopped. Jamie walked for several steps before he realized she was not with him. He turned.

"Hey. You coming?"

"Are you going to send me away?" Maria stared at the ground in front of her feet.

"No." Jamie shook his head. "Why do you say that?"

"You said you were going to send me away to school." She looked up at Jamie. There were tears in her eyes.

Jamie saw it, then. "No," he said. "You're with us. You're not going anywhere. School would be like with the Helpers or at Rachel and Ibrahim's cabin. You'd go there for the morning or the afternoon and then come home afterward." He put down the go-bag, walked back to the girl and put his free arm around her. "Hey, sweetie. You're part of the family. You're my girl, just like Lydia." Maria wrapped her arms around Jamie. Her tears left wet marks in Jamie's shirt, and Jamie felt like his skin had been removed and he lay exposed to the entire universe.

* * *

There was no line at the hospital tent, and Jamie went right in. Ramona was sitting at a table just inside the door, leafing through a big book.

"Hey," said Jamie.

"Hey, yourself," said Ramona. She smiled at Maria. "Hey, squirt."

Maria ignored the insult and leaned on the table. She studied a drawing in the book, a precise rendering of a plant.

"What's the matter? Lydia sick?"

"Yeah. I think she has a temperature. Feels warm." Jamie turned so Ramona could put her hand on Lydia's forehead.

"Is she sleeping at all?"

"Nah. Just fussing. She's either crying or fussing all the time."

"When did it start?"

"Yesterday after dinner. It was a rough night."

"I'll bet. Everything else normal?"

"Seems to be." Jamie nodded.

Ramona took Lydia and laid her on the table. She unwrapped her and checked her over carefully.

"She looks OK. Not measles or chicken pox, thankfully." She went over to a cabinet and pulled out a syringe and a bottle. "This is liquid Tylenol. Give her this much," she indicated a mark on the syringe "orally, three times a day. It'll help with the fever and if she has any aches or pains it'll help with that, too. You guys might be able to get some sleep."

"Great. Thanks," said Jamie.

"Here. I'll show you how." She filled the syringe and showed Jamie how to drip it into Lydia's mouth.

"Where do you get this stuff?" he asked.

"Patients bring it in. We put out the word that we'll take anything medical, medicines and stuff, as payment. Look at that." She pointed to the book in front of Maria.

"What is it?"

"It's an illustrated catalog of medicinal plants. Came in just this morning. In about a year, that'll be all we have. It's gonna save lives."

"Wow. That's scary." Jamie repackaged Lydia and picked her up.

"I know where that is," said Maria. She pointed to the picture of a plant.

"Really? Where's that?" asked Ramona.

"It's growing out behind the storehouse."

"Can you show me?"

"Yeah," said Maria.

Ramona checked her watch. "How about tomorrow right after lunch?" She looked up at Jamie.

"Yeah, that would work," he said.

"I'll bring the book." She turned to Maria. "We can sit down together and I'll show you stuff to look for. It'll be like school."

"OK," said Maria. She looked up at Ramona. "I learned a new word today."

Jamie smiled.

"Oh, yeah?" said Ramona.

"Stevie taught me."

Jamie stopped smiling.

"Oh?" said Ramona.

"Microscope," announced Jamie. "You learned microscope, right?"

A look of resignation came over Maria's face, an expression of infinite patience tested by intolerable aggravation.

Ramona looked from Maria to Jamie and back. "Well, that's a fine word," she said, and winked at Maria who grinned back.

CHAPTER 47

The fall sunshine was warm on Jamie's face. Emily and Eva had left earlier that morning with another load of venison jerky, honey and firewood to trade down in the valley. Jamie sat on a bench next to the empty smoking rack, unzipped his fleece and tipped his head back. The sunlight fell on the pale skin of his throat. He closed his eyes.

Ibrahim walked up and sat next to him. Jamie turned to him. "Hey, Ibrahim."

"Hey, Jamie."

They sat, silent, soaking up the sun.

Jamie sighed.

Ibrahim looked over at him. "How's fatherhood?" he asked.

"It's good," said Jamie. "All good." He nodded his head.

Ibrahim waited.

"But it's scary, in a way, you know?" He squinted at something in the distance. "She's just so... small, you know, so vulnerable. And it's like, I'm supposed to be her father? Like I'm supposed to protect her and feed her and, like be wise?" Jamie lifted his hands, open and empty. "I don't know shit."

Ibrahim grinned. "Most fathers don't know shit, habibi. But the race seems to survive." And then he looked away from Jamie and frowned. His lips moved and Jamie recognized Ibrahim's Inshallah, God willing.

"And it really doesn't make any difference if I am a good father, does it?" said Jamie. "I mean, if this virus doesn't get us, something else will, right? We'll all get sick with something, eventually, or a tree falls on us or we just get old and die." Jamie shook his head. "I can't stand it. I mean, for myself, OK. But not for Lydia."

"So, what's new, habibi? Hasn't it always been this way?"

"That's the point, Ibrahim. There's no reason for joy or happiness or love. We're all doomed, and it has always been this way and always will be."

"Yeah, Jamie. We've always been doomed. There has never been any excuse to be happy or to have hope. It is all baseless. There is no reason or cause. Unhappiness, it has a million causes, habibi. Everything causes unhappiness. Happiness, joy, love, these things have no cause. They are not because of something else. They just are." He looked at Jamie, and then tried again. "It's like when Allah created the universe, he made it out of love and joy. The universe is made of love and joy. And that's just the way it is." He grinned. "No reasons. It just is."

Adele walked up behind them, and Jamie turned his head.

"Can you take Lydia?" She unloaded the bundled-up baby and Jamie took her in his arms. "I gotta go help Rachel." She turned and started off across the open area. "She needs burping," she called over her shoulder.

Jamie arranged Lydia who was beginning to fuss. He patted her on the back and she quieted down, then spit up on his shoulder.

"Oh, shit," he said, but it wasn't like it was a ton of stuff and he had smelled worse from her, so he simply switched Lydia to the other shoulder and continued patting her on the back. She tucked her head down in his neck and her little body seemed to melt into his. She slept.

Someone across the way called for Ibrahim. He waved and got up. "I'm having lunch with the Helpers. Rachel and I are hosting dinner, tonight. See you all there?"

"Yeah, yeah. Great," said Jamie.

Ibrahim walked toward Peter who came to meet him. Peter waved to Jamie and then the two of them turned and started up the path.

A breeze came up the valley and breathed through the dark fir trees on the hillside. Jamie arranged Lydia's blanket so her head was covered, and folded his arms around her like dark wings. She shifted and smiled.

I'll never be enough, he thought. Never in a million years. But maybe this is enough. Just this.

He tipped his head back, closed his eyes and turned his face up to the limitless blue shining of the clear autumn sky.

* * *

Jamie sat at the dinner table, opposite Adele who was breast feeding Lydia.

Adele looked up at him. "What?" she asked.

Jamie was silent for a moment. "I was thinking about some projects, stuff around the cabin. Some things that would be good for next summer, maybe. And then it struck me. We might make it," he said. "I mean, we might grow old. Lydia might grow up, have kids, and the whole thing might start all over again, like before."

Adele stabbed a brussels sprout with her fork but then put it down and sighed. "Not like before," she said, "But, yeah. Ever since Lydia I've been thinking about that."

"It used to be I just wanted to make it through the day." Jamie stared at his hands resting on the table. "And then I just wanted to make it through the week, and then just through the winter." He looked up at Adele. "And we made it. We made it. We made it through the winter." He looked amazed by the fact. "We know how to do it, now." He watched Adele and Lydia. The only sound was Lydia suckling.

"Did you know Miriam brought in another orphan today?" asked Jamie.

"No. Where is she finding these kids?" She shifted Lydia and dropped the brussels sprout on the floor where Spot lay in wait. He had learned that being around Lydia was a good bet.

Jamie shrugged. "Out in the woods. Ibrahim says most of them are a little strange. Like they've been kicked out of their community because they see too much or something."

"How many is that now?"

Jamie shrugged. "Five or six? Peter's talking about setting up a school. It's like the Helpers want to start an orphanage. Peter and Ibrahim were talking about a mission statement and taking care of the kids would be one of the main things."

"A mission statement..." Adele rolled her eyes.

"They're thinking about it, too."

"Thinking about what?"

"What comes next. You know, what are we going to do? How are we going to live." Jamie got up and took his dish to the sink. He turned around and Adele looked back over her shoulder at him. "They're gonna have group meetings to talk about it, figure it out," he said.

"I want in on that." Adele looked down at Lydia. "I've got a vested interest."

Jamie smiled. "Yeah. Let's do it," he said. "Ibrahim said we should come." Lydia's eyes were open and she seemed to focus on Jamie. She waved her little fists and kicked her feet.

"Ow!" said Adele.

"Hey, you little stinker," said Jamie softly. "You go easy on your mama."

* * *

The bell sounded deep up and down the valley and the evening air seemed to hold the note so Jamie could feel it even after he could no longer hear it.

"You ready?" asked Jamie.

"Yep. Let's go." Adele put Lydia in her sling and Jamie grabbed the backpack full of Lydia's supplies.

"Hey, Maria," called Jamie. Maria and Spot came from her bedroom and the girl pulled on her fall jacket. She checked Lydia and seemed satisfied. Jamie slung the hunting rifle over his shoulder and the whole troop, Spot included, started up the road to the Helpers' settlement.

It was still light when they went up the stone steps from the road to the terrace. A few people were ahead of them, ducking into the meeting hall where most of the Helpers were already assembled, sitting on chairs and on the floor. Maria spotted Stevie sitting with Rachel and Ibrahim. She walked over and sat down next to him. By the time Adele and Jamie joined her, she was already picking a fight.

"Hey," said Jamie. He made Spot lie down between the two kids.

Ibrahim grinned at him. "You are most skillful, habibi. Perhaps you should run the orphanage?"

Jamie gave Ibrahim a yeah-right look. "So, how's this work?" he asked.

"We start with fifteen minutes of silence, and then we open it up to whatever comes up."

Jamie looked at the little, brass bowl and the small stick sitting on the floor in front of Ibrahim. "You timing?" he asked.

"Yeah," said Ibrahim. He picked up the stick and hit the bell three times, pausing to let the high, sweet sound fade to silence before ringing it again. The various conversations in the crowd died out and the room was quiet. A child fidgeted. Spot jumped up and scratched furiously and then lay down again. The silence seemed unbroken, throughout.

Then Ibrahim rang the bell once, and the room stirred again. Some gave the traditional Buddhist bow, palms pressed together, a few bowed until their foreheads touched the fresh boards of the floor, some crossed themselves.

A couple of the younger orphans went to a table at the far end of the meeting hall where some art supplies were laid out. Stevie, Maria and Spot joined them.

Ibrahim spoke up. "So far, so good." He paused. "We've got shelter for the winter." He raised his hands to the walls around them. "We've got a huge woodpile, thanks to Wynston and his crew." He nodded to Wynston and the crowd clapped and whistled. "We've got plenty of food and the medical team is receiving more donations all the time." He bowed to Ramona and Peter, and everyone present bowed as well. The two bowed back, deeply. "The question is, what next? It looks like humanity might survive. It looks like we might survive." Ibrahim looked around the room. A squabble broke out at the art table and Ibrahim smiled. He held up a hand. "What world do we want for them?" he asked and waited.

A young man stood up. "This world," he said. "We want this world. What more could we want? This can be a good life for us. We have the technology that we need.

It's simple, but it works and it isn't destroying the earth. Let's work and have babies and dance after dinner and drink hard cider. Let's meditate and chant. Man, let's be innocent again. We never needed big, honking pickup trucks that never got dirty and to hell with cell phones and computers." He sat back down, and the room erupted in applause.

When it died down, Ramona stood and looked around at the healthy, tanned faces of the young people. She held up two fingers. "I have two words for you," she said. "Primitive dentistry. All this mindless, happy talk will crash and burn when you have your first tooth ache, let alone when we have our first real medical emergency. What happens when one of us dies in childbirth? What happens when we've exhausted the supply of leftover antibiotics? The only thing worse than having technology is not having technology." She sat down.

The debate was on.

ACKNOWLEDGEMENTS

I am deeply indebted and profoundly grateful to the many people who have contributed to this work. Sara Stamey shared her expertise and insights as a professional reader and writer, and I hope I have done her comments justice in my revisions and rewriting.

My writing group – Lexie Lamborn, Susan Miller, Teru Lundsten, and Mark Lundsten – have read much of the novel and I could not have completed the work without their encouragement. I am a better writer thanks to the always gentle but always spot-on critiques of this group of fine writers and fine people.

Debbie Cole and Hilary Haberow-Stuart have both read early versions of the story and have made many helpful suggestions and corrections. I especially appreciate Hilary's thorough reading and the thoughtful responses and questions she has shared.

My family has been very supportive of my odd projects. I learned to love stories as my father read to me as a child and I aspire to the lively and vivid writing style that my mother displays in her pieces.

Finally, I bow in deep gratitude to my wife, Jan, who would not normally read a during-the-apocalypse story, but who read The Dark multiple times. Her comments were always perceptive and helpful. Her presence and our life together are really what the story is all about.

Made in the USA
Middletown, DE
30 September 2021

49372167R00168